1

2

THE GOOD QUEEN

MATILDA OF SCOTLAND, WIFE OF HENRY I

By J.P. REEDMAN

Copyright Herne's Cave/J.P. Reedman, 2023

4

Note—Matilda was originally named Edith and only changed her name upon accession to the throne. Throughout the book she will mainly be referred to mainly by her birthname, Edith.

CHAPTER ONE

The frowning stone block of Malcolm's Tower lifted over the gardens, casting a long, finger-like shadow. Winter had slipped away, dragging its snowy mantle back to the Highland hills, and lambing season was on the horizon, with promises of spring bloom and warmer winds. Emerging from the cold like hibernating animals, the castle nursemaids had finally allowed me and my younger sister Mary to gallop over the empty flowerbeds, shrieking in childish delight as we savoured the weak, wobbling sunlight that stroked our winter-pale cheeks.

Mary and I had been cooped indoors for months, stuck with the reek of hearth-smoke, wet dogs and festering rushes, listening to the hacking coughs of sick servants and the wild gales skirling about the walls, making sounds to terrify a child at midnight's hour, tapping and rapping and wailing.

Now released from our smoky, dank prison, the two of us bounded around like fawns, galloping about the tangled bushes and evergreen shrubs, our skirts flying and our shoes sinking deep in the muddy ground. Our Lady Mother would be horrified if she saw us, for she was a woman so good and soft and saintly that she spent most of her time in prayer or aiding the poor in the nearby town of Dunfermline. Dirt, such as the claggy mixture on our shoes and legs, was an ungodly and unwholesome blight to see on young maids and unbound hair was frowned upon too, for some priests believed it attracted the attention of fallen angels. But Mother was enclosed in the Tower's stout walls and could not see or hear a thing through ten feet of stone.

Malcolm's Tower was built by my father, Malcolm, King of the Scots. Many years before my birth, he had moved the seat of power there, raising the circular tower upon a sharp promontory of land with a steep cliff tumbling down one side. We children were never allowed near the cliff-edge of course, for it was a dangerous place. Animals had fallen over it, and one or two youths who had imbibed too many tankards in the taverns of Dunfermline. The cliff had old, frightening legends attached to it, too—an *Each-Uisge*, an unearthly water-horse, was rumoured to come galloping out of the Tower Burn at the foot of the hill, grabbing its victims in its teeth before leaping over the cliff's edge and letting the unfortunates fall to their doom...

"Children! Edith, Mary!" My sister and I were so engrossed in our unbridled frolics, we had not noticed that Mother had left her endless prayers and come into the garden, perhaps wishing to feel the sun on her face too. Mother, Queen Margaret, was tall and slender, her dark gold hair shrouded by a white veil. Below a golden circlet, her face was serene and peaceful. One could scarcely imagine she had borne eight children over the years. She always said she was blessed by God and so she was.

Immediately, we ceased our rough play, patting down our rumpled skirts and putting our hands behind our backs to hide the mud beneath our nails. Together, we curtseyed deeply, respectfully. "Lady Mother," I said, eyeing her. "It is good to see you this fair morning."

Today her usual calm seemed a little ruffled; a strange expression rippled across her even features and her eyes were shadowed as if she had not slept well the night before. "I must talk to you girls." Her voice was low and smooth, but had a slight quaver I had not heard before. "About your future."

I blinked, not understanding. Mary and I knew we were princesses, but I was only six summers and Mary only four. Our futures, whatever they might be, seemed far in the future; we knew nothing but the roar of the burn, the gales that screeched over the height, the shrill cries of eagles that soared into the nearby forest, their wings dark frills against the moving skies. The Tower was our place; we needed and wanted no other.

"Let us go inside," she said. "Nurses, bring them along." She nodded towards our nursemaids, who hurriedly ran over to tidy our hair and wipe our hands and cheeks with much tutting.

Made suitably clean, we proceeded back into the Tower with Mother in the lead, her long woollen robe, blue as the Virgin's gown, trailing on the floor. Inside the castle, it was, as ever, smoky, heavy blue coils rising from a central hearth to exit through a shunt in the roof. Twenty rooms it had, the topmost reserved for the King and Queen, a second shared by my older brothers, and a third designated as the nursery, where I dwelt with Mary and baby David. Two of my brothers, Edgar—whom we called Ned—and Alexander were in the cramped dark hall, clattering away at each other with broken wooden swords. Alexander, only eight, was being sorely trounced by twelve-year-old Ned, but he continued to fight courageously despite being a foot shorter than his brother. "I'll smite you down as Father smote down old King Lulach the Foolish!" he shouted, striking his sword against Ned's battered shield.

"*Ha!*" Ned cried, dancing in circles around him and prodding him with the blunt tip of his makeshift sword. "Well, any man might easily kill a silly Fool...but I will smite you as Father smote Lulach's *father*, Mac Bethad mac Findlaích!"

Alexander gave a roar, dropped his toy sword and lunged for Ned. The boys both froze as Mother swept towards them, frowning. "Take your rough play outside," she said curtly. "I must have an important discussion with your sisters and do not want the distraction of your shouts."

Florid with shame, our brothers bowed, took up their wooden arms, and hastened to the door. Mother led Mary and me on through the Tower into her private solar. It was hung with furs and woven hanging placed strategically to protect from the bitter cold of a Scottish winter. Dried rushes mixed with the faded remnants of pressed flowers covered the floor in a series of mats. There were oak-wood chests in which Mother kept her treasures—fine enamelled pendants, necklaces of polished crystals, brooches with the faces of the sun and moon, all inherited from her royal Saxon family. A folding iron chair stood by the bed with its down-stuff mattress; Mother sat upon it, straightening her skirts, and motioned for us to sit on two small nearby stools. Her tiring women, working on a loom near the back of the room, rose, curtseyed and left the room.

Mother sat looking at us, hands folded in her lap, her expression sorrowful. I began to fret, fearing that she might have dire news to impart. Father was at home, so he was safe and well, but my eldest brothers, Edward, Edmund and Ethelred had been sent away to various noble households to continue their education and training. I also had three older half-brothers from Father's first marriage to a Norse woman called Ingibiorg: Duncan, Donald and Malcolm. However, they were strangers to Mary and me—the elder we had never met, since he was surrendered as a hostage to King William of England in 1072, while the younger two had only appeared at Father's Tower once or twice, giant men with reddish-yellow hair and jutting jaws and brows, who cared for nought but the hunt and the feast.

"Oh, my dear daughters," Mother said at length, "I know not how to begin, but begin I must..." She toyed with a jewel she wore on her intricate girdle, a heavy golden cross inlaid with thick purple and green stones that Father had given her as a Yule gift. "You remember, don't you, the tale of my own youth, of how I was born in Hungary, far, far away from my sire's homeland of England?"

I nodded and so did Mary, although being only four she was likely just mimicking me. Mother had told us her family story and visiting bards also had recounted poems about her earlier life around the Tower's ever-burning hearth. When her grandsire, King Edmund Ironside, died, some say killed horribly while sitting on the privy, his successor and one-time rival, Cnut, sent Edmund's two sons, Edward and Edmund to the court of Olof, King of Sweden. Rumour had it that Cnut implored Olof to quietly kill the boys and let them disappear from memory, but Olof was no butcher and instead sent them on to his daughter, Ingigerd, Grand Princess of Kiev, who cared for them in their tender youth. Later, the exiled princes made their way to Hungary where, once he was grown, Edward wed our grandmother, a noblewoman named Agatha, and had three children, Mother, her sister Cristina, and her brother Edgar Atheling. The family returned to England when the old King, Edward the Confessor, in poor health and without sons, put forth our grandfather to be acclaimed as his heir. Sadly, our grandpapa died within days so never wore a crown, but Mother remained at court and was eventually betrothed to Father, while Cristina became a nun and then an abbess. Edgar, briefly, was named as England's King, although he bent the knee to the Norman that men name 'the Conqueror' and renounced his title…

"Then you will remember how I had to leave Hungary for what was a strange land to me. I knew no other place than the court of King Andrew yet I was compelled by duty to leave familiar things behind…To leave friends, to grow up, to assume the role of an English princess." She sighed as if the memories pained her. Her fingers caressed her bejewelled cross.

"Yes, Mother, I remember. Your journey sounded… frightening." And so it had. Uprooted by the wishes of a dying monarch, a journey over the sea to reach a land of squabbling princelings…and then the head of the family dying within days of setting foot on English soil.

"In the end, despite grief and sorrow, our family's return was the best thing possible," said Mother. "After the Duke of Normandy usurped the throne, Edgar, Cristina and I fled to Scotland for safety…and I wed your father and was raised to the royal dignity, which had at one time seemed lost to our line. In due time, all my wonderful children were born, all in quick succession and all alive, a sure sign that the Almighty smiled on our marriage. Some things…" She smiled a tight smile and I noticed a glimmer at the corner of her eye—was it a tear? "Some things require great sacrifice, and it is the duty of the children of Kings to fare far from their birthplace and make suitable, honourable alliances…"

I went cold even though a little fire blazed in a brazier near my feet. I knew girls were sometimes betrothed at my age, but even though they would not enter their husband's households for many years, such a thing was still a horrifying thought. The man might be old and battle-scarred, or spotty with a bad attitude like my brother Edmund. Was Mother going to tell me and Mary that husbands had been chosen for us already? Without realising, I reached over and clasped Mary's hand. Her palm was sticky and hot as she wriggled nervously on the stool.

"Do not look so apprehensive, my daughters." Mother leaned forward in her iron chair, which her brother Edgar had given her upon the occasion of her wedding some ten years before. "Your sire has found no husbands for you as yet. However, your Aunt Cristina at Romsey Abbey has written to me, reminding me of the need for a good education for you. A princess' education. Nowhere in Scotland could teach you as well as my sister at Romsey."

I breathed a sigh of relief that no marriages were arranged, but apprehension still gripped me. Romsey was a long way, far in the south, and Mary and I had never met our Aunt Cristina. Mother had told us that she was even more devout than her, which seemed near impossible, for no one loved the Lord more than Queen Margaret of Scotland. People in the towns often tried to touch the hem of her robe and called her a living saint when she went on her progresses from town to town.

Mary had started to weep, knuckling the tears away from the corners of her eyes. "I don't want to leave Scotland, Mother."

"I know, my daughter; I had no desire to leave Hungary, but it was for the best and decided by my Lord Father. Your sire, the King, has conferred with me and also agrees that an education in England would ensure you both make marriages of note when you are older."

"When will this take place, Mother?" I asked, my voice little more than a breathy whisper. In my heart, I already knew what her answer would be.

"Your Aunt asks to receive you as soon as possible. The journey is long, though, and we will have to make certain you are well-protected on the road. The lands you travel through are treacherous, and many unworthy men would happily kidnap a royal-blooded bride."

I gulped at that and a lump grew in my throat. I vowed not to cry, though I clutched Mary's hand all the tighter.

Mother rose, seemingly relieved that she had unburdened herself. "There—no tears now, my daughters. You must be brave. You represent Scotland and the hopes of peace between many kingdoms. Remember, too, you are not only of Scottish blood but of English stock too, granddaughters of the valiant Ironside, kinswomen of The Confessor, and descendants of mighty Alfred, whom men call 'The Great.' And as for the Normans who now rule England, much has changed since Senlac—King William's own son, Robert, stood as Godfather to you, so you will come to no harm among them. Queen Matilda, William's wife—God assoil her—she too attended your baptism, Edith, and you tugged upon her headdress with your tiny hands, making men whisper that it signified your own future as a Queen." She smiled, more to herself than at me. "I would like to see you made Queen someday. The rightful blood of England seated on England's throne…"

A chariot was readied for Mary and me, covered in tautly stretched hides, oiled to keep out the weather, and filled with heaps of furs, cushions and blankets to keep us warm on the road. Father ordered two hundred men to march alongside, protecting the 'pearls of Scotland' as he called us, from both our own brutish clan-lords and the English over the borders. We were dressed in our best, our hair brushed and plaited, mine the colour of palest wheat-Saxon hair, my mother said, and Mary's a deep reddish-brown like our Father's, a touch of the fox as he called it. Four nursemaids of good character came with us to see to our needs.

Mother and Father had said their private farewells to us the night before; they smiled and spoke comforting words but there was lots of stern-faced lecturing about 'best behaviour' and 'duty.' Mary and I had hugged baby David, and bade our resident brothers, Ned and Alexander, a fond goodbye, noting with some dismay that they seemed more excited by our departure than sorrowful.

"If you can," said Ned thoughtfully, "ask about the sword of Offa that was given to our grandsire Ironside or the silver-hilted blade presented to Eadwig. Our uncle Edgar, for whom I am named, might know…"

"He's not going to give them to you, Ned," I said primly, "even if he has them or knows who does. Besides, you have forgotten—he has left England and gone to Italy, unable to bear the Conqueror's rule. He may return someday, but…"

Edgar reddened. "How do you know such things? You are but a little girl! Girls do not know about such things!"

"Yes, they do," I said, pursing my lips. "I stay quiet like a mouse and hear things said by Mother and Father and important visitors."

"You're an earwig then, Edith!" he cried, going red and sticking out his tongue in a very unprincely fashion. "A sneaky little eavesdropper!"

"No, I am a princess, and maybe one day I'll be a Queen...if I'm lucky! I'll need to know *everything*; about friends, about enemies..."

"You'll probably end up a withered old nun instead," retorted my hot-headed brother, placing his hands on hips. Next to him, Alexander pressed his hand over his mouth to hide a titter.

Our chief nurse, a brawny, no-nonsense, red-headed woman called Muriel, tutted in dismay at our only half-serious spat, and then Mary and I were packed off to get an early night before our journey.

At dawn the next day, grey and with a chill wind whistling through the nearby trees, we clambered into the chariot with the nursemaids and our adventure began. Side by side, Mary and I sat holding hands as we watched the Tower grow smaller and smaller in our vision, a grey monolith against clouded skies, with our brothers Ned and Alexander tiny ants on the stout wall encircling the bailey. I thought Alexander waved once, the bright red sleeve of his tunic flaring out like a vivid flag.

"I'm scared, Edith," said Mary in a small voice as we rounded a bend in the road and the pointed turret of the Tower sank into a haze of greenery.

"Do not be! All is part of...God's plan for us." I patted her knee, trying to give comfort as our Mother might, although my own heart beat fast and my head felt light at the thought of leaving the Tower, leaving Scotland. Leaving Mother and Father, and even our brothers, who, being boys, could act appallingly and torment us with snakes and spiders and our dolls impaled on eating knives.... However, I forced myself to show a confident face, for I was Mary's elder and must show my sister a princess's decorum.

"What if we do not like it in England, Edith?" Mary asked, her round hazel eyes filling with tears. "Whatever shall we do?"

Overhearing, Muriel the nursemaid cleared her throat and gave us a stern stare from under shaggy red brows. "You will do what you are told, that's what you will do. You are royal princesses, not hoydens from the local village with muddy bare feet and rude manners. Although I dare say Grisell would let you run amok as she did the other morn when your Lady Mother found you traipsing around like piglets in a sty." She glanced at one of the other nurses, who blushed to the roots of her hair; she was the youngest, and aye, she had let us get away with plenty. But that was in the past…

Mary looked even more upset, if that were possible, for she had not expected Muriel to listen in on our chatter, and now she was shamed as well as sorrowing and homesick.

I put my arm around her shoulders and gave Muriel a haughty glare; she did not need to be so unkind. The large woman sniffed, seeing my expression, and gazed out the narrow window at the passing countryside.

I leaned over to give Mary a quick hug while the termagant was not watching. My sister was fiddling with a lock of her auburn hair as she always did when nervous. "Don't fret, Mary," I told her. "We're going to Mother's sister, Cristina, remember? Family."

"D-Does she have children? Girls like us?" asked Mary, releasing the tendril of hair.

I blushed for her ignorance; she was so young, so innocent. "No, Cristina is a nun, a great and powerful abbess. Have you forgotten that nuns are Brides of Christ and not earthly men? But no matter, surely she will be just like Mother…and love us nearly as much as Mother does!"

Mary seemed content at that and clutching her tatty old doll, Cannie, she fell into a restless slumber. Watching her, I picked nervously at my nails and hoped I had not told her a comforting lie…

We crossed the disputed border into England after several days of travel and made good speed toward the south. There were stops along the way at gloomy border fortresses and bastles, at towns where people would emerge from cramped houses and stare at us, sometimes with unfriendly expressions, although on one occasion, a haggard woman, recognising the banners fluttering above our company, burst into noisy tears and cried, "Bless these children, the scion of Great Alfred of old! May their sons and sons' sons reign over us one day, our own people!" She was swiftly hauled away, by a gaunt-cheeked nervous husband. I was surprised by her outburst, although I had heard Mother say that many English folk were still pained by the loss at Senlac, the battle that saw the Conqueror take the throne and caused her family to lose its position.

As our party passed further along the roads, I saw first-hand why feelings still ran so high in the north. William of Normandy had ravaged those areas, punishing those who had risen against his rule. Villages lay empty, the blackened houses long fallen into ruin, and crows spiralled up from toppling shells as our company passed by.

"Are there dead people in there?" whispered Mary as she peered out at the blighted landscape, empty of crops, of standing buildings...of human life. Only the weeds held sway, tangling around the jagged walls of burnt-out ruins. The weeds and the crows, cawing mockingly as they flitted overhead.

"No, what happened took place a long time ago, Mary, before we were born," I told her. "The people...most will have fled away. And those that did die; I am sure their kin gave them good Christian burials...somewhere."

I had told Mary another comforting tale, but I was not sure. I imagined those ever-present crows, their beady eyes ravenous, picking amid the ruins with their daggered beaks to find bones or other hidden morsels...

Muriel, listening in as was clearly her wont, gave a pained sigh. "It was wicked what King William did. He punished innocents along with the guilty, the poor folk tilling the land as well as rebellious lords. He ordered cattle and sheep slaughtered and villages burnt to the ground; he took tradesmen's tools and shattered them; he stole people's winter supplies and scattered them, trampling their food beneath his horse's hoofs while women and babes wailed. Nought would move his hard heart that winter, not even when folk were reduced to eating their dogs, cats and horses, some say even each other..."

Mary released a cry of horror and covered her ears.

"Muriel, I beg you, do not." I did not particularly want to hear this grim story either, although I believed it my duty to learn the history of this land where my blood kin once ruled.

But Muriel was caught in some unpleasant reverie, her face hard and stretched, her lips drawn into thin lines; I wondered if she had lost family or friends in the disaster of which she spoke. Mother once told me Muriel had mixed English blood, which was why she chose her as our nurse.

"They call it the Harrying of the North," she murmured, "and it will live in infamy until the end of days. God will surely punish William *le Batard* for the evils he wrought; may he burn in Hell's fires!"

"Why do you tell us such things when we are to dwell in England?" I asked. I thought of my godfather, Robert Curthose, the Bastard's own son, who attended my Christening with his mother, Queen Matilda. Mother seemed sure he would smile upon me and Mary, but I was not so certain, listening to Muriel talk of his father's black deeds. After all, Robert had never visited Scotland since my infancy and I would not recognise him in a crowd.

The nursemaid looked at me and Mary, wrapped together under a fur. "You need to know the truth. My little princesses, I do not speak to you in this manner to frighten you, although frightened you may be. I tell you because you will need to know…for if you remain in England, within a few years you shall be entering the world of these Norman men who rule the country with an iron fist. You must know how they behave, what they are capable of."

I nodded, the understanding a cold dart in my young heart…and I dragged the drapery across the chariot window, hiding the blighted land that William Bastard's forces had destroyed with all the savagery the *Orcneas* and *Etins*, the monsters that haunted the early fables of the Saxon people.

We travelled onwards and eventually the charred ruins and abandoned villages disappeared. The landscape grew tamer and grassier, a patchwork cloak of green dotted by white, fleecy sheep. The wind was less fierce here and its breath less bitter. Little churches, some wooden, others recently rebuilt in stone, stood on rises and hillocks or in leafy coppices surrounded by clusters of huts.

Occasionally we would stop at a larger town where Mary and I gaped from the window at the locals, dressed so differently from us, and in turn, they gaped back, eager to gaze on royalty, especially once word had spread that we were of royal English lineage.

But our company never stayed in one place for more than a night, and soon we journeyed with the setting sun toward the west, passing through the great city of Winchester where many of my kingly forebears, including King Alfred, lay buried. Mary and I could not take our eyes off the grandeur of the city, our mouths open in awe as we passed through a gate set into the steadfast Roman walls and saw the turrets and tiles and towers of buildings beyond number. Dunfermline, the nearest town to Father's Tower, was tiny and mean in comparison as were the other towns we had passed. Trundling up the busy street, we could see the keep of a stone and timbered castle, built by the Conqueror to prove his might, and the clustered spires of the half-finished New Minster and the convent known as Nunnaminster. Bells rang out from the nunnery and other monastic houses, mingling with the strident clangs from other churches that clustered like lesser children around their feet.

"Our travels are near behind us." Muriel had climbed down from the chariot to purchase some hot pasties from a street vendor. She gave them to us, then handed us clean linen strips to wipe our fingers and faces. "Romsey, and the nunnery where your Aunt Cristina is Abbess, is not so far hence now. And thank God for that, I smell like a pig and my back hurts as if a mule had kicked it!"

I squeezed Mary's hand. "We'll soon be there and we won't be cooped inside anymore…"

Muriel gave me a wry, almost pitying smile. "Remember, Edith, you are going to a nunnery, not a nursery. You will have to share quarters with other maidens and I doubt the sisters will let you play in their herb garden. It will be a life of learning and prayer."

Mary trembled a little and I bowed my head and squeezed her fingers all the tighter. I understood the truth in the nursemaid's words, but we were boarders, not destined to stay forever in the convent. Surely our aunt, sister to our beloved mother, would not treat us exactly as she would a pack of unruly novices?

Muriel cleared her throat. "Smile now, girls; your aunt will not want to see sullen faces." She gestured to the soldier leading the cavalcade and the chariot started to roll forward, pushing against the swell of the crowd.

Briefly, I entertained a mad thought—to take Mary's hand and leap to freedom, running through the little alleys and winding lanes to a church where we might beg for sanctuary. But it was a foolish child's dream—and I knew it. We'd be handed back in a moment.

Sighing, I pulled the curtain closed as we exited the town gate nearest Winchester Castle and set out on the open road once more.

After an indeterminate time, where I slept, woke, slept again, I heard a shout from outside our carriage. "Romsey ahead!"

My heart beat a little faster. Soon we would find out exactly what was expected of us. I tried to keep my invented version of Aunt Cristina in my head—a saintly woman, smiling with benign gentleness at her sister's children. That had to be true, didn't it? Surely she would not have asked for us to board at Romsey Abbey if she did not truly want us there. However, I was aware, even though I had lived only six summers, that it was prestigious for a convent to have two princesses under the nuns' tutelage…

The path the entourage rode on grew narrower, through areas heavily gowned in leafy green trees. Muriel said we were on the edges of the New Forest, which King William had designated as a vast hunting ground for royalty. Oaks dominated all, looming over elder, alder and birch. I saw a deer, dappled by sunlight, between the ivy-swathed boles; nose twitching, ears pert, it stared back at me for a moment, before bounding away into the shadowed undergrowth. I longed to go with it, free…

The tree cover ended abruptly and the ground began to grow boggy, making the carriage lurches and judder. The horsemen at the front of the procession swerved around patches of sodden ground; off the beaten track, almost against the treeline, I noticed slimy pools full of reeds, while the scent of rank water reached my nostrils. Romsey meant Rum's Island, so I surmised water must have always been present near the settlement, perhaps even forming a now-vanished mere.

Continuing on, the company reached a wooden palisade, its posts whittled into sharp spikes. Watchmen stood guard on precarious turrets; seeing our banners they waved us on without preamble into the little town circled by the palisade.

Romsey was close to the size of Dunfermline but the houses were different, more timber or wattle, no stone, and less insulated against the weather. Muriel said it seldom snowed heavily in England's south and Mary and I might not even see a flake for years. It was unlikely we would ever be shut in by snow as we had been on occasion at Malcolm's Tower. Those Scottish winters had proved hard; food was rationed and the Tower stank to high heaven with all manner of folk and animals crammed inside. I would not miss that at all.

"There is the abbey, girls!" Muriel pointed through the chariot window-slit. Mary and I clambered over each other to gaze upon our new home. Romsey Abbey was a large, solid building, faced by stonework, its arches and bell tower high and massive. The Vikings had razed the town to the ground once and burnt the old nunnery down in retaliation for the St Brice's Day massacre of Danish settlers, but by all reports, the rebuilding had given it even lovelier form, spiting those heathens who had burnt it.

The entourage entered the abbey precinct through a gate manned by a sallow-faced nun. Servants arrived to collect our baggage, quiet, dutiful lay brothers and sisters in dull brown robes who performed their tasks with bowed heads and did not look in our direction.

A young nun in black habit and scapula emerged from the cloisters and walked purposefully in our direction. The breeze picked up her white wimple, making it flap as if it were bird's wings "I am sister Agatha." She halted a few yards from Mary and me, gazing at us whilst ignoring all the others in the entourage. "I will take you to the Holy Abbess Cristina." No smile broke her sharp features and my heart sank—I thought our aunt would come out herself to greet us and make us welcome.

Muriel made a little noise of dismay, and I glanced at her and saw naked concern on her features, surprising me for I had thought of her as a hard woman, a stickler for rules, for propriety. "Muriel, whatever is the matter…" I began, forgetting Agatha, who frowned like a gargoyle in the background.

"My princesses." Muriel bent to embrace me and then Mary. "I've done my duty to your mother the Queen and brought you safely to Romsey. Now I must go and let the sisters and the Abbess take charge of you. Be good…that's all I can say to you…and if I ever admonished you in the past, please know it was not through cruelty, but because I wanted you to do well and survive in a wicked world."

"You are leaving so soon, Muriel? This very day?" I was horrified. Surely it was appropriate for her to stay a week or two while we settled into our new environment. Who would dress us and see to our needs? Who could comfort us with stories of our old home in Scotland?

"Yes, I must go; the Lady Abbess told your mother a quick and complete separation was best" Muriel wiped her eyes on her sleeve before her brisk demeanour returned. "Now…listen to me, your Lady Mother the Queen will expect letters from you every now and then…and so shall I. Believe me, I will be waiting to see the fruits of your education at Romsey soon."

She stumped away then, her shoulders sagging as if burdened and climbed awkwardly back into the chariot. "Away to the abbey's hostel, fellows," she ordered the two grooms who held the horses. "Two nights we are permitted to rest, then we must begin the journey back to Scotland." The captain of our entourage nodded, and the carriage rolled back toward the wooden gate and the town beyond with Father's soldiers tramping around it.

Stricken, Mary and I stared, watching the vestiges of our old life roll away. At our side, the nun Agatha made a rather impolite cough. "Lady Edith, Lady Mary, it would not do well to keep Abbess Cristina waiting. She is an extremely busy woman."

Agatha turned on her heel and started striding away, robes swishing in the wind of her speed. I hurried to follow her, Mary puffing at my heels. The nun led us into a cloister of round-headed arches, the supporting pillars laced with flowering vines. In the centre of the quadrangle grew a garden where vivid flowers bloomed in abundance. My heart lifted a little at the scent and cheerful brightness.

"The flowers are fair to gaze upon," I said, hoping to break through Sister Agatha's coldness, "and their fragrance is…delicious."

"Hmph." The nun's thin shoulders rose in a dismissive shrug. "I suppose that is true enough…but we have no time for smelling flowers here at Romsey. You may contemplate the wonder of God's creations in these cloisters, but anything else is…indulgence and thus sinful."

Afraid to speak again, I bowed my head and walked on in silence.

At the end of the cloister was a narrow passageway lined with large, glossy flagstones. Agatha led us down its length to a narrow chamber hollowed out from the thickness of the wall. The stones surrounding the doorway were a rusty red, different from the rest of the building; I assumed they had survived the fire when the old abbey was burnt by the Danes. An oak door banded with iron stood closed, flat and unfriendly. Agatha rapped on it with her bony knuckles, the sound echoing down the corridor.

There was no answer in reply to her knock but Agatha opened the door nonetheless and curtly beckoned us forward. Once we'd inched past her, she whirled about and disappeared, a black crow flapping towards the cloisters.

Mary and I teetered on the first of three large steps bent in the middle from the passage of countless feet, which descended into the chamber. The room was lit by several expensive candles nearly as tall as we were, but it had not even a solitary window-slit and hence was oppressively dark.

Ahead, I made out the faint line of a desk, with a cowled figure sitting behind it. "Enter," the figure commanded. The tone was impatient, not at all like Mother's gentle speech.

We stepped down the stairs slowly, fearful of slipping in the gloom. On all sides of us stretched wall-paintings, barely discernible in the shaky light—saints being martyred in horrible ways, mostly—St Edmund filled with Viking arrows, Lawrence flayed on the gridiron, Catherine spinning on a spiked wheel while her tormentors jeered…

Cloth rustled and another candle fluttered to life followed by another. I gasped as a beautiful visage appeared on the wall behind the desk—a radiant saint, neither bloodied nor brutalised, her rose-gold hair streaming out from her head like the blessed corona, her gown green as spring leaves, her eyes blue stars full of the light of heaven. I had no idea which saint the painting represented, yet she called to me in a strange way; the first welcoming face I had seen at Romsey Abbey. I took a step forward. The burgeoning candlelight revealed a figure of another girl at her side, also saintly, but clad in blue, her head covered by a white veil. The main figure's arm circled the shoulders of the smaller girl in a familiar gesture, as if the two saints, whoever they were, had known each other. It was an unusual pose for a religious painting and I wondered if they were sisters like me and Mary.

"Why do you stare so, child?" The darkness parted and another taper bloomed, lifted on high in a metal cup. A woman's face floated in the flickering candle-glow, the eyes darkly hollowed by shadows. There was a vague resemblance to mother, but the lips were thin and downturned while two heavy lines ran from the narrow nose to the chin. Light caught off the jewelled pectoral cross lying against the blackness of her robes.

Aunt Cristina.

Quickly I curtseyed and Mary followed my lead.

"I asked you why you stared." Cristina strode from the desk, still holding up the candle. "Do I frighten you?"

She did, but I dared not admit such a thing to a kinswoman. My hand rose, shaking a little, gesturing to the murals behind the desk. "Forgive me, Aunt Cristina. I was entranced by the paintings behind you…"

Her expression softened a little. Turning her head, she peered up through the moving shadows at the two images. "These two saints are early patrons of Romsey Abbey, Merewenna and Elflaed. Merewenna was appointed abbess by King Edgar the Peaceable on Christmas Day in the year of Our Lord 974. Elflaed was Edgar's daughter and Merewenna became as close as a mother to her. Their lives were full of charity and good works, and after death miracles were wrought before their tombs. It would do you well…" she glanced sternly at us again, "to learn from their examples. Maybe you will find calling as nuns too."

Startled by her words, I blurted, "Oh no, Aunt! Mother said nothing of joining the order! We are here to be educated to a standard befitting a King's daughters!"

Cristina eyes darkened; the irises looked almost black in the uncertain light. "Oh did, she? Your mother was always a gentle soul, kindly...but, in my opinion, tender-hearted to the point of foolishness. No doubt it is in her mind for you and Mary to wed Norman princes or wealthy barons! Hidden away in Scotland, she is well shielded from the doings of these men. I tell you, child, once you've seen their lasciviousness, their violence, you might well beg to take the veil! They are not like...like us...like *our* people...."

Frightened by her intimidating words, I began to sweat despite the chill in the chamber. I did not want to believe my beloved mother would send her two daughters into danger. Surely Cristina was being too harsh...but would an Abbess, a woman of God, lie about such matters?

"A-aunt C-Cristina," I managed to stammer, "one of those Norman princes is my godfather. If he agreed to such an honour, surely he would see that I came to no ill at the hands of his fellows."

Cristina laughed harshly, throwing the candle holder onto the desk so violently the taper fell over and was extinguished, the wick filling the room with a tallowy scent. "Curthose...Robert Curthose is your godfather," she spat with contempt. "King William's least favourite son; a thorn in his side, lazy and rebellious. William called him 'Short Boot' for his diminutive size and the name soon became 'short hose' to everyone else. A laughing stock and an unfaithful son. He will do nought of value for you, child...that's if he remembers your existence at all. Added to his other deficiencies, I imagine he would not dare set foot in England now, since he recently joined in an uprising against his sire."

My face fell and suddenly bone-weary, I stared at my feet, my churning emotions at this unpleasant first meeting causing a wave of crippling fatigue to engulf me. "Edith!" Mary clutched at my sleeve, her little round face fearful as I swayed as if about to faint.

Cristina's hands shot out, grasping my shoulders, her fingers biting into cloth and flesh as she pushed me over to a stone bench that ran down the side of the chamber. "Sit, Edith, and get hold of yourself. You're not sick, are you? Have you been in contact with any bearers of contagion? If not, you are merely having a foolish swoon."

My head spun and my legs felt wobbly but I managed to murmur, "I will be fine, Aunt Cristina. It is the long journey. I did not mean to alarm you."

Cristina went to her desk and lifted a little brass bell which she rang three times. Its sharp clangs sounded throughout the room and echoed down the dim corridor beyond, reaching into the heart of the cloister.

Minutes later, a pair of nuns appeared, upright and brisk, no friendlier than the first one we'd met, Agatha. "My Lady Abbess?" inquired one. "How may we do your bidding?"

"My nieces Edith and Mary have arrived from Scotland to begin a proper education. Take them to the boarders' dormitory and see that they are fed. You may allow them a little more meat than is usual. Edith is clearly weak; she nearly fainted at my feet."

Still shaken, I clambered from the bench. The taller of the two nuns gestured for us to leave. I caught Mary's elbow, holding tightly.

With a heavy sigh, Cristina returned to her desk and the documents spilled across it. "Tomorrow your tutors will begin lessons—Latin, the French of the Court, the Gospels, the histories of England, Normandy and great empires of old. You will also assist the sisters in their work with the poor and afflicted and tend the gardens and the kitchens when asked. You will have no airs and graces because of your rank…and if I hear that you do, I will beat such prideful notions out of you. Do you understand?"

I nodded dumbly.

"Say it!" barked Christina.

"I…we understand! Both of us, Aunt Cristina."

She smiled a chill, unfriendly smile, lips drawn in a long, hard line. "Good. I would not like for us to start out on the wrong foot.

CHAPTER TWO

At first, it was hard to adjust to the Abbey's rigorously enforced rules. The canonical hours were hard to keep, especially for young Mary, and the dormitories were colder than we were accustomed to in Father's Tower, where the central hearth blazed night and day. Thank the Lord it was warmer in Hampshire than in Scotland! There were other girls there, though, the daughters of nobles of the realm, and soon we became friendly with them—Oriel, Richenda, Sybil, Gunnora. Together we learned not only languages and deciphering religious texts, but also writing, calligraphy, music and even geometry and mathematics. Of the latter, I was a dunce, the numbers jumbling in my head, but I excelled in most of the other subjects.

By the following year, Mary and I had settled in as much as we were able. Cristina kept a sharp eye out for any misbehaviour and would often chide us or administer a slap if she thought we were slow, impudent or lacking in attention—but now that we had the measure of her and expected no kindness, we did not mind so much and learned to avoid her whenever we could. She was Mother's sister, but something in her had soured, and we could not change that, we could only deal with it as best we could.

In the summer, the nuns allowed the girl students into the town, under the strict gaze of Sister Ivette. We walked through the busy marketplace, wondering at the displayed wares from all over the county and hovering around the bakeries and cookshops with their forbidden delights, savouring the scents of baking cakes and meat pies. Our diet in the abbey was wholesome but plain and we had both lost weight.

Later that same summer, news reached the abbey of important events far beyond our walls. King William had sailed to Normandy to oversee his various castles and holdings, but while he was there, the King of France subjected him to a barrage of mockery which stabbed his pride like a dagger and made him grow vengeful.

Sybil, one of our fellow students whose father had journeyed with the King, was full of these tidings, which were imparted to her in a letter sent by one of her brothers. She was a little older than the rest of us, and liked to gleefully recount that her family was notorious...

But it was not her kin up for discussion that night. "You'll never guess what King Philip did to annoy King William!" she whispered, as we huddled in our dormitory after dark.

"What, what?" everyone pleaded as they sprawled on their paillasses, blankets drawn up to chins, trying to keep to whispers so as not to risk a beating from the nuns.

"He said the King was FAT!" Sybil smirked.

Titters filled the room. "But he IS fat," said Oriel, who claimed to have seen him once when he was on his way to a hunt in the New Forest. "He is *enormously* fat."

"But you don't tell a king he's fat, do you?" Sybil tossed back her wavy nut-brown hair. "Not if you want to keep your head on your shoulders."

Another wave of giggles ran about the chamber, a little nervous this time. Sybil crawled out from under her blanket, her short legs pale in the light of our solitary cresset. "Anyway, Philip didn't just say he was 'fat'...he said something even worse! Do you want to hear?" She glanced around the dormitory, revelling in being the storyteller, the knowledgeable figure of importance.

"Yes, yes," we clamoured. "Tell us, Syb!"

"Hush then!" She put a finger to her lips. "Or we'll get ourselves thrashed by that witch Cristina..." She glanced over at my pallet. "Oh, forgive me, Edith, but she can be..."

"A witch. Yes, I know," I said, rolling onto my stomach, my white-blond hair spilling out over the edge of the bed in a pale cloud. "I will likely burn in hell for saying so...but it is the truth."

"Just go to confession, Edith; you'll be fine," said another maid, Richenda, sniffing. "It's not as if calling a nun an unflattering name is a mortal sin, is it?"

Sybil sighed, exasperated with our toing and froing when she was bursting to continue her tale of the King. "Do you want to hear the rest or not? I don't have all night. I need some sleep to keep my complexion smooth and fair..." Animatedly she brushed back her hair, pursing her lips and trying to look sultry. "So my father can find me a rich husband. If I grow ugsome and black-eyed, well, I will end up locked in this abbey forever!"

More snickers filled the dormitory. "Go on, Sybil", said Oriel. "I'm listening even if the rest of these gabies aren't."

The laughter died away. Sybil folded her arms around her bony knees, her white linen nightgown foaming around her. "The King, God knows why, went to Mantes intending to capture the town, which I must say is rightfully part of King Philip's domain. He failed in his effort, was thoroughly humiliated, and limped back to Rouen to lick his wounds. Whilst there, Philip was heard to jibe..." She made her voice deep in a ridiculous imitation of a man. " 'The King of England is lying-in at Rouen, like a woman waiting to deliver her brat.'"

Richenda uttered a shriek of mirth and quickly covered her mouth. We all fell silent, expecting to hear the nuns bustling in to administer chiding or punishment. A few moments later we relaxed again; no thundering angry footsteps rang in the corridor and all was silent save the scurry of night-active mice and the sough of wind through cloister arches.

"I can see why the King is angry," Mary put in. "My father would go mad."

"Any man would," said Sybil. "I mean, a seasoned warrior likened to a birthing woman! Grotesque!"

A little thread of unease twisted around me. "What is King William going to do?"

"Lose weight!" cried Sybil. The other girls tumbled about, giggling again.

"I'm the King!" crowed Gunnora, shoving a cushion under her baggy nightgown. "Look at me! About to give birth to...a kingdom." She gave a theatrical groan and the pillow was hurled across the room.

"Is this true?" I asked. "William is forgoing feasting to reduce his belly?"

"I do not jest," Sybil continued. "My brother Hugh told me and he's in Rouen. William intends to cut down his paunch by denying himself ale and wine and certain cuts of meat. He is planning to exist on gruel like a toothless old monk! Of course...this deprivation of culinary delights will only serve to make his temper even fouler and the whole episode will only lead to one thing…"

"What?" Oriel said. "A new name for His Grace? King Baggy-hose the father of Curthose?"

"Revenge! Philip will be sorry he ever made a jest at King William's expense. You know how hot our King's temper runs; he will return to Mantes and burn it to the ground!"

With Sybil's tale finished, we all snuggled under our thin blankets and against each other and sought sleep. I could not drift off, though. Mary's breath was hot against my ear and Gunnora turned over, grumbling in her sleep, and flung one arm over my hip.

I thought of the King, fat, ailing, angry. Under the covers I shuddered, remembering how he had once burnt the North. At least, I supposed, this latest carnage was not in England or my homeland. Closing my eyes, I mouthed a little silent prayer that the King would not commit any atrocities in revenge for a galling but silly jibe…

Bells clanged in the tower of the abbey church, deep, sonorous, solemn. Waking, I scrambled onto my knees, my pale yellow hair sticky to my face after the muggy September night. The cacophony above was not the usual call to one of the Hours and the insistent stridor of the bells tolling sent shivers up my spine.

Next to me, Mary was awake, eyes heavy-lidded, struggling to free herself from the covers. "What's happening, Edith? What time is it? I am frightened."

Bare-footed on the rush-covered flagstones, I staggered towards the door. Sybil, the eldest and by far the most forward, was at my side, and Richenda, Gunnora and Oriel a few paces behind, expressions fearful.

I clutched at the door-ring and flung the door open. Peering from the doorway towards the cloisters, I saw that it was still dark, the sky made gloomier by cloud cover. However, nuns were running hither and thither, almost resembling the bats that often nestled in the church tower in their flittering robes and wimples. Even as I watched, torches bloomed into life, illuminating the running women. The bells continued to boom, incessant, ominous.

Sister Wulfwynn, the nun who taught us hymns and arranged the choir, went flying by, oblivious to the wide-open dormitory. Darting out, I caught her sleeve, inadvertently spinning her around and nearly making her fall onto the flagstones.

"Oh, goodness, Edith, you frightened me!" She reeled away from me, hand on her chest, gasping for breath. "I did not see you there!"

"Sister, we were woken by the noise of the bells. We are all afraid," I stared up at the pale, strained circle of her face. "Is there a fire? Are attackers besieging the town?"

Slowly she shook her head. "No, child. We have had important news, news that will bring changes to all of us. All the nuns have been summoned by Abbess Cristina to pray for a departed soul."

"Oh!" I exclaimed. "The deceased must be very important for all the nuns to be roused at this time of night. By the colour of the sky, I deem it long past Lauds…but still far from Prime."

My mind began to whirl. Was it one of the great Bishops who had died, Lanfranc or Thomas of Bayeux, or some powerful lord, a Montgomery, Tosney or Warrenne, a Giffard, Clare or Montfort?

Sister Wulfwynn nodded, bleakly, her trembling hand reaching to clasp the rosary beads dangling at her belt. "It is someone of utmost importance, child. King William is dead."

The warlord men called the Conqueror was gone. As he fired Mantes in his quest for revenge, burning church and abbey alongside the homes of humble men, his mount took fright amid the hellish flames and flung him forward as it stumbled over the edge of a deep ditch. The great gut that had brought him mockery and shame now proved his doom; he struck the pommel of his saddle and it jarred the innards within his belly, rupturing them. Roaring in pain, he was carried back to Rouen, where he summoned the leading Bishops to his bedside along with two of his sons, William Rufus, named so not just for his flame-touched hair but his ruddy countenance, and the youngest, Henry, of whom I'd heard little. Having warred with his sire, Robert Curthose, my godfather, was away in self-imposed exile, reportedly seeking some rich heiress to wed.

King William had, at the last, repented of his anger towards Robert, though. On his deathbed, he declared that his eldest son would have the Duchy of Normandy as his patrimony. Rufus, however, would become King of England. No one knew how Robert might take this; Normandy was the richer land but the position of King held the higher dignity. The youngest son, Henry, was given no lands at all, but a great amount of silver, which he apparently counted out very carefully, afraid that the full amount would not be paid.

"So we now have another King William," I said, a few weeks after that fitful night when the bells had rung and the nuns scurried through the corridors like terrified mice. "I wonder what he is like?"

"Face as red as blood I've heard," said Sybil, ever knowledgeable on the deeds of famed knights and barons. She was shrewd and jocular, supposedly in the mould of her dead mother, Mabel, a rumoured poisoner. "When he gets angry, he looks as if he is about to burst! I've also heard he does nought but hawk and drink and that he has the most awful companions, devious, violent and uncouth."

Gunnora, the second oldest and most level-headed of the convent's boarders, tutted and rolled her eyes. "Rumours are just that…rumours. It is unwise to speak badly of one's sovereign. Who knows, we may all marry his closest advisors and have to see him every day at court. Maybe…maybe he will even decide to wed one of us when he takes a queen." Her glance skimmed over me and Mary; as members of Scotland's royal house, it was a distinct possibility he might, far more than the other girls, who were noble but not as useful for alliances. My ears grew burned and I am sure my cheeks were just as scarlet as those of the fabled William Rufus.

"My older brothers say Rufus isn't the marrying type." Sybil gave an impudent grin. "He spends all of his time with other men…if you understand what I am saying."

Most, if not all of the rest of us, did *not* understand, and stared at each other, mystified. "But a king must marry," said Gunnora uneasily. She bore some royal English blood, even as I, although not so much or as high.

"True," said Sybil, "and no doubt he will eventually...but it would never be what I'd call a true marriage. And ugh, how horrid, to have to look at that great, red, sweaty face in bed!"

A few giggles emerged at the mention of the bed, but then we all fell silent, hearing the sound of approaching feet outside our dormitory. Moments later, in walked Sister Sacrist, who maintained the convent church, making sure that its statues were cleaned and repainted, the walls free of mould, the butts of old tapers removed and old wax chiselled away. A little, bird-like woman with piercing blue eyes, she looked straight at me. "Lady Edith, I come with a message from the Reverend Abbess. She summons you to her office without delay."

A cold sweat broke out on my neck, although I knew I had broken no rules of the abbey. Without waiting for my reply, Sister Sacrist turned about and stalked off towards the church.

"Edith, what have you done?" Sybil's eyebrows were raised, curious. "Drunk Holy Water from the stoop?" The older girl was fighting back laughter...but I knew there was nothing to laugh about if Cristina demanded to see me alone.

"I've done nothing wrong," I mumbled. "You're all near me day and night and know I am blameless."

"Mayhap you blocked the privy,"

Mary ran over. "If you go to Aunt Cristina, I want to go with you."

"No, Mary." I patted her hand. "I fear that would just inflame her ire if indeed she is wrathful."

"She's always wrathful," sighed Gunnora, who recently had her knuckles rapped for knocking ink onto a manuscript the Scriptor was compiling.

I smiled wanly. My aunt's mood was usually sour, but surely she would not punish me for an offence I did not commit. "I had best be off to see her. If I am tardy, she will indeed have something to complain about."

"Good luck to you, Edith," I heard Mary whisper as I took a deep breath and departed the dormitory chamber.

Aunt Cristina's office was dark, as she preferred it, smelling strongly of incense and tallow. Silent as a mouse, I slipped through the door and down the chunky, age-smoothed stairs. The Abbess had her back to me as she rummaged through a small wooden chest on the floor. For a long time, I just stood there, watching, while she ignored me. My cheeks burned with embarrassment and nervousness as I shifted from foot to foot.

Eventually Cristina turned around, her steely gaze latching onto my face. "Edith, I must speak to you. Much has changed since the old King died and a new King ascended the throne. I will speak frankly now, and want no word of our conversation to pass back to those gabbling chits you room with…Do you understand? If any of them were to pass on to their families what I am about to say, it may not go well for us. For you, me…and the entire convent."

Completely dumbfounded, I nodded.

"The new King…he is a devil. Yes, a devil, Edith. An unnatural man, as are many of his favourites. They are known to have no respect for religious foundations, even setting them to the torch—not here in England, not yet, but he will without his sire to hold him back. The Conqueror was cruel and ruthless but at least he had some modicum of respect for the church. Rufus has none. He and his cronies raided the treasuries of abbeys in Normandy…and some of his men carried off young girls such as yourself from convents. Many of William Rufus's men would be delighted to find themselves royal wives to boast about in this new regime. Do not imagine your young age would dissuade them from taking you, so evil are they. They'd lock you in a tower till you reached the age of twelve, the age of consent or…who knows, they are lawless brutes. Their actions are touched by Satan himself." Piously, she crossed herself.

"What can I do?" Helpless, I held out my arms, wondering why Cristina saw fit to burden me with this terror.

My aunt turned back to the chest on the floor and drew out a bundle of black cloth. "I had these made for you, Edith. A nun's habit and wimple. I want you to wear them at all times in case any Norman visitors come to Romsey." She thrust the bundle into my hands and then seated herself, watching me intently.

I stared at the raiment, coarse and uninviting. Nun's garb. I began to shake. "But Aunt, surely it is wrong to just pretend I am a nun. I-I think my father and mother would not be pleased."

Cristina made a huffing noise. "Let me deal with them. Your mother may be tender-hearted but she is well aware of how these Normans treat Saxon women—like cattle. I won't have that happen to you. You should thank me for wanting to protect you."

"I-I do, Aunt. But what about Mary? Are you going to make her dress like this too?"

"Not yet; she's really little more than a babe in arms, so I believe she is safe for the moment. You…you are tall and look older than your age, more like ten than seven. Also, you are the eldest daughter of King Malcolm, so your position outranks your sister's. You will be the one they come after, especially with that near-white hair of yours, which marks your English heritage."

"I…I do not agree to this…" Words burst out of my mouth, garbled and rushed. Cristina's eyes grew wide and enraged. "If I am seen in nun's garb, men may one day believe I was truly a professed nun, and none would dare marry me for that reason, even if I claimed otherwise. Your plan to keep me safe could destroy my chances in life, Aunt…"

Cristina shot up, leaning forward, her hands splayed on the desk, the candle flames making dark, threatening shadows leap across her hollow cheeks. "I am trying to save your honour, girl! Your mother has given you free reign to display insolence and stupidity, I see. In any case, would it be so terrible if you did become a nun, serving our Lord Jesus Christ in chasteness and humility?"

"No, of course not," I cried, "but a nunnery is not the path I would choose and my father would not wish it either."

"You do understand one day you'll marry a Norman lord then—the oppressor of your mother's people," Cristina spat. "He'll look upon you as lesser and treat you accordingly. A wife's lot is not an easy one at best of times, let alone when her husband is from a cruel, conquering race. You have no idea what you are desiring, child."

"Nonetheless, I do not wish to be a nun, or pretend to be one," I whispered. My hands were hot and sticky on the clothes she had given me. "I have no calling. Take this back…" I proffered the garments to her.

Cristina flew at me, knocking over the candle. Its flame licked at her hem and she gave a very ungodly curse and kicked the taper aside, extinguishing it. The room was midnight, full of moving shadows. My aunt grabbed my upper arm, her fingers clawed, and shook me as a terrier shakes a rat. "You will not disobey," she shouted. "*Put them on*…or I will strip you naked, thrash you, and put them on you myself."

Tears came now, large, fat ones that rolled down my cheeks. Embarrassed, I peeled out of my kirtle and let it fall to the floor, then picked up the coarse black nun's robe from where it had fallen. Yanking it over my head, the rough cloth abraded my skin, itchy already. Any heat would make it unbearable. Biting back sobs, I took up the rumpled wimple and thrust it on my head, although I did not know how to fix it properly in place. Cristina grasped me again and fiddled roughly with the headdress while shoving my braids inside its folds.

"Not one hair must show," she said. "There…that is better. You will blend in with the other novices well enough…as long as you wipe that sulky expression from your face."

She released me and returned to her desk, covered with wax from the overturned candle. "You may go now. Once you've reached the dormitory, I want you to contemplate what has happened this day and learn from it. You will, in future, cede to me in all such matters—as your kinswoman, your elder, your intellectual superior, and as the Abbess of this House."

Crying in silence, I stumped up the stairs to the cloister walk, my head hanging low and my habit, slightly too large, trailing on the flagstones. I felt so embarrassed to show myself to my companions dressed in these hideous, unwanted black rags. But I had no choice.

Entering our chamber, all of them turned towards me with mirthful faces, eager to find out what trivial infringement Cristina had punished me for. Expressions turned from mirth to shock.

Mary gave a high-pitched squeak and leapt from her pallet. "Edith…you…you're a nun. They've made you a nun!"

"No, they haven't!" I cried and tore the hated wimple from my head and flung it on the floor where I stamped upon it in a frenzy while the other girls stared, open-mouthed.

My fury spent, I ran to my paillasse and threw myself on it, sobbing as if the world was ending.

Over the next months, it did indeed seem as if the world was ending and not just because of the wretched costume I was forced to wear. Not long after the new King's coronation at Westminster, where Bishop Lanfranc placed the crown upon his brow, the weather turned foul, wet but warm, and crops were ruined, everything growing damp and mouldy. It was as if God himself had voiced displeasure at the crowning of this new Red King. The loss of the crops was followed by a terrible fever that raged through the towns and villages and eventually even found its way into Romsey Abbey. Old and young alike were felled, skin burning as if in the flames of hell and wracked by violent coughs—and a number of the nuns and novices died. Of our little group of scholars, we lost a newcomer, Petronilla, who had only been there a month; I was stricken, lying flat on my bed, gasping for air and soaked in sweat, while Sybil grew sick, then recovered swiftly...but lost her hair thereafter, weeping like a babe as clumps came away in her hands, leaving short bristly tufts all over her head. She was never quite so jovial after and became surprisingly introspective.

When I finally recovered, I was weak, feeling as if the joy of my youth was sapped from me, and I walked glumly with an old woman's shuffle to my daily lessons and to prayers. I was too worn out and disheartened to fight with Cristina over wearing the nun's attire, so I kept it on as she had dictated. The fever had left me often feeling cold and shivery, and at least the heavier fabric offered some warmth.

As time dragged on and the last dregs of my illness mercifully abated, I still continued to wear the nun's robe, although I took the wimple off whenever I could get away with it. For the first time, I had seen Norman men, friends of the King, staying as guests at the abbey as they travelled to and from his court, and I began to think maybe Aunt Cristina was right in her fears about their behaviour. They were arrogant men, the older ones with the back of their heads shaved and glossy bowls of hair above, almost giving them the look of shorn monks, though there was nought monkish in their leering and their display of rich garments and jewels. The younger ones, especially those said to be favourites of William Rufus, were quite different in appearance, wearing their hair even longer than my Saxon kin; they also sported shoes with ridiculously long toes and raiment as bright as a peacock's feathers.

One such was Robert FitzHamon, and it turned out he was there for Sybil. He had supported Rufus in the Rebellion that broke out in the months after old King William's demise, and Rufus had awarded him with the Barony of Gloucester, so he was a wealthy man. His sire had been Sheriff of Kent and his grandfather was known as Hamon Dentatus—for his large rabbit-like teeth. Hamon had quite prominent teeth too, though not disfiguringly so. And he was looking to see if Sybil would make a suitable wife. Quite inappropriately, he stepped into our dormitory to get a look at her.

"I know this is unusual, Abbess," he said in a pompous drawl, "but I have never wed before and want to make certain my future wife is suitable."

"She is well-educated and has a lively mind," said Cristina, her tone waspish, as she pushed in behind him, eager to make certain he kept his hands to himself.

"I am not so bothered about that," he laughed, "but I'd rather not wed a maiden who resembles a sow or a horse."

"She is of high-standing ancestry, a Montgomery," said Cristina. "That should make up for any deficiencies in her looks, although she has none. Well, one, but only a temporary one. Sybil, come forward girl."

Sybil stepped from the shadows, glaring. The torchlight glinted off her tufty locks, which had grown a little but were still ragged and sparse.

FitzHamon blinked. "God's Teeth, what happened to her hair?"

"Its loss was a consequence of the great fever that travelled around the land. We lost many sisters to it…Sybil lost only her hair, praise be to God."

"You are sure it will grow back."

"Yes," Cristina said stonily. "Sister Infirmarer says it will just take time."

FitzHamon stepped over to Sybil, who looked furious; she was embarrassed about her hair and this suitor had acted the perfect fool, rubbing her face in her temporary affliction. Now, though, he oozed with sudden sweetness as he captured her hand in a sword-callused paw and brought it to his mouth. "I have spoken with your father, Lady Sybil, to see if a match can be made between us."

"So I understand," she said. "Are you sure you still want such a burden? You seemed...horrified at the sight of me."

"It...it came as a surprise to see you shorn.... That is all, my lady," he stammered, reddening.

"You do not think I am too much of a pig o to wed?" Defiant, she stood with hands on her hips.

"I-I beg forgiveness for using such rude words, Lady Sybil. I jested...I fear I am foolish from my long ride and have drunk too much at the Abbess's table. Now that I've seen you and spoken with you, I would be truly pleased if you would become my wife. What say you?"

"If my father had already agreed, and it seems he has, then my agreement, or not, means little," said Sybil. "So, yes, I will marry you, Robert."

"All is well then," said Cristina, clearly glad there would not be a scene. "Come to my offices and we will talk the more, and I will write on your behalf to your father, Sybil."

They exited of the dormitory and when the door was closed, we all gathered round, laughing and gossiping, although nervously. Soon we knew many of us would be likewise pared off to men chosen by our fathers, in alliances for money and stability.

After a while, Sybil returned. We all went silent then, not knowing what to say to her, whether she would be angry or sorrowful...or even glad.

"Why is it so quiet in here?" she asked, glancing around the chamber.

Gunnora cleared her throat. "I hope it is not wrong to congratulate you..."

Sybil burst into laughter. "Oh, it's wrong…but there's no sense in crying about it. Father had decided on FitzHamon long ago. I made Robert agree that once we are wed, the first good deed we should do is build a grand abbey church at Tewkesbury. He agreed readily. I will soon have him wrapped around my finger, mark my words. And if, by some misfortune, he turns out utterly repulsive and brings me ill…Well…" She gave a fiendish grin, quite unladylike and made even more so by her short hair. "I shall do as my mother did to her foes and fill his cup with poison!"

Sybil left Romsey later in the year, and Gunnora and Richenda went too, to join the households of their betrothed husbands. Mary and I continued our education; I enjoyed embroidery and would make altar cloths, while Mary enjoyed singing under the tutelage of Sister Cantor. And so time passed, as time always does. For some reason, as months stretched to years, Cristina's feelings worsened towards me, her reasons known only to herself. I caught her glaring from behind pillars, watching my every move. If I forgot to wear my wimple to hide my hair, she would drag me to her quarters for punishment and smite me with a rod she hid in her desk. My knuckles and buttocks would smart and bruises dappled my skin but I refused to cry out or let her see my pain and dismay.

Although I bore these beatings without a word, rage boiled within my heart, for I had done nought to deserve them. Again, Cristina prattled at me about how I was at risk from Norman knights and nobles, and once she even admitted what was in her heart and behind these assaults on my body and my dignity, "I would advise you take the veil, Edith. A convent is the best place for you. Surely you have seen what these savage men are like. You saw the fool who has now wed Sybil de Montgomery. Do you want to be a broodmare for such as he, breeding half-Norman children till you die?"

"But my father and mother do not wish for me to be a nun," I returned, my fingers stinging from the latest caning. "I have told you this before, Aunt Cristina, and it has not changed. I do not wish to join the order, either. Any vows taken by a girl forced into the church are not binding, I'm sure. I beg you not to speak of this matter again."

A great melancholy fell on me, as was common in girls of my age, which was then almost twelve, and I thought I should never be released from Romsey Abbey. Missives from my parents in Scotland had dwindled almost to nought, and I felt the world was closing in upon me, for of late Cristina did not permit the lay boarders to visit the town, claiming it had become too dangerous. I begged my tutors for news of the outside world; astounded a child my age was interested in such, they tutted and frowned but I nagged them until they relented and told me what I wanted to hear. "I am a King's daughter and one day may be a queen," I said with as much seriousness as a twelve-year-old could muster. "I must know of the trials and follies of the outside world lest I become learned only in religion and Latin and oblivious to all else."

And so, after a period of reluctance, the tutors told me of the King's latest exploits, how he'd sailed across to Normandy on his longship, The Sea Snake, adorned with golden dragon figurehead on its prow, intending to bring Robert Curthose, now returned from exile, and his younger brother Henry to heel. Robert FitzHamon, one of his favourites, had gone with Rufus—I suspect Sybil was pleased to have him out of the way; from what we had heard she was throwing herself heart and soul into the building of her abbey.

At night, I often pondered on what would happen if Rufus fell in battle and Robert became King—could I write to him, my godfather, and get him to release me from Cristina's care? I dared not speak of such a thing with anyone, though, not even Mary. Thinking of the King's demise was close to treason.

As it turned out, the King survived his battles, although he was not exactly victorious. The tidal flats of Saint Michael-in-Peril-of-the-Sea foiled his siege, and nearly killed him when he was roistering on horseback with his knights—he fell from the saddle and was dragged facedown through the sand—but he managed to come to an agreement with Robert. Henry, holed up on the heights of Mont Sant Michel, agreed to terms a few weeks later.

But if I thought William Rufus' return to England, with the threats from Normandy at least temporarily halted, might make life somewhat calmer at Romsey, I was incorrect. Cristina still followed me like a black shadow, insulting almost everything I said or did, shaming me in front of the nuns and the other maidens residing at Romsey.

I began to lose weight, my dreary clothes hanging sack-like on my limbs like a sack. My face grew waxen and wan, the colour in my cheeks draining away. Concerned, Mary would try and tempt me to eat the rare treats we were allowed, but I could barely stomach them. In desperation, I began to pray fervently to the two saints of Romsey abbey, Merewenna and Elflaed, whose images graced the wall of Cristina's chamber. At least my aunt could find no fault with my piety.

One of the old nuns, Sister Edburga, also had a special devotion to St Elflaed. Edburga often met me in the church choir and we would walk through the cloisters while she told of the saint's life and the miracles she had performed in Romsey. Edburga was a kindly simple soul; she was also much crippled by arthritis, her steps painful and dragging, and sometimes her mind wandered. Yet she was much loved for her good heart, even by my aunt, and none dared complain of the time we spent together. After all, it was part of my religious education to learn of the holy saints.

"Have I told you of Elflaed's miracle when she was but a girl your age?" Edburga asked as we strolled outside in the gardens. It was summer, the lawns patchy and yellow, the flowers high, filling the bee-haunted air with jewelled radiance.

"I…I can't recall, Sister," I lied; she'd told me different versions three times and had forgotten. I was quite happy to listen again if it kept me from Cristina's wrath.

Edburga smiled and rubbed her hands together. "Well, then…legend says that Elflaed had a tutor who was a vicious and brutal nun, delighting in beating her charges."

I grinned to myself, imagining Christina's sour visage. "Poor, hapless Elflaed," I said. "Do go on, Edburga."

"One day, this tutor was displeased with Elflaed over some triviality, a flaw in her Latin, a missed note in Evensong, a minute's lateness for Matins…I don't know what. But the tutor's rage was terrible; she swore and shouted in a way no good Christian should."

I bit back a snicker. Once or twice, I had seen Cristina possessed of such rage she seemed almost unholy.

"Locking Elflaed within the dormitory, the angry nun thundered off to the orchard to cut switches, intending to lash her charge and any other maidens who riled her. In despair, Elflaed, reeling from her tutor's tongue-lashing, sat down with her head in her hands and prayed for guidance. Suddenly she smelt the sweet scent of heavenly roses and glancing over at the wall, saw that it had miraculously become as clear as glass. Through it, she saw her tormentor cutting the switches and hiding them beneath her robes. When the nun returned to the abbey, Elflaed prostrated herself on the flagstones and begged her not to beat her and the other girls with the branches she had cut in the orchard. The sister reddened and asked how Elflaed knew what she had been doing. 'I saw you,' Elflaed told her, 'and I know you carry switches hidden in your habit.' The bad-tempered nun was shamed then, and full of wonder, for she realised God must have sent Elflaed a vision. Filled with remorse, she cast away the offending switches, vowing to curb her temper and stay her quick hand…"

I wished Aunt Cristina would learn such lessons, but she believed she was right in all things… I suspected she would argue with Christ himself if he appeared! I sighed, remembering the sting of her beatings and the bruises yellowing on my calves.

"Things are that bad, are they, little Edith?" Edburga put out a hand to touch my shoulder in a comforting manner. Perhaps she was more perceptive than she let on…

Filled with the sudden urge to confide, I began to speak…but at that moment a shriek echoed through the cloisters and the sound of rushing footsteps. Edburga and I halted and stared in alarm. To my horror, I saw my sister run from the abbey into the garden where she hid behind a large, manicured bush.

Edburga saw too; her hand rose up to flutter at her throat. "Whatever had happened…we must go to the poor mite."

She choked on her words as Cristina stormed into the gardens, holding, just like the wicked tutor in her tale, a long, painful-looking switch. "Where are you, child?" she cried. "How dare you run from me, your aunt and your superior. You have received lenient treatment owing to your young age...but now no more! You must obey or suffer the consequences!"

Red rage filled me. I strode towards the abbess, who had not yet noticed my presence. "What is going on, Aunt?" I cried, furious to see my sister cowering in the bushes. "Why are you shouting at Mary?"

Cristina jumped and whirled around to face me, her switch held up in a threatening manner. "None of your business, you interfering minx. Mary defied me and ran away like a common hoyden; she needs to be punished, to learn that girls should be meek and biddable."

At the sound of my voice, Mary had crawled out of the bush, greenery threaded through her hair. Racing to my side, she caught my arm. "Edith, I am so glad you are here! Aunt Cristina tried to make me wear a nun's garb, even though she promised..."

"You are older now," interjected Cristina. "And the world has changed, becoming more sinful, more dangerous."

"Enough of this!" The angry flame still burnt inside my breast. Snatching Cristina's switch from her hands, I broke it in two. "You will not beat my sister. If you must hit someone, give me her punishment. But I tell you this now—you will not force her to wear nun's garb."

"It has kept you safe!" Cristina argued. "Ungrateful chit! I am ashamed that my sweet sister Margaret birthed such a hellion as you."

At the mention of my mother, my eyes flashed. "I will write to Mother...and to my sire, the King of Scotland. So far I have told them comforting lies; told them we were happy here. And I tried to be happy, but you would always spoil any joy with your harsh ways. Now I am going to tell them the truth. Why should I continue to protect someone like you?"

Cristina's cheeks blanched. "Edith, no, do not be so silly. This has all got out of hand. Sending a message full of tittle-tattle is unnecessary."

"No, it is *completely* necessary. I will write to my parents and let them decide if the 'care' you give us is the type that they imagined. You may write to them too, of course, to tell your side of the story. I think that is fair, don't you?"

"You…you arrogant…creature," she stammered, spittle flecking her mouth.

"I will write my letter tonight and want it sent upon the morrow. Is that agreed? If you do not send it, I shall find out, Cristina, and remember, one day I will be free of this abbey and dwelling in the world beyond …"

"You are threatening me?" Cristina snapped but I could smell the fear beneath her bluster.

"No, I warn you, Aunt; that is all." I took Mary's shaking hand and we both walked off, heads held high, leaving Cristina fuming in the garden.

"You were splendid!" Mary whispered as we entered the cloisters. "You sounded just…just like a Queen."

CHAPTER THREE

Mary and I were leaving Romsey.

Letters to that effect had arrived from Scotland by swiftest courier. I had been overjoyed to read in Mother's own hand that she believed my grievances against Cristina and hence decided to move us to the Abbey of Wilton, an even more established place of learning than Romsey. While journeying home would have been my preference, at least we would be far away from our aunt's malice.

Cristina had received a letter at the same time as I, only hers was sealed by Father. I was not privy to its contents but I could see the contents had disturbed her; her eyes were red-rimmed as if from weeping or sleeplessness and her face whiter and more pinched than usual.

She did not even leave her chambers to bid me and Mary farewell when our leaving day came and we clambered eagerly into a chariot paid for by Father. I shrugged as the carriage rolled through the abbey gates and away onto the road beyond. I had learnt a valuable lesson at Romsey, sure enough—you could not always trust even those of your family to do right for you.

Our journey into Wiltshire left behind the long, haunted tracts of the New Forest, where King William loved to hunt, and entered Squabb Wood instead, a little grove where the trees were humped like skulking trolls, passing near King William's manor at Mottisfont before finding a well-worn route not far from the river. At first, I watched villages and hamlets pass by, cows lowing on streambanks, sheep spaced out like standing stones on bare hillsides, enjoying what felt like freedom. However, by eventide, I was tired, my eyelids heavy and I fell asleep, Mary cradled against my side.

The next thing I knew a hand was shaking my shoulder. It was dark outside and wind was battering the cover of the chariot. A nun was standing at the entrance, a dusky horn lamp swinging in her hand. "You are at Salisbury, Lady Edith, Lady Mary. I am Sister Mildred and I have come from Wilton to greet you. It is after nightfall and the rain and wind are fierce, so you shall stay here for the night. I will escort you to Wilton Abbey on the morrow. Let us just hope the river we pass on the way does not break its bank tonight."

I clambered from the chariot, handing Mary down after me. In the gloom, we spotted dozens of houses, lit by torch and firelight, and beyond them to the right a handsome cathedral, blurry through the rain and on the left massive earth ramparts topped by fences and a castle rising behind on a huge mound.

"The Abbess Hawise has arranged accommodation at the cathedral with permission of Bishop Osmund, the kinsman of old King William, God assoil him. Come along and I will lead you there."

With servants carrying our baggage, we walked the last few feet to the Bishop's Palace that stood near the cathedral cloister. Osmund was not there, being on business at Winchester with the King but his attendants brought us in from the rain and the gale and took us to sumptuous chambers.

Sister Mildred stayed with us, although she refused even a truckle bed, preferring to lay on the floor in her robes as a mortification of the flesh.

Despite the warm room and fine bed supplied by the Bishop, neither Mary nor I could rest. The gale howled outside and the whole palace vibrated. With every gust, there was a great clanging of bells, wild and discordant.

"Is it always like this, Sister?" I asked Mildred.

The nun nodded. "The gales score the heights eternally, breaking apart stones and sending statues spinning from their niches in the face of the cathedral. The bells here never stop; when hands ring them not, the winds take over. If they are tied down, they invariably break free again. This hilltop was perhaps not the best place to found a town—not only is it windy but the water supply is poor. I believe Osmund thought God would provide, but He has not seen fit to."

Mary drew the coverlet on the bed around her ears. "It's not so loud now, Edith."

"Yes, try to block the noise," said Mildred, "and get some sleep if you can. Wilton is not far away but it will be an exhausting day for you, I am sure."

I must have looked nervous at that, for Sister Mildred cast me a heartening smile. "Do not fear, Lady Edith. Abbess Hawise is as kindly as she is wise. Your weariness will only be from taking in all you must learn."

The journey from Salisbury to Wilton was not over-long, although the road crossed a bridge where a deep, fast river flowed, before snaking up a steep hill that had the horse drawing our carriage puffing in distress. A brief patch of woodland greeted us before we reached a busy little town, full of churches and full of people going about their daily business. In the days before the Conqueror, Wilton had once been the capital of Wessex, but now its fame lay in the Abbey of Saint Mary, Saint Bartholomew and Saint Edith, which was one of the wealthiest in all England.

The Abbey lay in extensive lands a little way from the town centre. A stone gatehouse two floors high fronted it, its outward aspect carved with images of its patron saints. Receiving clearance from the porter who lived on top of the gate, our carriage advanced under its arches into a courtyard. The vast abbey church, perhaps the largest I had ever seen, gleamed like a floating ship of heaven, the wan sun, lighting pale yellow stone brought all the way from Caen. Mingled scents wafted through the air—luscious aromas of fresh bread from the bakehouse, fuggy smells of fermentation from the brewhouse, fresh, floral fragrances from the herbarium and flower garth.

Mildred helped us from the chariot and we entered the cloister. It was brighter and more spacious than that at Romsey and I marvelled to see vines on its pillars bearing grapes. Such delicacies, which I had tasted only once or twice at feasts, did not grow in Scotland and, indeed, were rare throughout most of England, save the southernmost parts.

"Wait here!" said Mildred, and she left Mary and me while she went to find out where we should be taken. She returned shortly.

"Abbess Hawise is available to see you right away. As I told, you, do not be afraid; the Abbess is a kind and holy woman. In temperament, you will find her very different to your Aunt Cristina." She smiled crookedly and I smiled back; obviously Cristina's ferociousness was known beyond Romsey's walls...

Mildred guided us to the chapter house where much of the nunnery's business was conducted. It had a stupendous entrance: red and green pillars covered in carved stone vines through which strange beasts peered—cats with human grins, bulbous-eyed dogs, horned dragons—into an airy, domed room painted with bright scenes from the Old Testament. Stone benches stretched along the walls, where the Abbess, the Dean and members of the Chapter would meet daily after Morrow Mass.

Abbess Hawise, recognisable by her ring and large pectoral cross stepped away from the nuns she was talking to and motioned them to leave. Mary and I approached her with polite curtseys. Hawise was a short plump woman with a face that fairly beamed with the love of God. Her lips curved up in a kindly smile, and relief flooded over me. Mildred was right. She was as unlike Cristina as it was possible to be and of that I was endlessly glad.

"Welcome to our Abbey, Lady Edith, Lady Mary," she said. "I received letters from your royal parents detailing your...issues at Romsey. I pray you will be content here in the continuation of your studies. Our community is a happy one and as long as there are no major infractions—lying, stealing, immorality or extreme insubordination—we do not chastise our charges. However, I must mention one thing that may be contentious. The wearing of garb like unto that of a novice or professed nun."

My heart sank. Surely I would not be required to walk about swathed in those hateful, itchy black robes again.

"You will not be required to wear such items in most daily tasks or in your schoolroom. Your aunt's measures at Romsey were unorthodox we might say—but she was correct about one thing, such attire can and does deflect unwanted suitors. Wilton is visited by many and on a few occasions, we have had unseemly scenes. I would advise you to dress in such modest garb when and if certain great men lodge at Wilton, as they often do. It in no way means that I shall push you to become Brides of Christ! Is that understood?"

I was still leery of wearing garments to which I was not entitled, fearful that it might be believed I'd secretly taken vows, but Abbess Hawise seemed much more reasonable on the subject than Cristina, so, with slight reluctance, I nodded and Mary followed suit.

"Good," said Abbess Hawise, "now you both may retire and rest in the boarders' dormitory. Your education will resume on the morrow."

A little novice called Martha, not all that much older than me, appeared as if from thin air and beckoned us to follow her. First, we visited the abbey refectory, where we were given small trenchers of simple fare—beans flavoured with fat, rye bread, slices of hard cheese. Once we had eaten, Martha pointed out the reredorter and the abbey's warming room, before leading us to the dormitory, which was on an upstairs floor. The novices and nuns dwelt in little cells while the boarding students lived in an adjacent area closed off with painted screens.

There were three girls in there when we arrived, all around my age. One was reading from a missal, another was sewing, while another held some kind of book which she shoved under her bed-pallet as we stepped into the room. The novice Martha pointed out paillasses and a few quilts and covers, then left us to adjust on our own.

"So you are the Scottish princesses," said one of the girls, maybe a year my elder, willowy and pretty-featured, with a mane of golden-brown curls. "Should we rise and then curtsey?"

I did not know if she mocked me but forced a smile. "No need for formalities. I hope we can all be friends here."

The girl got gracefully to her feet, smoothing down her skirts. "Welcome to St Mary's. My name is Adela FitzOsbern. Abbess Hawise told us you were on your way from Romsey. She designated me to show you around on the morrow."

"I am Pernel," said the second girl, a plump, bird-bright creature with a snub nose and freckles. "With me is my sister, Richilde, who is hiding a book…"

Richilde glanced at her sister, scowling. "Pernell! What if they tell?"

Pernel put her finger to her lips and glanced at me and Mary. "You will not tell, will you?"

I blinked. "Tell what? Are books forbidden?"

Pernel smiled slyly. "Some are. Ones that aren't…religious. Ones that have kissing…"

"Or worse," added Richilde.

Pernel suddenly reached down and grabbed the book from where Richilde had attempted to secrete it. It fell open before me to reveal a drawing in the margin of a nun picking disembodied male privy parts from a tree!

I blushed to the roots of my hair and Mary gave a horrified little gasp. The other three girls burst into laughter which they hastily contained before reburying the book under the pallet.

"You won't tell, will you?" said Richilde plaintively. "I do not want to get expelled…My father would beat me."

"Your secret is safe with me," I assured her. "I know how to be discreet."

Richilde looked both relieved and grateful.

Adela gave a brittle smile and folded her arms. "Well, we shall see. Maybe, just maybe, we can be friends, even though…" She tossed back her mane of curls. "Even though the rest of us are not princesses."

The next day, after Mass and an early Latin lesson, Adela guided me around the abbey. The cloister, the brewery, the kitchen where we were allowed a hot pasty each, and the herb garden with its pungent scents of lavender, mint and rosemary. At the last, we visited the abbey church and the shrine of Saint Edith, wrought in gold by the order of the grateful King Canute, who had survived a storm at sea by crying out the saint's name.

"Were you named for Saint Edith?" Adela asked as we knelt together before the shrine, laden with jewels and other gifts brought by noble visitors including a cloth embroidered by Edith Godwin, sister to the slain King Harold, who had been educated at Wilton Abbey and financed a rebuilding of its church.

"I do not know," I said honestly, "but my mother is very pious and it may be so. Saint Edith is, of course, a kinswoman."

"Of course she was." Again, that cynical tang in Adela's voice. "How foolish of me to forget you are both of Saxon royalty."

I held my tongue and Adela continued, somewhat less waspish, "Some nuns are rather…severe. Cheerless. Saint Edith was different. She never forgot she was a princess as well as a nun. She eschewed the habit and wore rich raiment…although she wore a hair shirt below, in case she grew too proud. I heard that you scorned the wimple when you were at Romsey, Edith."

"So my 'fame' has preceded me," I said with a wry grin. "Yes, I fought with my Aunt Cristina over it. She wasn't just trying to hide me; she was desperately trying to make me a nun despite my resistance and my parents' wishes. It is the reason Mary and I have been sent here."

"We sometimes do wear nun's veil, though," said Adela, "when unsuitable men are in the vicinity."

"Does it happen often?"

Adela shrugged. "Quite. The abbey is famous and has many visitors."

"I wonder how Saint Edith dealt with it when she was a girl?" I mused, peering through the haze of incense smoke towards the shrine.

"She probably terrified them!"

"Terrified?" I arched an eyebrow.

"Saint Edith had visions. They could be terrifying. She would fall down in a fit and cry out. Once she had a dream that one of her eyes fell out…"

I grimaced. "How horrid."

"She took it as an omen that something bad would befall her brother, King Edward. And then news came that he was stabbed to death at Corfe Castle." Adela licked her lips. "The shrine you see was built by King Canute, but years before, he was not so pious and doubted Edith was a saint. He said her father was a violent lecher, so he doubted she could be holy and pure." She gave me a sideways glance as if testing to see if I reacted to this assessment of my distant kinfolk. I kept my gaze fixed straight ahead on the smoke, the winking rubies and emeralds, the gold embroidery of Queen Edith.

Adela cleared her throat to get my attention. "Canute ripped her tomb open so that he could assess her saintliness—I presume he was checking to see if she was incorrupt and expecting to find a heap of mouldy bones. But a miracle happened—Edith rose from the grave and slapped his face. That quickly made him a believer in her powers." Adela pointed to a small object, encased in glass and bound with gold, that stood at the heart of the saint's shrine. "Do you see that? Do you know what it is?"

I squinted into the candle smoke and shook my head. "I suppose it is a relic. I do not know what."

"It is her thumb...Edith's *thumb*. It is incorrupt. The rest of her apparently fell to dust after her tussle with Canute, but the thumb remained intact. She was noted for making the sign of the cross with it in a certain way."

"I am not sure about that story about King Canute," I said. "A dead saint attacking him? I thought most saints would be *saintlier*...even if offended by an unbeliever. Miraculously healing the sick and distressed and that sort of thing."

"Oh, Edith," said Adela, rolling her eyes. "Not all saints are sweet and kind. St Julian was a murderer before he found God, don't you remember? Anyway, Edith did heal people too. Less than thirty years ago, Abbess Elfgiva's failing eyesight was cured here at this very spot. During her lifetime, Saint Edith founded a hospital in the abbey grounds. If you want, I will take you there."

I was tempted to ask if I could go alone but decided this might make Adela take against me. Already she seemed to have judged me and found me wanting. "I would love to see," I said with a wan smile.

We left the shrine and walked out across the verdant lawns surrounding the nunnery buildings. At one point, we passed a ramshackle enclosure, which held a few scruffy goats and pigs. It appeared to have once formed part of a greater structure for a number of empty pens and cages stretched along part of the abbey's retaining wall.

"Saint Edith had a bestiary," Adela explained, waving her hand in the direction of the pens. "Her own private zoo. The nuns didn't keep it up after her death—a shame, for it would have been nice to have some pets."

Just past the empty pens, we took a turn towards a row of thick, high bushes carefully pruned, creating a shield that hid whatever lay behind from sight of the abbey. Sliding through a rounded opening clipped into the hedge, I viewed a neat, compact, grey building with arched windows and a worn statue of a female saint above the apex of the door.

"This is St Magdalen's hospital," said Adela, "where Saint Edith gave succour to outcasts, cripples and the poor. A few nuns do still tend the sick here. I don't want to go any closer and I don't think you should either… Some of the residents are loons who paw at you or drool, and some have had their hands or feet chopped off."

I ignored her and, as if drawn, walked toward the hospital door, where an old toothless man was hoeing the ground in a little herb enclosure. His leg was encased in a bandage and stuck out at a strange angle. Several nuns were giving him instructions about where to hoe and how to plant. He took them gladly, nodding: "I want to be useful, you know. Like I was afore a cart crushed my leg. 'Tis least I can give back for the aid I've received here." On benches nearby, other residents of the hospital sat in the wan sunlight—an old woman with palsied hands, a blind youth clutching a cane, a young girl with a facial deformity who giggled as she waved uncoordinated hands at a butterfly that drifted past her nose.

So these were the people Adela felt so repulsed by. Out of the corner of my eye, I saw her hovering by the hedges, arms folded and looking cross. I decided to ignore her. I had watched my mother washing the feet of the sick and when I asked her why, she had smiled and recounted the words of St James: *Let the sick call the elders of the church to pray over them and anoint them with oil in the name of the Lord. And the prayer offered in faith will make the sick person well; the Lord will raise them up. If they have sinned, they will be forgiven.*

I had not forgotten the gratitude, the relief, in the eyes of those she ministered to. I would not turn from them either.

Approaching the hospital door, I was stopped by a nun who emerged carrying a large bowl full of water and soiled rags on her hip. "You are the new boarder, the Lady Edith?" she asked as she poured the water into a gully along the side of the building and wadded the rags into a ball which she threw back into the bowl. "I am Alice, Sister Infirmarer."

I nodded. "Yes, I am Edith. Today I am touring the abbey to learn its workings. Of all I have seen so far, this St Magdalen's intrigues me the most."

"We have beds for twelve paupers here," said Sister Alice. "Many have always been poor, others have suffered ill health, injury or other misfortunes. John..." She nodded toward the man with the hoe, still hacking the rich earth, his tongue half out of his mouth in concentration. "John was hit by a cart and his leg did not set correctly afterwards. He managed to labour on for some years, but with age came severe pain; he could no longer lift, carry, or walk far. He could no longer earn an honest wage, so he ended up here. The boy with the stick is Ailwin—struck blind by *Morbilli*, one of the spotted diseases that take so many children; the old goodwife is Gerd, a widow whose house burnt down in a cooking fire, and the maid is Leofgifu—Love-gift in the Saxon tongue. Her mother abandoned her at birth owing to the affliction of her face, and her mind never developed beyond an infant's—but she is the most innocent and sweet of God's children, and truly a gift to the abbey."

Sister Infirmarer walked back toward the hospital. "You may view the interior if you wish, Lady Edith. Come with me." She stepped over the threshold, and I followed on her heels.

Inside there was a long hall lit with rushlights. A large Rood carved from oak, blackened by smoke and age, hung on the back wall amid faded wall-paintings of the Virgin, Saint Michael weighing souls and other religious scenes. A series of simple straw-stuffed pallets lay in neat rows, six to a side. Some were empty, their occupants outside letting the sun warm their frailties, but the rest held the most poorly, invalids who were having broth or porridge spooned into their mouths by young novices.

"My mother, Queen Margaret often helped with the sick," I said as I watched.

"Yes, many have heard of the good deeds done by the Scottish Queen. Some liken her to a living saint."

"I...I would like to help at the hospital if it is permitted," I stammered. "I would like to emulate my mother's deeds and make her proud."

Sister Alice smiled. "It will have to be cleared with the Abbess, but I would welcome another pair of hands."

Together we left the hospital, chatting to each other about salves, unguents and tisanes. The simple girl, Leofgifu, bounded up to me, plucking at my sleeve. "Are you comin' 'ere, Lay-dee? Your hair so pretty..." She reached up to touch a strand of silken near-white hair that had escaped my tight braids.

"I may do," I told her, "if the Reverend Mother agrees. Alice told me that your name is Leofgifu. Mine is Edith."

The girl's face lit up with joy, and in that moment, she almost appeared...*beautiful*...despite her deformity. She radiated true, pure joy that was born of her eternal innocence. "The saint, you's the same as the saint...Are you the saint come back to us?"

"No, I am no saint," I laughed, patting her shoulder, bony beneath the worn cloth of her woollen kirtle. "But I would gladly emulate the good deeds my namesake Edith did long ago."

I walked back to Adela, still loitering by the hedges. "Why did you go in there?" she asked as we walked back towards the cloisters. "I thought you'd never return. I told you it was awful."

Her attitude was truly beginning to grate; her disdainful manner was evident from the first time I set foot in the boarders' dormitory. "You offered to show me what Saint Edith built. I was interested."

"Weren't you afraid in there?"

"Afraid of what?" I frowned. "I saw only unfortunates, not a ravening horde of murderers and thugs."

"Afraid of *illnesses*!" She sighed as if she was tired of explaining. "What if you picked up some horrible disease, something disfiguring like leprosy. Your nose might drop off ...."

It was my turn to heave a deep sigh—one of frustration "None of them have leprosy, Adela. If they did, they would live in a lazar house outside of town. Most are just poor folk who have grown too frail to work. Someone has to look after them, Adela, and there is no reason why one such as I, born into privilege, should not give back to the common folk."

"Never thought of it that way," she sniffed. "But still...I could not do such a task. Boils and burns, drooling and dropsy. Ugh."

She traipsed back into the abbey complex, frostier than ever, saying not one word. I did my best to ignore her and ran to join Mary in the school room to tell her what I had experienced and to find out how she had managed on her first day.

Abbess Hawise allowed me to assist Sister Alice as I wished. Every day, after lessons, I would trudge down to the hospital to begin my duties. I was not permitted to tend any of the male occupants, owing to my status and my young age, but I changed dressings on the injuries of the women, combed the hair of invalids, spooned frumenty into the mouths of the bedridden. It was hard work, no doubt about it, and one quickly learnt to have a strong stomach, but at the end of my day, when I returned to the dorter, I had a sense of accomplishment and a warm glow of satisfaction that filled my entire being. I had never known such sensations before; it was almost like a religious experience, as if Saint Edith herself guided me in my new endeavours.

One day, though, my ministrations to the poor and sick were abruptly cut short. I was braiding young Leofgifu's hair and helping her into a newly laundered shift when Richilde burst into the hospital hall, breathing heavily. She had been running. "Edith," she gasped. "Abbess Hawise wants to see you at once."

"I am nearly finished my duties..." I began.

"No, *now*," she insisted. "The Abbess said it is an important matter and cannot wait. Not for anything."

Apologising to Sister Infirmarer for my hasty departure, I hurried back to the abbey. I found the abbess waiting in the Chapter House, a furrow of consternation crossing her brow. Her usual motherly smile was absent.

"Reverend Mother?" My voice trembled. "Have I done something to displease you?"

"No, Edith," she said, "but I thought you should know. You will soon have your first suitor."

I gasped loudly, feeling as if all the air had been struck from my lungs. My head swam, the candle flames on the candelabras going blurry in my vision. "W-who?" I managed to stammer.

"William de Warenne, second earl of that name. It seems he is eager to marry into royalty. He is very wealthy and only in his twenties."

"Do my father and mother know of his intentions?"

"I have not heard from them; messengers from Scotland can often be long delayed. Of course, they would have to give their permission if a marriage was to be contracted, as would King William. But in the absence of any instructions from either, you are rather on your own, Edith."

I began to pace nervously on the flagstones. "I know not what is the right course to take, Lady Abbess! I beg you—counsel me!"

"Meet him. Wear your nun's cowl, as we decided to keep his ardour cool. You never know, Edith; he might make a splendid husband for you."

I nodded, trying to appear brave and mature, but in truth, I felt like Daniel approaching the lion's den. "Send to the Earl then, Reverend Mother, and tell him that I shall meet him."

A week later, Earl William arrived in the middle of a rainstorm, a small entourage trundling miserably behind him in the mud. From a hiding spot by a cloister pillar, I saw his coat of arms flare brightly against the dismal grey of the surrounds, *Chequy or and azure*, checked gold and azure-blue, as the gatehouse porter admitted his company into the abbey grounds where they dismounted before scurrying towards the abbey guesthouse, eager to get out of the wet. Through the downpour, I could not tell which one was de Warenne; all I could see was a cluster of sodden heads.

Breathing heavily, I yanked on the wimple the Abbess had given me, tucking every strand of hair under the brim, and strode towards the Chapter House where I would meet my suitor. *Do not be afraid, you are a King's daughter!* I told myself. *Show valour like your brothers would in a battle!*

I was the first into the Chapter House; Hawise had gone to give the Earl greetings and escort him to meet me. I paced around, wringing my sweaty hands like some vapid lady in a romance tale. I'd only been in there for minutes but already it felt like hours. Suddenly, footsteps sounded in the corridor beyond—the light tread of the Abbess, the scuff of a man's heavy boots. Taking a deep breath, I hauled myself up as straight as I could in an attempt to mimic the regal stance of my mother and face the doorway. Into the chamber came Abbess Hawise accompanied by a young man of middling height with curling brown hair and a pale oval face.

"Lady Edith," said Hawise, "I present to you the Earl of Surrey, William de Warenne."

The Earl stepped forward and bowed stiffly while Hawise retreated to a bench in the rear of Chapter House and assumed an attitude of prayer. I was gladdened that she was staying; if these Norman men were truly as wild as reported, a chaperone was surely necessary.

"Lady Edith." William took my hand and kissed it, his sudden motion almost making me pull back in fright. "I have long heard of your beauty..."

Liar, I thought, suppressing an urge to laugh. "Oh...thank you, my Lord," I murmured, "although I cannot imagine where you heard such a thing. I was only six summers when I left Scotland, and since then I have not once set foot at the royal court. I have spent all my time with nuns and maidens, and I hardly think they have fared abroad to speak of my 'beauty.'

He flushed red; he had an extremely fair complexion, pink beneath the pallor, the kind that would burn and blister in the sun. His brows were unusually thick over blue eyes that bore a pained expression and were a little bit too close together—they reminded me of furry caterpillars, and I had to choke back another peal of mirth at the thought.

"My Lady...are you all right?" He blinked at me, his pained expression changing to one of concern. The hairy eyebrows waggled, drawing together over his high-bridged nose.

I could barely control myself now; my eyes watered with the effort. I feigned a spell of coughing. "Yes, yes, thank you, Earl William; it is the air in here that ails me—so dry and dusty."

The Earl cleared his throat with a great deal of hacking. "Yes, I agree, it is rather warm and dusty in here...so, I will not keep you here long, but will explain the reason for my visit. I will speak plainly—I want to marry you, Lady Edith, if you are amenable. It will be a good match."

My brows lifted; I simpered beneath my ugly nun's hood. "I do not want to sound as if I am prideful, Earl William, but I am a princess born and my father's eldest. I had, truth be told, expected those who desired my hand would be princes or kings."

"Well, Rufus is unlikely to desire you, since his tastes run more to..." He halted, flush deepening, clearly appalled that he had somehow let his tongue run free and slandered his monarch...not that I truly understood the meaning of his words, though I pretended to by nodding sagely. He began to breathe heavily, his anxiety obvious; I saw sweat gleam on his forehead. "Forgive me, I should not have said those words, especially before a high-bred lady..."

"Oh, Earl William, you can trust me to keep your secret. The nuns taught me that one should always be silent and discreet."

"But you're not a nun, are you?" He leaned forward, his gaze fastened on the oversized wimple rammed on my head. "Or is there something you have not told me? I have heard rumours that perhaps you decided..."

"A bride of Christ is an honourable job, is it not?" I sighed. "But no, I have not made any firm decision about my future. That will be between me and God, and, if earthly marriage is to be my lot, between any suitor and my father, the King of Scotland."

"I have great wealth," he puffed, suddenly looking as if he wanted to fight...*something*. Not me, but maybe my sire...or even God? I chewed on my lips, striving to maintain a solemn countenance. "I not only own countless lands in England but the fine castles of Mortemer and Bellencombre in Normandy. You would want for nought, Lady Edith, fairest of women."

More flattery but now I did not laugh. I could see that he was quite serious, which worried me...for I had quickly ascertained that I did not wish to marry him. He was young but too callow, and his boastful account of his worldly possessions did not exactly endear me to him. Maybe I was just not ready for such a step…

"Well, you will have to ask my father what he thinks of such a match," I told William. "If he considers it appropriate, I will bow to his wishes. However, I would ask that our betrothal, should it take place, be a long one; my education at the Abbey is not yet complete."

"Why do you need more education?" His furry dark brows knitted once more. "You know how to put your mark on a document and can sew and embroider, I trust! That is more than enough; I want to wed a seemly, decent wife, not some would-be scholar with her nose fastened to a book." He snorted with derision.

I truly disliked him with that last comment and wished he would leave. On my head, my wimple was growing itchy and I longed to tear it off and hurl it in his face but I was too well-mannered for that. "I believe you also have to ask King William's permission before any steps are taken."

"King William will agree!" said the Earl with vehemence, but I saw a shadow slip over his face. "I—I helped him defend Hugh de Grandesmil from the depredations of Robert de Belleme and the Duke of Normandy."

"Robert Duke of Normandy is my godfather," I said flatly.

His colour deepened yet again. He looked blotchy, like the time Pernel ate strawberries and came out in an awful rash. "I-I did not mean…"

"No offence taken, Earl William," I said, but with such breeziness I knew he thought I was indeed offended. No need for him to know the last time I was with Duke Robert was at my Christening.

"I shall leave you in peace to consider my suit." He grabbed his hat and backed away from me as if grown eager to get away.

"Go with God, my lord." I cast him a beatific smile. "This has been a…a most *interesting* meeting."

He gave another sharp bow and almost fled the room. I wondered if he might stay the night at the abbey, but heard him shouting for his retainers, and soon the cries of men and whinnying of mounts filled the air, followed by the clang of the abbey gates opening to let the Earl out. I assumed he'd had enough of the ways of nuns and would fare to Salisbury instead where his men could carouse in the inns and he could drown his own sorrows.

I ran over to Abbess Hawise who was finishing her impromptu prayers "What on earth did you say to him?" she asked. "He ran out of here like a frightened hare."

"Nothing untoward," I assured her. "But… for numerous reasons, I do not believe he is suitable. May I write to my father and mother on this matter to make my feelings clear?"

"You may, Edith…but I must remind you. Earl William may be your first suitor, but he certainly will not be the last. And one day you must accept some man of rank to be your lawful husband. Make sure you choose wisely and well."

CHAPTER FOUR

I wrote to Father to tell him of Earl William's visit and how I did not deem him a suitable husband for I liked not his false flattery or manner. However, the couriers had a wasted journey. Before I had a chance to hear back from my sire, a missive arrived from the Earl. He had asked William Rufus if he would grant him permission to further his suit—but the King had refused his request. There would be no marriage under any circumstances. So much for Surrey believing that the King owed him favours for his assistance against his enemies.

Happy with this outcome, I returned to my studies and duties at the hospital of Saint Magdalen. I attempted to forget about my unwelcome suitor; at the moment, I had no wish to marry, not him, not anyone, being but thirteen summers. However, the peace I found in books and ministering to the unfortunate was soon to be broken again.

I was at the hospital, teaching Leofgifu how to plant cabbages and beans. She loved to thrust her hands in the warm rich earth and feel mud well between her fingers. I was wiping the dirt from her nails before we planted the next seed row when I heard my name shouted and turning my head, I saw Abbess Hawise herself entering the hospital enclave through the manicured bushes

"Reverend Mother!" I finished with Leofgifu and sent her inside to get her daily bowl of broth from one of the lay sisters. "I am surprised to see you here. Should I call Sister Infirmarer…"

"No, Edith," said Abbess Hawise in a low voice, "it is you I come to see."

"I am nearly done here for the day." I wiped my hand on my apron. "Once Leofgifu's garments are changed and I've put a poultice on Old Mother Ascelina's boil…"

"Sister Alice can deal with that," said Hawise. "Tell her that I need to speak with you."

She was obviously ill at ease, which made my own worries arise. Nodding, I hurried to the hospital door. Alice was inside on a wooden stool, spooning pottage into the mouth of one of the most debilitated elders who had suffered elf-stroke and could no longer feed himself.

"Forgive me," I said, taking off my dirt-speckled apron and placing it into a tub for the laundresses. "The Reverend Mother awaits without. I'll be back when I can."

"If the Abbess calls, you must go, there are no two ways about it." Alice wiped spilt food from her patient's bristled chin. "It must be important."

"That is what I am afraid of," I mumbled.

"God go with you, Edith," said Alice, crossing herself.

Abbess Hawise took me into the abbey church. On the wall, the sun through a window slit illuminated a painting of the blue-robed virgin, stars under her feet and sun rays streaming gold behind her head. "Edith, I have had a letter from His Grace the King of Scotland."

Fear gripped me. "Is it my mother? Is someone hurt?"

"No." She shook her head. "Here…he has also written personally to you." She handed me a parchment, a red lion roaring on the seal. I broke the lion in twain in a shower of crimson wax, unrolled the parchment and read it…then, stunned, read it again.

Dazed, I glanced up at Abbess Hawise, letting the parchment fall. It coiled up, rolling across the cold tiles of the floor. "My Lord Father…he is suggesting a betrothal. A man called Alan the Red. This Alan is Lord of Richmond in the north of England and my sire believes an alliance between our families would be useful…for protection of Scotland's border." I thought it prudent not to tell her the full reason why he desired that match, which was unlikely to have been stated in the letter she received—that King William would not relinquish lands in Cumbria that Father claimed were rightfully his, and a wealthy northern baron would make an ideal ally to wrest them from Rufus.

"How do you feel about this, Edith? I brought you here instead of my private office so that you will tell me your true thoughts…here in the presence of God."

I blinked back a shameful rush of hot tears. "I cannot go against my father's wishes if he truly wants this match, but I have never met this Alan at the Scottish court, or heard any word of him before now. A good man or a bad, I know not. All I can ascertain, from this letter is that he is incredibly wealthy, with many loyal brothers and soldiers at his disposal. I-I thought Father would at least suggest a possible match, rather than already speaking of betrothal as if the deal is already done."

"I have some knowledge of this baron." Abbess Hawise heaved a sigh. "Alan the Red came to St Mary's several years ago when the abbey was holding a prisoner called William de St Calais before his trial at Salisbury. Alan had travelled south to escort de St Calais to the town. Alan's conduct while he stayed at our abbey…was less than admirable. There was one of the novices…" She pursed her lips, clearly unwilling to proceed with the details of the tale, although I guessed what they might be. A lover's tryst…or, worse, an unwilling ravishment of a nun or boarder.

"Far be it for me to interfere with the King of Scotland's wishes, but from what I have witnessed, I do not think Sir Alan would make a suitable match for a gentle maid of such high breeding. To my mind, he is far less suitable than William de Warenne. So, I say only this, wear the hood again, as you did in de Warenne's presence. Find out the mettle of the man. But I will also warn you in advance, not only is his behaviour questionable, but he should have long ceased such wild antics as I witnessed for he is at least fifty summers old."

To say I was shocked by that revelation was an understatement. Once again, I felt a stab of utter betrayal. My father, my merry, laughing giant of a father, would surely never give me to a disreputable man old enough to be my grandsire. Not for a few more soldiers and a parcel of bleak, debatable lands at any rate. But yet…it seemed that is exactly what he would do.

"I can see you are distressed by King Malcolm's letter." Hawise placed her hand on my shoulder, her touch giving me strength. "Pray to God that He might guide you when Alan the Red arrives. All will be well; all will be as it is meant to be. Have faith, Edith."

Alan, Lord of Richmond, reached the town of Wilton about three weeks after the arrival of my father's unsettling letter. Overdressed and over-confident, his company processed through the narrow streets, the trumpeters blaring out a brash call that screamed of desired attention and adulation.

"What an awful din!" exclaimed Pernel, covering her ears as Alan's entourage was ushered through the abbey gate, while the trumpets blared on and on, although there was really no need for such an ear-splitting display within the abbey grounds.

"I've heard a rumour Alan the Red is here to marry Edith," said Adela spitefully. After our first days together at the abbey, she had either ignored me or made barbed jibes. Pernel thought it was because Adela felt that I made her look weak, snobbish and un-Christian by taking on earthy duties at the hospital when she refused to dirty her fair white hands.

"Won't that be exciting?" she continued, dancing around me like a malevolent faerie. She was a pretty girl, the comeliest amongst us, but she was vain and often touched by envy. "Our little Edith will go to the cold north to dwell with the sheep. I am sure Alan will keep her warm, though—if he doesn't fall asleep before the fire first. He's over fifty, I hear! An old man nearly in his dotage!"

I ignored her waspish words while Mary and Pernel scowled in her direction. "You're a shrew, Adela," said Richilde. "You shouldn't laugh at Edith—your father might wed you to a greybeard too, for all you know. And Alan the Red's hardly in his dotage, for all his years. He's a powerful landowner in the North."

Adela made to make a retort to Richilde, her eyes flashing angrily, but a timely knock on the door interrupted the fight that was brewing. Sister Cellarer stood outside, a burly nun who puffed from the exertion of climbing to the upper floor of the dorter. "It's time, Lady Edith. Mother Abbess is in the guest house hall with Lord Alan. He desires to make your acquaintance."

Brushing down my dour black robes, I drew on a veil to conceal my hair. I was sure I looked pale and sickly, for I had not slept a wink the previous night, tossing and turning on my pallet with unsettled thoughts streaming through my mind. Hopefully, a wan, drawn appearance would dissuade Alan if I found him particularly obnoxious. Perhaps I was not entirely fair to the man; he might be brave and stalwart, able to lead and guide me in a fatherly manner...but I suspected he was anything but. Not after what Abbess Hawise had implied about his past conduct. Not after his showy entrance to the abbey.

Sister Cellarer led me to the guesthouse, ushering me into the bright little hall, lit by beeswax tapers by the dozen. Abbess Hawise sat on a carved seat, heavy with cushions, while Alan the Red lounged on a bench, his favourites around him like a pack of fawning hounds. As Hawise had warned me, he was an older man, his visage ruddy and mottled from the wind and peeling from the sun. His eyebrows and lashes, from what I could see, were almost white, spikey and unappealing, giving him the look of a blind mole. The bushy, though receding, hair on his spotted pate showed how he got his name—it was a pale orange-red, although mixed with strands of grey.

As I entered the chamber, he stood; a tall man, whipcord-thin, his surcoat checked and garnished with a pattern of ermine tails. He grinned at me, his teeth small and black, his ice-blue eyes disappearing into a haze of sun-wrinkles as he did so.

"Greetings, my dearest Princess Edith!" He swept up to me like some kind of foppish courtier, grasping my cold, limp hand and pressing it to his bristly lips. "It is an honour to meet you at last! Soon, hopefully, with consent from all those involved, I will bear you north as my bride."

I cleared my throat, even as it threatened to seize up. "Welcome, Lord Alan. You must excuse me if I am not full of wise words and easy discourse. I am young yet, and my father the King did not inform me of your intentions till very recently."

"Not to worry, dear child," he said, his smarmy tone making me cringe. "There will be plenty of time to get to know each other once we are wed. Do not be frightened..."

He grinned at me with a lascivious glint in his eyes, and I scowled. *I am not so much frightened, you old goat...I am repulsed...*

"You will soon learn that I am a man of great prowess, both on the battlefield...and elsewhere..." Sitting back down, he cast a knowing glance at his men who all laughed raucously. Abbess Hawise's lips became lines and she frowned. "I was a boon companion to the Conqueror himself and fought in the vanguard with the Breton forces at Hastings. It was for my good service that the late King, God assoil him, bestowed upon me the Honour of Richmond."

"So you are Breton? I thought I could not place your accent."

He nodded. "Son of Eozen Penteur, Count of Penthievre, and Orguen of Cornouaille."

"Cornwall?"

"No, another place founded of old by a prince from those western lands. My native language is much the same as it is in your Cornwall. But now, I prefer to use the Norman tongue."

"I believe my father has agreed to this match to be assured of your support along the borders. Is this true? Do you have enough followers and influence to keep that promise?" My question was provocative, but I wanted to ascertain that he was indeed ready to provide what Father needed and that I would not warm the marriage bed for nought.

Alan looked surprised and hesitated, while his men smirked, amused that their lord was being questioned by a young girl "Yes. Of course," he answered after a moment or two. "My half-brother Ribald is Lord of Middleham, not so far from Richmond. My other half-brothers Bodin and Bardolf are Lords of Bedale and Ravensworth respectively. They are all ready to bring retainers to any conflict the King of Scotland might have. But…" he cast me one of his repulsive grins, his little black teeth glistening in the candlelight, "you need not worry about any troubles in the north. You will be safe inside the walls of the great keep I am building at Richmond. You will not be lonely either. My old wetnurse, Orwen, holds lands nearby and I am certain she will be the ideal female company."

Orwen. In my head, I imagined an old witch with tangled grey hair and a wen bursting out on her chin. To have been Alan's wetnurse, she was surely nigh as old as God himself!

I cleared my throat. "Before negotiations for my marriage proceed, I must tell you something, Lord Alan. Something even my royal father does not know about."

"What is that, sweet Edith? I have heard rumours you want to complete your education; if that's your wish, I will have tutors sent to you when we marry. However, I will not leave you with the good sisters, if that is your desire; I want you with me in the north. I need a son to inherit after me...just as your sire needs allies to keep the border peace."

I cringed, hating this man more by the second. "Lord Alan...there may be a reason why I cannot wed you."

"What reason can there be?" His voice grew harsh, the crooked, cracked-tooth smile fading.

I gestured to my wimple. "I tend the poor and ill...I-I think I may have a vocation, a calling."

"Are you telling me you are contemplating becoming a nun? And you've told no one?"

Folding my hands, I stared at the floor, attempting to look guilty. Silence would talk for me and then I would have spoken no lie.

Alan jumped up, his earlier false *bonhomie* vanishing like the sun behind storm clouds. "Or is it worse than that? Have you taken vows of some sort? Are you promised to the cloister? Abbess Hawise..." He whirled about, his thin flame-coloured hair flying out around his bony head. "What do you know of this matter?"

"I...I know nothing," Hawse stammered, her usual calm demeanour vanishing. "She has not taken any vows here at Wilton, although she does administer to the sick with Sister Infirmarer. However..." She shot me a keen look under her brows, "I cannot say for sure what took place at Romsey when Edith was in the care of her aunt, the Abbess Cristina. I heard that the aunt was eager for both her nieces to join the order..."

Enraged, Alan ground his teeth. "This is outrageous! I have travelled many leagues, and now it seems my prospective bride's eligibility is questionable. I dare not wed her as her contentious state would cast a cloud over the validity of any marriage...and worse, over any children she might produce! Pah..."

He rose in a flurry, gesturing wildly at his men, and stormed past me towards the door. Abbess Hawise took a step towards him, then retreated into the shadows, for he looked crazed, as if his emotions had become ungovernable.

Once he had vanished, Hawise approached me, worry etched on her features. "Get you to the dorter, Edith. I will not be happy until Alan the Red and his entourage have left the convent. Men like him are not used to having their wants denied."

I curtseyed to the abbess and hurried to the boarders' dormitory, rushing in with such speed I almost bowled Mary and Pernel over. One of the novices came running up behind and ordered us to bar the door. She then stood guard outside it, with others coming in to join her or give her time to use the privy. Our food and drink, which would normally have been taken in the refectory, was brought to us by a nun who left the platters on the floor and fled.

Ignoring the food, my fellow boarders clustered around me, eager to hear what had happened with Alan the Red.

"Maybe he'll try to carry you off in the dead of night," suggested Adela rubbing her chin thoughtfully as if musing about whether it would be a good idea.

"No, I don't believe he wants me anymore," I said. "My nun's cowl scared him off. What a relief."

"Was he terribly ugly?" asked Pernel, stretched upon a pallet with one of Richilde's forbidden books open atop a cushion.

"Quite so," I replied. "His teeth were stumps and his breath was bad."

A chorus of horrified noises of disgust arose from the others, except for Adela, who had perched herself on the edge of a bench by the window where she began combing her long, silky hair. "You'll have to marry sometime, though, Edith. You won't be able to fend off every suitor who isn't pretty enough for your tastes."

"If I wanted merely 'pretty', I could have encouraged William de Warenne's suit," I said coldly. "It is not about Alan the Red's appearance, but rather his other failings."

"I wouldn't lecture Edith about marriage if I were you, Adela," said Pernel. "After all, you're older…and no one has even so much as looked at you so far. It's as if your father has forgotten you exist."

Adela gave an outraged gasp, then turned her back on the rest of us, clutching her comb as if she were debating on using it as a weapon. I shook my head at Pernel who seemed eager to continue the verbal lashing; the last thing I desired after today's unsettling events was further conflict.

The rest of the evening we lay abed, listening to sounds of the retiring convent outside the door—swishing robes, a tinkling bell, soft pattering feet, a thin singing from the church's choir. As midnight's hour approached and the noises of daily activities completely died beyond, we were able to hear the gossip of the two novices guarding our chamber door, their voices echoing in the corridor. "Did you see Gunnild's face, Egidia? She was creeping about trying to catch his eye."

"Do you think she'd go off with him? I thought she got over that nonsense last time…She was doing penance on her knees for months after."

My ears pricked up. There was only one novice in St Mary's Abbey called Gunnild. She was of royal Saxon blood; her father was King Harold, cruelly slain at Senlac, while her mother was Edyth Swan's Neck, whom Harold had married in the fashion of the Danes—which meant, in the eyes of the church, that they were not truly wed. Gunnild had dwelt at Wilton since the Norman took power; she was a tall, spare woman, perhaps thirty summers old, with cropped honey-coloured hair beneath her wimple; a woman who seldom smiled but might have been considered fair if she did. She had entered the abbey for both education and her own safety, but had only decided on a religious life after the visiting St Wulfstan healed her of a mysterious case of sudden blindness. She had never become a fully professed nun, however.

I pressed a hand over my mouth in shock. Abbess Hawise had mentioned a previous incident concerning Alan the Red and a novice. By the gossipy whispers outside the door, the Princess was almost certainly the woman involved in the scandal.

I said nothing of my newfound knowledge to the other girls and eventually the drama of the day slipped away and we all fell into slumber while the candles set in brass cups around the room burnt away to nothingness.

Later, how much later I could not say, I was woken by screams and the sound of a bell clanging noisily over and over—a warning bell, an alarm. I sat bolt upright, clutching my coverlet to me. Around me in the gloom, I heard mutters and the sound of bodies shifting. Hot breath touched my cheek. "Edith, what's happened?" Mary's tremulous voice sounded next to my ear.

"I do not know," I murmured, reaching through the dark for her hand…but then I smelt it. Smoke. Acrid, cloying smoke. I glanced in the direction of the chamber door—long tendrils of grey were seeping through the gap below.

"Jesu, no!" I leapt to my feet, dragging Mary up with me. "Get up, all of you! Get up. *Fire*…there's a fire!"

Around me the other maidens scrambled from their pallets, half-asleep, gabbling in fright. Adela was openly weeping, Richilde coughing till her eyes streamed.

"We can't stay in here!" I rushed towards the door, hefting the bar that lay across it and flinging it to the ground.

"But what might lie in wait outside!" Adela grabbed the sleeve of my kirtle, almost yanking me off my feet. "The fire could be fiercer beyond. Or those men…that came with Alan the Red, they …they might…!" She started to sob.

"Let go of me!" I tore my arm free of her clutching fingers. "If we stay in here and the fire worsens, we'll all die! The smoke could kill us…or the roof could fall in. We must risk leaving—if there are wicked men out there waiting to assail us, we must fight them tooth and nail!"

Leaving Adela in floods of hysterical tears, I snatched hold of Mary and flung the door open wide. A blast of hot air struck my face followed by a huge billow of acrid black smoke.

Rushing down the corridor, I mounted the winding stairs that led down into the cloisters. Mary stumbled along next to me, crying, while the other girls pushed and shoved at my back, wailing and choking on the smoke.

As we burst into the cloister, I halted. The peaceful abbey had become a place of horror resembling the Hellmouth of the Damned painted on many church walls. At two ends fires were burning, their red glow lighting up the pillars of the cloister arches, illuminating the carvings on the capitals—foliate heads with goggling eyes; beaked monsters, half-bird, half-cat; stylised wolves eating sinners with long stone teeth. Nuns and novices were rushing around in a mad panic, hurling buckets of water on the flames. It was a slow job, as the well was not close enough to the building, nor were there enough buckets for all. Those sisters who had no buckets or who were too frail to carry one stood aside praying fervently, their voices rising in supplication to heaven.

At first, when I smelt the smoke and heard the clang of the warning bell, I had hoped that the fire was accidental—a candle fallen in the church or in the scriptorium, or an accident of some sort in the kitchens or the warm room. Fire was always a huge threat to both monastic house and castle. However, two separate fires were burning in the cloister, and both seemed to have been started in piles of rags, sheepskins and other detritus, so it seemed as if the fires had been deliberately kindled.

I started running towards the nuns trying to douse the closest blaze. The red light of the flames made their terror-stricken faces look contorted, devilish. Ash puffed into the air and sparks flew as if from blown from Satan's own jaws.

One of the nuns, Sister Almoner, thrust her bucket into the hands of another nun and lurched in my direction. "Edith, you must not stay here. Take the other girls and go round the back of the abbey into the garden. Try to keep out of the way and…lie low till we find out who has done this evil and why."

I whirled around and shouted at the other girls, "You heard Sister Almoner. We are to go to the gardens at once!"

We all began to run as behind us flames flickered, water splashed in glistening rivulets over the cloister's flagstones, and the sisters sent up prayers to heaven in a tearful cacophony of strained, frightened voices:

Sub tuum praesidium
confugimus,
Sancta Dei Genetrix.
Nostras deprecationes ne despicias
in necessitatibus,
sed a periculis cunctis

libera nos semper,
Virgo gloriosa et benedicta!

Breathing heavily, eyes and nose burning, I burst out into the night-furled garden with the other girls at my heels. Everything seemed strange and unfriendly under the light of a hard moon, with shadows and smoke warring for predominance.

Adela flopped down on the grass, holding her head in her hands. Her tears stopped as anger took over from fear. Her shoulders started shaking. "This is an outrage!" she cried. "We were meant to be safe here. My father will…"

"Hush," I ordered. "And get up. Sister Almoner told us to hide ourselves until we know what is what."

Gloomily she clambered to her feet, her gown now stained with grass. "This is your fault!" she snapped, jabbing at me with her index finger.

"My fault? How do you come to that conclusion?"

"It is Alan the Red who has done this, I am certain of it. He'll burn the place down because you've offended him. Your father wanted a betrothal…you should have been a proper daughter and agreed to it instead of playing foolish games that have brought evil to us all!"

I had tried to ignore Adela's shrewishness, but this last insult was too much. "Be silent!" I snapped. "I tire of your barbs and sharp tongue. Remember your place, as a daughter of a mere knight."

She looked stunned, her mouth dropping open. It was as if I had slapped her. She put her hands over her face and began to wail.

"Oh, shut up Adela," chided Pernel, rolling her eyes. "If there are wicked men about, your howling will bring them upon us, and all will be lost."

Adela bit her lip, wiping at her eyes. Her wild weeping had ruined her usual prettiness; in the wan moonlight, her crumpled face looked like a deflated pig's bladder surrounded by a mass of tangled hair.

"Are you done?" I asked. "All of us must stay together and not act like fools!"

I beckoned for the girls to follow me, and single-file and night-shadowed they came, treading silently along the path that ran hard against the wall. To my surprise, I realised I had assumed some kind of leadership, and all complied with my directions, even Adela, though she trailed in the rear, face screwed up in misery.

Soon I found a spot I deemed safe—a place where we hid from our tutors on lazy summer days when one second more in the scriptorium or poring over Latin tomes was too much to bear. There was a niche in the abbey stonework, once containing a saint's statue, long since removed; a rose bush bearing scarlet blossoms grew in front of it, masking the shaded alcove behind.

"In there...all of you," I whispered. "Do not move, do not speak...till I come back to you and tell you that it's safe."

"Edith! Where are you going?" Mary gasped. "Don't go, please..."

"I will be back soon, I swear it—now do as I say," I said firmly, pushing my sister towards the alcove. Pernel took Mary's hand, even as she began to weep, and the four girls crowded in together behind the flowering bush.

With the others safely concealed, I began a quest of my own. Blending into the shadows and smoke in my nun-like garments, I inched through the darkness. I could hear a nun shouting from the cloister, "It's going out, the fire is going out! Praise God on high!" and I heaved a great sigh of relief. Smoke grew denser, spiralling out of the cloister like a night-mist, but the crackling of the fires had ceased and there were no more towers of sparks.

Suddenly, though, there was a flare of torches in the courtyard and the loud shouts of men. Diving behind some shrubbery, I lay flat on the dewy grass as a large party of mounted men thundered along the path from the Guestenhouse towards the abbey gate. As they flew by, harness jingling, the horses' hoofs sending clods of earth spinning into the air, I managed to catch sight of Alan the Red mounted on a black stallion, his face alight with almost malicious glee. To see him wearing such a fiendish countenance was not so great a surprise, but what shocked me was that a was woman riding behind him, her arms wrapped solidly around his middle. She was wearing nought but a scanty kirtle—so shameful—and her legs gleamed white in the moonlight where her skirts had ridden upward. She turned her head, perhaps to see if the conflagration was ongoing in the cloisters—and I saw the ragged cropped fair hair of Gunnild, princess, novice, and now captive. However, I do not think she minded overmuch—for the first time ever, I saw her smile as Alan the Red glanced over his shoulder at his prize.

Then the northern baron's entourage was gone, streaming out of the gates and rampaging through the quiet streets of Wilton town, causing dogs to bark and men to shout in fear and grab knives, pitchforks and cudgels for fear or looting and worse. But the riders had no interest in the poor goods, their woollens, axes and scruffy animals—they rode on, out of Wilton, away up the hill and into the far distance.

My heart, thudding like a drum from the moment I spied Alan, resumed a quieter beat. Dragging up my heavy, dew-drenched skirt, I hurried back to the hiding place of my companions. Pushing aside the thorny boughs of the rose bush, I grinned at them as they crouched in the alcove, almost invisible, Pernel's dark cloak drawn over them all.

"You can come out now," I said. "The fire's gone out…and Alan the Red has departed the abbey. And it seems he's taken Gunnild with him. Both of them seem happy enough. I do not think he's all that upset that he did not get to marry me after all."

CHAPTER FIVE

Omne trium perfectum. All Things that come in Threes are Perfect. So, the old saying went. I did not find it so, however. I agreed with the lore of the local peasants: 'It never rains, but it pours.'

Another unwelcome visitor was set to descend on St Mary's Abbey. King William Rufus himself. He was on his way to Gloucester to meet with my father and broker a new peace treaty. Tensions had escalated between the two kings since the spring, with not only Father's lands in Cumbria being under assault but his lands in eastern England, granted him by the Conqueror.

Again, whispers ran through the boarders, novices and postulants—that William was coming to view me as a potential bride. After all the tales told of his rapacious and un-Christian behaviour, such a union was not a pleasant thought.

Abbess Hawise's usual calm was shattered; I do not think she ever recovered from Gunnild's abduction and the fires set by Alan's soldiers. She must have felt her position of pre-eminence in her own abbey was gone, her authority denigrated even as flames licked the pillars of the cloister. Now she was pacing the floor like a trapped beast, barking orders in a way I had never heard before. Tranquillity had fallen before panic. Nuns and novices were scrubbing flagstones and church tiles and chasing every cobweb that fluttered in the eyes and mouths of carved saints and monsters. Old reeds and rushes were raked out and fresh ones plucked from the banks of the River Wylye laid down in their place. The privies were thoroughly sluiced out and freshened by herb bundles, as were the guest's chambers. Orders of delectable food were hauled in by cart from Wilton and Salisbury—a larded boar's head, roasted larks, plovers and pheasants, carp and bream in spices, young conies doused in gravy.

I set my hand to helping ready for the visit in both the convent and Saint Magdalen's hospital, which distracted me from the awful thought of the Red King turning his harsh gaze on me and finding me desirable, not as a woman, but as a tool to bring peace between our countries. I was no fool, such alliances were common, with no affection between bride and groom, just royal indifference, but Rufus' reputation was so foul I trembled at the thought. Some folk even claimed he was not a true Christian but offered flesh and blood to the gods of the Norsemen, who were, not so many centuries ago, forebears of the Normans, or to the ancient spirits of the forests, devilish beings who dwelt in oak, ash and elm before England came to be, before even the Romans stepped upon its shores and laid claim…

"Edith!" I jumped in alarm as a voice called my name. Consumed by my thoughts, I had drifted into another world.

I set down the slops pail I was about to dump out behind the hospital and saw Mary. "It's time," she said breathlessly. "The outriders have arrived. The King will be here within the hour. The Reverend Mother wants us all gathered together when he inspects the place."

"Safety in numbers?" I picked up the pail again and dragged it over to the sluice. A horrible thought struck me, as I returned the pail to Sister Infirmarer and cleansed my hands. What if Rufus were to pass me over…and set his eyes on Mary instead? She was only ten, so not yet the age of consent, but there was nought to prevent a lawful betrothal. My stomach sickened and nervous sweat began to creep under my arms.

"Are you well, Edith?" asked Mary, concerned. "You have grown suddenly pale."

"I am tired, that's all," I lied, forcing a smile that hurt my cheeks and must have resembled a death-rictus grin. "I will be glad when this royal visit is over."

She nodded in agreement. "We must pray, too, that peace will be made with Father."

"Yes. I admit it frightens me that we will soon come face to face with a man who is, as things stand, an enemy of our House. And Mary… I am sure you've heard whispers about why Rufus has decided to stop at St Mary's for the night."

Mary's eyes filled with tears. "May it be proved wrong. You would make a fine Queen, Edith…but not with him. I heard Sister Sacrist saying he was incorr…inc…"

"Incorrigible? So it would seem. As well as irreligious and irascible."

"She is hiding the abbey's treasures because the King and his band of bullies have raided religious houses ere now. His right-hand man, Flambard, although a bishop, steals from the both wealthy and poor to enrich himself and his master!"

"I have heard that, too, and likely it is true, but what can we do except try to be courageous? Oh…" A little moan escaped my lips. "Sometimes I wish we were peasant girls, Mary, not chess pieces in the games kings play. Some of the girls in town marry sweethearts they have chosen themselves. Boys of similar age…"

"But we are not peasant girls," Mary whispered, "and we are bound to duty."

I squeezed her fingers, cold and clammy. "Yes, we are. So let us not tarry, and hopefully this horrid day will pass quickly and the King will have more on his mind than finding a bride. If our luck holds, he will ride on to Gloucester tomorrow. At least we can presume he is unlikely to offer us, or the abbey any grave insult, since it would ruin his chances for an agreement with Father."

King William Rufus decided to view the abbey after he had dined in the fratery with his closest companions and the Abbess, Prioress, sub-prioress and some high-ranking clergy who had ridden from the cathedral at Salisbury, eager to curry the King's favour.

The nuns, novices, postulants and young women boarders were herded into a group by Sister Infirmarer and Sister Refector as the feast ended and lay sisters and other hired servants appeared at the fratery door, dragging voiders full of scraps and chewed bones to the midden outside. "We can keep an eye on you here," Sister Infirmarer—Alice—whispered in my ear. "On all of you."

Our group sprang to attention as the voices of the departing feasters grew louder, ringing through the cloister and breaking its peaceful sanctity. A harsh, deep voice, which we presumed belonged to William Rufus, the wheedling tones of old men—the clerics and bishops—and the deceptively calm and polite burr of the Abbess Hawise as she conversed with the monarch.

Robes swished, footsteps clattered on tiles, and the feasting party rounded the far corner of the quadrangle, disturbing the swallows that nested in the vines that furled the arches. Terrified, the birds sailed down the length of the cloister, then darted out towards the lightness and greenness at the centre. I watched their flight, wishing I could soar away with them.

The King strode past the elder nuns without glancing at any of them. I could only see him out the corner of my eye, a haze of crimson robes trimmed with miniver; even as a princess, I was not permitted to gaze straight into his face unless invited to do so.

Rufus continued down the cloister, moving rapidly but then halted only a few feet away. I stared at my feet, my cheeks burning and my head unpleasantly giddy.

"Which one is the elder daughter of Malcolm Canmore?" the King asked Abbess Hawise.

"Lady Edith, come forward." Hawise gestured with a hand for me to face the Red King.

Slowly, I left my place in the lineup and approached his royal person, struggling to keep my breathing slow and even. I wore my disguising black robes and hood in the hope they made me seem unattractive and insignificant. Clumsily I curtseyed to the English ruler, averting my eyes as was customary.

"You may look at me, girl," said Rufus, curtly, as if I were a skivvy from the kitchens. I did not like his tone; disrespect oozed from him. I could almost hear his thoughts. *English. Saxon. Inferior...*

Steeling myself, I raised my chin and stared as boldly as I could into the King's face.

He was every bit as terrifying as legends painted him. Fairly short in stature, his build was yet powerful, muscles bunched beneath the shoulders of his flowing robe. His long, straight hair was bright yellow touched with a hint of fire, and his face, beneath a heavy moustache, was extremely red, as if he had spent too much time in the sun. His moustache and beard were of darker hue than his locks but also shot through with wiry, coppery strands. Like his sire, the Conqueror, he was inclined to fatness around his mid-section, his belly jutting forward and making his jewelled sword belt strain.

But it was his eyes that frightened me the most—I had never seen such they before; they were of two different colours. One was blue, the other a greenish-grey; both were flecked with gold that seemed to sparkle. Somehow, they reminded me of a wild animal's eyes, feral and lacking human warmth.

"So you are Edith of Scotland." Rufus looped his thumbs into that straining belt and stepped closer with what could only be called a swagger. "Hmph."

The last sound he made was dismissive, decidedly rude; his visage was frowning, the gold lights cracking in his wolfish eyes. "Does she always wear the veil, Abbess?" he asked Hawise, his gaze fixed firmly on me, pinning me to the spot as a spider pins its prey. "I thought she was only here for her education."

"She is, Sire, but over time, Lady Edith has joined in with the duties of the sisters. She tends the sick and poor, even laving their feet and tending their infirmities."

The King gave another grunt, clearly not impressed; indeed, he seemed quite repulsed by what Hawise was telling him. "I see. Well, I have seen enough, Abbess. Lead us on to our bedchambers. I am weary from the ride hither. My companions and I shall leave for Gloucester at first light tomorrow."

One of William's lackeys, drifting around his master like a rank smell, made a flipping motion at me with his hand, indicating that I should step back into the crowd of nuns. Rufus had finished with me.

I made another quick curtsey but the King did not notice. He was already striding toward the door to the courtyard, Hawise hurrying to keep up in her heavy robe and his crowd of toadies and sycophants buzzing about him like flies drawn to dung.

As he departed, one of his followers, trundling at the rear of the party, suddenly stopped in his tracks, a younger man with near-black hair and a neatly trimmed beard. He peered at me and, to my surprise, smiled, his straight white teeth flashing. He then gestured toward the retreating back of the King and shrugged, as if to say he too was puzzled by William Rufus's behaviour.

Despite myself, I smiled back, ever so slightly.

He grinned then, but only for a second. A moment later, he whirled about and proceeded to chase the royal party out into the convent's grounds.

"Edith! What in God's name is on your head?"

A month after the King's unwelcome visit, I was drawing water from the well in the hospital gardens when I heard an enraged voice bellow my name. A man's voice. A leonine voice raised in a ferocious roar. A fearsome, wrathful, but familiar voice...

The late August day was hot but grey, the sky filled with boiling scuds of thunderclouds that held a sick, jaundiced tint. The air felt oddly charged; my hair bristled beneath my hood and along the back of my sweat-damp neck. Bees buzzed in the nearby lavender bushes while other flying insects stuck to my sweating flesh...

I wiped my brow with my sleeve. The one bawling my name could not be here, not at St Mary's Abbey. Was I dreaming? Hallucinating from the intense heat? One of the nuns had told me that eating cheese could give one strange fancies and I had eaten a rind at noon.

"Edith, God's Teeth, girl, have you gone deaf?"

The angry bellows were closer now, along with the sound of heavy feet thudding on grass, and I knew I did not dream.

Dropping the hoe, I whirled about to see my father, King Malcolm of Scotland, striding purposefully towards me. His fire-hued hair and beard flowed in the wind of his speed, while his freckled face was contorted in a scowl.

"Father!" I ran in his direction, while Sister Infirmarer and the residents of the hospital all stared in surprise. Leofgifu let out a high-pitched peel of laughter and clapped her hands. "The great lord comes for our Edith...the great lord!"

Father halted as I approached him, my arms outstretched. I slowed my pace as I realised that he was not about to reciprocate any embrace. His threatening scowl was directed straight at me. Never had he looked upon me with such wrath before.

"Lord Father?" Nervously I peered up at him. He towered over me, boiling like the storm clouds.

"What, by the Rood, is that upon your head!" he shouted, and then one arm swooped down and tore the black nun's hood from my hair. For a moment, he held the veil in his hands, staring at it with a livid countenance, and then with a loud tearing of cloth he ripped it to shreds. Casting the pieces on the ground, he trampled them beneath his boot heels.

"I…I…" My tongue would not work; fear dried my mouth and throat. My Father's rage had never been directed at me before; he seemed a stranger, volatile and even dangerous.

"You told us your Aunt Cristina wanted you to wear a nun's wimple but that you refused…yet here you are wearing one. Do you claim the abbess here forced you, too…or were you lying all along? Did you really intend to join the church, but at a more prestigious foundation than Romsey!"

"No…NO!" I insisted, shaking my head, causing my blonde hair to break free of its coiled braid and spill over my shoulders and back, almost reaching my waist. I must have looked a wild, crazed thing, standing there, shaking with fear before my own sire. "Cristina did force me and beat me if I refused. I only wear this raiment now because I realised it was indeed a good way to dissuade rapacious men of evil intent."

"And any suitor you found unappealing…Am I correct?" His tone was still threatening; sweat beads glistened on his broad forehead. "Like Alan the Red? Alan, who had promised me men and protection of the borders if he could wed you? Alan, who you gave cold treatment to and had called the whole plan off?"

"Alan of Richmond!" Fiery anger leapt up in my heart; although more my mother's daughter in temperament, at times my father's noted temper flared in me too. "Have you not heard what he did when he was here? He set fires in the cloister, making us all fear for our lives! He carried off a would-be nun of royal ancestry and is now living openly in sin with her. Is that kind of man what you would truly want as a son-in-law? Do you think he could ever be trusted to keep any promises he made to you?"

Father gritted his teeth but the fury in his gaze was slowly receding. "Alan was a fool; I will not deny that. Still, I'd rather have seen you go to his bed than cloistered away forever with a pack of nuns. Even if he kept his whore in the house, I should have given you to him. Not that any of it matters now…Alan the Red is dead."

"Dead!" I gasped in surprise, though in all honesty, I could not find it in myself to sorrow. Not one bit.

"Aye, at the beginning of the month. Died suddenly, only God knows what from. Sent to Bury St Edmund's for burial. The Archbishop of Canterbury wrote to that slut Gunnild and told her she should kiss Alan's teeth in his rotting skull since she was eternally damned for breaking her vows to commit fornication."

I winced, nauseous at the harsh words of Archbishop Anselm. He was a great and holy man, ascetic in all his tastes and such condemnation would make Gunnild an outcast in polite society for life.

"Do not worry about that wench, Edith—hell-cats such as she always fall upon their feet. But you, Edith…I no longer know what to think about my own daughter. About your honesty, your fidelity to me, your father, who made you and whom you should honour with obedience and compliance."

"You must believe me, Father, I have done nought to shame you. Truly I am no nun. I never considered joining the order for a solitary moment. I have always desired matrimony and children…though not with someone loathsome and debauched like Alan the Red."

He must have seen the panic and distress in my face and recognised that I spoke no lies. He gave a loud sigh. "Yes…yes, stop looking so woebegone, child—I do believe you. Your mother taught you never to lie, even if the truth was unpalatable. I know she taught you well."

His stance softened, his shoulders drooping a little, and finally I dared to fling my arms around him to show that I was glad he had come. After all these years, it was strange—he did not seem quite so gigantic while his middle was wider than I remembered and flecks of grey glinted in his hair. "Gladness fills me to see you, Lord Father…but I am surprised you have come to Wilton. I thought you were set the meet King William at Gloucester?"

Again, rage darkened his clear blue gaze. "We met. We argued. We parted. He wanted me to pay homage to him…for my own lands.

For my own bloody lands in the north. When it became clear I'd not bend the knee, he refused to receive me for further talks, the pompous bastard."

I dropped my hands from his waist, confused. "What does this mean, then? For Scotland and England? And…for us?"

He glowered, and above the churning sky let out a tremendous boom of thunder that set bells in the churches and priories in the town jangling. Warm damp air struck my face; the earth seemed to shake beneath my feet. Rain, sharp as darts, driven by the storm wind, needled my cheeks and flooded my eyes.

"War may be the outcome," growled my father, as the ascending gale lifted his hair like a war banner and whipped it against his sunburnt cheeks, "and so I have ridden here to take you and Mary home. Home to Scotland."

CHAPTER SIX

My return to Scotland was full of both wonder and grief. My heart sang as our company neared Dunfermline; my thirsty eyes drank in shadowy, misted hills and deep green forests, well-remembered from childhood; red deer and roebucks leaping through twisted tree boles; peregrines, kites and mighty eagles with huge wingspans soaring against a sky still holding onto the vague warmth of passing summer. Heather brought a jewel-like glow of royal purple; legends told how the ground the plant grew on had never been doused with blood from any battle.

The entourage went to Dunfermline town itself rather than Malcolm's Tower, for Mother was visiting Holy Trinity, a Benedictine House that she had founded. A cavern wound into a rock face that reared behind the abbey—a hermit's grotto where she was wont to pray in peace and solitude, the sounds of the outside world muffled by the craggy walls. She had gone there to pray for her daughters' safe journey home.

Mother was exiting the cave with her ladies-in-waiting as our chariot, surrounded by soldiers, pulled up by the cavern entrance. The sight of her as I disembarked the carriage was like a dagger to the heart. She was thin and grey-faced, her beauty robbed, the colour washed from her golden hair. She leaned heavily on the arm of her favourite maid, Alesoune; however, her face beamed, lantern-bright as Mary and I hurried towards her, trying to keep some decorum in our approach but wanting nought more than to fling our arms around her.

"My girls," she said, voice heavy with emotion. "I prayed to God for a safe return for you, and now you are here, unharmed and as beautiful as I remembered. Even more so, now that you are both near enough grown women."

Mary and I began to weep at that, despite our best efforts, and Mother waved Alesoune discretely aside and drew the two of us into a warm embrace. My tears flowed the harder, though, when I felt the sharp bones of her ribs and hips beneath her heavy robe of robin's egg blue.

"Mother...what ails you?" I asked, standing back after a minute or two.

"Nothing ails me...now that I have my daughters with me."

"I am not a bairn to be pacified with soothing words," I said, wiping tears from my cheeks. "It is clear that you are unwell. That is why you seldom wrote to St Mary's, isn't it?"

Mother made a face and shook her head. "I had no wish to interrupt your studies over a triviality. You would have worried needlessly."

"I would have come to you at once!" I said fiercely.

She sighed, folding her thin arms; her sleeves hung like dangling shrouds. "I feared exactly that. There is nought you could have done for me, Edith. I have physics here and herb-women a-plenty."

"And have they helped you?"

She sighed again. "Y...yes, as much as is possible. Do not dwell on it, Edith. If it is my time to die, then that is the will of God, and I will gladly go to my Creator. I am content."

"Mama, surely you are not..." Mary's face screwed up in fear and she buried it in her hands.

"No, man—or woman—is privy to the exact knowledge of the hour of his or her passing," said Mother, both gentle and stern. "But come, girls, our reunion should be a happy one. We are here together for whatever time is given to us".

Any brief happiness found in the reunion with my parents soon faded, even as summer dwindled into Autumn, with high gales, driving rain and flurries of blood-red leaves. Father had brooded and stormed about the keep, mulling over the insults he had received from William Rufus at their meeting in Gloucester, and finally, in a fit of impassioned temper, decided he could take no more. His kingship and dignity had been insulted; he would seek vengeance on the hellish Red King. He began raising an army to go on raids over the border.

"I beg you, do not do this, Malcolm," Mother implored, wringing her hands. "I fear no good will come of it."

"Wheesht, woman," he growled, the harsher side of his nature bursting to the fore. "I will show that catamite in the south that he was unwise to cross me. Northumberland will go up in flames—a merry *Samhuin* bonfire with any luck!"

Mother had collapsed in her chair at those words, hugging herself, rocking slightly. "I fear if you go on this raid, we will never meet on this earth again."

He softened slightly, pulling her to her feet and crushing her to him. She looked like a frail doll in his thick-muscled arms. "Now, Margaret, my fair Meg, don't you fret. I am leaving the best physic with you, and the Abbot Turgot, who is most loyal to our family."

She stared up at him, eyes fixed on his face, imploring. "Is there nought I can say that will sway your course, husband?"

"No."

"Then it is all in God's hands," she murmured, seeming to slump in his hold. Candlelight slid down her face, shadows circling her eyes; she resembled a living skull. "Everything we ever strove for."

Father escorted her back to her seat, where the tiring-women wrapped sheepskins and furs around her. She was trembling whereas she had never minded the cold before. It was like watching an old woman huddled before a fire, seeking the last bit of warmth before the chill of the tomb.

It broke my heart but I dared not interfere.

"I do not think it's safe for you to remain here at the Tower with the girls," Father continued. "Most men of fighting age will travel to Northumberland with my army."

"Where do you counsel that we go then, Malcolm?" Mother's voice was a cracked whisper. Alesoune brought over a mazer of warmed spiced wine and pressed it to her dry lips, mumbling soothing words to her distraught mistress.

"Edinburgh," Father replied. "Windy, alas, but almost impregnable, with cliffs on one side and a boggy marsh on the other. A good safe place for you and the girls, and David, Alexander, and

Edmund. Ethelred is leaving his abbey to give you more comfort too."

"And what of Edward and Edgar? What part have they to play in all of this?" Mother glanced up, a ripple of pain crossing her fine features.

"We are going to war with Father." Edward walked into the smoky hall, followed by Edgar, moving like a shadow in his wake, two tall, handsome boys in the flower of their youth. Edward boldly swaggered the way young men as yet unblooded by warfare often did, oozing over-confidence, while Ned gazed up at his older brother like an adoring pup. "I am more than old enough to fight and I long to wet my sword with English blood."

Mother winced. "English blood? Oh, Edward. It runs hot in you too, my son. Remember where you came from, my son. And the great saint whose name you bear."

Edward flushed red to the roots of his long fair hair. "Forgive me, Mother. My words were clumsy. I should have said 'Norman blood' for that is what Rufus is, despite his unlawful claim to be 'King of the English.'"

Mother managed a wan smile. "You are forgiven. I fear one day soon the line between 'English' and 'Norman' will be blurred forever, for good or for ill. It is the way of things."

Edmund, who was kneeling by the hearth, cossetting one of Father's hounds, suddenly sprang up and strode over. He was the most temperamental of my brothers, grey-eyed and auburn-haired, with a strong, square pugnacious chin cleft by a deep dimple. "I do not think it fair that I am not permitted to join in the raid with my brothers," he complained. "I'm as good a swordsman as Edward, maybe better. I am fully of age and eager to prove myself. Jesu, you are taking Ned, and he is younger than I…"

"Edward is my *tanaiste*, my chosen heir," said Father, "so it is his place to come. As for Ned, do not envy him; he is unlikely to see much fighting—he'll squire his brother and clean his armour and weapons! I will be straight with you, Edmund; I thought about taking you along, but you are too rash. You've learnt to control a sword but not your temper."

Edmund's face flamed to match his hair. "What about our half-brothers?" he flung back. "Some of them are going, are they not?"

"They are a fair bit older than you and far more experienced in the field." Father suddenly slammed a hefty fist down on the nearby table. The hounds lounging around the hall yelped in fright and scuttled away, tails between their legs. "Don't argue with me, Edmund. You are upsetting your Lady Mother. You will fare to Edinburgh with her. If you want a high position…well, then, I appoint you as protector of your mother and sisters. Do you understand?"

Edmund glowered, folding his arms defensively. "Yes, Lord Father. I understand."

"Good!" barked the King. "Edward, Ned, come with me—the war council is to begin. Margaret, make sure all your necessary supplies are packed and in the wains. I want to see your entourage on the road to Edinburgh by tomorrow's dawn."

Edinburgh Castle loomed against the skyline, a craggy crown on the brow of a steep hill. Its stones were black and weathered; its towers jagged against the clouds. A long, cobbled road ran through the city to its gates, lined with tall, teetering houses. People emerged from houses, hostels and taverns, from tanneries and dyer's shops, from silversmiths and goldsmiths, from churches and priories, to watch the royal party ascend the steep incline of castle hill. It was a rainy day, blustery and cold, just before the Feast of Allhallows, and the weather made everything about the town seem gloomy and unfriendly. The narrow street upwards funnelled the wind into our faces, and its howls and shrieks added to our discomfort and drowned any cheers that might have erupted from the soaked bystanders. Gutters brimming with rainwater burst, turning into unsavoury little rivers filled with leaves, detritus and unmentionable things.

Wrapped in a sheepskin, Mary huddled in the back of our carriage, not wishing to look out, but Mother and I sat by the opening at the back and waved at passersby every now and then. Mother continued wan and pale, her cheeks sunken, and I tried to convince her to join Mary deeper in the chariot and keep warm, but she refused. "It is my duty to show myself to our subjects, Edith. They expect it. We are their servants as much as they are ours. We have to give to them in return for what they give to us. You would do well to remember that."

The chariot creaked along, canvas roof flapping in the wind, ascending the last steep section of the hill. Street urchins raced alongside, muddy from head to toe, almost appearing as otters from the river as they dived in and out of the streaming gullies on the roadside. Stony bells clanged throughout the town, heralding our arrival.

At the hill's summit, bleak and bare, rose two thick round gate towers with fanged crenelations and pointed turrets stained the red of old blood. The rain bounced off them, causing spray to fall into the courtyard below.

Men shouted, mechanisms creaked and groaned, and the portcullis was raised for our passage. The carriage was conveyed in, the sound of its large wooden wheels amplified by the close black walls of the gatehouse, and then we were out in the bailey. Which was flooded. Grey water coursed between the cobblestones in a dirty tide.

The governor, Bartolf de Lesthlin, Earl of Ross, a brave and brawny man who had journeyed with Mother's family from their refuge in Hungary and later married Beatrix, Father's baseborn half-sister, emerged from his quarters to greet us while servants rushed about in the rain like startled ants, hurrying to remove our chests and other goods before the deluge claimed them.

"Oh Bartolf, it is good to see you again." Mother held out her hands and Bartolf duly clasped them—it was a great honour to touch a Queen and he grinned from ear to ear. But Bartolf and Mother were old friends and did not stand on ceremony.

"Remember when we rode out on your first royal progress, your Grace," he said. "It was raining like this—no, far worse; one could scarce see a hand's breadth before their face. You were riding pillion on my mount, as was custom back then, for the Chamberlain's duty was to protect his Queen at all times."

"Yes, "I remember." A little smile brought a moment's glimmer of happiness, of bygone youth, to mother's pallid visage. "I was terrified and clung desperately to your waist, praying to God that I would not fall off. But when we got to the burn, which had broken its banks, I was certain I was doomed. The water was up to your steed's belly, pulling at my skirts. I thought for sure we'd all be washed away to our deaths. I grabbed as tightly as I could to your belt…"

"And you cried out, 'Will your belt buckle hold!'"

Mother laughed. "Yes…yes, I did. What a foolish thing to say when one is close to facing one's maker."

"And I spurred on my mount and told you to 'Grip fast!' and so we made the far shore, with the wind blowing the current and the riverbanks crumbling and uprooted trees crashing into the stream."

"We laughed when it was over. Your belt had held and saved me from death in the flood."

His eyes twinkled. "I have a new motto, my Queen. 'Hold Fast!' I have also added two more buckles to my belt to make sure, no matter what befalls, it will never break."

"Husband!" Lady Beatrix darted over the slick cobbles from the hall block, two ladies holding a canopy above her. "Surely you are not talking about old times out here in this rain-storm. Look at Her Grace, she has come far today, and needs a hot meal, a hot bath, and a rest."

Beatrix took Mother to the royal apartments at one, supporting her with a steady arm. Mary and I were given a room on the floor above and our brothers yet another chamber. Edmund was none too thrilled when he found he must share not only with Ethelred, who had ridden in from his monastery, but also our two younger brothers, Alexander and David.

"This is not right!" I heard him roar in the distance. "David should still be in the nursery." Edmund's moodiness and ill-temper rarely abated these days, although I understood his pique better than he realised—it was hard for a youth to be overshadowed by his brothers. Ethelred had his life at the monastery, Alexander and David were still just children, living a life that veered between play and learning—while Edmund had nothing, no lands, no wife, no money…no status.

I settled down early with Mary, wrapping ourselves in warm coverlets while a servant stoked the fire brazier, making it pop and crackle. "I hope we can go back to the Tower soon," Mary said plaintively. "I don't like it here. Listen to the wind…" She paused, head on one side.

Outside, the wind had risen to a gale, skirling about the dark, damp walls, making eerie hoots and whistles through the jagged crenels.

"It sounds like ghosts…" Mary licked her lips; they looked dry and chapped and her cheeks were flushed. I prayed she was not coming down with a fever. God forbid we should all be struck down with some malady…Mother was so frail…

"There are no ghosts here." I tucked the covers around her, trying to assume a motherly demeanour. "I promise you that. Edinburgh is a good Christian place where no ghost would dare tread. On the morrow, if you feel like it, we can go exploring. I am sure once we are familiar with the castle, it will not seem so daunting!"

She nodded but threaded her hand through mine, holding on tightly. At one time Mother might have sung to her, but we were considered too old for such cossetting now, and besides, Mother had taken to her bed early, with possets and stones warmed in a fire and wrapped in cloths to keep her feet from freezing.

So I sang instead, an ancient lullaby, close to the pink shell of Mary's ear so that she could not hear the wails of that unfriendly wind outside,

"Lullay lullow, lullay lully,
lullay lullow,
Lullay lully,
My fair bairn, sleep softly now.

I saw a sweet and seemly sight,
A blissful maid, a blossom bright,
That morning made and mirth among.

Lullay lullow, lullay lully,
lullay lullow,

*Lullay lully,
My fair bairn, sleep softly now.*

*A maiden mother, meek and mild,
In cradle keep, a radiant child,
That softly slept; she sat and sang.*

My fair bairn, sleep softly now."

The next day Mary and I were brighter and more cheerful. The sky had changed from dark cloud to light, wispy strands flying like a lady's veil over the feeble sun. We walked the castle walls with our kinswoman Beatrix, the constable's wife, who pointed out the castle kitchens, the Great Hall and the chilly little chapel, primitive and quite unadorned, where the wind whistled through cracks in the walls, pressing icy fingers to the spines of those who prayed on their knees within. We noticed there was a marsh on one side of the castle, sucking the hill's foot. Long reeds grew there and birds shrilled, their voices eerie even by day. From the far wall, facing inland, the view changed dramatically—a sharp green hill jutted from the land like the prow of a foundering ship. It demanded attention from all who viewed it.

"See yon green hill?" Beatrix waved a gloved hand at the distant hill, shadows playing over its flanks, a low rim of thin cloud floating over its summit. "It looks like there should have been an opposing castle up there, does it not?"

I strained my gaze into the distance. "I suppose so; it would make a formidable place to defend against one's foes."

"It is called *Suidhe Artair*, the Seat of Arthur. It is said that centuries ago the war-leader Arthur built a fort there, back when this castle and town was called Dun Edin rather than Edinburgh. It is long gone, alas, but you can still see the earthen ramparts of this fortress on the outcrop called Samson's Ribs."

"I cannot see anything…" I squinted, the pale sun dazzling my eyes.

"No, not much is visible today—the ridges are battered by time and today the cloud hangs low around the head of the dun. Mayhap when your sire and Lord Edward return from battle, they will go hunting in the nearby Forest of Drumselch and take you and your poor mother, the Queen, along. Her Grace is so weak and pale, she could use some air and some pleasure...if I may say so without giving offence."

"No offence is taken." How could I take offence when she voiced the thing I feared too? "I am so concerned, Beatrix. She will not tell us what the physics believe is wrong and grows ever weaker. She is very pious, but her constant fasting and prayer in cold chapels for hours is taking its toll on her too."

"The chapel here at Edinburgh is indeed draughty," said Beatrix, downcast. "I wear my thickest shawl whenever I attend Mass. It is old, almost like a hermit's cell in its comforts; maybe when our troubles with the English King are settled, it can be rebuilt anew."

Rubbing my arms, I stared away into the distance again, uncomfortable, feeling suddenly exposed upon that towering height. Where was Father now, and Edward and Ned? In Northumbria, harrying the English, far from their true home. I wished they were here and all feuds settled. Father committed himself to these raids to protect his honour; but to the minds of many, they were counterproductive and would only infuriate William Rufus, who was equally as ruthless as his sire, the Bastard. What if he brought a massive army north, as his sire had done, and razed to the ground every Scottish village he encountered, sparing neither men, women, children or beasts? Father had severed his ties with Rufus, likely forever, when he had stormed out of their meeting in Gloucester and snatched Mary and me from St Mary's abbey. Archbishop Anselm was filled with a blinding rage upon hearing that Father had absconded with us, Mother said; Anselm had even sent letters demanding we be returned to the nunnery at once or suffer hellfire and damnation. Father had snorted with furious anger before ripping these letters up and hurling them on the fire.

Beatrix was looking at me solicitously. "You look cold, princess. You and Mary must take care; I advise we go down where the wind is less scathing—Jesu, sometimes up here it feels sharp enough to scrape the flesh from one's bones! I plan to go into town later to collect some gowns I ordered and to visit the market; would you like to come? Tomorrow is All Saints Day, the next day All Souls and the town is busy. The bakers will be making Soul Cakes and all the young ones out to celebrate around the bonfires."

I glanced over at Mary; I could tell by her expression she wished to see this spectacle. In Romsey and Wilton, All Saints and All Souls were very solemn occasions, in which we knelt and said prayers before the altar all night and throughout the day, offering for the souls not only of the heavenly saints and martyrs but for the faithful still waiting in Purgatory; those not fully cleansed of sin and who had never attained the Beatific Vision. The earthly faithful could bring about the transition of these ancestors through praying and singing the Offices of the Dead. Amongst ordinary folk, especially in country villages and in Scotland as a whole, these feast days were quite different. Although Mass was also attended, there were bonfires, games, dancing and delicious cakes marked with crosses to aid the transition of the dead into the blessed afterlife. Some priests decried such activities as sinful, for not only were the saints and waiting souls remembered on those two feasts but also creatures from bygone heathen times—witches and fearsome elf-folk shooting flint arrows, croaking toads oozing poison and malicious revenants who would drag victims to the grave unshriven.

"We will go with you, Mistress Beatrix." I squeezed Mary's shoulder. My sister gave me a grateful look. "The games sound like fun, even if we can only watch. And who doesn't like a slice of Soul Cake?"

Dusk fell early on All Saint's Eve, its rapid descent heralding the advent of the winter months. In the more remote Scottish villages and towns it was known as *Samhuin*, which meant 'summer's end.' Mother had told us that to the Saxons of yore, it heralded the start of 'Blood Month', when sacrifices of cattle were given to the ancient pagan gods.

Blue-tinged shadows and night-fog swirled in and the streets of Edinburgh took on a sinister twilight haze where it was hard to tell what was real and solid and what was not. Beatrix hardly seemed to notice, going from stall to stall, shop to shop about her business. On the far side of the city, flames leapt to the sky, orange in the gloom as a cheer went up. Mary and I both gasped and clutched each other's arms.

"Fear not," Beatrix said with a distracted smile, as she deliberated over the contents of a pastry stall manned by a toothless old woman with a crumpled brown face that resembled a withered apple. "That fire is the traditional Samhuin bonfire on Calton Hill. Other will be lit on every green space…to keep unfriendly spirits away."

Beatrix purchased a number of pastries and handed them to one of her servants to carry. Then she turned to Mary and me, pressing a little cake into each of our palms. "A penny soul cake for each of you upon this blessed night."

The cakes with their little crosses had not long been out of the oven and warmed our cold hands. Raising them to our lips, we nibbled tentatively on them, careful not to burn our mouths.

Younger people were filling the marketplace now and many of the stalls were dismantled for the night. Tradesmen and hucksters were still trying to make sales, however—buoyed by the influx of celebrants who had arrived, sometimes from places far from Edinburgh by their manner of attire. The winds died and a heavy fug hung over the town, rich with the scent of burning combined with flax, hemp and heather. Fishmongers were gutting their wares in side wynds, adding the iron tang of blood to the air, and near them furriers hung pelts of newly-skinned animals stretched out on the front of their shops. A deathly, fleshly smell emanated from them, making me retch, and little trails of blood dripped down onto the cobbles. *Blodmonath*…the Blood Month. My belly heaved.

"Come along, Lady Edith, Lady Mary," said Beatrix, noticing my queasiness. "Not the proper sight for young ladies' eyes. Besides, the watch will be around soon to see that these traders have paid extra taxes to accommodate a good cleansing of the square. These rough men seldom react joyously to such a visit, so it is best we start making our way back to the castle."

Surrounded by Beatrix's attendants, all wearing the colours of the Governor's household, we began our journey up the sloping hill towards the castle's gatehouse. Several members of our company were armed and mailed, but the press of bodies had grown very thick, and the noise riotous. Drums banged and pipes wailed and yowled, while torches and rushlights flared all over the streets, lighting up drink-reddened faces, some painted, some masked, all becoming hazy, surreal and sinister as true darkness drew in.

Suddenly the crowd gapped apart. My gaze was drawn to two cloaked and hooded figures passing through the throngs of revellers. Two men, wearing sombre green, walking side-by-side in a commanding manner, as if they had embarked on an important mission.

There was an odd familiarity about them, although they walked stiffly, rigidly, almost as if reluctant to go wherever their destination lay, but aware there was no time to tarry. The head of the taller of the two swung in my direction and I gasped in shock—the half-concealed visage resembled that of my brother Edward! He hesitated a moment as if sensing my presence, but the man at his side reached out to clamp a hand on the other's shoulder, turning his attention back to his fellow. And the hand, though pale in the gloom, looked exactly like my father's hand—the scarred knuckles, a gold ring engraved with scrollwork on the small finger.

With a cry, I pulled away from Mary and Beatrix, pushing through our startled attendants into the milling Samhuin crowd. "Edward! Father!" It had to be them, no one else could look so like them. They must have returned in secret. Perhaps strong opposition from the Northumbrians had caused them to retreat back to Edinburgh unannounced. But why were they walking away from the castle instead of towards it?

Behind me, Mary screamed my name. The sound was carried away on the wind. I did not glance back. Driven by an unexpected determination, I plunged through the stream of revellers after Edward and Father. After a few hundred yards, I leaned against the wall of an old craggy house, panting. I had lost them…

No, wait! A little wynd ran beside the next house, twisting down like a worm into another area of the town. The hem of a green cloak swirled, beckoning. Blindly, I ran after it. I could no longer hear Mary's frantic cries and the noise of the revellers had become a dull roar. The night grew dimmer, full of heavy bonfire smoke hemmed in by the lowering clouds. White wisps coiled like hands around old, decrepit buildings. Occasionally I caught people staring at me from windows and alcoves, unfriendly faces smeared with dirt and ash. I ignored them and raced onwards, seeking Edward and my father.

I emerged onto an adjacent street that wound alongside the river Leith, a name that filled me with foreboding, as I remembered from classical studies that 'Lethe' was a river of the underworld in the myths of the pagan Greeks. Fires burned hot and red on the banks and the figures of dancing, capering men and women were silhouetted against the flames. Some wore masks topped by antlers of cow's horns; it was a devilish and macabre sight. Panicked, I stared this way and that, seeking the men in the green cloaks, the men I felt sure were my brother and father in disguise.

No one. Instead, along the shoreline trudged a funeral procession. Mourners carried two shrouded bodies on a bier. Tapers flickered at head and foot of the corpses, and rushlights fluttered in the hands of the wailers and weepers who trundled along, slipping in the slime of the riverbank. "*Ochone, ochone!*" cried the veiled women, a terrible lament of grief and sorrow.

"Who has died?" Words tore unbidden from my lips as the cortege approached, the bier swaying, the wailers still keening their dismal dirge. All the mourners wore deep hoods, their faces furled against the weather and the gloom.

One of the women glanced towards me, her rushlight held up in a bony hand, exposing an ancient visage within her hood, craggy and toothless, her hair spun silver. The look she gave me was fearsome, warning me off. "Who has died? Someone's father, someone's son. So it will always be...*Viam universe carnis ingredi.*"

The Way of all Flesh.

Growing horror filled me and as a sudden rain shower sluiced down, extinguishing the candles and rushlights illuminating the bier,

I began to tremble and shake, my legs growing weak as a newborn calf's. I fell to one knee in the gutter and the procession carried on as if I had become invisible. "*Ochone, Ochone!*"

A moment later the blackness of the night had sucked it into its heart, consuming it utterly, the wails of the mourners drowned out by the growing cheers and chants of Samhuin revellers.

I stood, alone, breathing heavily, my head in a whirl. What madness had possessed me that haunted night? What fey fancies had made me rush off into the back alleys of Edinburgh unaccompanied, following two men who resembled my kinsmen, but who could have been brigands or murderers...or even phantoms on a night like tonight?

Braids dark with water and my shoes seeping, I stumbled back the way I had come, but with the fey glamour of the night dropped from my eyes, I saw how unsavoury, how dangerous the wynd was, packed with rogues and drunkards and bawds who shrieked as they hooked up their tattered skirts and touted for business.

I crouched in the lee of a building, uncertain of what to do. If I did not follow the exact path back, I was likely to become lost. If I stayed here, I was prey for anyone of ill intent...

At the end of the path, a lantern bucked into view, spilling greenish light through its horn slats. I shrank away...but then saw the angry face of my brother Edmund, and next to him a worried Beatrix and Governor Bartolf, followed by a cluster of armed guards, their helms glinting blue as rainwater splashed over them.

"Edmund!" I cried, stumbling forward. Reaching him, I fell into his arms...but there was no welcoming embrace.

Instead, he grabbed my shoulders and shook me roughly, as a terrier shakes a rat. "You stupid girl! Why did you run off like that? Mary is inconsolable, she was sure we'd never find you alive! You've shamed us before the governor and his wife and brought members of the garrison away from their duties!"

"Oh, Edmund," I wept. I could not tell him what I witnessed; I knew it would fool his fury." "What I saw...Oh, you would never understand!"

"Living with those nuns all those years has made you foolish and unworldly," huffed Edmund, hands on his hips in the manner of a scolding fishwife. "You're right—I care nothing for your fantasies. Now, come, give me your arm; I'm not letting you out of my sight. We must hurry back to the castle…not only is everyone in an uproar over your disappearance, Mother…" He took a deep breath and distress momentarily replaced his wrath. "Mother's illness is worse. She has taken to her bed and the physician has been summoned."

CHAPTER SEVEN

Mother had caught an ague, which added to her other unknown malady. Her ladies fussed and wept; the physics came and went with possets and potions. Coriander brews were given to her, to calm her fever, and other brews of marjoram and honeycomb to heal her harsh cough, while wormwood was administered for the pains that clawed her belly.

After several days, I, too, fell ill, maybe having breathed in some noxious air from the nearby marsh or from the riverside when I engaged in my mad, frenzied journey. Head pounding and lungs burning like fire, I huddled in my bed, consumed by guilt because my own illness brought extra worry to my ailing mother. Also, I could not banish the memory of the All Hallow's funeral procession—the swirling candles, the swirling river, the swirling cloaks of the men who had resembled Father and Edward. Could they have been Fetches, ghostly doubles that foretold death? I could ask no one, not even Mother's private chaplain or Brother Turgot; I was certain they would chide me for even considering such heathenish things.

The week dragged on and soon my health was restored, my nose growing less fiercely red and my cough abating. Mother, too, rallied, casting off the ague, although her limbs remained weak, but the pain in her belly remained, a wyrm that gnawed her innards with unseen fangs.

I did not go to the town again, having lost the heart for it, and busied myself embroidering in the solar with Mary and Beatrix. As time crawled on, I began to feel like a caged beast, full of frustration and ill-tempered with it. The dank walls kept enemies out but also kept me in like a prisoner. I daydreamed of Wilton Abbey, of kindly Abbess Hawise, of the little hospital with the laughing, moon-mazed child Leofgifu, the girl who would never grow up but who had the innocence and purity of a saint. I wondered if I would ever see either of them again and hated myself when tears stung my eyes. I also wished Father would write from his campaign in Northumbria, but unlike Mother, he was not one for book-learning although he valued it in his children. Edward and Edgar, however, were both lettered, and I grew quite cross that neither wrote. No doubt they were too intent on blooding their swords to think of their womenfolk, the thoughtless knaves.

November drifted onwards, and from the sullen heavens snow drifted down, thin white flakes twirling on the everlasting breeze that soughed over castle rock. Below the fortress, the marsh was frozen, quelling its evil smells; the birds who tenanted the reed beds mostly fled away. A gull skimmed across it, shrieking; I followed its flight with my gaze until, in the far distance I could see the stormy expanse of the North Sea, greenish-grey and frothed with white caps. The sight of it made me feel restless—if only news would come to Edinburgh, whether by land or by sea!

One eve, shortly after Martinmas, the Feast of the Soldier Saint Martin, I had gathered with the rest of the family to listen to the *Filidh* telling tales in the hall. Mary, Alexander and David huddled together by the firepit, while Edmund glowered in the back, flagon in hand, and Aethelstan and I sat on benches next to Mother, who was wrapped from head to toe in furs, her colour white as the snow outside, her cheeks stained by an unhealthy flush. Her thin hands, blue with veins, twined round a rosary of jet, the polished facets of the black beads twinkling in the muted torchlight.

The *Filidh*, a thin man of middling years with a taut, sun-bronzed, ageless face and raven's wing hair, stalked across the rushes, mood changing from merry to sorrowful, from sly and sinister, to proud and noble, as he used all his dramatic skills to tell warriors' tales from the Kingdom of Reged in Cumbria, which was part of the disputed lands in the Old North that Father sought to win. In his hands, the *Filidh* carried a horse-skull with the jaw strung on; he clacked its huge yellow teeth together in time to the cadence of his poems.

Lo! Listen now to this ancient tale... Clackety Clack.

Ebon shadows swept back from the storyteller's lanky frame, capering around the chamber, while the firelight made his deep-set eyes sparkle like a raven's beady eyes and cast an eerie glow over the sharp, high planes of his face. The name by which he was known was Albannacht, and some of the elders crossed themselves when he told his tales and sang his songs, for he was deemed fey, almost a supernatural creature of woodland and wild lands like the Ghillie Dhu. He swept from castle to castle like the north wind, halting for a while then journeying on with more coin heavy in his purse.

I found Albannact's eyes unnerving, so ignored him as he capered with his skull and looked over to Mother, frail and wasted, scarcely seeming to breathe. Pressing sweetmeats into her hand, I coaxed her to eat with smiles and forced jollity. In the background, the winds wailed outside the keep…and *clackety clack*…the rattle of bone horse teeth sounded loud, ominous.

My whispered ramblings to my failing mother could not completely block out the words of the Filidh's latest poem, however--a tale of old battle, of death, of red ruin in the ancient north:

Savage men in war bands I beheld
After morning's fray, the torn flesh.
(Clackety clack!)
Hordes of invaders lay dead;
Joyous, wrathful, the shouts the victors heard.
(Clackety Clack!)
Defending the White Valley one saw
A high rampart and lone weary men.
At the ford I found men stained with blood
Cheeks pallid…

A loud clatter sounded in the corridor outside the Great Hall. Voices burbled, some raised. Beatrix glanced nervously over one shoulder, her brow furrowing in consternation; Governor Bartolf had left the chamber earlier to inspect the garrison before night set in. Rumours had reached the castle of war bands roaming in the fields and glens below Edinburgh; they carried no banners or recognisable insignia hence no one knew if they were friend or foe…but their presence and secretive movements aroused every suspicion.

A moment later the Governor himself appeared, walking swiftly towards his wife without glancing right or left. He took her hands, clutching them tightly, as he whispered close to her ear. Colour drained from her cheeks and her lips parted. She shook her head and staggered to her feet, almost falling in her haste.

Aware that the room had grown quiet, I also made to rise. Albannact the *Filidh* stood silent now, the macabre horse skull dangling from his hand, the jaw swinging uselessly back and forth, back and forth.

Beatrix and Bartolf came over and knelt before Mother, who sat as if she had been turned to stone, her hands gripping the arms of her seat. "Your Grace," said the Governor, "I bear evil news, of which I must tell you, although it splits my heart in twain. A battle has taken place at Alnwick, and...and his Grace King Malcolm had fallen in the fray. God have mercy on his soul. He was a great-hearted King and a good man."

Mother's breath scraped through her teeth as she bit back a moan of pain—not of physical pain, although that gnawed at her constantly with dragon's teeth, but the pain of a heart breaking in two. "Christ and his Saints preserve us all. Oh, this is a wicked, wicked day...What news of my eldest son, Edward?"

Beatrix hung her head and began to weep now, as only a mother would. She had a son of her own, named Malcolm for Father. Bartolf placed a hand on his wife's shoulder and looked steadily at Mother. "Prince Edward fell at his sire's side, fighting bravely unto the end."

Mother slumped in her chair; I thought she might faint, but after the initial shock, she rallied. "And my other boy, Edgar? Does he lie dead alongside his sire and brother?"

"No, your Grace," said Bartolf, "and thank Christ Jesu for that small mercy. He has taken a sword cut on his arm and is even now in the care of my personal physician. The cut is not deep, and it is thought he will recover without disability."

"So, Ned is here at Edinburgh?" Despite her frail condition, Mother sprang from her chair. Athelstan and I both grasped hold of her as her knees threatened to give way. "Take me to him!"

The Governor bowed his head. "I most certainly shall, my Queen, but before I take you to his chamber, there is one more thing you must know—the King's brother, Donald Bane, is approaching Edinburgh with a vast army, seeking to claim the throne. In the old manner of kingship, he would have been accounted Malcolm's heir, and it seems he has taken the opportunity to fight for his position once again."

"The news grows evermore evil!" gasped Mother, shaking her head. "If Edward is dead, Edgar should take the throne."

"And if his wound is grave, I should be the King!" Edmund staggered over, dizzy with drink and with shock. His pugnacious face was mottled red and white, his eyes shining with a mixture of tears and selfish fury.

"But it is not, Lord Edmund," said Governor Bartolf.

"Who are you to say?" yelled Edmund, suddenly throwing his drinking vessel across the chamber. "The wound could fester and turn black, as often happens. He'd die! Or his arm might need to be sliced off to save his life—of old, it was said that no King could rule with a bodily infirmity."

"Edmund!" Mother stared at him, horrified. "Why do you speak so foully of your brother, who lies sick within this very castle? Where is the grief for your father and brother Edward? You were so close to Ned once and now…" She leaned forward, convulsed with grief.

Angrily I glared at Edmund. "You should be ashamed. Mother is ill, our father lies dead, and you…you rant like a lunatic. If you mean to set yourself forth as a prospective king, you are doing a poor job of it."

For a moment, I thought he might strike me for his hand curled into a fist, but Athelstan and Alexander both strode towards him with purpose and he backed off. He reeled into the doorway, propping himself up against the frame and glowering as if he despised us all, and then with a wordless bellow of wrath, he flung himself out of the chamber, knocking over a servant carrying a tray who was on his way in. A wine carafe fell, clanging; redness splattered floor and walls.

"He is upset; I spoke too harshly," panted Mother, unwilling to believe the worst of her son.

"Let Edmund calm himself and worry not on his behalf." I slipped my arm around her waist. "Let us go to Ned's bedside and find out how he fares."

She nodded weakly. "Mayhap he can tell us of the last hours of my dear husband and eldest boy. If he is well enough."

A sad little crowd, the family of Malcolm Canmore exited the Great Hall. Athelstan's face was long and strained, while all my younger siblings wept and lamented openly. I had shed no tears yet; my eyes were dry, burning. I moved slowly, like an old woman, feeling as if a weight had fallen on my shoulders.

And though I had spoken up for Edmund, excusing his outburst…something had changed in him of late, filling him with spite and jealousy. I felt it every time we met—his hooded eyes, the slight sneer he often wore, his unwillingness to join in with any pursuits we indulged in to pass the days in Edinburgh Castle.

Blood though we shared, I no longer trusted him…

Edgar lay upon a bed, face leached of colour, hair spread out upon a heap of cushions propping him up. A bandage swathed his left arm. Bruises ran up onto his shoulder, where his shield had been smashed in against his flesh, and as he struggled to speak, I noticed he had lost a side tooth and his cheek was black and blue.

"M-mother…" he stammered as Mother and I approached, "I do not want you to see me like this! I should have been with my father and Edward at the end…" He began to weep.

"No." A servant brought Mother a stool and she slumped down at Ned's side and clasped his uninjured hand. "It was God's Will that you alone survived. You are meant for another purpose, Edgar. Perhaps a higher purpose. Who are we to question God? Although it is hard, so hard…" She choked back sobs.

"I do not believe in God anymore!" Edgar's voice rose in a tormented howl. "Not after what I saw! How could a loving God see a just King die!"

Everyone in the room gasped in horror at his sacrilegious words, fearing he might damn himself, as he lay with wounds that might not heal. "He speaks thus through grief and pain!" cried Mother, beckoning to the black-robed physician standing near the foot of the bed. "Do your job, man…or…or I'll have you flogged!"

More shocked gasps ran around the bedchamber. Mother never spoke thus. Punishments were anathema to her; she preferred forgiveness.

The physic, white, shouted at his servant to bring his bag of remedies. He scrabbled through it, then found a brew he claimed took away pain. Edgar snatched it with his good hand and downed it. Slowly, he began to grow calmer, falling back in exhaustion against the bed's bolster.

Mother stroked his brow, his hair as she would a small child. "Unburden yourself to me, my son. Tell me all there is of that fateful day, Ned. Tell me of the last moments of my dearest husband…and…and…" Her voice trailed away.

"Lady Mother, surely in your condition…" he struggled, searching for words. "It is not a tale for the ears of gentlewomen, let alone a Queen!"

"Is it because I am a Queen that I must know," she said. "It is my duty to know. Speak, Ned, if you will. Then I will leave you to sleep…and go to the chapel to mourn alone."

Ned took a deep breath, wincing as he did so; through gaps in his thin linen shirt, I saw the blooms of more dark bruises where his own mail had been driven into his flesh from an impact. "How could I deny you, Lady Mother…though it pains me to speak. But speak I will."

He pulled himself up a little higher on the bolster. "Our journey began with high hopes. We raced through the Cheviots and set the planes east of them aflame. No one opposed us and Father's mood was merry as he galloped onwards beneath the lion banner. 'We will teach the Northumbrians a lesson…and send a strong message to William Rufus!" he had chuckled as he led us to the walls of Alnwick. The fortress there was well-built and I had some misgivings, but the hill on which it stood was slight and led only down to the river Aln. Father ordered that we make camp on the rise above the valley, north of that river. We sent a message to the castellan, asking for surrender but no response came—we did not truly expect one."

"So Malcolm decided to attack the castle," said Mother in a whisper.

Ned nodded wearily. "The town was abandoned as the residents had taken shelter within the castle and we raided anything of worth left. The soldiers on the castle battlements pelted us with stones, oil and boiling water, but they were too far away to cause much damage...but equally we could not reach the foregate to force it without exposing ourselves to the enemy. Still, Father remained cheerful. 'They will give up soon when their bellies grow empty,' he said. 'If they capitulate quickly, I may even be merciful.'"

Mother shifted uncomfortably. She knew war was expected of a King but she had never truly approved of Father's incursions into foreign territory. "What happened?" She reached for Ned's fingers, squeezing, giving him strength to go on.

"A messenger slipped out of Alnwick under the cover of night to inform Robert de Mowbray, Earl of Northumbria, about the siege. De Mowbray marched from his fortress of Bamburgh, his speed almost unnatural, and caught us unawares as we smote the gate of Alnwick with a makeshift ram. Fighting ensued...Father led the vanguard but it was overwhelmed, crushed between the newcomers and Alnwick's walls. Arkill Morel, the steward of Bamburgh, saw Father's horse fall, pierced by an arrow, and took advantage..." Ned pulled his hand away from Mother's weak grasp and wiped his eyes. "He speared him with a huge lance that he carried. Father fell near a spring, and it ran red with blood..."

Mother beckoned me nearer, falling limply from her stool onto her knees. "Support me, daughter," she rasped. "Come, too, Mary. I want you at my side...to hear the end."

Ned pulled himself even higher onto the cushions, gritting his teeth. "Ale..." he ordered one of the pages loitering at the back of the room "My tongue, I fear, will not work otherwise. It is as if all strength has left me; even the strength to talk."

The page hurried over with a horn cup and placed it in Ned's grasp. His battered, swollen fingers shook. Black blood clotted beneath the nails; though whether his or some opponent's I could not say.

Thirst quenched and his mouth wet, the chapped lips almost feverish red, Edgar continued his story. "Edward was close to Father when Morel rode in and slew him with the lance. He leapt from his steed—the brave, stupid fool—and fought on standing over Father's fallen body. A lowly man-at-arm smote him...here..." He touched his shoulder and then gave a great gulp as if he might be sick. "He struck him with an axe."

"Jesu!" Mother's tears fell like rain now, as Mary uttered comforting words and wiped her face with a linen kerchief.

"Battle is an ugly thing," said Ned. "I never realised how ugly till that bitter day! But Edward was not killed outright. The survivors of the vanguard gathered round and carried him from the field. The priest who travelled with the army was brought and so he did not die unshriven."

"At least that gives me some small comfort," whispered Mother, white-lipped. "Where…what had been done with their bodies? I pray…I pray the enemy has not mutilated them."

Edgar shook his head. "Our troops were scattered; there was no way of bringing the bodies back without risking my life and that of other survivors. De Mowbray behaved with honour, if such a thing may be known of the Normans, and had them taken for burial at Tynemouth Priory."

"Tynemouth!" Mother flung up her hands. "So far away…but I suppose it matters but little as their souls are now safe with God."

"If…if I ever should get the chance, I will have them disinterred and reburied, either in Dunfermline or Iona. Or Edmund will, as he has a claim to the Kingship, now that Edward is no more. Where is he anyway? Is he not with you in Edinburgh?"

"He deals with his grief differently from the rest of us," I said, hoping that Edgar sensed my disapproval of our brother.

"He should be here…" cried Ned in agitation. "Donald Bane, father's brother. He is on the move. He is coming here to claim the crown for his own."

"We have heard these evil tidings about Donald already," said Mother. "Whatever happens is now in God's hands. We can only pray that the high rock of Edinburgh can hold against Donald Bane's army. Now…I must go to rest, and you should do likewise, Ned, that your body may heal."

Mary and I helped Mother to rise and she bent to kiss Edgar's brow. The physician then closed in on him again, bringing poultices made of vinegar and honey for his wounds and Saint John's Wort stewed in oil for the bruising.

The rest of the family left the bedchamber and escorted Mother to her own apartments where Alesoune and other ladies took over, guiding her to her bed, where she lay like a small, white doll, stiff with sorrow.

After we left her, I went with Mary to the castle wall-walk. "I need to take the air," I told her. "My head is full of dire thoughts and my heart is sore."

Buffeted by the freezing November wind, we walked along the stony stretch together, hand in hand, united in our sadness. Father had lived a good life, an eventful life, and had seen over sixty summers, but his loss still bit into our hearts like a knife blade. To say nought of Edward, young, proud Edward, so eager to blood his sword…

The winter turned the tears to ice on my cheeks…or so it felt. The sky was hard and clear overhead, the constellations bright, blue-white hoar frost gleaming on the castle walls.

I looked over the breastwork, away towards the distant sea, smelling a faint tang of salt amidst the more usual odours of castle life. Then I turned my head towards the town and saw the streets were a mass of light—torches, hundreds of torches in all directions, and in the far distance, a ring of fires. The wind shifted direction and my ears were assailed by the sound of neighing horses and shouting men.

"Mary!" I gasped, clutching the balustrade. "Look."

She flew to my side, peering over. "What…what is it?" she whispered.

I began to shiver within the folds of my heavy fox-fur cloak. "It's him, Mary. Our uncle. Donald Bane has come to claim the throne."

CHAPTER EIGHT

Boom, boom!

The din of Donald Bane's battering ram as it slammed against the iron-studded gates of Edinburgh Castle sent pain searing through my skull. I had not slept since his army had arrived, fearing that soon he would gain entry, and my head was gripped by a ceaseless pounding. I believed he would not harm us women, but I feared for my younger brothers—it was different for them as they were all contenders for the throne. At best, they might live out their lives in a remote monastery or be sent from castle to castle with a gaoler, released only when broken enough to accept Donal Bane as King. At worst—mutilation was a possibility, or a quiet, secret death. As for me, I would end up married to a chosen laird in return for his loyalty or betrothed to my cousin, Donald's bastard son, Ladhmann. Mary would no doubt suffer a similar fate. As for Mother...I bit my lip. She might be forced to wed too, even in her sickly state. A nunnery would be the kindest option—but was Donald Bane kind? And would she even live to find out her fate?

Mother's condition had declined further since the enemy army arrived at the gates. Scarcely able to walk, she had insisted her maids dress her in a hair shirt so that she might further suffer for her sins. She refused to eat and drank but little, taking medicines only when the pains in her belly brought unbearable torment, and sometimes her mind wandered. She had visions of sights beyond the boundaries of the world, heaven's angels and the blessed dead...and sometimes demons that brought her to tears and anguished, frantic prayer.

She was dying. I knew not the hour or day, but I knew it would be soon. The death of my father and brother had started to sever the increasingly thin chain binding her to life...

"Lady Edith!" A knock sounded on the chamber door, its stridency adding to my throbbing headache.

"Enter." I put down the missal I had been trying to read for an hour, though the words made no impression upon me in my nerve-ridden state.

My mother's maid Alesoune appeared in the doorway, taut-faced and sorrowful. She visibly shook, her hands knotted together. "My Lady, you must come at once. Her Grace the Queen…she's in the chapel."

I did not even hesitate to ask the reason for such urgency. Throwing a cape over my robe, I went to Alesoune. "Has my sister been informed? My brothers?"

"Mary awaits your arrival, Lady Edith," said Alesoune. "The Lord Edgar is being roused from his sickbed. David and Alexander have been fetched."

"And Edmund? What of Edmund?" My eldest surviving brother had lain low since his embarrassing antics when Ned returned from battle bearing grievous tidings. I had seen him once, perched on the battlements like a gargoyle, a black silhouette against snow-burdened skies, but he had spoken to none of us and no longer partook of meals in the Hall. We all tried to excuse his behaviour, but I suspected there was more to it than just sorrow.

Alesoune flushed and shook her head. "A message was sent to his chamber, but the Lord Edmund was nowhere to be found."

"We must search the castle!"

Nervously she cleared her throat. "It has already been done, Lady, by the Governor himself. It seems, for whatever reason, he has slipped out of the castle through the postern gate. An inspection of his room showed he had taken many of his possessions with him."

I gasped loudly, thunderstruck. "The guards let him go? Just like that?"

"The Governor is having them interrogated. It is though Lord Edmund paid them handsomely to let him pass or else tricked them in some way."

I exploded in anger. "The traitor; the worthless cowardly little traitor!"

"My Lady?" Alesoune looked perplexed.

"He's gone to join Donald Bane, I am certain of it," I said bitterly.

"But why would he? It's his crown, surely, that his uncle wants to usurp."

Misery filled my heart. "Yes, but Edmund knows what might happen to him if we continue to hold out against Donald and are, at the last, taken prisoner. No doubt he wants to lap at our uncle's feet and offer his support—as long as he is made Donald's heir. My uncle has no legitimate offspring, only two bastards, a girl called Bethoc and a son called Ladhmann. He is over sixty summers old so it's unlikely he'll ever beget a legal heir."

"Oh, my Lady..." murmured Alesoune. "How has it come to this?"

Unable to answer, with rage, grief and fear welling in my heart, I shook my head and pushed past the maid into the corridor. All I cared about now was reaching my mother's side.

When I arrived at the castle chapel, nobles, clerics, knights and ladies milled around, some openly weeping. My heart pounded; was I too late? The throng fell back as I approached, ill-attired in a thin robe, a cloak flung loosely around me, my hair streaming loose in wanton disarray to my waist. Ignoring those who gawped and stared, I thrust my way through the crowd to the chapel door and entered.

Mother knelt before the high altar, deep in prayer, wearing a circlet and robes of blue that resembled those of the virgin. Her colour was yellowish, her complexion waxy, yet a peaceful air hung about her emaciated form—she had resigned herself to her impending mortality and felt great joy at the thought of being received into Our Lord's presence in heaven. The beeswax candles standing in the nearby sconces burnt brightly, making a ring of gold, a nimbus, an aureole about her bowed head.

She was a saint. I felt it then. My mother and yet far more than that. A true daughter of Christ and His church. Noble Queen, but also a generous patron of the monasteries and other foundations, a champion of learning for women, a blessing to the poor and afflicted whom she supplied with food, medicine and raiment, treating their diseased flesh without hesitation.

I began to cry, my hands curling into balls. I did not want her to leave me but I knew she must, and that she would take her place with the blessed saints. I stumbled to her side, kneeling beside her in prayer, while Mary and Athelstan, followed by Ned, breathing heavily and still weak from his wounds. Our younger brothers stood behind accompanied by a nursemaid.

Mother reached out and clasped my hand before reaching for Ned's. I wondered if she realised Edmund was not present and hoped not. "My children, my beautiful children…God's gifts," she murmured, her voice a mere crackle in her throat. "Through you, the blood of the Saxon kings will go on, whether in Scotland…or in England." She looked straight at me, her eyes strangely unfocussed but gleaming, unearthly, the candle flames shivering gold on their surfaces.

"Yes, Mother," I whispered back. "I pray I will soon wed so that the seed of great Alfred is carried on forever."

Mother smiled but suddenly jerked sideways as pain gripped her innards. Her hand tore free of mine and she slumped in a heap before the altar. Turgot of Durham, her confessor and confidant, hastened to her side as Ned and Athelstan rushed to raise her into a sitting position, her slackening face turned towards the glory of the Rood.

Turgot drew a cross on her brow with Holy Oil and murmured, "Through this holy anointing, may the Lord in his love and mercy help thee with the grace of the Holy Spirit. May the Lord who frees you from sin save thee and raise thee up."

Mother's eyelids fluttered; the light in her eyes was waning, a fading candle, blue skies dimmed by eventide. Her mouth opened but no words she spoke; instead, there was an inhalation of breath, a gasp that savoured of awe, as if she saw the Light beyond the sinful mortal world and walked into it with open arms.

Then her eyes closed and her head fell forward.

She was gone.

Mary cried out, her voice a high wail that echoed through the chapel.

I fought back my tears. I must be brave now; I must be like my mother. But…what would happen to our family now?

Mother's body was washed, packed with fragrant herbs and shrouded in preparation for burial. It was then placed on a bier before the chapel altar, surrounded by a sea of candles and covered with a pall fashioned from golden cloth.

I went to pray there each day but found it gave me no peace. Mother needed a proper burial before too long, for the usual reason—unless God should see fit to make her mortal remains incorrupt like many of his Saints. Donald Bane was still at the gates, hammering or sending over rocks in a trebuchet that scattered across the inner ward so there was no chance of bearing Mother hence to her final rest.

And then, one morning, the booming of the ram against heavy wood fell silent; the trebuchets were drawn back, their throwing arms empty of missiles. With Mary at my side, I ran out onto the covered wall walk, which was now sagging and precarious, damaged by blows from flying stones. Far beyond, through the hazy blue smoke that hung like a pall over Uncle Donald's war camp, I spied a grand pavilion with riders clustered in and around it. Shading my eyes against the brightness of the sky, I strained to see if I could recognise any flags or standards. It was too far away, alas, but I surmised that the flurry in that area was made by newcomers. I wondered darkly if Donald Bane had received reinforcements to assist in taking the castle.

I returned to the solar with Mary, where we read and sewed and embroidered. Words on the page seemed to have no meaning and the bright illuminations looked drab and pointless. Our stitchery was poor and ugly as if untutored children had stabbed at the frames with needles. We worked steadily, barely speaking and rarely pausing, enclosed in our own private world of mourning. The future was bleak and uncertain—neither of us wanted to think of what might happen next.

As evening fell and torches were lit through the castle, I began to sense a change in the atmosphere amongst the servants—an air of expectancy mingled with trepidation. It was still quiet outside the wall—the hammering of the ram against the gate had not resumed. I had grown used to its rhythmic bangs; now the silence began to make me uneasy.

Something had taken place or was about to, and I wanted to know what it was. Leaving Mary with instructions to remain in the solar, I sought out Governor Bartolf who was presiding in the Great Hall. To my surprise, Ned was with him, still wincing in pain from his wound, but looking much sturdier and more determined.

"Edith!" he cried, rising from a bench to greet me. "What do you here?"

"I cannot sit and wait like a lamb to the slaughter. I can tell there is something afoot, Ned. I hope to find answers."

Edgar took my hand, squeezing my fingers. "Yes, you are right. Something is afoot. The Governor and I did not wish to bring more worry to you at this time."

I looked my brother straight in the eye. "I am not a little child any longer, Ned. If my fate is under discussion, I want to know so that I can make my peace with whatever I might face."

"So be it," he said. "I will tell you. Our Uncle Edgar has ridden in from England and is treating with Donald Bane, hence the cessation of the siege, at least for now. We pray he comes to some arrangement that will guarantee our safety and freedom."

I shivered. "Let us pray the discussion does not end in daggers." The ruthlessness of men such as Donald was well known; my father himself had not walked away from killing, taking bloody revenge after the murder of his own sire by MacBethad.

"It would be ill done to harm an emissary who is there to parley," said Ned, but he shrugged. "But in these times, men's hearts are cold and cruel."

We both fell silent as a guardsman marched into the Hall, bowing to us and to the Governor. Bartolf drew him away from us and they spoke together in low, urgent voices.

When the guard had delivered his message, Bartolf returned to our seat. "I go to open the gate. An arrangement with Donald Bane has been agreed upon."

I held my breath. His words sounded promising, but I was afraid to drop my guard. We might have our lives but end up with little else.

Ned nodded toward Bartolf. "Go and see what Lady Fortune brings us."

The Governor left the Hall, and Ned and I sat in silence, listening to the muted noises from the bailey—the clank of the drawbridge being raised, the clatter and bang of the gates as the barricades and bolts were thrown back.

Then an uneasy silence took over, but fortunately not for long. The sound of swift-moving footsteps in the corridor brought us both to our feet as our Uncle Edgar, Mother's brother, strode into the room, hair windswept and his countenance weary and white, with dark bags low beneath his eyes.

"Uncle!" I stepped in his direction. "Come, sit here near the fire—you look so cold. You have journeyed a long way, in mourning as we are…and facing great danger on our behalf."

Uncle Edgar slumped onto a bench, letting his damp cloak fall to the floor. He stretched his legs before the central fire pit as a servant boy brought in a goblet of heated wine.

Ned and I sat near him, watching the colour return to his cheeks as he drank. We did not question; he would speak when he was ready.

Finally, he set down his cup. "Donald Bane has agreed to lift the siege and allow your mother to be respectfully buried at Dunfermline Abbey. However, his terms are absolute—all of Malcolm's children must leave Scotland and go into exile. Save for my bastard nephew, Edmund who is now Donald's lapdog, fawning at his heels…" Edgar spat into the rushes in disgust.

My brother Ned leapt up, his fists clenched, grimacing as pain ran up his wounded arm from the sudden motion. "This is outrageous! How dare Donald Bane order such a thing! As for Edmund, brother or no, I'll…"

Frowning, our uncle held up a hand for silence. "Edgar, enough. If we do not comply with Donald Bane's wishes, he makes no secret of the fact he will besiege Edinburgh again once the burial is over…and that if he is kept waiting outside through the winter, he will not only fire the town but kill the garrison when he gets inside. As for what he'd plan for all of you…I would not like to think."

Ned was almost weeping with rage and pain, clutching his arm with his uninjured hand. "What shall happen to us? Where can we go?"

Uncle Edgar sighed. "Where do you think, boy? All of you shall come to England with me. We will go to the court of William Rufus."

"Rufus!" I cried. My uncle had bent the knee, first to the Conqueror and then his eldest son, but it seemed, well, *odd*, for a troupe of displaced Scottish princesses and princes to flood his court. I had not forgotten, either, the whispers that the unmarried King may have once desired me for a bride...

"I understand you may have heard tales of the immorality and violence of his court." Edgar's lips drew into a grim line. "I dare say most of them are more than exaggeration. But he has offered a safe haven for you, and I would not turn his offer down—such largesse is unlikely to be offered again. You may not need to stay there overlong, either...for hearing the dire news of Malcolm's death, Duncan is readying to march to Scotland and contest Donald Bane's claim to the throne. Donald is unaware of this as yet...so I warn you, you must hold your tongues on the matter. No one knows what spies he might have, even here."

"Duncan," I murmured. Duncan was my half-brother, son to Father's first wife, the mysterious Ingibiorg. One of the sons whom Father has treated well enough—except that he removed all three from the succession in favour of Mother's children. I had only met him once or twice and knew that even if he prevailed over Donald, nothing would ever be as it was before. He would establish his own line of succession, and our family would be cut out of it forever. He might allow a return to Scotland, with conditions...and again, he might decide we were too great a threat to his rule.

Ned was still in shock at our uncle's tidings, his emotions still in turmoil after his injuries and the death of our parents and Edward. He slouched onto a bench, hiding his head in his hands; I suspected he hid bitter, angry tears. I went to him, pressing a comforting hand on his uninjured shoulder. "We will survive this, brother," I whispered in his ear, "one way or the other. Have faith."

Ned did not answer but his head bobbed slightly in agreement.

I glanced up at Uncle Edgar. "Uncle, send to Donald Bane and tell them the children of Malcolm and Margaret, of blessed memory, agree to his terms. We will go into exile as he wishes…but not till after we see our mother the Queen buried in Dunfermline."

Edgar rose, an expression of relief on his face. "I will tell him, Edith. I will tell him tonight."

It was as exiles and orphans the children of great Canmore left Scotland, accompanied by Uncle Edgar and the loyal Prior Turgot of Durham, Mother's friend, who swore to see her children safe from harm. Royal we were, but travelling with nought but what we could carry in our small baggage train. Even through our misery, there was a vague sense of relief as we passed over the border into England. Scotland was too volatile for us right now, with Donald Bane snatching the crown and Edmund waiting at his shoulder, having been declared heir presumptive by the usurper, to say nothing of Duncan readying to march north and press his own claim with the sword. We were too young, too vulnerable to be caught in the midst of such a fray; the boys were liable to imprisonment or even death, while Mary and I would become hapless pawns. Yes, William Rufus was a cruel ungodly man, but at least we would be under his royal protection, with Uncle Edgar making sure that no harm befell us at his riotous court. Whether the English King still felt any inclination to wed me, I was unsure…but I refused to dwell on such a possibility. He might well consider me too far below him now, anyway, with my family ousted from the throne of Scotland.

After many grey, dull days of travel, battling wintry rains, muddy tracks and a nasty flux that felled each of us for a day or two in turn, our tiny, pitiful entourage reached Wilton. My heart jumped with joy to see the abbey's retaining wall, the gatehouse with its façade of stone saints, even though rain sluiced over their faces, making them appear to weep. Well, maybe they wept for joy at my return, as I nearly did when I saw that treasured place, which I had thought never to see again.

Abbess Hawise called for me after I had bathed and eaten in the guestenhouse. Wearing modest garments, but as a princess rather than the lay boarder of old, I hurried to her closet. "My Lady Edith," she said, looking me up and down, "how pleased am I to see you back here. I have heard the grievous news of your parents, the King and Queen of Scotland. I have candles lit and masses said for their souls in Saint Edith's shrine every day."

"You are too kind, Reverend Mother," I said. "You were always good to my family."

"Perhaps too kind." Her eyes twinkled, bright amidst the nest of fine wrinkles. "Archbishop Anselm was most distressed that I let you and Mary leave."

"We could not disobey our father," I said. "The only one we would obey above him would be our Heavenly Father."

Hawise let out a chuckle which she hastily stifled. "And what are your intentions now, Edith? Your situation has changed drastically with the passing of King Malcolm. Perhaps you and Mary will now consider joining the order and taking vows? I realise this was never your original intention..."

I sighed. "Mother Abbess, I fear I would make a terrible nun. I am not obedient, pious or retiring enough. I desire a different life. I believe it's my duty to marry someday and carry on the line of Alfred—the line of English kings. I believe Mary thinks likewise, although I would not speak for her; you may ask her yourself."

Hawise chewed her lip thoughtfully as she mulled my words. "So...if you are not to stay here at St Mary's Abbey, where will you go? To the house of your Uncle Edgar?"

I lowered my head, aware that she would not like the answer to her question. "The King has offered us places at his court." I did not tell her that Uncle Edgar had written to Archbishop Anselm to ask if he could convince Rufus to financially support Mary and I at St Mary's...but the King had told Anselm he would not pay for tutors or any niceties. The only thing he'd grant us was a small pension covering our board. Upon hearing this, Edgar had decided court would be our best option. "At least you will live in some comfort," he said, "and are more likely to find fitting husbands, though I'll need to keep an eye on you."

Abbess Hawise had gone quiet at my words; silence hung heavy between us, Then, sighing, she rose stiffly from her stool. "Well, what will be, will be. You are a King's daughter; I suppose it is fitting you spend time at a King's court. But such a King...You will remain in my prayers, Edith, and the door will lie ever open to you here at St Mary's."

She motioned that our meeting was over. "I know it is late, Reverend Lady," I said, "but may I visit the hospital of Mary Magdalene before I retire? I would visit those I cared for one more time."

She nodded, with a smile. "Go, with my blessing, Edith."

I ran out through the gardens to the hospital. Dusk had just fallen and the torches were lit, hazy and sputtering in the drizzly night. Most of the residents were already abed but I could see Sister Infirmarer standing with a familiar figure—young Leofgifu, the moon-touched girl who was forever innocent. She turned towards me as my shoes whisked over the damp grass and her soft, round face broke out into a beatific smile. "Edith…jus' like Saint Edith!" she cried, pointing. "Edith comes back to us. And lo…look Sister…" She grabbed the sleeve of Sister Alice's habit, tugging. "Her head…it shines… shining… like a crown. She has a crown! Queen Edith!"

"Hush, Leofgifu." Alice gave the excited girl a gentle shake. "You must curtail such fancies. What you see is only the torchlight, reflecting on such pale tresses."

But Leofgifu would not be calmed. She danced around the herb garden, uncaring of the cold, damp weather, crying out in a sing-song voice, "Queen Edith, Queen Edith'.

I called to her, begging her to stop, but the girl continued to dance, a ragged figure in the rain, mud up to her ankles, with her proclamation clear as prophecy rising up to the brooding skies

CHAPTER NINE

The children of Malcolm Canmore joined the Red King's court in the town of Winchester, once ruled by my own kin, and before that a bastion of the Roman legions. In the half-completed new castle, one by one we were presented to William Rufus, seated on a throne draped in golden silks from the east and wearing his crown. He spoke us fair, with well-rehearsed pleasant words that rang throughout the Great Hall, desiring to show the gathered spectators that he could be kind and magnanimous, even though he had parted from my father on bad terms. He swore that that we would receive the best of care in his house, and the Hall, packed to the brim with his barons and knights broke into raucous applause.

I trembled as I dropped a curtsey before him, remembering our brief, unnerving encounter at Wilton Abbey...but if he had truly considered me a marital possibility then, he clearly did not do so now. His glance as it fell upon me was dull and uninterested, almost as if he did not recognise me at all. Maybe he didn't without my nun's veil, and of that I was glad.

Uncle Edgar led me to the quarters I would share with some of the other women of the court—his own illegitimate daughter, Margaret—nicknamed Meggott—and his concubine, an English woman of lower rank called Goodeth. Mary also shared the space, and several tiring women who would see to dressing us, repairing our garments and arranging bathing and other needs.

At court, I soon met my half-brother Duncan, former hostage to the Conqueror but now a staple of Rufus's court. He was big, like Father, his features heavy and prominent, his brow beetling, but his hair was sandy without any hint of flame. I found it hard to believe he was kin, for he had become Norman in dress and manner and, it transpired, had even spent time in Normandy. No hint of the Scot hung in his deep, gravelly voice, let alone in his dress and mannerisms.

"Dear sister!" he had said, kissing my hand in a courtly way, but then he dismissed me, not in words but in action, to talk excitedly with Ned about Father's last battle and the usurpation of Donald Bane.

"The King has lent me a good Norman force to take to Scotland," he said with ill-suppressed excitement. "I will put Donald Bane to flight."

"Will the King himself go with you?" asked Ned, rather shrewdly.

Duncan harumphed. "No. He has other business...here. I could scarcely ask for more than his Grace has given. You do not understand, Edgar; you are too young as yet and unfamiliar with the ways of our King."

I noticed his lips curl, almost contemptuously, and Ned stiffened, though he kept his visage friendly and unperturbed. "How odd you call him 'our king' when you long to be a king in the country of your birth," he said softly. "Will you be a king in name only, or will he let you truly rule your lands?"

Duncan's eyes snapped fire for a second but he restrained himself. "You do not understand," he repeated, full of condescension. "You will learn, my young brother...you will soon learn what must be in King William's court."

I tensed; above his bluster, he was making it clear that Ned was to stay here while he headed north to attempt to wrest the Scottish crown back from Donald Bane. He was also making sure Ned knew that he, Duncan, was the only fitting candidate for kingship and that he had displaced him in the succession, just as our dead brother Edward had displaced Duncan by Father's own decree.

Ned beckoned for a servant to bring wine. "To you, then, my brother," he said, raising his goblet. "May you win against our uncle and may the crown bring you all the happiness you deserve."

Duncan looked confused then, not knowing if Edgar was insulting him or not, but the situation had no time to escalate for Duncan's wife Ethelreda thankfully appeared in the solar, with Duncan's little son, William.

Her presence broke the growing tension and it was clear Duncan, for all his faults, doted on the little sandy-haired lad, who pulled away from his nurse and climbed upon his knee. He forgot Edgar's ill-conceived jibe and began to boast of how his lad was already showing signs of great courage and had beaten off a vicious dog in the marketplace.

Ethelreda was the daughter of Gospatric, who had once held the Earldom of Northumbria, although his title was stripped from him when he joined a rebellion against William Bastard. Gospatrick was of English blood, of the line of Ethelred Unraed through his mother, Ealdgyth. Our similar heritage made Ethelreda eager to befriend Mary and me and also to act as a chaperone and companion at court where needed.

"I think I arrived just in time," she whispered to me, nodding towards Duncan, who was still dandling his boy. "He can have a hot temper, my husband."

"So, too, our sire, Malcolm," I said, "but..." I added, "Ned's tongue is too hasty and he was impertinent to his elder brother."

Etheldreda smiled over at me. "He was promised a crown once—of course he is impertinent. But King Malcolm did wrong, Edith—he should never have discarded his elder sons as if they were fit only for the midden, just because he had some grievance with their mother, Ingebiorg."

"I never knew exactly why he found her so distasteful," I said. "Neither of my parents would ever speak of it. But it is not necessarily the way in Scotland that the eldest son follows his father. It is not always that way with Normans either—or we would have a King Robert instead of William."

"Mm," mused Etheldreda, "if it had been so, maybe we would have had fewer conflicts in this realm...but these Normans are a fractious bunch, are they not?"

"Men are fractious, no matter their background," I grinned. "Swords into ploughshares was not a lesson they learned well."

Her face darkened. "You don't think your brother Edgar would...come after Duncan if he claimed the Scottish crown, do you?" she said worriedly.

"Oh, no!" I shook my head, although I lied. I could not say what ideas my brother had about his lost crown. "I am certain, that like our Uncle Edgar, he will grow to enjoy the English court and find a place here."

She breathed a sigh of relief. "I am glad to hear your thoughts. I truly would not want Duncan to have to kill him…Edgar is quite a handsome lad …"

At that moment, Duncan swivelled around his seat. Small William had been denied a pastry and had set up a red-faced roaring, thrashing the air with his fists and scrunching up his visage until he looked like a scarlet turnip. "Etheldreda! Wife! Do something…"

Etheldreda hurried to his side, the nurse joining in, and there was much cooing and fussing over the tantrum-ridden babe. I felt a sense of relief as Duncan left the Hall with her, and left Ned to his own devices. A young Norman lord named Hugh wandered over and asked Ned if he wanted to visit the mews and kennel to see the hawks and hounds. Ned looked relieved to be away from our half-brother and his talk of claiming the Scottish crown, and hurried after his new-found companion as eager as any ordinary boy of lowly birth.

As he departed, I wondered if Mary and I would ever truly belong here. Meggott, my cousin, was shy; her mother suspicious and perhaps slightly envious, as her daughter was born of a man who might have been King of England, but Meggott would always be tainted by her illegitimacy and would have neither the rank or the marriage expected for Mary and me. Ethelreda was kind enough, but if Duncan prevailed against Donald Bane, she would go to Scotland to be crowned Queen. It was difficult to imagine her taking our mother's place wearing her crown, sitting on her throne…

A pang of grief gripped me and I whirled about to retreat to my chambers before tears came to shame me.

And I almost bumped into *him*. Henry, the younger brother of the King. I fell into a clumsy curtsey.

"Why so sorrowful, Lady Edith?" he asked. He was clad in riding clothes; he smelt of horses and rain but it was not an unpleasant fragrance. His dark, almost black hair, was poorly cut and tousled, as if he never used a comb, not even his fingers. Close up, he was short and rather barrel-chested for a young man, but his visage was pleasant enough. He was personable in a way William Rufus was not, and I suspected of higher intellect. He was said to be brave in battle, even though enamoured of books; his main defect was his ceaseless lust for women—young, old, maidens or widows, it mattered not to Henry. Rumours abounded that he had a handful of bastards already. I wondered if he would try to charm me into his bed—well, there was no chance of that. I would not give up my virtue so easily.

"I am not sorrowful," I said to him. "A little lonely, as might be expected when one has had to flee into exile. I cannot even visit my mother's grave."

He bowed his head. "An unpleasant time for you. I, too, have known family strife...and I am certain more will come, for the sons of the Bastard...are bastards!"

"Lord Henry!" I raised my brows.

He chuckled. "Forgive my rough speech. I am a soldier and not a courtier."

"Obviously...my lord."

"I hope you will not hold my crudeness against me. I am not used to the presence of such highborn ladies."

But not so high women, girls, serving wenches...a different story, I thought, with a little tight smile.

"There...I've made you smile, princess!" he grinned. "Things cannot be so bad. I remember you from Wilton Abbey, you know. So clever to wear that cowl to dissuade my brother—his advisors had almost convinced him that he must take a bride, although he has no...desire for women."

"I know the King is a war-like man," I said, "but I am astonished he has not wed, even if only out of duty. Surely he desires an heir?"

"Maybe it will be a godsend to me if he does not," laughed Henry, his deep brown eyes gleaming in his tanned face.

So...there it was. Like all such powerful and ambitious men, Henry sought that most dangerous lure, a golden crown. I imagined that if William should die prematurely, Henry would fight his elder brother Robert for England's throne.

"Is that not a dangerous thing to say at court, my lord Henry?" I murmured in a low voice.

He leaned in close; powerful, almost overwhelming. There was an energy about him that reminded me of lightning, swift to strike and deadly to those it struck. "Perhaps, but as the youngest of the Bastard's sons, I have learnt to live with danger." He then backed away from me, his mood lightening. "Have you ever ridden in the New Forest, Lady Edith?"

I shook my head. "Never. I lived with the nuns, remember. We were not out gallivanting with hawks and hounds. I have heard the Forest is a devilish place anyway, filled with unclean pagan spirits. But I have also heard your brother the King frequently hunts the deer there…"

Henry slapped his thigh and loosed a roar of laughter. "Pagan spirits! I have never seen any…but some might call my brother pagan. He loves not the church, nor does the church love him!"

"Ranulf Flambard seemed to love him well, and he is high in the church," I countered.

"Ah, but Ranulf is not your usual dour churchman like Lanfranc or Anselm. Can you believe he was captured by pirates once…and escaped? He keeps the Royal Seal, and devises all sorts of interesting ways to gain revenues…"

"You mean extortion."

Henry leaned in again to look straight into my eyes. My breath caught in my lungs. He was so close, improperly so…yet somehow, I did not mind. "For one so young, you are very astute, Edith."

"My parents spoke of such matters freely; my mother wanted me to be knowledgeable, not ignorant."

"This is wise and I am sure you will have a fine future, my Lady. But do not be too free with your tongue."

"But you were, my lord—were you not?"

"Yes, b…but…" he stammered and I forced back a smile. I had thrown him off course, dinted the confidence that radiated from his stocky form.

"But what?"

Another grin broke through the close-cropped hair of his dark beard. "But there is a difference! You could not raise a sword to defend yourself if challenged for your unwise words! Or, perhaps with your English ancestry…you could!"

I goggled at him. "Whatever do you mean by that?"

"A compliment, my Lady, not an insult. Your ancestors, men and women alike, were brave and fought bravely, even when they did not prevail and lost the day. I admire that, you know. I do not think the forest wights you speak of would dare show their devilish faces to you if you rode there. One day, pray God, I may be able to take you to the forest...with the other ladies, of course. Not to deer hunt, for that is a man's sport, but perhaps to hawk? But not now, alas...for I fear my brother and I must soon fare away to Normandy."

And with that, he turned on his heel and strutted away like a short, burly peacock, leaving me staring at his mantled back.

After Henry and King William had sailed away to Normandy, eager to quell the unrest amongst the proud and land-hungry barons, another maiden arrived at the court at Winchester—Nest, a Welsh Princess, the daughter of Rhys Ap Tewdwr, who had fallen at the Battle of Brecknock. She was an unfortunate girl—after Rufus conquered her father's kingdom, Nest was brought to England as a hostage—no doubt to become someone's marriage prize in due course. Nest was a few years younger than me but strikingly fair to behold with long, curling near-black hair and wide, sky-blue eyes fringed by sweeping dark lashes. She looked older than her age and acted it too, which often drew the attention of the King's unsavoury companions. Thank God, they never touched her, though—gossips said he had warned them that if any took her maidenhead they would be castrated, blinded and then hanged.

When she first arrived, Nest spoke to few except her old nurse, Rohaise, with whom she shared a separate chamber, but with the King gone and the court emptied of overbold, pugnacious knights, she quickly began to thaw.

I was in the garden when I spotted her by a pond, playing with a ball of golden twine like a kitten. She sang to herself in the strange Welsh tongue, of which I knew nothing. One time my sire's people had spoken an old tongue a little like Welsh, but he had decided upon English at court, not just to please Mother but for the advantages of trade. Soon though, we were hastily learning the Norman's version of French as the tongue of the English was consigned to the serfs beneath the Conqueror's iron rule.

"What were you singing?" I asked. "It had a pretty melody."

Nest jumped, not realising I was there. A blush stained her cheeks. "Oh, it is nothing...an old song from my homeland," she said in broken Norman French. Her voice was musical, lilting, something I noticed in all the Welsh and Bretons that I had encountered...except for odious Alan of Richmond!

"I am Edith of Scotland," I said. "We are of similar age; perhaps we could be friends. There are not enough women here at court, and though my brother's wife Ethelreda is kindly, she is older and has a son to see to, and soon, God willing, she may become Queen of Scotland."

"I know of your brother, Duncan. The very tall one...with a chin like a mountainside!"

"Half-brother," I corrected, laughing. "My family is complicated."

She threw back her pretty head and laughed too, the sound like the tinkle of faerie bells. "So is mine." Then suddenly a shadow descended over her face and those blue eyes darkened. Tears brimmed and she turned away, blinking.

"Oh, Nest, what is wrong?" I asked. "Have you been mistreated here?" I felt pity for her and also understood her sorrow well. She was far from her people, spoke only rudimentary Norman French, and had the promise of beauty and early maturity—a combination potentially lethal among crowds of hungry young Norman men, of which Rufus's court was full. At the moment, she was forbidden to them, but at some point, one of these bravos would claim her, with William's smiling permission.

She took a deep, shuddering breath. "My father was killed in battle at Brycheiniog, which you English call Brecknock. My youngest brother, Gruffyd, was rushed away to Ireland for his safety. He is only a babe, Edith. My mother and my brother Hywel were taken as prisoners to Arnold de Montgomery's castle...and I have heard dreadful things about his family. He is brother to that knave, Robert de Belleme, who men say is the devil's son. There has been no news of my kin since the day we parted, and mam was with child…"

"Someone must know." I tried to show comfort. "I am sure even de Belleme's kinsman would not be base enough to harm a pregnant woman." (I deliberately made no mention of the unfortunate Hywel.)

"I had two half-brothers as well; sons of my father's mistress. They…they were killed." Reaching up, she wiped her eyes. "Goronwy…We were close once. I do not even know where they buried him…or if they buried him at all. His head might well stand on a pike at a town gate somewhere."

"Nest, do not think on it. You must not. Such dark thoughts will sicken you in body and mind." I put my hand on her elbow, guiding her through the garden to a little stone bench that leaned against the castle wall. We sat together, Nest with her head bowed; her long raven braids, streaked through with silver-white ribbons, hid her face.

"I lost my parents too, only days apart," I told her. "My sire died in battle even as yours, along with my brother Edward. My other brother Edmund turned his coat and brought the ruin of our family. And so I am an exile from my homeland, too."

"Edith, what shall become of us?" Nest raised her head and leaned back against the wall, warm from the sun. "The King and his brother may be in Normandy now, but I hear they will soon lash Wales with their fury yet again, their lackeys raising their great stone fortresses upon the hills and grabbing cantrefs from rightful lords. The land of the Cymry has fallen indeed, and even the rocks cry out with agony…"

"I cannot see the future, but I am sure a time will come that is better for us all."

"Do you?" asked Nest. "I have listened in on conversations, heard men squabble over me. I expect one of these base Frenchmen will be my fate, curse them…. It is grotesque and unfair. They even tried to change my name, calling me 'Agnes'. My name is Nest, not Agnes, and always will be!" She sprang up, grown fierce rather than sorrowful; I could almost imagine her with a spear in her hand, fighting off the Normans hordes.

She whirled back towards me, face falling, and gripped both my hands. "It shall be your fate too, Edith. I should not cry out like some ninny and bewail my fate when others around me must face the same. Yes, we should be friends. We may need each other for companionship...and for a shoulder to weep upon. Do you still wish to befriend me, Edith?"

I gave her hand a squeeze; her long, graceful fingers were cold. "Yes. We shall be friends."

It turned out that Nest became more of a friend than Ethelreda or shy Meggott. Duncan won his coveted crown, taking an army of mercenaries and borrowed Norman knights to Scotland, where he faced down Donald Bane and managed to drive him into the Highlands. He had himself crowned at Scone and sent for Ethelreda and his son, William. Flushed and joyous, she set forth in her chariot, her entourage carrying the banner of Scotland before them on the long journey north.

I waved farewell as the new Queen's entourage left the town, wondering if I would ever see her or Duncan again. "He should have made it decisive," I murmured to Nest, who stood watching the departure beside me. "He should have hunted Donald down...and killed him. Donald will not lie low forever. Once he has licked his wounds, he will seek the crown once more. Scottish lords are prideful...and fighting is seen as honourable"

"Welsh nobles are much the same," Nest whispered back, with a tight little smile. "Honour is everything; debts must be repaid—sometimes in blood."

In the failing months of 1194, news arrived from Scotland, bringing new grief to my family. Duncan was dead. As I had predicted, Donald Bane had crept out of hiding and raised another army from a sea of various malcontents. Our treacherous uncle had sent my brother Edmund to offer terms for a lasting peace. Instead, Edmund laid a trap, and Donald's soldiers fell upon Duncan in a place called Monthechin. A great battle was fought, with no quarter given to either side and no thought to honour in warfare. A lackey of Donald Bane called Malpeder struck the fatal blow that brought Duncan down, his hopes and aspirations sinking into a pool of mud and blood on a trampled field.

Duncan had not proven popular in Scotland; his years at Rufus's court had made him seem more Norman than Scot. He was hot-tempered and also had the arrogance of the Normans he had resided with for years. Nonetheless, as befitting his rank, and in accordance with ancient laws, he was buried as a King on the Isle of Iona having ruled only seven short and troubled months. Panicked and deep in mourning, Ethelreda immediately fled Scotland with her son and sought out her brother Waltheof in Allerdale in Cumbria. Soon she married again.

King William returned from Normandy, leaving his brother Henry to deal with the ongoing unrest within the province—renegades ravaged and burnt, thieves robbed humble priests and nuns; churches were abandoned and villages set ablaze. Castles were passed back and forth like pieces on a bloody chessboard; Robert de Belleme switched sides from Curthose to Rufus and the French King, Philip, became involved, storming de Belleme's castle of Alencon, and taking scores of knights as prisoners, before marching on Eu in the hopes of capturing William Rufus himself. Such a confrontation never took place for unexpectedly Phillip withdrew, fearing the three sons of the Conqueror might band together at the crucial moment to topple him. As Philip retreated and Robert Curthose backed off, licking his wounds, King William sailed for England, harkening to the reports of rebellion in both Wales and Scotland.

After his arrival, I espied the King once, stalking through the bailey of Winchester Castle as he inspected the building work and the state of the household servants and the guards. He looked older and more hardened, his mismatched eyes burning like fire out of his ruddy, unsmiling visage. I quickly retired to my quarters where I engaged in nervous embroidery, hoping he would not decide to inspect me and the other girls...

Fortunately, King William paid no attention to me, Mary, Nest or Meggott; we were just pretty adornments to brighten his court and bring a little civilisation to the Great Hall when various dignitaries visited. He had no interest in women, not even as marriage pawns to please his barons, at least not as things stood in regards to Robert Curthose and the uprisings of his opponents in Wales and the North. Such 'niceties', the distribution of wealth and women to the most loyal, would come in a time of peace, as an afterthought.

The King did not stay long in Winchester. The trouble in Wales drew him away, Nest's prediction sadly coming true, and when an uneasy peace settled again, and more stern fortresses thrown up, built by the Montgomeries and their ilk, Rufus was sailing back from the port at Hastings to tumultuous Normandy.

During that time, I often thought of Henry fighting his brother Robert, my godfather, in Normandy. Word often reached Winchester of his deeds—how he had swiftly erected a huge stone keep and a priory, bringing in the best stone masons and urging them to build quickly but with skill. For an unknown reason, I felt a certain flush of pride upon hearing of the prince's works. Although he was a prince by blood, of the three Conqueror's sons he alone had no titles or lands, but rather than brooding upon the deficiencies in his father's will, he worked out strategies to ally himself with important men in all walks of life. Still only in his twenties, he planned warfare and the building of castles and religious houses with abilities usually seen in men much older.

Henry returned to England shortly before Christmas. The court had removed to London for the Yuletide feast, an exciting time for me, Mary and my brothers. We had heard how London grew in size and strength and was soon expected to overtake Winchester in importance. Men said the streets were paved in gold and a poor man could become as rich as a king. Shops sold imported goods from fabled lands and men in strange costumes from far abroad loitered on the wharves. Bishop Gundulf had built a huge Tower there in the Conqueror's Day, its impregnable walls gleaming white—this castle was held by the king now, a palace and a prison, a symbol of strength and, to some, oppression. Rufus himself was planning to set his own mark on London by building a feasting hall alongside Westminster Abbey, where he and his sire had been crowned. It would be the largest such structure known to man, according to the King.

When the court had settled into the newly-built palace of Westminster, there was some dismay when tidings were received that the King had not arrived from France as expected—no one knew why, whether he was laid low by illness, engaged in battle or held up by inclement weather. This put everyone into an uneasy mood for we had no idea whether the expected Christmas revels would take place.

Then, to the court's surprise, Prince Henry turned up, having ridden pell-mell from the port of Dover. I'd heard the ruckus of newcomers at the palace's main gate but had not thought it of importance till Henry burst unannounced into the Hall, windswept and rain-dappled, treading mud across the dried rushes.

"My lord Henry!" I blurted in surprise, breaking away from Mary, Nest and Meggott, and dropping into a low curtsey. Around Henry's sturdy form, the gathered servants were bowing. Startled faces peered from side doors and from the gallery. "What do you here? When did you arrive? This is most unexpected. You should have sent a rider from the port; we could have made a finer welcome for you."

"I need no better welcome," he said with a grin. "Why waste time cooling my heels at a port? As for my business in England… I am home till the King sends me elsewhere."

"Is his Grace with you?" I peered over his shoulder, half-expecting to see the Red King stalk into the chamber, flame-faced and uttering his favourite oath, "By the Face of Lucca!"

"No, not yet, Lady Edith. William is on his way home, but whereas I set sail before the storms set in, he was caught amidst the tumult. With the weather so foul…" He slid out of his sodden cloak, heavy with rain, and tossed it to a young squire. "His homecoming is regrettably delayed, so he has decided to hold his Christmas court at Wissant in Normandy this year, instead of Westminster. So those of us in England must make do without him. We can make our own merriment, I am sure. Do you not think so?"

Eyes bright, he winked at me…and I lowered my head in maidenly modesty, blushing, not daring to answer such a question.

Henry turned from me, staring down the body of the hall, which was filling up with those who had heard of his return—clerics, prelates, knights and barons who had not accompanied William to

Normandy through infirmity or because they had been left to govern in his absence.

"Come, my fine fellows!" he roared, his voice echoing up to the rafters. "Your King cannot join you this Christmas, but that does not mean we must mope and be stingy in our celebrations of the birth of the Christ child! I declare that all jollity will go on, just as if the King were here among us."

"I hope he's paying for it, then," one grizzled old veteran called out. "'Cause I cannot."

"Ah, the treasury is full enough to pay for a month of feasts," said Henry. "Just ask William Mauditt. Or Herbert the Treasurer."

"We can't. They're still in Winchester," someone chortled.

"I shall send them the bill, then," laughed Henry. "We will not go without this festive season. I shall oversee the arrangements as if I were King myself."

Likening himself to William Rufus was an audacious thing to do, some would say almost treasonous. I saw the older lords with their gleaming bowls of silvered hair glancing at each other and frowning, but Henry paid them no heed.

He turned back towards me, grinning, and my heart beat a little faster.

Preparations began for the traditional Christmas feasting, which would begin on Christmas Day and run through the Twelfth Night. Mary, Nest and I even helped decorate the Hall with greenery—armloads of holly, ivy and mistletoe—setting all the servants chattering, for it was not a task expected of King's daughters.

Candlers had been contacted in the town and dozens ordered to keep the Hall bright, and salt simnel bread baked, and tuns of claret brought from the cellars deep beneath the palace. Hugh the larderer brought venison and pork from the slaughtermen, followed by chicken, geese, swans and braces of rabbits, much loved by the Normans who plucked them from the large warrens that the English called coneygarths. Fishes were purchased from the local fishmongers, an array of bream, trout, pikes and herring…and the ugly eels with a single nostril known as lampreys. A cook called

Anscar, apparently famed for both his good cooking and his terrible temper, took over the kitchens, smiting and shouting at the scullions and the turn-spit, an unfortunate boy with a face blistered by flying grease from turning the meat over.

The first feast on Christmas Day was small but merry. Henry sat at the top table in his brother's absence, though he was not presumptuous enough to sit in his chair. Mary and I sat near the prince in our best gowns, glowing like two jewels; Nest sat with us, dark and lovely in an emerald-green bliaut, her hair in waist-length braids held back with a circlet of Welsh gold. My brothers, bold and handsome, took their places on the opposite side of Henry's seat, ever more princely in look or manner as they blended into the royal court. Ned had recently spoken in earnest to all who would listen about avenging Duncan and becoming King of Scotland himself. King William had agreed to lend military support if Ned paid homage to him.

Fiddlers played and musicians made sweet melodies on rebec and lyre, and without Rufus's most influential barons, the overbearing brawlers and calculating side-changers, the atmosphere in the hall was less strained than it often was, even pleasant.

Ale and claret ran free, and soon my head grew giddy, even though my drinks were watered down as was customary for women. I laughed like a loon and spoke nonsense to Nest. Mary looked mortified but Nest was amused and started giggling herself. The next thing I knew, the minstrels had begun playing a different, livelier tune, and a swift and jubilant dance was taking place in front of the high table.

Before I realised what was happening, Henry was out of his seat and leaning over me, bowing with mock courtesy. "I would have the honour, noble princess," he smirked. "That is, if you know how to dance after all those years in the confines of a cloister."

"I know how!" I cried drunkenly, full of affront. "I was never a nun and I...I am more cultured than you think, Lord Henry!"

"Oh, are you now?" He swept me away onto the rush-matted floor between the long trestle tables. "I was worried that day I saw you at St Mary's with that black rag on your head, hiding away like a meek little nun."

"And why did you care?"

"From the moment I saw you...I thought you wouldn't make a good nun."

"Oh?" I felt doubly offended, although I had never had the inclination to be a nun, as I had told many. "Did...did you think I would be better off marrying your brother?"

"No, definitely not that!" he cried, surprised, as he stepped around me, taking my hand. The music rolled over us, the vielle and psaltery joined by a thudding, incessant drumbeat. My head began to throb too...the effects of my indulgence. "William would make a terrible husband. I would not wish such a fate on any woman, truth be told. Just imagine—my brother, Flambard and a blushing bride...all in the same bed."

"*What*?" I almost screeched at his astounding statement and blushed to the roots of my hair, which Nest had braided with strips of winter ivy, green against the near-snow of my tresses.

Henry reached out to touch a strand...*presumptuous*...yet I did not push his hand away. "I should not have spoken so," he admitted. "But my brother is not like...me..."

No, that he was not. I was still too young and naive to fully comprehend the rumours that ran rampant about William Rufus, but I certainly understood Henry's sins. He was the gossip of Winchester, a constant source of speculation by bored women at the court. Mistresses and concubines galore, from the great to the humble—a list of names 'as long as his arm' my tiring woman Helicent said. "His arm? As long as something else, I think!" her sister, Emma, had chuckled. I remembered some of these concubines over the past months had even met a few—Gieva, Sybille, Ansfride—and to my chagrin, two Ediths. I realised I should be very careful around him, for my honour was the greatest thing I possessed, but...somehow, I enjoyed his company, even if he was the Norman lecher my shrewish Aunt Cristina warned me about.

The dance ended. Red-faced, and not just from exertion, I pulled away from Henry and returned to my bench where I downed some more wine, pretending to be engrossed in the contents of my goblet.

"What's wrong, Edith?" Mary nudged me. "Did he ...say something inappropriate to you? Your face is the colour of fire!"

"No!" I barked, a little too stridently. Mary's clear eyes widened.

Across the Hall, the musicians had begun to play another lively air. Henry was still on the floor, scarcely out of breath from the last swift dance. Now he was joined by Nest, her green robes belling, her feet light on the rushes. I saw all men, young and old, crane their heads to watch her, so poised and pretty despite her youth. I hated that they gawked so, for she was not even old enough to be lawfully wed. I especially hated that Henry looked down, smiling, into her pert face as they danced.

A knot twisted in my belly, a muted rage mingled with despair. I recognised it as something not laudable in a lady of breeding—jealousy. And I did not understand why I was jealous. Henry was royal, but a younger son, trying to prove himself but still landless. He had low moral character where women were concerned. He was short and probably would grow stout like his sire. To add to all that, William Rufus would never agree to a match between us, even if someone should suggest it.

Never...

I clutched at the table's edge, propping myself up. "Are you ill, Edith?" asked Mary, concerned.

"Just a megrim," I muttered. "I am going to retire for the night."

"But-but you can't just leave like this! What would I tell Prince Henry?"

Angrily, I rounded on her. "Tell him? He's not a king, we do not have to curtsey to him and ask permission to leave the room. Tell him? Tell him the truth."

Mouth pursed, she folded her arms. We rarely fought but it was clear she was angry. "The truth? That you are in an evil mood and behaving like a shrew?"

I stared at my little sister, who suddenly seemed not quite so little and meek anymore. "Why you...I don't believe..." I stammered, and then, my cheeks growing rosy and hot, I rushed from the hall, afraid I would make a complete fool of myself if I stayed.

The King returned a few days later, blowing in on the gale like some raging old god of the north. "More troubles with the Welsh I hear!" he cried in a voice high-pitched with rage.

He glowered at poor Nest as if she was personally responsible for her countrymen's failings, and it gave me a reason to hurry her away from all the unwelcome activity and hide in our chamber with Mary, Meggott and our maids.

Men's business had begun in earnest, and soon all the court ladies were herded like cattle into chariots and sent back to Winchester. Nest fretted the whole journey, fearing the King would destroy the remnants of her family, while I sat sourly in my heavy cloak, wondering what part Henry would play in his brother's plans.

He had spoken to me only once briefly before I'd left Westminster. "I had hoped to spend longer in London, but the King wants me at his side and he's eager to get marching."

"The Welsh again, I hear. Nest is disconsolate."

"Yes, the Welsh, but other issues are making my brother as pleasant as a rabid dog. There are problems with Anselm."

"The Archbishop. Is he well?"

"He's his difficult old self," laughed Henry. "He's asked to go to Rome and get a pallium from the pope."

Frowning, I bit my lip. "Which pope?" England had officially been without a pope for around ten years, ever since Pope Gregory died and there were two contenders for the role in Rome, Urban and Guibert of Ravenna, known as the Anti-pope. Urban was recognised in France and Italy but it was by no means a sure thing English would do likewise.

"The Archbishop favours Urban as do most…but it irritates my brother to hear Anselm naming him before it is made official. He has done this without royal license, which makes it seem as if he is trying to sweep the crown off William's head and make archbishops higher than kings. Naturally, the very idea has made my brother extremely angry."

"He won't harm the Archbishop, will he?" As I knew myself from past experience, Anselm could be curmudgeonly, but in my heart, I knew he was a good man, more interested in the care of our souls than the likes of money and power-hungry Flambard.

"Oh no, he's not a complete fool," said Henry. "William has called a council to decide the matter."

"May it all end well."

"Aye," he nodded, "and once it's over, I can relax and go hunting in the New Forest. I promised to take you there with me one time—do you remember, Edith?"

I mumbled unintelligibly, not wanting to seem too keen lest he thought of me as one of his trollops...but not wanting to appear entirely disinterested either.

"Well, *I* have not forgotten, Lady Edith. I will be back soon enough...to claim the pleasure of your company."

CHAPTER TEN

Despite his words, I did not see Henry for a long time. He went to Wales with the King but there was little to be done there now—the native Welsh had taken back many of their original strongholds; one by one, Norman castles fell and the Welsh rejoiced and burnt effigies of their Norman overlords in the streets of towns and villages. Vowing to deal with the Welsh 'problem' later, William Rufus marched to the castle of Rockingham to thrash out the problems with Archbishop Anselm. While this council was in progress, the King bellowing at the Archbishop, Anselm warning him of God's wrath with waggling finger and steely eye, Henry sailed for Normandy which was, as ever, in danger of falling into violent rebellion.

By the summer, the King was at war with one of his barons, Robert de Mowbray of Alnwick, who, along with William of Eu, had plotted to depose Rufus and set his cousin, Stephen of Aumale, on the throne. De Mowbray's disloyalty came as no surprise to anyone; he was a man I hated beyond all reason, for it was at his hands that my father and brother had perished. I blamed him for Mother's death too; she had been ill, but grief had pushed her into the open grave. I therefore took an 'unladylike' interest in news of the conflict drifting out of the north as the remnants of the court moved between palaces and castles in London, Windsor, and Winchester. I could not bear to sit doing nought but embroidery while momentous things were afoot, so I prowled the halls like a stray cat, listening at doors, paying close attention to men's conversations in the hall, even eavesdropping on the gossip of other women whose husbands were away with the king.

I learnt from Meggott that her father, my Uncle Edgar, had written to her to advise of his return from pilgrimage. Hearing of the King's northern campaign against de Mowbray, he had marched with a band of knights to join him at once.

"What else does he say?" I needled her as we sat beside the brazier in our chamber, combing out our braids. Mary was slumped on the bed in her under-kirtle, listening in.

"Nought much, really, Edith," said Meggot. "Just that he would join us at court when the troubles are over. I hope he brings me a lovely gift…"

"He's at war," Mary scoffed. "I doubt he will have time to think of such niceties. What would you have him bring you—a severed head?"

I made a face at my sister. Being at Rufus's court, Mary had certainly lost her timidity.

Meggott reddened, stuttering. "O-of course not! Why do you mock me? It is natural for a maid to have no interest in the affairs of men!"

Our cousin was not particularly bright, I had found. I shook my head at Mary; it wasn't worth upset and argument.

"You will tell me if you hear anything more, won't you, Meggott?" I asked sweetly.

"If you wish." She blinked. "But why would you want to know about killing and cutting off heads…and…"

"I need to know what is happening, ugly or not. Remember, de Mowbray killed my father and brother…your cousin Edward. And Mother died too, her grief at their deaths killing her as surely as a dagger. They were your family too, Meggott; you were even named for my mother…Margaret."

Meggott blinked slowly, stupidly at me with her big grey-blue eyes. It was as if she had never even contemplated that fact before. Uncle Edgar clearly cared for her and provided for her and his mistress, but unfortunately, he seemed to have been remiss with her education. Or perhaps she had fallen on her head as a babe…I could think of no other reason for her slowness.

Seeing my expression, she grew even redder and began to stammer. "I-I've displeased you, h-haven't I? I'm not a princess like you…I don't know many things." Tears began to well in her eyes, and now I was sorry I'd spoken.

I sighed and patted her on the arm. "Do not worry about it, Meggott. Do not be upset. I'll find out what I need to know…elsewhere."

A few nights later, long after the curfew bell had rung in the town beyond, I heard a rustle in the corridor outside the bedchamber and, always a light sleeper, I woke at once. A castle was never a quiet place but the footsteps had stopped outside the door, as if whoever was outside had contemplated entering but held themselves in check. They were not gone, though; I'd heard no departing footsteps. Now there was only a chilling stillness. Immediately I was wary. I did not appreciate being spied on and was loathe to think of even more nefarious possibilities.

But I was the daughter of great Malcolm Canmore, killer of MacBeath, and although I tried to emulate Mother in her attitudes toward the poor and sick, I was still the daughter of a warrior-king with his blood burning hot in my veins.

Sliding from beneath the covers, careful not to wake anyone else, I flung a cloak about myself, grabbed the metal poker from the brazier, and crept towards the door.

I could see a sliver of light shining below the door, cast by the torches bracketed in the corridor, and two long shadows side by side…shadows cast by someone's shoes. My breath hissed through my teeth and pushing aside the latch, I lunged into the hall with poker ready.

"Edith! Stop!" Waving the poker, I almost fell atop my brother Ned.

"Ned!" Furious, I shut the door behind me. "Is this some kind of foolish jest? A dare between you, Alexander and David? It is most improper to be lurking around women's bedchambers, especially as one day you may be raised…"

"It is that of which I wanted to speak!" he said excitedly. I noticed he was flushed, his hair mussed. "I did not want to have all the other girls listen in."

"What about Mary?"

"She's young yet and more likely to find herself unable to hold secrets. Let her sleep, Edith. Come with me."

Together we slinked down the corridor to the chamber he shared with my other two brothers, trying to avoid the servants or anyone else still wakeful in the castle. While we were kin and there was no law against brother and sister taking counsel together, we did not want to arouse curiosity or inflame gossiping tongues. In Rufus's court, where true wickedness often abounded, our family was seen as amusingly virtuous anyway—so if we were spotted by the wrong people, much rumour-mongering would doubtless ensue.

Inside Ned's room, the fire was burning and Alexander and David fully awake, looking excited and pleased. Alex pushed out a stool for me to sit upon, while David passed around a platter of sweetmeats.

"So, what is this all about, Ned?" I asked, stretching my legs out before the brazier.

"Uncle Edgar has written to me from Northumbria." He reached into the breast of his tunic and drew out a parchment, waving it in my direction. "It arrived this morning."

I shrugged, popping one of the sweetmeats into my mouth. "He has written to Meggott too."

"But I would wager he hasn't told her what he's told me." Ned's visage was triumphant. "He is showing loyalty to William in return for the King's help once de Mowbray is vanquished. When all is done, and the rebellion firmly crushed, Uncle Edgar plans to invade Scotland with Rufus's backing. Donald Bane shall be deposed once and for all…and I shall be King of Scotland!"

He grasped my hands, pulling me up and twirling me around the chamber. "We shall be exiles no more! Our positions in the world will be fully restored!"

I tried to share his excitement but no flame would kindle in my heart. Scotland's already bloodied soil would end up drenched with gore yet again. And what if Edgar was called to fight against Edmund, who was still supporting Donald Bane? Brother against brother, fratricide to go hand-in-hand with all the other bloodshed.

"What of Edmund?" I pulled my hands from his and drew away. "He will oppose you!"

"Will he? Maybe he will turn his coat again when he sees my army approach."

"Perhaps, but I think the die is cast for our brother. He has moored himself to Donald Bane's cause and pride will keep him from ever admitting he was wrong. Remember how hot-headed and stubborn he could be?"

Ned's eyes grew steely. "If he does not submit, I will do what I must to subdue him. Even if…"

"No!" I said sharply, making both Alex and David jump. "Edgar, you must promise to spare his life. Our Mother, God have mercy upon her soul, would be heartbroken to think one of her sons would slay the other."

"If he is captured, he can never be set free," said Ned between gritted teeth, shaking his head. "You cannot be tender-hearted as a woman if you are a king."

"But you cannot act as a rabid beast either, without mercy or justice…" I fell silent, thinking of Rufus, who seldom showed either of those qualities save to his closest companions.

"Imprisonment for life then." Ned folded his arms. "Maybe take an eye…"

"No! No mutilation either. Promise me!"

"What would you have me do?" His voice was sharp.

"Force him into holy orders. Tell him he lives only if he is to become a monk in some remote priory in England, far from Scotland's borders."

Ned rubbed his chin, looking thoughtful. "Yes…yes…that might work, but I can promise nothing, Edith; not until I have taken control of the bastard. Now, do you want to hear the rest of Uncle Edgar's letter or not? The northern campaign sounds so exciting; I wish I was there with Edgar. I'd challenge de Mowbray to a duel and smite his head…"

"No, you wouldn't," I interrupted "He is the King's quarry now. Like the deer in the royal forest, de Mowbray is his alone to hunt down."

Ned sighed. "I suppose that is true. I must try to hold back my battle-ardour and follow Uncle Edgar's advice. Oh, you should hear what has been going on, though—glorious! De Mowbray's castle at Monkchester taken, his man de Merlay's small fort at Morpeth overrun, both garrisons imprisoned."

"And de Mowbray himself?" I sat back down on the stool, with David paying squire and bringing me a cup of watered-down wine. My mouth felt suddenly dry…things were once again changing for the children of Canmore. If God smiled on us this time, my brother might soon be the rightful king and Alexander his heir apparent. As for me and Mary, our marriage prospects would be greatly heightened. No longer would we be orphans suffered at a foreign court.

"De Mowbray has fled to the coast. To Bamburgh, with his wife and children. Rufus has built a wooden castle near Bamburgh's walls and threatens him with a siege tower he calls Malvoisin…"

"The Evil Neighbour," I laughed. "I pray it is every bit as evil to him as he was to our family."

I could not ill-wish de Mowbray's wife, though, caught in troubles not of her making, as women often were. Perhaps she would be glad if he fell in battle. I had heard that not only was he murderous and disloyal, but hairy as a woodwose, swarthy-browed, grim and unsmiling, his thought only of gain or warfare. An ogre.

"De Mowbray stands no chance," said Ned with confidence. "He will fall…so will Donald Bane, and I will be King of Scotland at last! To me!"

He lifted his own goblet and toasted himself. Alex and David did likewise and eventually, caught up by their emotion, I raised my own chalice.

"To Edgar, King of Scots!" I murmured.

Uncle Edgar wrote to Ned again a short time later. De Mowbray had escaped Bamburgh under the cover of darkness and ridden like a madman for Tynemouth, pursued by the King's men. Once he reached his destination, he found could fly no further and was captured after taking an arrow wound to the thigh. Bound in chains, Rufus's men hauled him back to Bamburgh where his wife Matilda still oversaw the ongoing siege.

Ned put down the letter, his eyes glittering. "What do you suppose happened then, Edith?"

"I can think of many possibilities, none of them pleasant."

"The King threatened to put out de Mowbray's eyes unless Lady de Mowbray opened the gates."

It was a fitting punishment but a brutal one. I tried to imagine the world in darkness—the fear, the isolation, the loss of autonomy. A living death. He deserved it if anyone did, and yet…

"What did Lady Matilda do?"

"Opened the gates," said Ned triumphantly. "A full surrender was given."

"And now what? Is de Mowbray dead?"

Ned shook his head. "The King gave him his life…as long as he agreed to become a monk at St Alban's Abbey. An annulment is already being sought for his marriage, in order to let Lady de Mowbray wed again."

My brother began to stride around the chamber, "These are trivial events, though…"

My eyebrows lifted. "Are they? It does not sound so to me."

He placed his hands on my shoulders. "Edith, in two days I leave for Norham. Alexander and David are coming with me. I will meet with Uncle Edgar there. I will grant Berwick and other estates to the bishop of Durham and the good monks of Saint Cuthbert. Our old friend Turgot, who did so much for our family when in need, is coming with the monks to witness the charter. Alex and David are also to be witnesses—so, their first step towards being princes."

"This has come very suddenly." It felt as if the floor tilted slightly beneath my heels, my world rocked once more. I grasped his arm. "I wish I could come with you, Ned. Our family should stay together. And…without you at court, it is less safe for Mary and I to remain here."

"Oh, come, you are a brave girl. You stood up to our Aunt Cristina, the old harridan!" He put his hands on his hips and laughed. "Most of Rufus's terrorisers are away with him, you are here only with the old and less-than-bold servants, churchmen and men half in their dotage who can do nought but mumble toothlessly about their prowess in the Conqueror's time. Besides, who would dare to lay a finger on you, the sister of Scotland's next ruler!"

He would not be persuaded to take me with him, that much I could see. I kissed his cheek, now covered in a fair beard. "Go then, and may Our Lord smile upon you," I murmured. "Maybe the next time we meet, our father's crown will lie safely upon your head."

It took two years for Ned's desire to come to fruition. In the meantime, the Pope had called a Crusade against the Saracen in the Holy Land. Robert Curthose decided to take the cross, and Abbott Jarento of Dijon came to England to discuss peace between Curthose and Rufus in the Duke's absence. The whole idea of this Crusade brought unrest throughout England, even amongst the clergy—the Abbot of Cerne encouraged his monks to set out for Jerusalem and other abbots followed suit, causing immense distress to Archbishop Anselm, who ordered Osmund, Bishop of Salisbury, to prevent any more such actions in the west of England. Other bishops across the country took their cue from Anselm, forbidding monks from leaving their monasteries with threats of heavy sanctions.

It was not a happy time. The King invaded Wales again, at Easter and Whitsun, polluting those holy days with bloodshed, as he swore to root out and kill every Welsh male of battle age. Nest was near hysterical; it was all Mary and I could do to keep her calm. It seemed the King was near-hysterical too; his campaign was not going well, and he wrote furious letters to Archbishop Anselm, tearing into him for sending 'badly trained and poorly armed' soldiers and threatening him with charges next time he held court. Not all was dire gloom, however—apparently, a monk either brave or foolhardy, followed William all the way from Normandy, needling the King over a chasuble Rufus had promised to his monastery. Surprisingly, the King gave in and admitted his error, and the monk walked off with a length of rich purple cloth. Even poor Nest managed to laugh at that tale. I was gladder when I heard the good brother had immediately set sail for Normandy, his cloth safely with him—Rufus's temper could be mercurial and he was well-known for changing his mind; at Salisbury he had William of Eu, a conspirator with Robert de Mowbray, blinded and mutilated, then sent to his manor at Hastings to die. Eu had thought he'd receive leniency like Robert de Mowbray...how wrong he was.

In Scotland, however, things looked up for my family at last. With Rufus's permission, Uncle Edgar took control of an army recruited from amongst the King's men and marched to meet the gathered forces of Donald Bane.

Donald's luck had truly run out this time; at Rescobie a battle was fought and his army overwhelmed. Captured, he was brought into the presence of my uncle and Ned.

I had the miscreant blinded, Ned had scrawled in a missive sent by courier from Scotland. *I fear this may offend your tender heart, sister, but it was necessary. It was that or execution. He will now spend the rest of his days in a cold dungeon, contemplating the fruits of his treachery towards his kin. Soon I am to be crowned at Scone; the people cheer for me, Edith, calling me 'the Valiant'. Would that you were here, but the land must still be secured and made safe first.*

God Protect You, Edith,

Your brother, Edgar, King of Scots, Rex Scottorum

"Do you think Ned will summon us to Scotland?" Mary asked after she had pored over our brother's jubilant letter. "Will we go home?"

I made no answer but stared intently into the flames on the hearth. Uncle Edgar had also written, his words straight and plain, less joyful than those of my brother. Ned was only king by the grace of William Rufus; he was William's vassal, a client king. William had said nothing of releasing us, his wards, back to our family. Ned might risk asking such questions when he was well-settled in his new regal position and had proved himself loyal. In truth, I was no longer certain I wished to return to Scotland. Half my life had been spent in England and I had grown accustomed to it.

Receiving no response, Mary tucked the letter away and sat in a small heap, arms around her knees, looking pensive. "Do you…do you know what has become of our brother Edmund?"

"He is safe," I informed her. It was not a lie. In Uncle Edgar's letter, which I had kept from Mary, he told how he had subdued faithless Edmund, making him watch as Donald Bain was blinded, screaming in agony as a heated dagger jabbed his eyes, not quite enough to kill but near enough to bring on fear of death, bringing him eternal darkness, the life of a cripple, a half-man. A king fallen to the estate of a lowly beggar. To see his uncle so mutilated had sent Edmund to his knees before Edgar and Ned, weeping and begging.

As he had promised, Ned spared our brother sending him under guard to a small, English monastic house in Montacute, where he agreed to become a tonsured monk and spend the rest of his days contemplating the deeds that brought him low.

"If he's alive, where is he now?" Mary asked.

"I do not know." This was a lie and my heart knotted with guilt, but wanted to keep Edmund's whereabouts secret. Montacute was not so far from us when we were at Winchester or Salisbury, but I did not want Mary to attempt to visit or communicate with him. He had been given a new chance at life serving God, so I deemed him as one dead, our brother no longer but a brother in Christ.

Mary rose from the floor, brushing ash from the hearth off her skirts. "I know he did evil, but I wish we could see him, and ask why he hated us so."

I put my arms around her, drew her close. "Perhaps it is better not to know. Sometimes temptation proves too much…especially when there is a crown involved. Whatever the case, our lives change from here on…and Edmund is no longer part of those lives."

With William sailing forth to Normandy after Robert Curthose's departure on Crusade, life at Winchester was quiet and subdued. Wherever the Red King fared was filled with violent discord; a peace of sorts came only in his absence. Some months before he left, he had feuded once again with Archbishop Anselm, this time over Anselm's desire for church reforms. He proposed strong measures against priests who were wed or had concubines, abbots who committed simony, nobles who married closely related women without dispensation, and any man who committed sodomy. When the King refused to listen to his request, doubtless taking affront over several of the points raised, Anselm then asked permission to journey to Rome and speak to Pope Urban.

Rufus had mocked him, saying, "Why would you need to go to His Holiness, Anselm. Have you committed some terrible sin that you need to get absolution from the Holy Father? Or are your counsellors so foolish and mutton-headed, you must go ask His Holiness for advice? I would scarcely believe you'd need to, though, for you are always so full of 'advice', Archbishop, I deem you'd be counselling the Pope!"

Anselm was enraged by this mockery; the King met his anger in a violent outburst of his own, implying that the Archbishop had broken his fealty to his monarch…and Anselm, surrounded by a party of monks, had departed into exile.

Having little else to do, I threw myself into quiet arts such as embroidery; the English style was gaining great popularity not just in England but in Europe too. As I was no longer a very young maid, and now the sister to a King, I had slightly more leverage in what I did, especially with Rufus absent. I travelled frequently to visit the nuns in Wilton, with a little band of court ladies, including Mary, Nest, Meggott and my maid Helisent, who was the most skilled embroiderer of us all. I offered to Saint Edith and prayed for peace and good fortune to my favourite saint, St John the Evangelist. When I had time, I even assisted for a few hours at the little hospital. Sadly, Leofgifu was no longer there. Sister Infirmarer told me she had died the previous winter after catching an ague. I picked some flowers growing near the wall and laid them on the spot where the unclaimed dead were buried; white daisies and yellow buttercups, white for her purity and gold for the music of her innocent laughter.

On one visit, it happened that Bishop Osmund of Salisbury was there to speak with the Abbess Hawise. He was an ancient man, frail with age, his close-cropped hair white as snow and his back bent beneath his rich robes. However, his eyes were still keen and bright in the lined parchment of his face and he gazed on me with interest as I entered Hawise's study.

I was a little flustered, fearing I had made an unwelcome intrusion. "Forgive me, Reverend Mother, Your Grace…Sister Helena did not tell me you were conducting business. She must have erred in her times. I shall leave at once…"

"There is no need, Edith." Hawise gestured me over towards her desk. "Bishop Osmund heard you were at St Mary's and was interested in meeting you."

The Bishop drew closer, shuffling, holding a candle in a brass folder near my face so that he could see me clearly with his weak, rheumy eyes. "I have seen you from afar, Lady Edith, but we have never spoken. I send, through you, felicitations to the new King of Scotland, your brother Edgar."

"Thank you, your Grace," I said. "It has taken seven years but God has seen fit to place the rightfully anointed on Scotland's throne once more."

"Have you made any decisions as to *your* future, Lady Edith?"

I blushed. "My future is not for me to decide, your Grace, as surely one of such great learning must now. It is in the hands of King William, whose court I abide in." I shifted nervously. "He was...kind...to give my family succour after my parents died and to assist Edgar's assumption of the Scottish throne."

"Would you rather have remained at St Mary's Abbey, Edith? I heard your first stay was a pleasant one, where you had laudable commitment to the sick, skill in the art of embroidering altar cloths, and proficiency in the reading of texts both secular and holy."

"I thought of my blessed days many times," I admitted, "and that is why I still visit when I may. But it is essential for me to take my place amongst royalty and nobility, so it is best to learn such courtly ways as I can to aid me in my future life."

The Abbess gave a little cough. "Of course, the King was also...unable to pay for more than the scantiest sum towards your board should you have stayed here as a lay boarder."

"I know it has been asked of you before, Lady Edith," said Bishop Osmund, "but would you take the veil if you felt the choice was solely yours? Or...did you at any time wear it, as I heard you once did, with intent to become a vowess?"

My cheeks burnt. I had no idea why Osmund was questioning me in this manner. Beseechingly, I glanced at the Abbess. "No...no, never. The Reverend Mother will vouch for me. I wore a nun's wimple only to keep unwelcome advances away from my person. I was very young, very innocent..."

"I have told Bishop Osmund this." Hawise gave me a little smile. "But he wanted to hear it from your own lips."

"I swear it is true," I said. "If it is important to you, your Grace, I shall swear an oath upon the Bible."

"No, no, there is no need." Osmund shook his head and blew out his candle. "You are a princess and your mother was of saintly bent—I would not expect a daughter born of such a godly mother to lie about such an important matter."

I wanted to ask him why my former disguise was of sudden interest. By now, I thought everyone had forgotten my childhood foibles. Yet I did not dare question, and could only assume the old Bishop was pressing for me to join the order, perhaps on behalf of Archbishop Anselm, who had reacted so furiously when Mary and I left Wilton for Scotland, insisting we had taken vows and were runaways.

Bishop Osmond gave a contented sigh and glanced first at Hawise and then at me. "I have heard much of your love of learning, Lady Edith. Some may think too much schooling is not fitting for royal maidens but I disagree. Beauty and charm alone is not enough, especially when one is called to the dignity of Queenship and is effectively the mother of her people."

"I have not had that… calling," I said, "but a keen mind and knowledge of one's letters can only be beneficial for any woman of rank. Such learning is more valuable than comeliness, I deem, which is fleeting as the autumn leaves."

I glanced down at the plain gown I wore, brown with yellow trim, no jewels to show my rank, save a solitary silver cross with several emeralds winking like a cat's eyes. Was I plain? I never had much faith in my looks, too round in face, too short-legged. My long pale hair I considered my best asset and that was coiled up demurely and hidden beneath a veil.

"Yes, yes, learning is an excellent pursuit. The Lord Henry is also a keen learner. I taught him myself."

"Lord Henry?"

"The King's brother. He once told me that he thought an unlearned king is no better than a crowned ass." Osmund chuckled. "I did tell him to be less free with his tongue…or his brother might get wind of his words and order it torn out."

I winced at the thought but my mind was awhirl. I had never thought of Henry as a studious kind of man. Some named him Beauclerc, a fine scholar, but in my ignorance, I had thought he was called such only in jest!

The rest of my meeting with Bishop Osmund and Abbess Hawise was spent discussing other less intriguing matters—a recent flood of the River Wylye in Wilton, the problems with the cathedral at Salisbury, which Osmund mournfully informed me was daily buffeted by winds so fierce they knocked carved gargoyles off the roofline.

Yet when I left with my entourage to return to Winchester, I found my thoughts returning to what Osmund had told me about Henry.

An unlearned king is like a crowned ass…

I was inclined to agree. We needed scholars as much as we needed swords.

CHAPTER ELEVEN

It was summer in the year of Our Lord 1100. England wilted in unusual heat; the fields dry, the crops golden in the sun, the peasants labouring with burnt faces streaked with sweat. The skies were dark azure, clear until nightfall, when clouds as threatening as siege towers suddenly spiralled up toward heaven and loosed vicious storms that clashed and clattered throughout the night before vanishing again.

King Rufus was back in England and determined to make merry. Every night, feasts were held in Winchester's Great Hall, accompanied by wild entertainments, not all of them savoury—bear-baiting, cock-fighting, tumblers who flung knives, dwarf jugglers who bared their buttocks and farted loudly, and *danses per haut*, frantic dances in which anything was permitted, including the removal of garments... Food of all sorts dressed the high table: pottage flavoured with almonds, salted and smoked beef topped by diced onions, laurices from the coneygarth brewed in oils and spices, rose pudding made from milk and the real petals of red and white roses. Drink was ever-popular and over-consumed, especially the imported wine from Normandy—English wines were more sour and less pleasant as the climate was not fitting to produce them

Mummers performed plays, fantastical in masks of devils and woodwoses, and women who bent and twisted their bodies into almost impossible shapes went wheeling and tumbling in sheer gowns that would have made a harlot blush. Rufus's men roared in delight and pounded the table with their mazers. They were a crowd hand-picked for proven loyalty, wealth, hunting skills or just the fact the King found them amusing. Dressed in red, his sleeves dagged and his shoes pointed, behaviour decidedly unholy despite his office, Ranulf Flambard was foremost amongst them, but other favourites included the de Clare brothers, Roger and Gilbert, handsome but acquisitive; Walter Tirel, a Frenchman known for his marksmanship; William Breteuil, a Norman lord with a fiercely bristling moustache; Robert Bigod from the east of England, garrulous and shrewd; the Montgomeries, descendants of the infamous Mabel de Belleme; the ever loyal Robert FitzHamon, husband of Sybil who was schooled with me at Romsey; William Giffard, a prominent landowner with a keen mind; Earl Simon of Northampton, puffed with pride till he looked like a toad; sweaty, porcine Bishop Gerard of Hereford, and Henry, Earl of Warwick, proud and hot-tempered.

When more ale and mead began flowing, the more formal dancing began, with Nest firmly at the centre of it. Fifteen now, her body and her beauty had bloomed, and she was well aware of it, using it to gain favours. She twirled with one de Clare and then another, her dark locks tumbling under a silver circlet, the cut of her dress lower than was considered decent for a highborn maiden—but she was in Rufus's court where almost anything was permitted.

The King himself would sit slouched on his throne, drunk, often belching from too-rich swan, one hosed leg dangling over the arm of the chair. Despite the frequent admonishment of the clergy about his attire and appearance, he still wore peacock bright raiment, spangled and bejewelled, and rings on every finger, their stones nigh as big as pigeon's eggs. He was perfumed with exotic oils from the east, redolent of fruit, but fruit almost no one had ever tasted in England. He still wore his hair long, flowing in shiny red-gold waves down his broad back, and his crimson beard was plaited into a point. Sometimes I caught him looking at me, and sometimes at Nest. I wondered if Flambard had pushed the idea of marriage and begetting an heir on him. I prayed Rufus would not listen.

Henry returned to court from Normandy partway through the summer, sunburnt and rough, with none of his brother's ostentation, although his near-black hair was long and his beard untidy. He often spoke to me, his speech plain with no condescension as some men showed towards women...but I noticed his eyes lingered on Nest, which made me strangely furious, even though I was aware of his reputation and the large number of bastards he had sired.

One hot, humid evening, though, he came to me, not Nest, while I was in the herb-garden seeking refuge from the sticky heat by dabbling my toes in the pond. I pulled my feet back as Henry appeared, covering them with my skirt.

"I was looking for you," he said, standing hands on hips against the crimson light of the dying day."

"Were you?" I asked. "Whatever for?"

"The King plans to do some hunting in the New Forest. I promised I would show you the woodlands, did I not? I have offered to see all is made ready at the lodge for his presence, and I would take you with me, to show you the woods. If you wish it, we could hunt with hawks."

"Did you truly mean it? It would be highly irregular for us to go off together."

"I have asked my brother's permission. We shall have an escort and you will have other women with you, Edith…Christ's Teeth, I am not going to throw you down and ravish you amidst the ferns! As Rufus said, you are far too valuable for just a tumble."

My cheeks blazed, imagining the two men having such a conversation about me. "I do not know whether to take that as an insult or not."

"Just a jest," he said dryly, "and not a very good one…although I do not think you found my words as offensive as you pretend. After all…" He suddenly moved his boot and flipped up the hem of my skirt, revealing my bare feet and ankles. "It is also highly irregular for a princess to go unshod in a garden, especially with no chaperone on hand. But I must say, I do not mind—such pretty toes and graceful ankles!"

I began to stammer a stern rebuke, but he held up his hand. "Tell me now if you will come, Edith…or I shall ask Nest instead. I cannot waste time with indecision."

I folded my arms, but my reply was quick, perhaps too quick. "Of course, I will go with you."

Henry and I, along with the de Clares, including Gilbert's wife Adelize, Walter Tirel, who was not only a famed archer but wed to Gilbert and Adelize's daughter, and a broad-shouldered falconer called Geoffrey, made our way down to the hunting lodge near Brockenhurst. I had two serving maids, for propriety; there were grooms, cooks, servers, and several armed foot soldiers to protect us from any outlaws or other ruffians, although the Verderers and

Foresters had managed to keep the New Forest safer than thieves' dens such as Sherwood and Barnsdale.

The hunting lodge at Brockenhurst was timber-framed and plastered white, with shiny grey slates from Cornwall upon its sloped roof. It had a chapel with a royal bench, a large bedchamber for the King and smaller chambers for his hunting companions. Next to the lodge stood a long wooden hall containing a kitchen, larder and granary. The stables, mews and kennels were behind the hall, out of sight but near enough to be reached in a hurry. The whole structure was surrounded by a wooden fence with the tops of each post whittled into points; a single great gate with a guardroom was the solitary point of admission.

I shared a room with Adelize, while the maids, Helisent and Emma, were given pallets outside the door to sleep upon. Adeliza, much older than me and a mother many times over, had little to say, having not long birthed a son with great anguish. She wanted nothing more than to rest...and talk of returning to Suffolk to see her child, who was weak and ailing.

With such a dull and unhappy companion, it was no wonder I grew restless and wandered away to explore. I could have taken the maids but oftimes I preferred my own company away from any chatter. Quietly, I crept through the lodge, a basic functional place although being filled with niceties to please the King on his visit. As I passed the little chapel, I heard the murmur of voices from within. I halted and then pressed on; the door was closed, and when I touched it with a fingertip, it appeared to have been barred from within.

Very curious.

Glancing around to check that I was unobserved, I thrust back my thick braids and pressed my ear to the wooden panels of the door.

Inside the chapel, I heard muffled speech...but no recognisable prayers. One of the voices was Henry's; he was speaking quickly, in a low, urgent tone. Another voice answered him; I recognised the younger de Clare...and then the French lord, Walter Tirel. All sounded serious but I could not make out any individual words. A shiver coursed down my spine and the day's warmth seemed to seep away.

It was as if they discussed something too serious, too dangerous to speak of in the open, hence they endeavoured to make it seem as if they were at prayer.

With no priest and no prayers spoken…

It is not your business, Edith! I told myself sternly. *Whatever intrigue Henry is involved with has nought to do with you!*

Straightening, I began to walk briskly down the hall while keeping my footsteps as light as possible.

And not a moment too soon. I had barely reached the corner of the hall when the chapel door was flung open wide and Henry strode out, his boots making a clatter on the floor. "So, all has been decided…you have placed your trust in me and I have placed mine with you. Do not fail me in this matter…if all goes well, your rewards will be higher than the stars. But if it goes ill for us…" he shrugged, almost nonchalantly, but his bearded face looked grim and aged, bone-weary but determined, "then God help us all."

I did not want to hear any more of this secretive talk; did not want to imagine what it might betoken… Scuttling down the corridor, I headed out of the lodge and towards the mews. Cages of the hawks and falcons rose around me—inside were Lanners, Peregrines, Goshawks, Sparrowhawks, Merlins, and even a regal white Gyrfalcon, used only by royalty. Perched on their cadgers, the silver tablets denoting their ownership glistening on their spindly legs, they scrutinised me with fierce red, orange and yellow eyes, as if debating whether I should be their prey.

I began to feel like prey and to regret my presence here at the Brockenhurst lodge. But surely…surely Henry would not try to involve me in some unknown plot? His invitation was kindly, making good on a promise made long ago…was it not?

My heart thudded in my ears as I heard the scuffle of boots on the ground. I pretended to admire the gyrfalcon, whose beady eye on its cocked head now seemed mocking rather than predatory. *You are trapped, Edith…* I did not turn, but I felt a presence behind me, a familiar presence…It was him. Henry.

He said nothing but his shadow enveloped me, stretching over me with a sense of menace. Beads of sweat burst on my neck, under the thick coils of my bound hair. Reluctantly, my heart hammering, I twisted around to face the prince.

"Edith?" He took a step in my direction. "I saw you...leaving the lodge."

I shifted uncomfortably from one foot to the other. I was not an accomplished liar. "Yes, I wanted to look at the Merlins. Ladies' hawks. I want to choose the one I will fly."

"Oh, I think there's more to it than that." He folded his arms over his burly chest, expectant. "You tried the door on the chapel."

"A chapel should be a safe place open to all," I said defiantly. "Yes, I tried the door; I wanted to pray. I left...because it was clear I was not welcome in God's House while you and your friends were in it. Is that a crime?"

"What did you hear?" His hand descended on my shoulder like a thunderclap. He was close, so close...*too* close. His eyes bored into mine, such a dark brown they seemed almost black.

"I have no idea what I heard, but if my presence was so upsetting that you must hunt me down like this, it was clearly nothing good. Unhand me, sir, or prince or no, I will strike you!"

He looked stunned at my last words and, for a moment, outraged, but then he grinned and his hand dropped to his side. "You are a feistier maid than I thought after seeing you, so demur, so calm beside such firebrands as Nest. You would make an excellent queen for some ruler, Edith. Someday..."

His mention of Nest rankled me for reasons I did not fully understand. "It has been seven years since my parents died," I said shrewishly. "I doubt at this point that I will marry at all. The King seems to have no interest in finding me a husband. Maybe I should go seek Aunt Cristina and tell her I repent—and take the veil. It would make her happy."

"No, no, you do *not* want to do that!" I was surprised to find a hint of worry in his gaze. "Edith, perhaps I over-reacted about the chapel door, but I was on men's business in the quietest part of the lodge."

"Men's business," I said dubiously, a trace of mockery evident in my voice.

He nodded. "I would not expect you to understand—not because I believe you are stupid but because you are not privy to the unrest in the realm. My brother becomes more dissolute as the years pass. Poor old Anselm is still lingering in exile. Clergy far and wide deem the king an ungodly man, carnal and lewd—and only a liar would say he is otherwise! Those he appoints to church roles are clearly unsuitable--men even say that Gerald, Bishop of Hereford, worships Satan instead of God. Apparently, he had a pig delivered to his house in York and proceeded to worship it in the privy. And Gerard's brother, himself a chaplain, claimed he was impregnated by a man!"

"Oh fie!" I put my hands on my hips, aware I looked and sounded like a sharp-tongued fishwife. "Nonsensical tales, invented by some oaf in a tavern." I sneered. "If not…what happened to the man claiming to be with child?"

"He died, Edith. The local priest refused to give him a Christian burial, he went into an unmarked hole outside the churchyard wall."

I rolled my eyes. "'Twas as I said—a nonsense. The poor soul's brains were clearly addled. In my work with the sick of Wilton, I encountered such swellings in the belly or other parts. A cruel and fatal illness afflicted that man, not an unnatural pregnancy."

"That may well be the truth, but others do not see it so and lay the blame for all evil at the feet of William."

"And do you do so as well, Henry?" I was audacious but could not hold my tongue.

"No, but he is not a prudent man and his moral failings do not endear him to many. He refuses to do what is best for England; he makes enemies with the church both here and abroad. He refuses to marry but will not name an heir—you'd think he'd do his damn duty in that regard even if he prefers a cock to a hen!"

I spluttered, shocked by his words. Yes, at court I had come to understand what the rumours about William Rufus meant. I had watched him laugh and carouse and make bawdy jests with his favourites, but I had seen little that hinted at sodomy save for his obvious preference for male company. Not surprising for a warrior-king. However, before he fared into exile, Archbishop Anselm had admonished the King and stated that he wanted to make a new law banning such sinfulness. He had done that for a reason.

"William had his eye on you at one time, Edith," said Henry.

I nodded. "I know…but I seem to have frightened him off."

A quick smirk lifted the corner of Henry's mouth before his expression became serious once again. "I am glad nought came of his plans. I said it before and mean it still—you would have been wasted on my brother. You are too fine, too intelligent.…"

His hands, rough with callous, dark hairs thick on the raw knuckles, were suddenly at my waist, on my girdle of golden wires clasping me tightly. Alarm, surprise, and other sensations I was loathe to admit to, flooded through me, and I gawked at him with a stunned look that probably did nothing for my beauty and instead made me resemble a terrified sheep.

On seeing my fright, he dropped his hands instantly. And so he should have. All knew of Henry's lechery, the countless women he'd tumbled since he was around fifteen, the stream of bastard children that came and went from court, large and small and in-between, dark-haired like Henry, blonde like the old Queen, his mother, with even one or two fire-tressed like some of the Scottish nobles I'd known.

But he would not treat me that way, a hasty rut and a hastier departure. I was a King's daughter and a King's sister and I would not let him treat me like some common drab.

He took a step back, his voice changing, his eyes suddenly shuttered, unreadable. "You will still ride out to hawk with me tomorrow, Lady Edith?"

I hesitated. Perhaps I should demand to return to Winchester at once; it would be safer than here, with these hard Norman men plotting God knows what.

But I did not. It was as if my lips moved of their own volition. "Yes…I would like nothing better."

The day dawned fair, though even in the early morn it was ridiculously hot, the ground steaming as we headed into the lodge's courtyard to take our horses from the grooms. The clearing where we would release the birds of prey was a mile or two inside the forest, through the heavy growth of oak, elm and alder. I rode side by side with Henry, while my female companions came next, Adelize de Clare looking pale and bilious and as if she wished she were anywhere but here. I wondered if what ailed her had less to do with recent childbirth and more to do with whatever her husband had conversed about with Henry. But that was all speculation on my part.

The head falconer marched along behind us, the birds in their cages carried on carts. The cadger ambled alongside on shaking legs; he would bring the birds' perches out into the field before their flights and gather a few coins from the lords and ladies for his troubles.

The path through the trees was narrow, the forest rushing up to embrace our party with green arms. Although the forest was named 'New' by the Conqueror, it was old, the roots of the oaks buried deep in the loam, gnarly and twisted boughs heavy with summer greenery. Sunlight slashed between stout boles, sending beams of light spraying over beds of emerald ferns. A fox poked his crimson ears up and with a yelp vanished into the safety of deeper woods. All around was a riot of greenery, smelling warm and summery in the hot breeze. Birds trilled in the branches, although they fell silent, sensing the danger, as we processed by with the hawks.

"They called this place Ytene once," Henry informed me, turning in his ornamented saddle. "A forest of the Jutes, the people who once dwelt in this region. It was thought to be a haunted place but my father loved it dear for the hunt was his greatest pleasure."

The Conqueror had driven numerous villagers out for the sake of that pleasure. Uncle Edgar had told me so with much bitterness in his tone. William had placed harsh laws upon those dwelling within the confines of the mighty forest—his precious deer came first in importance, not lowly peasants. The village folk were allowed to let their beasts graze on the commons and their pigs could root for beech nuts and acorns between September and November. Gathering wood and turf for fuel was also permitted. However, they could build no fencing that might impede a royal hunt, and if they were caught red-handed poaching deer, their hands would be cut off. Even those who innocently disturbed the forest beasts could face the punishment of blinding…

"Legends say a dragon dwells in the forest over on Burley Beacon," Henry continued, "and there's a Black Dog that betokens death."

"Have you ever seen either of these beasts?" I enquired, my lips pursed. "I mean, when you were not deep in your cups?"

"No," he grinned, "but..." His visage suddenly clouded, his eyes darkening. "There is something *strange* in these woods; something *old*, that perhaps does not welcome sons of the House of Normandy. Something that desires atonement, that wishes for our blood, royal blood..."

I glanced at Henry, expecting him to have assumed a mocking smirk—after all, he had just prattled on about dragons haunting the local hills. Everyone knew dragons had been extinct for centuries; Saint George had slain the very last one! But his expression had not changed; if anything, it had grown deathly serious, pale and ominous. A ripple of unease ran down my spine, cold in the heat of the day.

"What do you mean, Henry."

"Divine retribution...for what my sire did to your people, especially the innocents slain during the harrying of the north, for which he asked forgiveness on his deathbed. Retribution...but not from God."

"From local men?" I asked, confused. "They are only poor peasants, trying to eke out a living from the land. Their spirit, if they ever had any, is broken. They would not dare raise a hand...."

Henry shook his head. "No not ordinary men either, Edith...Can you not feel it, here in the forest? Watchfulness, evil spirits, old pagan gods..."

I swallowed. "If such demons ever existed, they are all gone now. Christ's Light swept them away..."

He let his horse drop back a few paces and reached out and touched my cheek. "So innocent you are, Edith. I truly do not think the old gods are quite as dead as the priests would like us to believe! Some say a giant called Yernagate walks the forest, and that he is the Wild Huntsman who chases the souls of the wicked with his band of red-eyed hounds."

Overhead, a small cloud scudded over the surface of the sun. The pleasant stream of sunlight faded in a flash and the verdant forest dimmed to sickly green robbed of its warmth. Bracken stirred as if trodden by unseen feet, the languid silver birches swayed like dancing spirits. Ahead rose a massive oak tree, a giant of the forest, its branches shuddering in the breeze that seemed to have sprung up from nowhere. It was an old tree, gnarled, its boughs heavy and sagging low, rimed with scaly knobs and knots. Its broad trunk was grey, lichenous, warped by nature and time into a scowling face— two goggling eyes, a broken limb for a nose, a yawning hole forming a dark, woody mouth. Even as I watched, a little robin flew from the 'mouth', his red breast flaring like blood in the green gloom.

"You have heard of my brother Richard?" asked Henry as our party trundled past the giant oak. Other oaks clustered around us now, nearly as large as the first and equally as disturbing—oaks blasted by lightning, black and skeletal, fungus clawing up their trunks, amid younger trees with strangely configured boughs that gave them the semblance of long, snatching arms or stag's horns jutting from their crowns.

"I have not heard of any Richard," I said, fiddling with my reins. "I thought William and Robert were your only brothers." My gentle mare was showing distress, her nostrils flaring, her hooves dancing on fallen leaves; she liked this sinister tangle of trees no better than I.

"He died, Edith…died here in the New Forest when he was scarce more than a boy. Like my father, he loved the hunt. He pursued a stag, they say, a stag white as death and fleeting as a ghost…and he was crushed between the hanging bough of a hazel tree and the pommel of his saddle. His body was carried to Winchester for burial."

"I did not know, Henry. Truly, a tragic accident."

He craned around to look at me again, that same solemn, dark expression on his features. "He is not the only one of my family taken by the wood. Another Richard, the bastard son of my brother Robert, was killed in similar fashion while hunting upon the first of May, an auspicious date for devilish goings-on and sacrifices, I am told."

I did remember this Richard, a swaggering youth who seemed to prefer his Uncle Rufus's dissolute court to his father's more sedate one in Normandy. He had been quick with his hands in ways that he shouldn't and vicious with his tongue, and most women of the court avoided being alone in his presence. No one had asked many questions or mourned his demise and his bones had been boiled free of flesh and returned to Normandy, wrapped in white linen.

"A-a tragic accident, I'm sure," I said, "and the day just a coincidence."

"Perhaps," said Henry, turning his head away and staring into the tangle of greenery, "but let us not forget, we are soon come to Lammas, another of the auspicious days when Christians celebrate…but others do so too and have time out of mind."

Soon we reached a bright and airy heath, covered with gorse bushes showering gold. Adelize de Clare started to sneeze and her eyes went red and teary. The sun had returned, burning like a coin in the dark summer blue of heaven's vault, but I could not shake off the gloom, the sense of foreboding that had enshrouded me within the forest. I shivered, despite the growing heat of the day.

As the old cadgers got to work putting out the hawks' perches, and the falconers tended to their birds, I dismounted my horse and waited, but in truth, the heart had gone out of me to witness such sport. The falconer brought me a peregrine whose name he told me was Merrywind.

"A peregrine?" My brows lifted in surprise. "I expected to fly a Merlin—they are known as ladies' hawks."

"Peregrines are stronger and fiercer," said Henry, with a grin, looming over the falconer's shoulder. "I thought you might enjoy a chance to handle something larger and fiercer than usual." He gave me a teasing wink that made me blush.

I tossed my head and glanced away, focussing on the falcon. She clambered from the falconer's gloved wrist onto my own, claws digging into the sturdy, decorated leather as the bells on her feet jingled musically.

Feeling Henry's gaze bore into my back, I walked out onto the common with its haze of scrub bush and yellow Asphodel. Ignoring him, I stared into the sky, scanning the horizons; from the dark fringe of the nearby trees, a handful of skylarks were flying, black dots against the blue.

Merrywind gave a shriek and danced nervously on my glove. I lifted the falcon up and then set her free. Swifter than an arrow, her wings a blur, she shot high into the sky, soaring higher and higher until she could barely be seen. I shaded my eyes, trying to follow her motions despite the glare. It would be hideously embarrassing if she vanished, never to be seen again, although the falconer would take the blame for poor training.

And then I caught sight of her, a small dot sailing through the heavens, with the skylarks that had emerged from the forest streaking through the air below, perhaps growing aware of the danger hovering overhead. Merrywind halted in mid-flight; I envisioned her wings beating furiously, keeping her aloft in that one spot while she focused on her prey. A moment later, she swooped, plummeting through the heavens like a dart sent from God, hurtling with terrifying speed toward her prey.

A high screech rang out across the common as Merrywind descended on her quarry, the force of her dive shattering all the bones in the other bird's body and killing it instantly. In a shower of feathers, the skylark's corpse began to fall, tumbling through the sky, but fast as lighting, Merrywind fell upon it, her sharp talons hooking into the shattered body.

There was a cheer as Merrywind landed on the common and began to rip at her kill. The falconer let her eat for a few moments, before striding out with a net to capture her lest she try to fly away. She shrieked and battered at the net, furious that her feasting was disturbed.

"A good catch!" cried Henry. "Well done, Lady Edith and Merrywind! It is my turn next. However, I…I prefer a kill less swift and of longer duration… so have brought the gyrfalcon."

His choice of bird surprised me; the gyrfalcon was a bird of royalty and although he was indeed a prince of the blood, this large white bird was surely meant for the King alone. I hoped his companions were able to keep their tongues still for Rufus would look darkly on having his property so used.

As Henry took charge of the gyrfalcon and walked out onto the common, a wave of dizziness overcame me. The day was hot and my white wimple and woollen gown were hot and oppressive. Pressure arose behind my eyes; my head began to throb. Glancing skyward, I saw clouds starting to bubble up, dark and bruised-looking. A summer storm was on its way.

I leaned back against the flank of my horse, wiping my sweaty brow with my sleeve. Adelize de Clare fanned herself, equally drained. "Why did they decide on such sport on a day such as today?" she complained. "My skin shall end up as red as fire. Why are we even here, Lady Edith? Oh well…" she flapped her hand before her face again; she had a small upturned nose and yes, it was already peeling, "Perhaps I can guess why. The Lord Henry gazes at you with eyes full of desire."

"No, no, you are mistaken," I insisted. My head gave a sudden, vicious throb. "He once made a promise to show me the forest, that is all."

She gave a knowing little smirk. "Dear Edith, he wants to show you much more than that. Surely you know of his reputation? Lots of his byblows are at court."

"His reputation is exactly why there will be nought ever between us," I said fiercely. "If he wants me, he would have to marry me!"

"Would you be averse to marrying him?" Lady de Clare queried with glee. "He is a prince, after all…and you are now twenty years old and unmarried. So unusual for a princess; I was wed at fifteen."

"He is a younger son with little to his name." I folded my arms, hating her questions, hating the muggy heat, hating the fact my head felt as if it was in the grip of a demon's pincers.

"That may be so for now…but it is unlikely that will always be the case. If William Rufus should die without an heir…"

"Henry is a prince, but unless Rufus named Henry his heir, Robert Curthose would claim the throne as eldest of the Conqueror's son."

Adelize's crimson nose wrinkled. "Curthose is in the Holy Land. For all we know, he may never return." The unpleasant smirk she had, tight-lipped and showing no teeth, returned. "He might wish to marry you himself if he does make it back."

"He cannot," I shot back. "He is my godfather. Oh, Lady, I beg you do not keep on with this tiresome speculation about marriage."

Shouts and cries from the hunting party drew our attention to the common. The white gyrfalcon was ascending to heaven, incandescent white against the brewing clouds. A large crane was moving on grey wings from the nearby trees where it had built its nest. It flapped slowly across the sky, an impressive bird with an enormous wingspan, a long neck and a fierce sharp beak.

Cranes were also considered a delicacy at table…

For the first time, Lady de Clare appeared excited. "The crane does not stand a chance against the gyrfalcon, but it will fight for its life and will not give over to death easily. It will be the Haut Vol, the high flight, where the gyrfalcon will battle the crane…and humble it."

Overhead the gyrfalcon had soared to dizzying new heights, just as the peregrine Merrywind had done, but higher, much higher. The crane seemed aware of the predator now; it hesitated in mid-flight then turned rapidly as if to hasten back to the forest's shelter. Its size and weight were not to its advantage here, as the gyrfalcon soared above, shadowing it, movements rapid, precise, deadly…

The gyrfalcon began its lethal descent, moving even swifter than Merrywind had. It struck the crane, tearing with its beak and suddenly there was flapping and birds shrieking, their distant screeches as terrible as the cries of men in battle. Feathers flurried in great clouds, grey and dark, as the white gyrfalcon latched onto its prey with its talons. The crane, though, was not ready to give up its life. Although sore wounded, its motions jerky, it managed to disentangle itself from the aggressor and peck wildly at the falcon's head with its rapier-sharp bill, perhaps seeking to put out the hypnotic red-gold eyes.

The men were cheering the gyrfalcon on, Henry the loudest of them all. Blood bloomed on the crane's flank and stained the white plumage of the gyrfalcon crimson, bringing ever louder shouts from the hunting party. More feathers flew, drifting down on the rising wind like rags of torn and desecrated angels' wings.

Borne on the hot wind, droplets suddenly sprayed across me and Adelize de Clare, crimson blots staining the fabric of our fine garments. I smelt hot iron, felt wetness seep through cloth to touch my skin.

"It is an evil omen!" hissed a pallid Lady Adelize, eyes hollow in a waxy face. Helisent and Emma were running about frantically, trying to wipe the blood from our raiment.

I could make no answer, for my guts gave an abrupt heave as the megrim I'd been fighting against all morning took control, squeezing my temples in a vice, and I felt myself falling as the first booms of thunder began in the west and heavy raindrops pattered on my ruined gown.

In silence, the hawking party returned to the Brockenhurst lodge. I still felt unwell and Lady de Clare moaned piteously the whole time, unsure which pained her more, the ruined gown or her fragile health. It was decided that as soon as the worst of the storm abated Henry should send us women back to Winchester. It would be for the best; it had been a mistake to invite us to a place with few creature comforts in the midst of summer storms.

I was happy to leave. Something unknown was brewing alongside the stormy weather—what, I could not say, but an ominous feeling crept over me every time I gazed upon the rows of oaks, the forest's sentinels with their half-define faces, tree-knot mouths, and snatching forked limbs.

Henry appeared unconcerned by my hasty departure, despite Adelize's assertion that he had his sinful eye on me. "It is nigh time for his Grace my brother to come here for his hunting pleasure," I heard him say to Walter Tirel, as Lady de Clare, the maids and I were hurried toward our wagon with its painted cover to protect us from the rain. "All is now prepared for his arrival and the great stag hunt that will follow, so it is just as well the women leave now. The King would not appreciate ladies cluttering up the lodge in his presence; you know how he feels about most of the fair sex."

Tirel gave a short rumbling laugh; a tall, muscled fellow, his eyes were black and his hair a shining bowl; and a long moustache dangled from a jutting lip. "No matter what he feels, it is best the women are kept out of the way. These ones here…they have served their purpose anyway, no?"

Perplexed by his words, I frowned. Whatever did the Frenchman mean by 'served our purpose.' I struggled to listen for more information while pretending to fiddle with my cloak-clasp.

Henry's voice carried on the breeze. "Walter, speak not too loudly. They are still here, and the servants always have eager ears…"

"My Lady…" A horse-face groom had handed Lady De Clare into the chariot and was extending a hand in my direction. I could delay no longer. I cast a surreptitious glance at Henry; he was deep in conversation with Walter Tirel, not looking in my direction at all. There was tension on his face and a strange, dark excitement that reminded me of the gyrfalcon's anticipation when spied its prey and dived in for the kill…

Shuddering, I climbed into the cart and settled in next to Adelize and the tiring women, who both sulked, disappointed that we would return to Winchester so soon.

As the carriage rolled down the rutted forest tracks and onto the main road to Winchester, the girls and Adelize fell asleep, listening to the warm summer rain patter on the canvas stretched above. I remained wide awake, however, the headache still nagging at my temples and the remembrance of Henry and Walter Tirel's words nagging in the back of my mind.

Once we had arrived back in Winchester castle, I retired to my quarters. Mary was already there, sitting by the window and playing on a recorder. She had been trying to learn but was not yet good at it—the instrument gave out an inharmonious blatt as I entered the room. "You are back sooner than expected."

"I'm unwell," I said shortly. "Henry sent me back…but I do not think he was upset to see me go."

"Why? Did you argue?" she asked.

I shook my head. "He showed me the forest…and then lost interest. It seems he had *other* things on his mind. Things I was not privy to."

"Another woman?"

"No!" I said crossly. "And I would not care a jot if it was true. But I do not want to talk more about Henry…I need to sleep!" I pointed to her recorder. "And I would appreciate it if you put that devil's tool away. My head hurts enough!"

I lay down on the bed and Mary, tossing her recorder aside, called for a servant to bring a basin of rosewater. She bathed my forehead with it after shooing the servant away. "You do look pale…" she murmured. "Did something else happen while you were gone?"

I dared not tell her my suspicions. Indeed, could not, for I could not yet verbalise them, for they sounded mad…and they were dangerous. Very dangerous.

I tried to change the subject. "How has his Grace been, Mary?"

"His usual self," she said with ill-disguised disgust. "Roaring and drinking and belching with his cronies. Falling out of his high seat, blind drunk. He spewed upon one of Robert FitzHamon's hounds, causing great mirth. He soon became bored, though, and was greatly pleased when your entourage arrived with the word that the hunting lodge was ready for his visit and well-stocked with meat, wine and ale. He plans to ride out for the New Forest before dawn; he is afraid he will miss the stags if he tarries here too long for the fat-time of deer starts on the Feast of St Peter's Chains…Lammas. It will certainly be more peaceful once he is gone."

I nodded. "Yes, once he is gone." Why did I feel like I had spoken word of treason? My head reeled again as I recalled in my mind's eyes the blood-spattered gyrfalcon, its breast incarnadine, and the spots of gore that streaked my gown, raining from above.

"You've gone pale again." Concerned, Mary put the rosewater bowl aside and brought a flagon of watered-down wine to my lips. "I've heard Lady de Clare is sick too. Maybe that will keep Nest from complaining."

Wiping wine droplets from my lips, I pushed myself up onto my elbows. "Nest? Why is she upset?"

Mary looked at me as if I were a silly ninny. "Can you not guess, Edith? Because Henry did not invite her to go to the forest, and left her here whilst taking you. She blames you more than him, the silly chit."

"Oh!" I had been unaware. Yes, Henry oftimes flirted with Nest and Nest with Henry, but then, as she'd grown older, Nest flirted with most men of any rank. She was beautiful and clearly was eager to gain a high-ranking husband ere long. Had she set her sights on Henry? That was presumptuous indeed for a daughter of a deposed Welsh King…A slither of annoyance ran through me; some might think I was just as presumptuous, but at least my brother had won back my father's throne, which raised my status, whilst Nest's royal inheritance was truly gone. It was foolishness even so—I hadn't presumed I'd wed Henry anyway! Nor did I want to…not at all…

"Let me rest, Mary," I said grumpily. "I will feel better after rest, I'm sure."

"Sleep well then," she said and swished out of the chamber.

Ill at ease, I tossed and turned on the bed. It was still humid, uncomfortably so, the air so thick it clogged one's throat and made breathing laboured. Somewhere in the distance, I heard the roar of King William's laughter, and then a shout, "By the Face of Lucca, there will be good hunting in the forest this Lammas!"

As if in answer, the clouds burst again, spewing heavy rain, and thunder shook the castle to its ancient Roman foundations.

CHAPTER TWELVE

Enfolded in a muggy haze, the King's hunting party headed out into a damp but humid morning that promised to become a scorching afternoon. Feeling more rested, though still not quite myself, I took up the embroidery I was working on and hurried for the coolness of the garden in the lee of the castle walls.

As I sat under a rose-laden arch, listening to birdsong and the tinkle of water into a pond, Mary ran out of the castle hall-block, and zigzagged towards me between the roses, lilies, betony and lavender bushes.

"I am glad I found you," she panted. "There are strange rumours abroad in the town. The servants are abuzz with them. Bishop Gundulf himself has spoken to some of the bearers of these tidings."

"What kind of rumours?" My fingers trembled on the needle.

"One is that a well at Finchamstead bubbled with blood!"

"Oh, that's not new," I sniffed. "It did so two years ago, I recall."

"It gets better, Edith. The devil himself has been seen lurking in lonely woodlands and wastelands. The Evil One spoke to travellers, warning them: 'The Red One shall fall, and his Flame-Bearer with him—clearly referring to the King and Ranulf Flambard."

I put the embroidery aside. "That last is treasonous talk, sister. Encompassing the death of the King. You must not repeat it."

"Everyone else is," Mary said mutinously, folding her arms.

"You were not raised to be a gossip. Just stop it, Mary. Do you understand?

"You are unsettled, I can see it in your face." She waggled a finger beneath my nose. "Ever since you returned from the New Forest, you've been as jumpy as a cat on hot cinders. I wish you'd tell me what happened at Brockenhurst to make you so unnerved…"

"It was not…what I expected, that's all," I said, snatching up my embroidery again. "This conversation is over."

The next day Mary, Nest and I went into the town of Winchester with our attendants, ostensibly to buy fripperies at the market, but the other girls were clearly eager to find out more about the rumours that were spreading around the country. I pretended to have no interest, but despite my aloof demeanour, I was secretly every bit as engrossed as they—perhaps more so after my stay at the hunting lodge, something I dared not speak of before Nest. She was cool to me; clearly, I was not forgiven for going to the forest without her.

The thunderstorms had abated for a while, a hot but watery sun shining through a halo of puffy black clouds that promised more downpours later. Heat made the paving stones steam and the sunlight cast pale yellow fingers on the towering market cross, where pedlars hawked buns, mortrews and dripping pigs' trotters alongside old women selling ribbons, cheap gewgaws and pilgrim's badges.

The air was thick, rancid with the heat and the scent of greasy cooking and slightly putrid meat. Gutters brimmed with mushy vegetables cast away after yesterday's market. Street urchins clustered around, fishing out any still-edible morsels before scampering away into dim side alleys between the stone houses.

Mary pretended to be interested in ribbons; Nest bought one for her from a toothless old woman in a soiled coif. The real focus of interest, for both my companions and the heaving crowd, was the preacher who was mounting the steps of the cross. His robes were monkish as was his tonsure, although it was shaggy and unkempt as were his garments. His sandalled feet were black with dirt, hard as horn, and his face bore a wild, mad look. The sun shone wanly on the sweat-dappled bald patch on his head. His skin was jaundiced, giving his bare pate the appearance of melting rancid butter.

On the top step of the market cross, he stretched wide his wasted arms in a dramatic gesture to keep the onlookers' attention. Staring heavenward, he thundered in a hoarse, deep voice, "Lo! The wrath of God is soon to befall this wicked land!"

"I bin hearin' that for years, shave-pate," crowed some wag in the street. "Tell 'im He best get on with it."

"Let me get me laundry in first!" chipped in a blowsy woman with a wimple flowing like a sail, to accompanying laughter from the throng.

The preacher stared around, eyes burning with fanatical intensity, and suddenly the crowd's mirth was quelled. A moonstruck fool…or one touched by God himself?

"The time is coming!" he cried. "England shall be freed from tyranny and sin! I saw in a dream Christ on a golden throne with a beautiful virgin kneeling before him. She raised her hands in sorrow and begged Him, 'Lord Jesus Christ, saviour of man, for whom you shed the Holy Blood, look with mercy upon your faithful, we beseech you. England groans beneath the yoke of William Rufus who despoils Mother Church and pollutes the position of God's Anointed. And the Lord replied unto that fair maid, 'Be patient, child, and wait a little longer. The Red King shall pay the full penalty for his crimes!'"

A hushed silence fell across the crowd. Then someone hawked on the steps of the cross, shattering the stillness. "Bloody monks, always seeing signs in the birds and the fishes and in damn dreams brought on by cheese and wine. You'll have to do better than that, brother whoever you are. We've heard it all before…for thirteen damn years, ever since that red-faced sodomite took the throne!"

The preacher looked furious, thrusting a bony warning finger towards the onlookers. "Thirteen the number at the Last Supper. One of his own shall lay him low, who has kissed his cheek in amity…"

"More likely his arse!" shrilled a youth clutching a wineskin.

The monk ignored him. His lanky frame suddenly trembled as if he might have a convulsion of some sort. Froth touched the corner of his thin mouth, and the melted appearance of his pate grew even more noticeable as sweat dribbled through the greying strands of his rough tonsure. I had seen men with the falling sickness taken by sudden paroxysms that made them tumble down, foaming from the mouth, and wondered if this monk would do the same.

But instead, despite his violent trembling, he muttered what sounded, not a mere dream, but a prophecy: *"The bow of divine vengeance is bent on the wicked, and the swift arrow taken from the quiver is ready to wound. Soon shall the blow be struck…"*

Silence descended again and dark, wary looks passed between the people gathered in the street. As I had warned Mary, it was treason to predict the death of a monarch, and the monk's words seemed awfully close to predicting exactly that.

"Let's go!" Nest dragged at my sleeve. "The mood here is no longer jovial; I fear they will either lynch this man or carry him on their shoulders as a prophet. In any case, there will probably be fighting." She nodded towards some angry-looking oafs, swaying from drink, who were attempting to thrust folk aside to get to the steps of the cross. "Where there's men and drink, there's always fighting. It used to be so even in my father's hall."

I motioned to our guards for our little party to move off. The armed men, their faces grim, hurried us through the teeming streets until we were almost running, as unseemly as that must have appeared to any onlookers. Our maids, my Helisent and Emma, as well as Mary's new girl Gillian and Nest's Rohaise began to weep in fear, sure that we were going to be attacked by the roused townsfolk…or perhaps the demons and devils hinted at by the strange holy man on the market cross.

Luckily, we reached the massive gates of the castle unharmed and raced inside, the huge doors clanging shut behind us.

Later, in our chamber, we dined on traditional Lammas bread, hot from the oven and swathed in new-churned butter, and gorged on fresh fruits such as blackberries and strawberries, and for a while our moods were light again.

But as the sun westered and fire-tinged storm clouds began to churn again, filling the creeping darkness with growls of thunder, a sense of unease spread over me once more and the monks' prediction returned to haunt my thoughts.

Soon shall the blow be struck…

It was late evening of the next day, the second of August, when a great commotion broke out in town and spread to the castle. Through the open window, I heard the whinnying of horses and the frenzied shouts of men.

I leaned out into the cooling but still humid air, so heavy it struck one's lungs like clay. I noted the castle gates hanging wide and streams of riders pouring through into the bailey. Torches flared as castle officials surged from the outbuildings, and in the flickering, uncertain light, I thought I caught a glimpse of a familiar face…

"We must go and see what is happening, Mary." I withdrew from the window and threw a respectable veil over my hair.

"Should we?" Her small, heart-shaped face was pinched and frightened. "If there is trouble, we should stay where we are, behind a closed and barred door. It's not safe for maidens…"

I thought of what I thought I had seen—a short, dark man, windblown, upon a lathered horse. Henry Beauclerc here…when he should be in the New Forest with his brother, the King.

"Mary, I must go!" I cried, and though she tried to drag me back, I pushed her off and throwing open the chamber door, ran down the corridor, my heavy skirts clutched in my hands so that I would not trip. Down a spiral stair I fled, leaning heavy against the sweating wall, and into a passage that led to the Great Hall.

Bursting through the arched door, I encountered a scene of pure pandemonium. Knights were shouting, guards striding by with drawn weapons, servants running, some weeping or with faces twisted in grimaces of pure fright. A fight broke out; I saw the steward fall from a fist to the chin; men stumbled through the firepit, scattering sparks; a table went over with a resounding crash, throwing platters here and there. A bench followed, hurled suddenly; striking a line of men, they hit the rushes like fallen skittles.

"My Lady!" Amable, one of the castle laundresses, recognised me as she dived for the door. "You must go back to your chamber, it isn't safe. They've all gone mad; the world has gone topsy-turvy."

I grabbed her arm, keeping her from fleeing out of the Hall. "What has happened, Amable? Tell me. I won't go till I know. I thought I saw the Lord Henry…"

"Yes…you…you did," she gasped. "He is here. Here at Winchester."

"Where?" I asked. If he'd been in the Hall, he was not there now amidst the brawling knights and soldiers.

Her rosy, dumpling face became the hue of curdled milk. "It's unbelievable, my Lady…He's heading for the Treasury…"

"The Treasury?" I shook my head. "Why should he do that? Where is King William?"

Amable's mouth opened and shut like a fish's, with no sound coming out. Finally, she managed to stammer, "The King…he…they say…he…" A harsh gasp tore from her lips and her eyes rolled back in her head before she crashed to the floor in a faint, dragging me down on top of her. Her basket of newly washed linens toppled over, tangling around us both like grave shrouds.

Hastily I freed myself and leapt back to my feet; the fighting in the room had increased, swords and daggers fleshing and clattering. Sparks from the trodden-on central hearth had caught in the rushes and were having to be stamped out, causing even more mayhem and producing clouds of heavy, rank smoke.

Nest appeared through the thickening smoke and careered in my direction. "Edith!" she cried, surprised. "Why are you here?" She did not look particularly happy about my presence.

"Why? I wanted to know what's happening!" I said. "I thought I saw Henry."

"So did I," she said. "That is the reason why I came." There was a certain challenge in her voice.

"Well then, we have something in common," I said. "I am told he is headed for the Treasury, to what purpose I cannot say."

Without waiting for her, I ran across the Hall into the opposite corridor, nearly tripping on fallen crockery and pushing between heaving bodies and wailing servants. This passageway was also packed by people, most gaping witlessly, but others were shoving and shouting in an attempt to press forward. I began thrusting my way through the throng, calling out, 'Make way, make way!' and trying to sound regal and officious. A few men and women recognised me as a princess of Scotland and backed away, fearing to give insult.

After what seemed a horrible eternity of jostling, shoving and shouting, I spied the passage's end and the round-headed door to the Treasury Tower. Here, the onlookers shrank back, afraid, for a confrontation was going on in the Treasury doorway.

I recognised William de Breteuil, one of King William's supporters from Normandy, blocking the entrance with an unsheathed sword in his hand. "You shall not enter!" he roared furiously, his eyes black with wrath. "This thing must not be done until Robert Curthose is back from Crusade. Remember, we both swore oaths to the Duke that we would support him as William's heir."

And that's when I fully understood. The prophecies spoken in the marketplace were true. William Rufus was dead.

And Henry, no matter what he had once sworn, was in no mind to cede England to his absent older brother.

"Get out of my way, Breteuil!" Henry bellowed, drawing his own sword in a flash of silver. "Curthose's rule in Normandy had been nought but rebellion after rebellion—only a fool would want him to bring such strife to England too!"

Teeth gritted, Breteuil took a menacing step towards Henry and I gasped in fear and pressed my hands to my mouth. Nest clung to my elbow, her own gaze terror-stricken.

"Think, man!" Henry shouted at him, raising his sword and deflecting a blow from William de Breteuil's blade. "If you continue to bar my way, you will see your head atop the city gates as a traitor to the rightful King. Stand back, and you will not only be pardoned but, in due time, be rewarded for good service."

Conflicting emotions streamed over Breteuil's visage. For a second, I thought he might lash out again. Instead, he gave a loud cry and with a sharp motion, dashed his blade to the floor and fell on his knees before Henry, head bowed.

Henry elbowed him aside and entered the Treasury where all the riches and wealth of England lay in coffers and chests. "I claim the Treasury this day!" he cried in a great voice so that all in and without the chamber could hear. "For my brother, William, Second of that Name, has been slain through misfortune in the New Forest, and I, his youngest brother, the only one of the Conqueror's sons to be born on English soil, do this day assert my Right to the Kingdom of England. What say you, folk of Winchester?"

Briefly, there was a hush. Then, Roger de Clare, who had ridden back from the forest with Henry, raised a clenched fist in the smoky air and roared, "God Save the King. God save King Henry, First of that Name!"

The crowd pushed forward slowly, and another voice cried, "God Save King Henry!" and then another. Before long, the whole castle rang to those shouts of acclamation.

Tears standing in my eyes, I too raised my shaking fist. "God Save King Henry, First of that Name!"

He came to my chamber early the next day. It was unannounced and improper, but who was there to tell him he could not enter? Henry Beauclerc, newly acclaimed King, thrust the door open and strode in with a swagger, telling Mary and our tiring women to leave.

"But my…my lord King," stammered one of the maids, "the Lady Edith, as you can see is still in her bed and near enough unclad. Men might think evil…."

"Let them think, then, woman." Henry jerked a callused thumb towards the open door. "Go; my time is being wasted. Soon I must ride to Westminster for my Coronation and I must speak to the Lady Edith ere I go, whether she is naked or not."

The maid, Helisent, curtseyed and fled, her cheeks stained deep scarlet. I was *not* naked thankfully but wore only a thin under-kirtle as one might expect in bed. I sat up, my pale hair coursing down freely, and clutched the embroidered coverlet against my bosom.

"Hen…y-your Grace," I stammered nervously.

"There need be no formality between us, Edith." Henry took a long stride towards the bed. "Call me by the name I was given at my birth."

"Henry," I began, "I can scarce take this all in. Last week, you were a prince, but a nigh-landless younger son."

"And now I am King," he said, "as God decreed."

"What happened?" It was bold to ask, but ask I must, although I suspected the answer might be constructed of half-truths, if not outright lies, and the facts of William's demise hidden forever.

Henry took a deep breath. "William arrived at Brockenhurst and, as was his wont, got terribly, uncontrollably drunk. He stumbled off to bed where he had a nightmare that left him screaming—he dreamt that he was sick and being bled by a leech, but his blood gushed forth in a column that reached to heaven and turned the very sun to blood and day to night..."

"How hideous!" I cried. I had not liked Rufus but felt some pity for the dead man. He may have done great evil, but his conscience must have gnawed at him. He was not an out-and-out villain, like his old friend Robert de Belleme, who maimed and blinded his foes for pleasure, and who kept his own wife, Agnes of Ponthieu, it was rumoured, as a prisoner in a tower.

"I had to calm him—he was calling for the Blessed Virgin, something he had never done before, and ordered all the candles be lit. Even with the room nigh as bright as morning, he did not fall back to sleep for hours, hence in the morning he rose far later than was usual for a hunt. His temperament was sour that morn and black bags hung beneath his eyes. He looked ill and feverish."

"He should not have ridden out in such a state."

Henry shrugged. "He soon recovered—he flung himself down at the table and drank more wine! He even laughed when FitzHamon told him that while William slept, a monk had accosted him within the forest, a foreigner on his way to Southampton port."

"A monk? Why would that upset a man like Robert FitzHamon?"

"The monk was in a state of great distress and eager to leave England, which he deemed a place of great wickedness, thanks to my licentious brother's rule... He warned FitzHamon of a nightmare he had the previous night, in which he saw William stride into a church and glare at the priest, before seizing the Rood and gnawing the image of Our Lord with his teeth."

I gasped in horror at the idea of this sacrilege, even if it was only in a monk's nightmare.

"The crucifix endured this unholy desecration for a time...but suddenly it struck back, kicking my brother to the floor before the high altar. Rufus opened his mouth to curse it, but from his throat issued gouts of flame and smoke that spiralled up to cloak the stars..."

"Surely William no longer laughed then, with his own troubled dreams only a few hours before."

Henry shook his head. "No, he continued to laugh and mock the words of the monk. He told FitzHamon, 'This man is a monk and his monkish dreams are to get money. Find him and give him 100s!'"

My eyes widened. "That is an exceptional amount of money for a stranger who has just dreamed that you will commit a sacrilegious act and spout fire like a demon from hell!"

Henry chuckled. "Yes, William could be extravagant. And perhaps, underneath the mirth and mockery, he was truly afraid."

Shadows passed over his face and he grew solemn. "You will want to know about…how my brother fell." It was a statement, not a question.

Before I even had time to answer, he began to pace around the chamber, hands knotted behind his back.

"I did not see it happen." He suddenly whirled toward me, making me jump and clutch the coverlet even more tightly. "The sun was already hanging low in the sky and the party was dispersing, men faring forth this way and that. Walter Tirel remained with the King; in the morn, William had given Tyrel two arrows, noting that Tyrel was known as a deadly shot. I was not far away; my bowstring had snapped and I had ridden to the hut of a local bowyer to get the string mended. As the bowyer restrung the bow, his goodwife asked his grandson who had come seeking her husband's skills. The lad told her, and she peered at me and murmured, 'Within the presence of a king I deem I stand.' I thought she was mad from age and, taking my restrung bow, returned to the glade where William had remained."

"And he was dead when you arrived."

"Yes," he said. "Walter Tirel was still there, then, as white as a ghost. He told me the King had seen a white stag across the glade and had shot at it, but missed. As he watched it go, shading his eyes from the late sun with his hand, another stag appeared in the greenery behind the first. Walter shot at it, but the King turned at that moment, and Tirel's arrow struck him full in the chest. William grasped at the shaft and fell to the ground on top of it, driving the arrowhead further in and ensuring a quick death."

"And what did you do?" I swallowed, realising my words might be taken as an accusation. "When you saw him, I mean."

"Checked that he was truly dead. When I ascertained that he was, I leapt astride my steed and told Tirel to flee for the coast and take ship for France, for his life was surely in danger, even though my brother was not greatly loved. I then climbed back onto my steed and rode like a madman through the forest, making for Winchester. I happened on the rest of the hunting party and some of them rode with me…while some, the fearful fools, left for their own castles, seeking to bar their gates against any trouble. What happened when I reached Winchester, you saw yourself, Edith."

"If you and the King's companions all rode away, where is the King's body now?" I asked. "Surely he should be laid in state before burial."

Henry stared at the ground, almost as if ashamed. "His body remained in the forest. However, it was soon found by a charcoal burner named Purkiss, who placed it in a cart and brought it hither to Winchester. Some say the blood from his body ran red on the road all the way from the New Forest to the town."

"It is claimed that happens when men are murdered! They bleed after death!" I murmured. It was a dangerous thing to voice, here in the presence of a man I suspected, but could not prove, was involved in usurping his unpopular brother's crown. But my Mother, God assoil her, had told me to speak plainly and to question rather than willingly accept what I was told, and I was highly disturbed by what Henry had told me, especially after my own visit to Brockenhurst Lodge.

I saw shock in his eyes and a flicker of anger but it was gone in an instant. "Such claims are often wrong, Edith; foolish superstitions. Many out in the streets of Winchester are saying that William deserved his fate, that it was the hand of God that struck him down, using William Tirel as his tool of divine retribution. Not many mourn my brother."

He sighed and folded his arms. "He will be buried soon, in a tomb in the crossing of the abbey. You may attend if you see fit. I must ride for London, where I will be crowned."

"So quickly…" I murmured

"So it must be. There is no time to waste. I must take the reins of power ere the barons gather into various factions, some of them conspiring against me. I must strive to unite the lords of England in my Coronation Charter, in which I will seek to establish a lasting peace. I have many new laws in mind, Edith…some of which you might well approve."

"And what are those?" I gazed at him with renewed curiosity.

"One is that if a maiden is placed within my guardianship, she will not be married off for my own gain."

I bowed my head, suddenly embarrassed. "That is a good, just rule…your Grace. Henry."

He reached out to me then, his hand on my half-revealed shoulder. His fingers burnt my uncovered flesh like fire. For a fearful few seconds, I thought he might tear my covers away and ravish me, despite the pretty words he had just spoken about maidens within the king's care not being sold for monetary gain to the highest bidder.

But he did not. Eyes shining, full of fervour, not lust, he stared down into my tense, upturned face. "I will be the Lion of Justice to my people. And I want you, Edith, to be my Queen."

CHAPTER THIRTEEN

Henry was in London being crowned. I remained in Winchester, in shock, hardly able to believe what had transpired. Henry had departed almost immediately after he had made his intentions towards me known, without waiting for my answer, clearly believing it would be 'yes.'

I had always assumed I would marry a king or great magnate, but now...I was afraid. I was all too aware that Henry was the son of the Conqueror, who had brought so much evil to the English people, and that he could, when enraged, be cruel. Some years ago, he had helped put down a revolt in Rouen, taking the leader, Conan Pilatus, captive. He had marched the rebel to the top of the castle keep and mockingly told him to look out at the green fields and fish-filled river and enjoy the view. Realising his intent, Conan had begged to confess his sins to a priest at least. Henry cared nought for that and flung him from the tower, ordering his men to tie Conan's broken body to a horse and have it dragged through Rouen's streets as a warning.

But...would I receive a better offer? Henry was aware, that as an orphan, I had no marriage portion. My only fortune was my bloodline, which I supposed was the main reason Henry desired a union.

Brooding on these trying thoughts, I attended the funeral of King William, along with other notables of the court. The burial seemed humble and mean, especially contrasted with the rich opulence of the cathedral's soaring roof, Saint Swithun's gem-encrusted shrine, and gaudily painted pillars. No tears were in evidence, even from his most faithful; instead, a sense of relief emanated from them all. One of his favourites had wrapped him in his own cloak, and he was hastily buried in that garment rather than a king's robe, and there were no symbols of his office—no funerary crown or ceremonial sword. Even the words spoken from Proverbs during the interment seemed harsh—*As a roaring lion and a ranging bear, so is a wicked ruler over the poor people. The prince that wants understanding is also a great oppressor...*

Numb, I returned to Winchester Castle as William Rufus lay in his humble coffin unloved and unmourned beneath the crossing of the cathedral's tower...

Back in the castle chapel, I prayed for guidance, but none came. Dust motes shimmered above the wall-painting of the Virgin but she offered no advice.

Greatly troubled in mind, I sought out Mary. She was sewing in the solar, her face taut with concentration, the sunlight through a window slit picking out the red strands in her brown hair, making it shine like copper. "Mary," I said, "I must talk to you in private."

I let my gaze slide over to Nest who was embroidering on the next window seat. Of late, my feelings towards her had changed. Increasingly, it felt as if she somehow vied with me—and that, in her eyes at least, I was wanting in some way and she wished to prove it. I found her flirtatiousness irritating

Mary nodded and gathered up her work, following me back to our bedchamber. I felt Nest's gaze follow us but at least she did not try to pursue. Once inside, I bolted the door, as my sister sat down heavily on the edge of the bed. "What is it, Edith?" she said. "You look ill at ease."

"I think we should leave court," I blurted.

She stared at me as if I had gone moon-mad.

"Why on...on earth?" she stammered. "William Rufus is dead. Henry, I am sure, will not run such a debauched court. He is fond of you; any fool can see it!"

"Too fond, perhaps," I blurted. "Mary, he wants to marry me!"

She let out a loud gasp but then her brow creased. "And you are not pleased by this proposal?"

"Yes! No...Oh, I do not know," I said miserably. "My head is in a whirl. The offer is a good one, no denying that, but...I still cannot forget who his father was, and how all the sons of William Bastard behave when provoked...and even when they *aren't* provoked. I...I need time to think, and I fear I cannot do that here in

Winchester. With Henry's men around, knowing his wishes, and Henry himself bound to return soon and finalise his plans, I fear I may be forced…"

"What do you propose, Edith?" interrupted Mary. Her eyes were wary.

I took a deep breath. "That we go to Wilton and abide at St Mary's. Take counsel from Abbess Hawise. It will only be for a short time, I promise. It will have to be…for surely Henry will want an answer soon."

"Won't he be angry, should he find us both gone without telling him? He…he's now the King. Who dares walk out on a King?"

I shuddered, recalling the legendary tempers of the Conqueror and all his male children. Frothing, writhing, biting…beating. It was said their father, the Bastard, once beat their mother Matilda black and blue in a rough wooing before they were wed.

"I will look upon it as a test," I said shakily. "If his reaction to my entering St Mary's is violent and I am fearful of his wrath…I…I will take the veil as a nun of the order."

"So after all the denials you made years ago, you might join holy orders after all?" Mary looked slightly disgusted. "I well remember the protestations you made to Aunt Cristina."

"I'll only take vows if I can see no other course," I said. "Will you come with me?"

"Why should I?" Her full bottom lip thrust out and I was reminded for the umpteenth time that she was no longer the biddable, quiet little girl who clung to my hand when we first left Scotland, but a determined young woman seeking her own place in the world. "I am happy enough here at court."

"Well, if Henry finds I am not available, he may turn his gaze upon a younger daughter of the royal houses of Scotland and England, Mary. But perhaps it would not be matrimony he offered you. Look at all the bastards and concubines that have appeared at court from time to time. Almost two dozen, I'd wager …"

A look of stark horror crossed her face. "I would NEVER…"

"You would. He is the King." He had told me he would make new laws so that the monarch could not profit from female wards...but he said nothing about him taking his 'dues' in other ways!

"Then I will come with you," she said with a heavy, disgruntled sigh. "I do not like your idea, Edith, but I do see what issues could arise at court. When shall we go, and how?"

"I will arrange it. No one will suspect. All and sundry know I still have strong ties to Saint Mary's, especially to the poor and ill in the hospital. If anyone questions it, we have sought the convent on a...spiritual matter. It is not exactly a lie."

In her chamber, Abbess Hawise greeted me with warmth and affection...but also with surprise. "It is a pleasure to see you, Edith," she said, but then she peered closely at my face. "However, I sense this is more a mere social visit."

I blushed and decided that, in this instance, it was best to speak the full truth. Lying to the Abbess would nearly be as sinful as lying to the Blessed Virgin herself.

"Reverend Mother, Henry...the King, I mean...he has asked for my hand in marriage."

She blinked, taken aback, but recovered her composure almost immediately. "And you are not pleased? He has done something to offend you?"

"No," I said, "but I have questions...about the death of William Rufus."

An indrawn breath from the old nun. "Yes, I have heard these...*rumours*, Edith, but they are only rumours. Remember, many holy men prophesied King William's death upon Lammas, an auspicious time; let us say, no matter how he came to die, it was God's vengeance that laid him low."

She emerged from behind her desk and taking my arm, led me down the familiar cloisters, splotched with sunlight that streamed through the leaves of vines coiling up the pillars. "You could do much good as Henry's Queen, Edith. Good for the people of England...your people, who dwelt here before old King William arrived to claim his crown. Many would look to you as a saviour, and you could intercede with Henry to grant them more rights and freedoms. You, my dearest girl, could be seen as a second Queen Esther."

"Esther? You flatter me indeed, Reverend Mother!"

"Oh, no, I never flatter, Edith. Think on Esther's tale—she too is a meek orphan who becomes the saviour of her people once she weds the Persian king."

Thoughtful, I stared down at the flagstones. "Do you truly think I could help in such a manner, Abbess Hawise?"

"Yes, I do. There is much of your saintly mother in you, but also the courage of your father's people. I cannot think of a young woman in England, France or Spain who is comparable to you. If I were in your shoes, I would gladly accept the offer of Henry Beauclerc, who told Bishop Osmund, God rest his soul, that he thought you were 'exceptional'!"

I blushed furiously. "Did he?" I said, and was embarrassed by the eagerness in my tone.

"Would I lie?" she said with mock sternness. "Go pray before the relics of your namesake saint, Edith. Maybe guidance will come to you from above."

Guidance did not come from the holy Sain Edith...but King Henry did the following week, riding in with the wind on a handsome grey stallion. Heart hammering against my ribs, as I walked through the cloister towards the guestenhouse where he waited with Hawise.

As I arrived, nervous and wary, the Reverend Mother cleared her throat and edged towards the arched door. "I will leave you to speak alone with the Lady Edith, your Grace," she said to Henry, who was standing in the shadows behind her, and then she swished out into the corridor with a gentle nod in my direction.

I stood before the new King of England like a naughty child, my head bowed...although I allowed myself a surreptitious glance at his face to gauge his mood. To my relief, he looked more perplexed and even uncertain, rather than wrathful.

"Edith, why are you here in St Mary's?" he queried. "I was...disappointed when I arrived back in Winchester and you were not there. Have I committed some sin to gain your displeasure?"

"No...no, I merely needed time to think, and pray, so that God and the saints could guide me in the matter of our possible marriage,"

He stepped back, a little tic in the corner of his left eye showing that he felt some agitation, even though he was holding it in check as best he could. "And what did God and the saints say?" His voice dripped with mockery.

I raised my head and met his glance, sword-sharp. "God was silent on the matter, but Hawise thinks I should become your queen and your helpmeet."

A huge grin split his face and he strode forward as if to catch me in a tight embrace, but I raised my hand in front of myself protectively. "Wait, my Lord King. Before I agree to become your bride, you must first agree to my terms."

"Your *terms*." He folded his arms over his chest and his lips tightened.

I cleared my throat, ignoring his vexed expression. "Yes. First, you must ease the harsh laws your father and brother set upon the people of England. You must promise your English subjects that they can still be governed by the laws of Edward the Confessor. You must earn their love with good leadership, not rule through fear. Norman and Saxon in the generations to come should become as one."

I feared my blunt words might cause his temper to erupt, but he looked triumphant instead and a little bit smug. "It is done already. Written as my Coronation Charter. The customs of the people will be upheld. Peace is what I desire most of all and a prosperous England."

"But that is not all, Henry," I continued. "Some who have behaved with malice in the past must be punished."

"That, too, is done, Edith. Ranulf Flambard...I have him confined in the Tower, charged with corruption. Others will follow."

"And what of our missing Archbishop of Canterbury?" I asked. "The holy Anselm. He has dwelt long in exile and he is no longer young."

"Once we are wed, you will find I am not a sleepy sluggard in such matters. Anselm is journeying to England even as we speak!"

I was impressed by how much Henry had accomplished in only a few days but refused to show it, for that would weaken my position with the King. I must demand and have assurances that what I desired would be done...otherwise, I would refuse the marriage.

"You must also send a message to my brother, the King of Scotland, and ask for his blessing on our nuptials."

"It shall be done. Tomorrow if you say me 'yea' in the matter of the marriage."

I made no answer, studying the floor tiles below my feet. A lion...he said he would be the Lion of Justice. A lily and a rose twined over a crown; symbols of the Virgin. Apt symbols for a royal bride. Was this an omen that I should accept his suit.

"Edith?" His voice was sharp, impatient.

Instantly I glanced back up. "I have made my decision. I will become your wife, Henry Beauclerc, and together we can make a broken England whole."

He gave a shout of joy that rang out loudly in the confines of the chamber. I forced back a smile as I imagined the nuns on the floor below racing about in alarm like black beetles, wondering what was going on and imagining all kinds of immoral scenes. Once again, Henry strove to embrace me, but I laid my hands on his broad shoulders, heavy with muscle from wielding the sword, and shook my head. "We must behave with the dignity of our stations. Those with evil minds and malicious hearts must not be given reason to see me as an unfit bride."

"Why would anyone think such a thing?" Henry roared, his happiness at my acceptance of his proposal fading to pure rage. "If anyone should slight you, I will kill him..."

"Henry, calm yourself, I beg you. It is understandable for some to doubt. Your barons...some may not appreciate a Queen of the old Saxon blood. They may stir up trouble. It is just the way things are; I am not offended. But let us not play into the hands of those who would hurt us. I propose I stay here, in the company of my sister and the nuns, until our wedding."

He ran his hands tetchily through his shaggy dark hair. "You are wiser than I, though you are young and a woman. Yes, yes, the nobility must be convinced there is no stain upon you, that you are the most fitting choice as queen. Stay in the abbey until all is arranged."

He made as if to leave, then suddenly swung round to face me. I thought he might insist on at least a kiss and was minded, now that he had agreed to my terms, to give him a chaste, sisterly embrace…but he did not draw closer.

"You have asked much of me, Edith; now I have one thing to ask of you before we proceed."

"Yes?"

"Your name."

"My…m-my name?" I stammered, unsure where this was leading.

"Yes. It is an English name."

"An esteemed one," I said, somewhat coldly, my eyes narrowing.

"But English nonetheless. You mentioned yourself that some men amongst my followers might not take kindly to one of the blood of Alfred on the throne. The time of the old Kings is gone forever, and you must realise that, Edith."

"What would you have me do?"

"Take a regnal name. Show naysayers that you may be English-blooded but that you are a true Norman queen. I would have you call yourself Matilda, the name of my mother, blessed in memory, a woman of excellent virtues and skills—as I deem you will be. She was, of course, your godmother, too."

"Matilda." I rolled the name around on my tongue.

"In private, you can retain your own name," said Henry. "It can remain between you and me"

Matilda… I murmured the name again. A strong name and one acceptable to the most powerful nobles in the land. It would harm me not at all to accept such a name, at least for my public duties as queen.

I reached out and caught Henry's hand; this time, I startled him.

"I will be Matilda," I said. "Matilda, Queen of England."

The tidings of my betrothal swept across the land. It should have been a joyous time, but it ended up a time of torment and unease. One from my past emerged to make my life difficult, one thought of as a holy woman who would never lie.

My aunt Cristina, Abbess of Romsey.

We had lost contact after my parents moved me to Wilton but she had not forgotten the spats that took place while I was within her 'loving' care. She had written to inform Henry that I was indeed a professed nun, and he would commit sacrilege if he married me. Any children we had would be cursed, for I was a Bride of Christ and not a bride for mortal man.

Henry came to Wilton himself to tell me of her letter. "She says you are a nun, Edith. And that I must ascertain the truth before I 'advance you to my bed.' I beg forgiveness for my bluntness but those were her very words."

He held out the letter; I snatched it angrily and read it through, shaking. "She is a liar. Do not believe her, Henry. I was never a nun, not at Romsey and not here at Wilton. I told her many times but she wanted a nun's life for me and would not listen to my denials."

Henry sighed. "The matter must be decided before we wed. I would not delay the marriage but it must be completely clear to all that you are free to marry. Otherwise, rumours will forever haunt our progeny."

"I know," I said, crestfallen, wanting to tear Cristina's cruel missive into shreds. "Whatever shall we do?"

"Bishop Anselm is on his way back from exile and should arrive in England in October. I will ask his opinion."

I grimaced. "Henry, he too thought I was a nun, no doubt through the false words of my aunt. When my sire took Mary and me from St Mary's, Anselm wrote an angry letter saying that we were sworn to God and must return. We did not, of course."

Henry's expression was grim. "I believe you, Edith, but this situation needs more than belief. There must be no question of your status. Forgive me."

Stiffly, he left the chamber without a farewell. I listened to his vanishing footsteps along the cloister walk and burst into tears.

I was miserable for the next few months, worrying about what the Archbishop of Canterbury would decide. As October came with high winds, grey skies and migrating geese screeching through the skies like hounds of the Wild Hunt, a courier finally arrived with a letter from Henry.

Hands shaking, I carried it to my chamber, broke the red wax of the royal seal and read the dreadful words I feared.

I send unhappy news. Anselm has returned and I have held discourse with him. Alas, he sides with the Abbess Cristina and firmly believes you are a vowed nun of the order. You will know that I argued with him, saying that I had sworn a solemn oath to make you my wife. He would not sway in his beliefs, the hard-headed fool. I will not give you up just yet, though. Anselm is on his way to visit the Bishop of Salisbury. I advise that you meet with him there and speak frankly and honestly to him.

God be with you,
Henricus Rex

I crushed the parchment in my hands; the wax crumbled, falling to the flagstones like droplets of blood. Tears started again, stinging my eyes. Why, oh why, did Cristina hold such hatred towards me that she would ruin all my chances in life? If only my mother had known of her sister's ill-will and kept me and Mary away...

I rode to Salisbury with a small entourage of nuns sent by Abbess Hawise. She was more cheerful than I was as she waved me through the abbey gate. "The truth will come out, Edith; I have prayed to the Virgin and Saint Edith on your behalf. Afterwards, in the early hours of dawn, I dreamt of a crown of gold and I am certain it is a sign that you soon shall become King Henry's wife. Naturally, I shall testify on your behalf if called to do so."

Salisbury was cold and windy, its walls standing grey upon the bleak earthworks that reared up like man-made mountains. Passing through the main gateway, the party headed toward the cathedral, bypassing the castle on its steep earth motte.

The cathedral was fair to the eye, but as usual the wind buffeted it fiercely shrieking through the ornamented pinnacles along the roofline. To my ears, the noise sounded like demonic laughter, and I pulled my vair-lined cloak firmly around myself. I was shivering with nerves but wanted none to notice my discomfort and start whispering.

Anselm was set to meet me in the cathedral's Chapter House. Dismounting my steed, a groom took her away to be stabled. "Good luck, Lady," whispered Sister Cellarer, who had ridden out from St Mary's to accompany me. "God will see things come aright."

"I hope so," I returned in a whisper. In my head, I had imagined myself striding in before the Archbishop and setting forth my case, my word being instantly believed...but I knew, in reality, that Anselm, though a holy man, was often tetchy and stern, especially in regard to the idea of vowed nuns running off to wed.

I entered the cathedral by the west door, under an arch rimmed with dizzying zigzag patterns and guarded by the roaring stone heads of fantastical beasts—no doubt the hellish creatures that would tear apart sinners after death. They seemed to observe me with their bulbous eyes. *You're a sinner*, they seemed to say. *Anselm thinks you are the ultimate sinner...and wants us to eat your damned soul...*

My lightly-shod feet glided across the floor; everything, floor and walls and arches, was patterned in green and white stone. Candelabrum burned, the scent of tallow and beeswax heavy in the air amidst wafts of incense; cressets flickered in the small chapels on either side of the nave.

A tall, thin monk, his face hawkish, strode out of the hazy gloom towards me, his long black robes rustling, the cross and beads bound round his middle clacking like dry bones.

"Lady Edith," he said, "you are to follow me."

He made a hasty about-face, not glancing back to see if I was following him, and marched towards the chapter house of the cathedral. I hurried after him, astounded by his brusque, almost rude manner and increasingly more nervous by the second.

In the magnificent chapter house, Anselm the Archbishop of Canterbury was seated on one of the benches that ran around the circular chamber. Glorious paintings shone like jewels behind him;

scenes of Abraham, of Moses, of the Virgin Mary and the Christ Child, of the angelic hosts set against a backdrop of royal blue sky and myriad stars.

The Archbishop was a small, old man, the white hair sparse upon his furrowed brow, looking almost like a swaddled babe within the cocoon of his lavish robes. He had suffered much ill-health during his exile and the strain of his bodily afflictions showed on his lined visage. But although he appeared hunched and frail, as he raised his head, his watery eyes were keen and discerning…and not altogether friendly.

"Come, daughter, come closer," he ordered, extending his wizened hand with his great episcopal ring upon it. I moved forward and bent my knee to kiss the jewel and then stood back, head bowed, waiting for him to speak.

"So…" he said, "it has come to my attention that King Henry wishes to make you his bride."

"Yes, your Grace."

"And that you desire to join with him in holy matrimony."

"I…I do, your Grace."

"I have grave doubts that you are free to do so," he said, his tone growing severe. "Your Aunt, the Abbess Cristina, has informed me that you took a nun's vows as a girl. If that is true, all the pleading and begging in the world will not release you of those vows, for you are a Bride of Christ and not for the carnal bed of mortal man."

"I took no vows, your Grace," I announced in a strong clear voice.

"You say that your aunt, an esteemed abbess, is a liar?" He cast me a baleful stare from beneath bushy grey brows.

"As painful as it is to say…yes, I do accuse her of lying."

"And why would she do such a thing, a woman of God?"

"How can I read the hearts of others and know their reasons to commit sin?" Imploringly, I held out my hands, hoping he would see that I was sincere. "I can only imagine it is because she hates the Normans and does not wish me to marry one, thinking such a union beneath a descendent of Alfred."

Anselm harrumphed. "Surely, Cristina is wise enough to understand that the children of an overthrown royal house must find their way within the system as it now stands. As it is said in Romans: *Everyone must submit to the governing authorities, for there is no authority except that which is from God. The authorities that exist have been appointed by God.*"

"I am content with the words written in Romans," I said, "but I cannot speak for my aunt. You must ask her yourself, your Grace, if you would know more about the reasons for her actions."

The Archbishop made a low grunt, his disbelief in my story still all too evident.

"I took no vows," I reiterated, my voice rising. "I was meant to enter the convent only to be educated. Cristina forced me to wear the veil for my own safety and I rebelled against it. I trampled it upon the ground when my aunt was not looking."

"What about at St Mary's?" Anselm continued. "You were also seen wearing a veil there. I have several reports."

"It was no true nun's veil but a skein of black cloth made to resemble one. I learned that such dour raiment, indeed chased off unwelcome suitors—rogues of ill-intent, who would only bring dishonour to my name."

"*Hmmm.*" Anselm stroked his chin, observing me closely with those flinty eyes.

He still seemed dubious.

"I have never been dedicated, nor did I wear the veil of my own free will at Romsey, only when my aunt bid me or when I thought it might protect my virtue. If I cannot convince you, holy Father, I beg you bring this matter before a Church tribunal. That I should ask such a thing surely shows you how eager I am to cast off the untruths and slanders of my Aunt Cristina."

Anselm rose from his bench in a swish of vestments. "I fear I cannot make a decision this day. The truth is not clear in my mind. As you have suggested, I shall bring the case before a party of bishops, abbots and patrons of the Holy Mother church."

It was not exactly what I wished to hear but at least he had not denied me outright and ordered me to the cloister to become a nun whether I desired it or not. Perhaps I had sown a seed of doubt about my aunt's testimony after all. "I will send a message to you at Wilton with details of the day," he said, as he swished past me, "but you will not attend in person so as not to sway any of the judges."

I returned to Saint Mary's no further ahead with my marriage plans than I had been. I chewed my nails with nervousness as I heard how a huge contingent of bishops and abbots, lords and barons were gathering at Lambeth to discuss my fate.

Eventually, two archdeacons arrived at the gates of St Mary's with the intent to question the sisters. I knelt in the chapel, praying that the truth would prevail, as, Hambald of Salisbury and William of Canterbury grilled the sisters as to whether they thought I was, at any time, a professed nun.

After the archdeacons had taken down numerous statements and then departed for Lambeth, Sister Infirmarer sought me out. Feeling sick and giddy, I leaned against a pillar in the chapel. "Do you think they believe now?"

"I cannot say," said Sister Alice, "but I chided them for listening to Cristina of Romsey. Abbess she may be, but your royal parents believed she was abusing you, so she is not a reliable witness and likely has vengeance on her mind. I also told Hambald, whom I've known many years, 'Just look at Lady Edith. She is not wearing the wimple now, is she? She's dwelt at William Rufus's court; if she had become a nun, she'd have surely run from such a Babylonic furnace as that!'"

"My thanks for your kindness," I said, genuinely touched, though rather amused by the reference to the 'Babylonic furnace'.

"Oh, it's not kindness, Edith," she said. "I only speak the truth, because if I should tell a falsehood, even to please Father Anselm, who seems to desperately want you in the cloister, *HE* would not look kindly upon me…and I cannot have that!" She pointed to the alabaster crucifix affixed to the wall of the chapel. "Besides…It will keep my patients happy to hear tales of how I once vouched for the honesty of the Queen of England!"

Hambald of Salisbury appeared back at the abbey a few days later, asking to see me and Abbess Hawise in private. Though tingling with nerves, I managed to keep a cool composure. "The bishops have decided that you did not wear the veil as a nun," Hambald told me. "Some spoke of how years ago Bishop Lanfranc advised the wearing of the veil to deflect unwanted male attention. It was, at one time, a known practice, and the Bishop had insisted these unprofessed women should always be permitted to leave their convents."

"So...is it over," I asked in a hushed whisper, relief flooding through me in a warm rush.

The Archdeacon smiled kindly. "Near enough, child. But Archbishop Anselm wants you to appear before the court when the decision is spoken and consigned to the records."

"I will have a horse and an escort made ready for you," said Hawise, rising from her chair. "You must not delay, Edith; not for one moment. The King must have his Queen."

London rose on the horizon, smoky and dim under banded layers of grey clouds. Thick and turgid, the Thames looped alongside the road our party took, its vast waters filled with punts and ferries. "We are nearly there, Lady Edith." Hambald gestured with a gloved hand. "You can see the top of St Mary's church ahead. It belongs to the Archbishops of Canterbury, who have lodgings next to it."

I peered into the murky day. Birds alighted from the river, shrieking into the wintry sky. The church of St Mary's had been built by Goda, sister to Edward the Confessor. The first structure had been wooden, but now the church was an austere block of stone with crenels on its tower. Still, it felt right to have the confirmation of my fitness to marry Henry given in a place beloved of my distant Saxon kin. A new start, a new day; rebuilding from the ashes.

Reaching the boundary wall, a steward arrived to lead me into the episcopal mansion. As I was announced and shown into the hall, a sea of male faces turned towards me, some mitred, some tonsured, some with long hair, beards and rich clothes. Their expressions were solemn, unreadable.

Maurice, Bishop of London, who was chairing the proceedings, climbed stiffly from his seat, cleared his voice, and began to read out the results of the debate from a parchment scroll. I heard how Anselm had resisted, only giving in when he realised old Bishop Lanfranc had admitted that a nun's wimple was a good protection for noble and royal maidens dwelling in convents. However, even so, he had spoken words that seemed both cold and cruel—"I fear England shall not long rejoice in the children Edith of Scotland might bear…"

"Is there anything you would like to add, Lady Edith?" asked Bishop Maurice, rolling the scroll up once again.

"Yes," I said, stepping forward. "I would like to make a short statement, if I may."

Anselm, seated on the Bishop of London's right, looked unhappy, his brows lowering, but Bishop Maurice nodded. "Speak, child!" He gestured toward a bowl-haired scribe who sat at a bench. "Record Lady Edith's words, scribe."

"I still feel there is doubt amongst some of you as to my suitability for marriage with the King," I said, my gaze passing around the room. "I will swear a public oath before you all that I have spoken nought but truth, beginning to end. I do not wish gossips and evil-minded people in the future to question the legitimacy of any future children I might bear."

"That will not be necessary," said Bishop Maurice. "It is clear to the majority on this council you did not take religious vows, and you are therefore free to enter marriage with his Grace, King Henry."

Archbishop Anselm scowled, then steeled his face into stony acceptance.

I looked straight at him, and said, "You still seem unhappy, Reverend Father, even though these learned men have decided in my favour. Will I not have your blessing?"

He sighed and then rose with the help of two attendants and shuffled towards me. "For all my doubts, Edith of Scotland, I would not withhold a blessing." He made the sign of the cross over me. "Go now, and inform the King."

"I shall be grateful to you all my days, your Grace," I said. Anselm said nothing but for a brief second, I could have sworn the corner of his stern mouth turned upwards. Then that tiny smile was gone and he was sweeping away with his attendants.

I left the Archbishop's London dwelling with a joyous face. The day was cold and drizzly, yet I felt not the cold, nor heeded the rain.

Henry was waiting for me at Westminster.

Upon the Feast of Martinmas, Henry and I were wed within the hallowed halls of Westminster Abbey. At the same time, I was crowned Queen. I wore a gown of blue for the Blessed Virgin, cinched by a golden girdle about my waist, its sleeves long and billowy, embroidered with roses and stars around the cuffs. My unbound tresses flowed in a pale cascade to my hips; the last time I would be able to flaunt it, save for ceremonial crown wearing. As our entourage reached the abbey, walking under canopies that rippled and boomed in the cold wind, I noticed the crowds of well-wishers pointing and exclaiming at its glory; I might not have the beautiful face of Nest, but the hue of my hair, inherited from my English forebears, certainly caused favourable comment that day.

After Archbishop Anselm had recited the marriage vows, stern-faced and mitred, glimmering in the candlelit gloom in his rich vestments, Henry brought forth a ring, plain gold, gleaming like fire, and slipped it on my right hand. I stared at it; it was done. I was his and he was mine until death parted us.

Then Henry stepped aside and I knelt while Anselm anointed me with the Holy Oil. Prayers were spoken, telling the stories of brave women in Biblical times—Sarah, Rachel, Rebecca and Judith, all the great matriarchs of old whom I must try to emulate. Esther was mentioned too, she who brought her people to salvation—I admired her tale most of all for it had great meaning to me.

Finally, the crown, once worn by Henry's mother, Matilda, was brought out on a tasselled cushion and set firmly upon my brow. I rose, slightly dizzy under the unfamiliar weight, and a sceptre and an orb was placed into each hand.

I turned to face the congregation as the choir sang the Ta Deum, its glorious words echoing through the vastness of the abbey. This was followed by a solitary singer, his voice pure as an angel's, who sang a poignant song that brought hot tears to my eyes:

> *Now by the Tree is deep thrust root,*
> *Like to bear fair flower and fruit,*
> *This Tree, men all may understand,*
> *Twines with the Kings of England.*
> *The root below is the King's seed,*
> *Whereof our rulers should sprout indeed.*
> *Now has the Tree had twined its root,*
> *And like to bring fair flower and fruit—*
> *Dame Matilda, our Queen and Lady.*
> *Wedded to our sovereign Henry…*

I was no longer, to the people and the court, Edith, princess of Scotland.
I was Matilda, Queen to the King of England.

Preparation for the Christmas Feast and crown-wearing at Westminster Hall, the huge feasting hall built by William Rufus, was in full swing, leaving me little time to recuperate from my joint wedding and coronation. Twenty oxen were ordered, numerous pigs and sheep, dozens of chickens and eggs, pickled herrings and Henry's favourite—lampreys. I found these eels shuddersome, their faces resembling demons with sucking mouths rimed by spiny teeth, and knew I could not watch him eat them when they were served! (Let alone eat one myself.) Hopefully, there would be some dancing or minstrels to distract me while he gnawed on the slimy creatures…

At night, Henry and I spent much time, as newlyweds often did, in the privacy of our spacious bed. I was shy at first, as befitted a maiden, but Henry was a skilled lover. "I *must* give you pleasure," he said, as he lay atop me, our sweat mingled, my hair sticking in pale damp tendrils to his body and to mine. "Not only is it my duty as a husband, I have heard tell that children are not conceived unless the wife enjoys the bedding as much as her husband."

"Well, you have done your duty in that regard, Henry," I laughed.

"I have had plenty of practice since Rufus bought me a harlot when I was thirteen…" he said, and then he flushed, for he realised it was not appropriate to speak of such past encounters to his new bride.

"Forgive me," he murmured, his hand flipping back the coils of my hair to curl around my breast. "I have lived a soldier's life as well as a prince's. I am not a courtier with pretty words always on my tongue."

"It is fine, there is nought to forgive," I said but my voice came out a little shrill. I understood that many men had huge…*appetites*, and my new husband was one of them, as proved by his numerous bastards. Most royal and nobility kept mistresses and this was not cause for a wife's complaint, although I might wish it otherwise. Better Henry's lasciviousness, than what had been rumoured about his brother William!

Henry must have noticed my pained expression. "I love all of my baseborn children," he said. "That is why I allow so many of them to reside at court. With them, I can also make strong alliances against my enemies. However, Edith, *our* children will be more precious to me than all the gold and jewels on earth. They will want for nothing."

"I did not doubt that," I said. "I just pray…it happens soon."

"It will if I have any say in the matter," he said, his voice a deep rumble in his chest as he pulled me against him once more, eager for another round of bed-sports. Although tired and sore, I reached out to draw him closer, enfolding him in my hair and my limbs. In my head I prayed, *God, make our union blessed. Give us a son to make England strong!*

The Yuletide feast was every bit as lavish as Henry had planned. The Great Hall, in all its immense beauty, was decorated in holly, ivy and mistletoe, the fresh scent of the greenery mingling with the smoke from the central hearth and the muted fragrance of the herbs strewn in the rushes. Archbishop Anselm was there and a special royal guest from France—Prince Louis, a tall but rather hefty young man of similar age to me. He sat between Henry and the Archbishop, chatting merrily to both.

I wore my crown, as was common for royalty at Christmas, and wore a gown of golden hue, set off by a necklace of red and green cabochons set in gold. I had officially made my tiring women from Winchester, Emma and Helisent, my ladies-in-waiting, and my sister Mary and Nest attended upon me as well. The latter I still considered a companion of sorts but she had grown ever more distant since Henry announced our nuptials. She had had her sights upon him once, of that I was certain. Well, she would have to learn that beauty was not everything a man desired, especially a King. He could have beauties anytime but would always come back to his Queen…

A horrible thought suddenly struck me, and I went cold despite the muggy warmth of the chamber. Spots danced before my eyes and my ears rang as the raucous shouts of the carousing mummers, maskers, noblemen and knights faded into the background. I clutched at my wine goblet, inelegantly slurping its contents in the hope that the wine would steady my nerves

"Edi…I mean Matilda," said Mary, still unused to calling me by my new name. "What is wrong. You're so pale…"

"Just a moment's giddiness, "I said, patting her hand. "It…it's far too hot in here. It will pass."

"Maybe you are with child," she said hopefully.

"Maybe," I murmured, although I knew I was not. My courses had come as usual, crushing my hope for that month…

Before the high table, a group of musicians had gathered, beginning the first notes of a stately dance. Prince Louis arose in a rush of deep purple robes trimmed by squirrel pelts and swept in my direction, smiling "If her Grace the Queen would give me this honour?"

"Yes, of course, Prince Louis." I rose, eager to get away from the table, from Nest, whose gaze had drifted from the contents of her trencher to Henry. Perhaps innocently, I had to admit; she looked bored, despite garnering the attention of all the young gallants of the court. Henry, at least, was not returning her stare, having turned to converse with Anselm after Louis left his seat.

Louis led me out onto the floor and the dance began. I was amused to see my old companion, from the nunnery at Romsey, Sybil Montgomery, who had married Robert Fitz Hamon. She grinned and leaned over as we passed each other. "You have done well for yourself, Edith…your Grace, Queen Matilda. Very well."

Then Louis spun me around and we were facing other couples, the massive, puffing Hugh d'Avranches and his wife, Ermentrude of Claremont, and Richard de Redvers with his new bride Adeliza, Roger Bigod with the beauteous Alice de Tosni, who had hair as red as fire and skin like lilies.

Louis was an accomplished enough dancer, but owing to his spreading girth became very florid and sweaty by the end of the dance. Bowing, he excused himself from the floor in order to sit down, take some deep breaths, and regain his royal dignity.

Henry was still engrossed in Anselm's pronouncements so motioning Helisent to accompany me, I sought the quiet of the outside courtyard.

It was dark in the spacious yard with its chequered paving. Westminster Hall loomed behind me like a slumbering monster, its narrow windows glowing like eyes in the gloom. Across from it, stood the Palace, first built by Edward the Confessor and much modified by his Norman successors, the two Williams. Servants and household staff came and went, barely visible in the gloom; a night mist, chill and smelling of foetid water, had risen from the Thames, making ghosts of living men and shrouding the battlements of Hall, Palace and the adjacent abbey

Helisent did not look happy, dragging her cloak close around her shoulders. "Your Grace, I must insist we return to the banquet hall. It's not safe for you…there are men about and by the sound of it, they have been drinking."

"Oh, fie, Helisent," I chided. "Who would dare attack me in the grounds of my own palace, with my husband the King in the Hall next door? We will not stay out here long, but the dance I joined with Prince Louis was frenzied and the air hot and smoky. My throat is on fire!"

I walked out along the side of the Hall, pulling up the hood of the cloak Helisent had brought for me to conceal myself. I noticed now that there were indeed a lot of men passing hither and thither, laughing, singing, cursing, drinking. Straining my eyes, I recognised several barons and other nobles. Particularly noticeable were a gaggle of members of the infamous Montgomery clan, Sybil's rapacious brothers. They laughed and jested with each other, roughhousing like undisciplined youths.

They paid no heed to me and Helisent, half-furled in the dense river fog, but as a sudden breeze shifted the dense vapours, their voices were carried to my ears, clear as a ringing bell.

"Christ's Tongue, why did he wed her?" slurred one. "A Saxon woman. And very likely a sworn nun, though old Anselm said otherwise in the end—I wager Henry offered him a few bags of gold for that!"

"Did you see them up on the dais together?" sniggered another Montgomery. "God's Teeth, it was like watching 'Godric and Godiva'. I almost expected the King to start speaking the language of the peasant rabble."

"Or wearing barbarian trousers," chortled another. "Christ, what next. Pigs rooting in the Hall?"

I halted, unable to believe my ears. They were taunting me and Henry, their sovereign, implying we were nothing but ignorant country peasants. Implying that I had contaminated their precious Norman king with my inferior English ways. Tears burned my eyes, hot and furious. I could have thrown off my hood and railed at them like a madwoman, or even had them taken prisoner and marched to the Tower…but I managed to hold my rage in check. Henry would not be merciful to such men if he knew they mocked him—not only imprisonment but mutilation might follow. I thought of the traitor he had hurled to his death in Caen long ago; I truly did not want him to start his reign in England with such violence, such needless bloodshed. I must accept the slurs, for now at least, and turn the other cheek as the Bible advises. I must win the love of the Normans as well as the ordinary English folk…and make them change their minds about my worth.

I would be a Good Queen. My mother's memory would guide me; I would follow in her saintly footsteps as best I could.

I gestured to Helisent, who, having heard the sneers of the barons and knights, looked like a terrified rabbit. "Come, let us return to the Hall. I trust you will be discreet about what you've heard tonight; word of these slanders would greatly anger the King. I do not want him to start his reign consumed by anger. I will change the opinions of those hateful men in time, Helisent, I promise you that."

CHAPTER FOURTEEN

I threw myself into working alongside Henry in the governance of the realm. He was appreciative and admiring; he did not want a wife who was unlettered and could only simper and sew. I sat in on gatherings of the Royal Council and issued writs and charters, using my own seal, which bore the image of a queen carrying orb and sceptre.

I began trying to build up a relationship with Archbishop Anselm, vowing that I would cast the doubts he held about my past at Romsey from his mind. Slowly, he came round to me—his letters were cool, like those of a stern father, but I could tell his stance had changed; he sought to guide, not to condemn.

England was at peace for once, but I was aware it might not always be so—and soon I was proved right.

I lay asleep in Westminster Abbey, Helisent and other maids snoring faintly alongside my bed on their paillasses, when I heard the clang of stony bells ringing out across the city of London. I stirred, staring at the narrow slit of the window with its frosty horn covering—no hint of light beyond. The hour was late.

Swinging my feet down, I hissed for Helisent, Emma and the newest lady-in-waiting, young Gracia, to arise. Blinking in the feeble glow of the embers in the brazier, they sat up, drawing quilts and furs against the cold. Their teeth chattered. "What is it, your Grace?" Helisent said sleepily, rubbing at her eyes.

"The bell," I said. "Do you not hear it? Bells, tolling."

"I do, your Grace," said Helisent, "and wish that I did not. 'Tis a warning bell, I deem; something terrible is happening in the heart of this great city. Maybe fire or an assault by raiders unknown…"

"What if it's Norsemen?" Gracia gulped. "You know what they do with women they capture."

I shook my head, dubious. "No, they never come so far south, not anymore."

Helisent was on her feet, pulling on a robe. "I think we should barricade the door," she said, "and wait until the King sends word that it is safe to emerge."

"Do not be silly, Helisent." I motioned her and Gracia over to dress me. "I was not raised to cower in fear. I will find the King and take counsel."

Fully dressed, I reached for the latch on the heavy oak door. Helisent shrank away, terrified. "I beg you, my Lady Queen—do not go!"

"If you are so fearful, I grant you permission to wait here for my return," I said firmly, "but it is my duty to stand beside my husband, the King, if there is turmoil in the realm."

I slipped into the hallway, banging the door closed. I heard the latch fall into position again. Cold wind whistled down the corridor, making the flames of torches in their sconces leap and dance. Shadows ran amok, twisting and writhing into strange and sinister shapes.

Holding up my heavy skirt so that I could walk faster, I hurried down the passage toward the council chamber. As I drew near, I saw barons and knights and servants flooding in, their faces tense and white, their hair standing upright where they had leapt from their beds without even reaching for a comb.

Henry was standing in the centre of the chamber near the firepit. The smouldering cinders glowed sullenly, like demonic eyes, the redness spilling upward over Henry's enraged face. For one terrifying moment, his own eyes looked the colour of blood. Then they became dark…and full of wrath.

I hastened to his side. "Henry, what has happened?"

He seemed surprised to see me there, and for an instant, I thought he might rail at me and send me back to my apartments, but then he set a firm hand on my arm. "Ill news, my Queen. Ranulf Flambard…"

Flambard, the Flame Bearer, locked behind the adamant walls of the White Tower. Flambard, William's money and power-hungry bishop…and, some whispered, more besides. Never had there been a churchman so unholy.

"Is he dead?" I asked. Many had hated the embezzling bishop; it would not surprise me to find that one of his foes had slipped in amongst the household servants and stabbed or poisoned the miscreant. Certainly, such an act would irk Henry, for such justice was his alone to dispense, but the ringing bells and the sea of concerned faces spoke of more than a knife in the dark to slay the hated bishop.

"Dead? I wish he was damn well dead," growled Henry. "I should have strung him up from the first, with no care to his position in the church. No, he's not dead, wife…the wily bastard has escaped."

"Escaped!" Astounded, I goggled at him. "But…but none has ever escaped from Gundulf's White Tower."

"Till now," Henry snarled. "I would almost swear there is sorcery afoot…"

"Sorcery!" I cried, aghast.

"Did you not know?" Henry's voice was sharp as the crack of a whip. "They say his mother is a witch. She has but one eye and that one needs putting out…for it gives the evil eye! The harridan got together a band of men who supported my brother's rule, and in the cold fog off the Thames, managed to get Flambard out of the Tower with a rope that a sympathiser had smuggled inside concealed in an ale keg. The Bishop slid down the rope, falling the last ten feet—I wish he had broken his bloody neck! But no, his supporters dragged him away into the fog to where his foul dam waited with fresh horses. He is no doubt well on his way to a port by now, bruised but all too alive."

"Can you not pursue him?" I asked. "Surely a fast rider…"

Furiously he shook his head. "Some time passed before the alarm was raised. There are many places he could depart from and many routes he could take to the coast and then into Normandy. I have lost him…"

"Maybe it is for the best that he is gone. Perhaps he will hide abroad and bother us no more."

Henry shook his head again, more strongly. His teeth were gritted, bared like a beast's, such was his rage. "Do you not understand, Edith? My brother Robert is returning from Crusade with, I've heard, a beautiful wife and raised hopes for an heir, and a lot of anger towards me…for he believes England is his by right. My bandy-legged, big brother Curthose, aided by that thieving, conniving bishop, will soon bring war upon us!"

I was with child. The midwife confirmed my suspicions on the very day that it was announced Robert Curthose, aided by Ranulf Flambard, was sailing towards the south coast. He clearly intended to attack Winchester first…and that was where I was domiciled, unwell as breeding women often were, my belly heaving at the scent of almost all food.

The situation looked grim for Henry. Robert's time as a crusader had raised his esteem in the eyes of his fellows, and his beauteous bride, Sybilla, daughter of Geoffrey of Conversano, had brought an extensive dowry that made Robert very rich indeed.

Henry's most loyal barons had also dwindled. Old Hugh, the Earl of Chester, had become sick unto death and entered an abbey he had founded, where he renounced the secular world and joined the brethren. A man of immense size, a lover of wine and meat, he had grown so large he could scarcely move and now his huge body was shutting down, stinking and full of putrescence even though life clung to him still.

Robert de Belleme had begun his cruel tricks also. Although he had sworn fealty to Henry at his coronation, he had quickly gone back on his word. Numerous others followed him in breaking their oaths, massing behind the Conqueror's eldest son instead.

Henry paced the halls of Winchester Castle, listening to dispatches from couriers, planning in close-quartered meetings with Anselm and those few who remained loyal.

He came to my bedchamber late one night after one such meeting, his face creased and weary, suddenly aged. I lay abed, Helisent fanning my hot face. Emma and Gracia had been trying to tempt me to eat small cakes and sweetmeats but all turned sour in my belly. I had been in and out of the privy all day, spewing until my ribs ached, which worried me for I felt unnaturally weak and sick. I was assured this was normal in a pregnancy, but I felt an ominous cloud descend over me as the day progressed. I had never feared death so much, and I clung to Henry's tunic in shame, embarrassed that I appeared so fragile.

"Curthose has arrived at Portchester," he told me in a low voice. "He marches inland even as we speak."

I pressed my hot, sticky hand over my mouth, unable to get any words out for a brief moment. Then, breath coming in gasps, I stammered, "Will…will he besiege the castle, do you think?"

Henry rubbed my shoulders, attempting to bring some small physical comfort…for his words could not. "I expect he will…if he comes here."

"Is there any doubt that Winchester is his destination?"

"I have sent a missive by swiftest courier, telling Robert that you are in Winchester and with child. He is your godfather. Maybe such news will move his stony heart. Do not count on it, though, Edith," he said, with a sharp bark of a laugh. "He is not known for tenderness, and he hates me, ever since William and I played a prank on him long ago when we were boys in Normandy."

"I dread to think what you did," I murmured, cradling my unsettled belly.

"We emptied a chamber pot on his head from a tower window. Ruined his garments and made him a laughing stock in front of his fellows," said Henry wryly. "He would have got over his shame, I think, but he could not bear that our sire refused to punish us. Father didn't like him much; he was the one who gave him his nickname Curthose and mocked his stubby legs. *No one* likes Robert, unless they find him useful in some way, like his good friend Robert de Belleme." His lip lifted in a sneer, recalling the ill-starred baron, who had defected to the side of his former companion, Robert.

"Anyway." He slapped his hand down on his thigh. "I must tarry no longer in Winchester but ride out to face my brother…wherever he chooses to meet me."

"Oh Henry, take care," I said, glancing upwards, bitter bile strong on my tongue, as fear—and another wave of sickness—gripped me.

"I shall," he said, surprisingly cheerful, as if he had not heard the concerned whispers that had proliferated through the court of late. Whispers that he could not prevail against Robert Curthose. Then he leaned and kissed the top of my head. "You rest, and try not to fret overmuch. Have the chaplain come to you and have your ladies sing soothing songs. You must take care, Edith. After all...it is my heir you carry beneath your belt."

His fingers drifted down to brush against my belly, swelling by the day. He gave a deep sigh, his jaw tightening with resolve, and then he strode from the chamber and away.

I burst into tears, burying my face in my hands. I had not thought his kingship would be challenged so soon, and twinges of guilt ate at me as well—the barons did not like him having an English queen for his consort, so my unwelcome presence was yet another reason to desert their sworn liege lord.

Helisent came to comfort me, and for a few hours the castle was full of the noise of war-like preparation—gates clanging, men shouting, horns blowing, horses champing and neighing. At length, the sounds faded, departing with the host that marched under the castle barbican to join the levies gathered in the nearby marketplace. The horns shouted out once more, brazen and fierce, echoing around the donjon, and then banners were raised and Henry's army, almost pitifully small, exited through the sturdy town gate nearest the castle.

From the window embrasure, I watched as best I could through the narrow crack. The light was warm and gold over Winchester, the dust clouds left by the passing host shimmering in the hot summer air.

Another wave of nausea gripped me, and the scene of walls and street and dust wobbled and blurred in my vision. Clutching the window's stone sill, a cold and clammy flush chilled me to the marrow, despite the heat of the day.

"Your Grace?" Helisent's nervous cry sounded both as loud as buzzing bees yet strangely distant at the same time.

A cramp needled my belly, sharp as if I had been stabbed. I stared down towards my feet, aware of a sudden, unnerving change.

Even as I watched, a tendril of blood ran down my ankle and spread around my jewelled slipper. I watched in horror as it grew, widening around me in a shallow pool, and then I was screaming...

The babe was lost. A tiny girl, her fingers nigh translucent, slid into the world on a red sea. The priest was there to baptise her and see her pass into heaven from the earth she had never walked. She took a few small soundless gasps of air, then fell still.

I called her Euphemia, the name of a saint who had faced the wheel, a pit of knives, a burning oven and an arena full of lions. Euphemia, sent before her time, had fought too, but had also gone to the glory of the heavenly Father. I wrapped her in white linen and then she was carried away to be anointed with sweet herbs and unguents before burial within the cathedral. Her grave would lie unmarked, save in my heart, and it was some comfort that she was near the resting bones of many of her illustrious ancestors, who had been moved there from the Old Minster nearby.

I was weak with grief and loss of blood, though at least my travail had been brief. I lay abed, managing to smile grimly when a messenger came with the news that Robert Curthose had indeed deliberately bypassed Winchester to spare his god-daughter the ordeal of a siege. He was now hurrying towards London and Henry was marching to cut him off. What would happen at that meeting was anyone's guess.

As I lay, aching and heartbroken in the summer heat, I did not much care about the battle's outcome. I thought only of Euphemia, those tiny gasps on those rosebud lips, the blue-veined eyes that never opened, the hands that glowed translucent in the sun as if filled by God's light. My firstborn, now lying in the dark beneath the flagstones of Winchester Cathedral.

Henry returned to the town a week or so later. Someone had informed him of my plight and he entered my chamber full of concern. It was not right he was there, as I had not yet been churched after the birth, but who would dare naysay the King? He was a Norman warrior; he would do as he pleased. If priests or bishops chided, he would do the penance and be done.

"I was informed of the evil news about the child when I reached Winchester," he said, seating himself on a stool near the bed.

"Forgive me, I failed you," I said weakly.

A look of anger crossed his features. "No, you did not, madam. Such things are common enough with women, I am told. We will have others...many others."

I laughed bitterly, on the verge of tears. I could not imagine going through such torment again...but knew I must. It was my duty, as a wife and a Queen.

"Not right away, of course," he said, noting my distress. "I am not a barbarian. I have spoken to the physic and your midwife and taken advice from them."

"Let us not talk of it." I struggled up on an elbow, wanting to talk of anything but babies and children. My body ached, deflating and shrivelling—battered, beaten and empty. "What of Robert Curthose?"

"I assume you know that my brother and I have signed a peace treaty."

"Yes, at Alton. I am surprised it ended without fighting."

He rubbed his beard. "Neither of our armies seemed much inclined to fight. It would be father against son, cousin against cousin ...brother against brother. Not a happy situation and not an event I would like in my first year as King if it could be avoided. So, we met in my tent and thrashed out an agreement between us...Robert has agreed to renounce his claim on England."

"Truly? What did you offer him?"

"A handsome stipend. Three thousand marks. And I have given him all my properties in Normandy, save one."

"Will he hold to the terms of this treaty?" I was dubious; it seemed too good to be true.

Henry shrugged. "Who knows? Like most of us, he needs money. His is sailing home, at any rate, with not one drop of blood spilt."

"A relief for us all."

"For now."

"So you *do* believe he will break the treaty after all?"

Henry shrugged. "My brother is unpredictable...but there was another part to the treaty that neither of us was keen on. It was the bishops who pushed us towards it."

"What was it?" My eyes locked on my husband's face. He looked uncomfortable now, shifting on his stool.

He sighed and his gaze met my own. "We swore to be each other's heir in the event one or both of us should remain childless."

I was silent, my hands knotting together, my heart hammering. Head bowed, I stared down at the body that had betrayed me.

"So, Edith," I heard my husband whisper, his voice hoarse, strained. "The fate of the kingdom of England may well depend on you. On a living child born from us both."

It was a hard, painfully hard, burden to bear.

As soon as I was fully recovered from the nightmarish loss of my daughter, Henry returned to my bed. Every night, often more than once a night. He was like a man driven, his desire for an heir overriding all. Occasionally he played the doting lover, bestowing me with kisses and caresses, slow and languourous; at other times he rutted like a boar, almost as if he had forgotten I was there, pinned beneath his muscled, sturdy body.

One night, he ran his thumb along my jawline, seeking. He wiped a tear that had come from the corner of my eye and made a sound of dismay. "Edith? Have I hurt you in some way? You weep…"

I opened my mouth to tell him that, although my body had healed, my heart had not, as yet. That in my waking dreams, I saw Euphemia, glowing as if filled with light, and heard those soft gasps she made, her first and last. But the words would not come.

Henry stared down at me, perplexed. "You do enjoy our bedsports, don't you? The physicians say it is imperative that women feel pleasure along with their husband, or conception often will not take place."

I blinked back more tears. "I have no complaints, my lord King," I said dully, knowing that if I expressed my true thoughts, he might grow furious.

"Good!" He let his hand drift along my thigh. "Are there any signs?"

"Not yet," I said.

He gave an annoyed sigh. "All these bastards I have and yet my own lawful wife does not quicken…"

I bit my lip and shut my eyes, holding him closer while I wished for him to spill his seed and leave me to find the solace of sleep. Though I knew there was no real solace; Euphemia would rise before me, near and yet so far, in my troubled dreams.

And then it happened. My moon-courses ceased and I had the same sickness in the early hours that I'd had with Euphemia. I dared not tell the King right away, lest the bleeding came or the sickness proved to be some temporary malady from spoilt food. But when a second month passed without courses, I knew I was indeed with child again.

Learning of the news, Henry immediately ceased his frequent trips to my bedchamber. In fact, he insisted I leave Winchester for peace and solitude at the manor of Sutton Courtney in Oxfordshire, where the air was purer and the streets less busy. However, once I was settled in, he sent me lavish gifts to show his pleasure in my pregnancy—missals and manuscripts, imported silks and fine furs, jewelled slippers for my feet, a dark green cloak with gold traceries, a girdle studded with red stones. Food and drink arrived at Sutton Courtney too—sugared dates, cherries and oranges from the south; tender kid and slices of chicken in vinegar sauce; wheat bread and pots of heavily salted butter; wine mixed with pomegranate juice, the latter from Spain.

Two midwives were hired to tend me at all times and advise me in my daily activities. They were far stricter than the old woman I had in Winchester and, truth be told, quite bossy, even though I was their Queen.

"You must not drink anything too cold," admonished one, tutting as she mixed a drink of warm dry wine. "For cold engenders girls…and we do not want that, do we?"

"I hope you remembered to clench your first when you lay in…congress with our Lord King," shrilled the other. "It is known that clenching your fist aids in the conception of boy children!"

"Make sure you never eat a fish's head at table," the first midwife went on to warn, her tone grim, "or, God forbid, a hare's head, no matter how nicely stewed. A fish head will give the child a downturned mouth while a hare's head will almost certainly cause a cleft lip."

I nodded at their ridiculous statements, not truly believing a single one, and let them get on with their ministrations. It was easier to just agree and hence there would be no stress to the growing babe.

The year passed on, seasons flashing by. My morning sickness vanished and I felt healthier than I had throughout my pregnancy with Euphemia. When the time of the quickening came, this babe was far stronger in its fluttering and shifting, almost as if it pounded the walls of my womb to let me know it was there. Showing me that it was strong, far more so than its poor, doomed sister. Showing me that it would come out fighting and win.

Henry's personal physician, Faricius, the Abbot of Abingdon Abbey, came every week or so to examine me. He was Italian, a short, spare man with wiry black hair and lively hazel-brown eyes that missed nothing. His skills in medical matters were so renowned he had rebuilt parts of his monastery with the monies paid by grateful patients for his cures and leechcraft. He was also a lover of books, which gave us common ground for conversation during my examinations. When he was away on the duties of his abbacy, another famous Italian physic, Grimbald, would come in his place. Grimbald was held in high esteem by my husband the King, not only as a doctor but as a dream interpreter.

I was not so certain of that art, finding it a little close to divination, which I considered sinful, but Henry liked the man so much that he often allowed him to sleep on a pallet in his bedchamber. When Grimbald was with me, we spoke mostly of medical issues and he further advised me on what I must and must not do while I was with child. One day, however, after my night had been full of strange and disturbing visions, I decided to ask his opinion on what I had seen in my sleep.

"Last night I dreamt of a flying crown. Not borne by angels or carried on the wings of birds, it was flying through the sky with an agency of its own. The sky behind was stormy, with lightning crackling and a great, roaring wind. Below was a battlefield, and two armies strove together, but I could not see the banners. The crown began to fall, spinning as it neared the ground, and then two hands shot out, each one grasping a side and striving to wrest it from the other. The hands were cut by the crown's tines and bled upon the earth…"

Grimbald folded his arms, frowning, deep in concentration for a moment. Then he lifted his head, nodding. "It is obvious to me, Highness…you dream of the crown that will one day be your son's legacy. Only it would seem he must fight for his right. Perhaps his Uncle Robert or his heirs might dispute his accession."

I did not tell him one of the hands looked too small and fine to belong to a man. This augury was unwholesome nonsense anyway, even if Henry was inclined to believe in it.

I sighed. "Well, I want no more such visions to trouble my rest, Grimbold. Can you not give me a draught to ensure sound sleep?"

"Aye, your Grace," he said, full of good cheer. "A tea made from valerian. Or, even stronger…lettuce soup."

My stomach lurched and I grimaced. "I will tell the midwives what you suggest…and endeavour to stomach it."

Grimbald left the chamber and in due time I had my lettuce soup simmering before me, unappetising but necessary. I spooned it up, deep in thought, trying to ignore the unpleasant taste.

Two hands clutching the same crown…one female… That image was burnt in my mind…but luckily, with calming teas and potions in my belly, I dreamed of it no more; not that night, nor any night to come.

My travail began in February, not long after Candlemas. Again, it was earlier than it should have been, but Faricius, in attendance with the midwives at his shoulder, told me that with good care, the child should survive.

I was not so fearful this time as the pains took me, great cramps that swelled and went. The baby was strong, all along I could feel it. Even though born early, it would live and thrive.

It would be a son. A future king.

The labour went on from noontide throughout the long night. Candles were lit and a girl from the village with a sweet voice was brought in to sing. One of the midwives cast down primrose and violet petals to freshen the air. I lay abed with Faricius hovering nearby. A holy relic of St Margaret, patron saint of birthing women, was placed into my hands. The Abbot had sent for it in preparation for the birth. The older midwife bustled in with heated water in a basin; the younger, once she had finished strewing her blossoms, tied an amulet in a little linen bag to my ankle. Made of pure virgin wax, the amulet bore magic words in Latin to help ease the baby out—*Maria virgo peperit Christum. Elizabet sterelis peperit Johannem Baptistam. Adiuro te infans si es masculus aut femina per patrem et filium et spiritum sanctum ut exeas et recedas ultra ei non noceas neque insipientiam illi facias amen. Videns Dominus flentes sorores Lazari ad monumentum lacrimatus est coram iudeis et clamabat Lazare, veni foras et prodiit ligatis manibus et pedibus qui fuerat quatriduanus mortuus.*

That done, the midwife rubbed a smooth piece of reddish-brown sard-stone, rumoured to ease the pains of childbirth, over my distended belly. It made no difference in the pain, but at least the stone was cool against my burning flesh; in the closed chamber, shuttered and with a fire burning, I was already awash with sweat, my unbound hair darkened by dampness.

The contractions within my womb grew stronger; animal urges overwhelmed all manner and breeding, and I grunted and puffed like a sow, almost unaware of my surroundings, wanting nought but for the agony to cease.

"Nearly there, your Grace!" cried one of the midwives. "A few more pushes!"

"Calm your breathing," ordered Faricius. "Concentrate. The child is nearly here…the top of the head is visible."

My heart was beating like a drum but I tried to concentrate on the task at hand—the most important task of a Queen. A violent spasm speared through me, and I gave a strangled cry as I bore down as hard as I could…

I fell back against the bolster, gasping…and suddenly there was a flurry of the midwives' aprons and then the shrill, fierce, angry screams of a newborn. Faricius, gestured to the midwives to clean the infant, then wrap it in linen. Once done, he took it from them and approached the bed.

"My son...let me see my son," I gasped, struggling into an upright position.

"Your Grace..." The Italian physician's face was expressionless. "You have a healthy daughter."

Henry had decreed that if he had a son he would bear the name of his father, William...but a girl, we had not talked of what she might be called. When couriers were sent to the King at Westminster, advising him of the birth, I sent a letter telling him that, as our daughter was baptised on the day of her birth, in the usual custom, I had named her Adelaide. I chose a Norman name for her, as that would be her father's expectation.

Henry wrote back immediately, full of joy that he had another healthy child, despite the disappointment of Adelaide's sex. He asked me to journey to Westminster with the baby as soon as I was churched.

I recovered quickly from the birth and was soon eager to leave my rather solitary existence at Sutton Courtney. A full month I had to wait, but the moment the *Benedictio mulieris post partum* Rite had taken place and the priest said, 'Go in peace', I ordered my goods packed in chest and placed on wains. When the packing was finished, the swaddled babe, wrapped in silks and furs, was carried by her wetnurse Goda into a waiting chariot. The chamberlain graciously handed me in after her and I settled down amidst the cushions and rugs. The roads were long clear of snow and ice, and no rain had recently fallen, so I hoped we would make good time on the road to London.

I watched the manor of Sutton Courtney through the window, fading into a distant haze of mist.

Londoners emerged in droves to cheer as my entourage passed through the city streets. At Westminster, trumpeters emerged to greet me, and carpets spread out for me to walk upon. I alighted from my chariot, a golden bliaut swirling around my ankles, my hair in ribbon-laden braids beneath a jewelled circlet and snow-white veil. A mighty roar rang out from onlookers both humble and noble. Women threw flowers into the air. Goda handed little Adelaide to me, and the cries of acclaim rang out again louder than the trumpets. I walked with the baby cradled in my arms to the door of the palace as the crowds cheered in delight. Although she was a girl, they had great love for her, it seemed, especially those of English ancestry, for in Adelaide, indeed, the blood of Norman and Saxon was commingled.

Henry was waiting in the Hall, hale and hearty in a red velvet robe, gold gleaming on his brow and around his throat. He took Adelaide from me and held her aloft to show the assembled members of the court. "My daughter Adelaide!" he cried. "My first legitimate child...though doubtless only the first of many if the Queen is as fertile as her sainted mother!"

The assembled crowd roared and I smiled wanly. The baby began to cry, agitated by the vast eruption of sound. "We have had a long journey, husband," I whispered near his ear. "Do I have your permission to retire early?"

"Of course, of course," said Henry. "I did not expect you to join the celebration after a long ride in a jarring wagon. Go to your rest and take our daughter with you; she's crying...no doubt she wants the pap." His gaze wandered over to the wetnurse, Goda, a plump, fair-haired girl, her heavy breasts straining at the lacing on her simple gown. He smirked, and I felt my belly knot up. I understood my husband was a man of lusty tastes...but if it was his nature, why so blatant, right next to me?

"Goda, come!" I ordered sharply and whirled towards the door leading into the inner recesses of the palace, with the poor girl, wondering what she had done wrong, trailing at my heels.

It was no lie that I was bone-weary and I slept for almost three days straight, Helisent and Emma tending me with gentle care. Adelaide had been taken to the palace nursery with her wetnurse. The nursery was farther away from my bedchamber than the spare chamber at the more homely Sutton Courtney, and I found myself pining for my daughter, wondering if she might cry, or ail, and fearful I would never hear her if she needed me.

I had seen but little of Henry, busy with the daily duties of a king—Mass, then meeting the common folk to accept their petitions and hear their grievances, followed by discussions about various policies with the nobles and clergy. The day would end with the court roistering in the Great Hall made by William Rufus, as large as a palace itself, where Henry would receive news from England's shires and from abroad before granting favours or removing them, giving gifts to the faithful, sealing letters and grants. Swan and venison would lie on the table, and the best musicians in London would play while the court ate and danced.

I had cried off as 'indisposed' which was not truly a lie. I felt unready to retake my place as Queen so soon. After losing Euphemia, I feared, like any humble countrywoman, that evil demons would spirit my infant away if I was not close by to fend them off. My chaplain told me all was in the hands of God and that I must not worry overmuch, as it might seem as if I questioned Him…but the fears in my heart would not disperse.

Henry, at least, had not insisted I front his feasts as yet…or return to his bed. Indeed, when he visited my apartments for brief moments, he merely kissed my cheek in almost brotherly fashion, although he brought me little gifts—a breviary, a jewelled pendant, furred gloves.

I began to ruminate, not just on the health and wellbeing of Adelaide, but on the infidelities of my husband. I recalled how he'd looked at Goda, how he had many of his bastards at court, and often their mothers too…

Disturbed, I could not sleep. While Helisent and Emma lay on their bed-pallets, softly snoring, I lay in my bed chewing my nails to the quick with nervousness, waiting to hear the wail of my babe…or maybe my husband the King's bold laughter.

I heard neither of these things, but, suddenly, there was the sound of furtive footsteps outside the door. A servant—no, none had been called. The King himself—no, he always sent a message prior to his arrival.

The footsteps passed on and then began to fade. I listened intently. A woman's feet, I deemed, wearing slippers that were soft and made minimal noise on the floor. I leapt from my bed as quietly as possible so as not to disturb the ladies in waiting, and drew a heavy robe over my night-shift. Drawing on my own slippers, as it was far too cold to go barefoot, I opened the door a crack and slid into the corridor beyond.

The torches in their brackets had burnt down; a smoky haze hung over the hallway, winding like the shroud of a wayward spirit. Silent, I moved along the wall, my hand pressing against the chill stone for support.

Up ahead, I spotted a flitter of movement, the swing of a robe's hem. A red robe. A kingly scarlet robe lined with ermine fur.

My belly lurched and I stifled a cry with my hand.

It was the King. My husband. And he was creeping about his own palace like a thief.

He did not want to be seen, I understood that from his furtiveness. And he did not wish to visit me, for he had passed on by.

My shocked sickness began to dissipate, replaced by a growing anger. How dare he go to some tryst almost under my nose? I strode after his retreating back, eager now to confront him, but also secretly hoping I would be proved wrong.

I reached the end of the corridor, which joined another leading to the nursery. Could Henry have gone to see the baby? I stumbled on, walking more quickly, growing clumsy as my fear and anger mingled.

No sign of Henry. He had gone. Even as I took a step back, thinking I had lost my quarry and having second thoughts about my plans to confront him, the door of the nursery drifted open, the candles inside casting a warm summery glow onto the floor.

Enfolded by shadows, I pressed myself against the wall. Goda stumbled out, hair wild, its fair strands glowing like gold in the candlelight, her dress dishevelled and open almost indecently. She ambled off in the direction Henry had taken.

My rage re-ignited, burning hot as a glede. It was as I had suspected. Henry lusted after Goda and was tupping the slattern while our daughter was left, alone and defenceless, in her cradle! I stormed down the corridor, almost blind with anger. At the end were the castle privies and then another long passageway through the palace apartments.

I rushed toward the garderobes...just as a sleepy-eyed, unsuspecting Goda appeared from behind a privy curtain. "Where...where is he?" I hissed, grabbing her shoulders.

"W-wha...your Grace. You're hurting me!"

"Why are you out here? Where is the King?"

"The King?" The girl looked genuinely bewildered. "I-I do not know, your Grace."

"Then why are you here, traipsing around with your paps half out like a harlot?" I cried, trying to resist the urge to shake her.

"Oh...oh no..." She grasped at her gaping dress, pulling the sides close together with her hand. "I didn't mean...I didn't think anyone would see. I was just stealing away quickly to use the privy."

"You have a chamber pot, don't you?"

She winced, embarrassed. "I ate too much at table and I—I..." Her cheeks turned crimson. "Well, I didn't want the Lady Adelaide to be assailed by foul humours until a servant came to take the pot."

Goda seemed so distressed and confused that I began to waver in my conviction that she was tupping Henry. As she started to cry, I realised I had made a terrible mistake. It was my turn to be embarrassed. "Go back to the nursery, Goda," I said. "Do not leave Adelaide again, do you understand? Other nursemaids are meant to relieve you throughout the night...although I understand you had a fair enough reason not to await them."

"Yes, my Queen," she gasped and fled down the corridor to the nursery.

I stood there in the cold, smoky gloom, staring at the three privies with their chutes that slid down to dump waste into the river as if I expected Henry to guiltily emerge from one.

He did not. I knew the wise thing would be to seek my bedchamber again, forget my mad flight through the palace, laugh and make excuses similar to Goda's if Helisent or Emma asked where I had been.

But I did not go back. What malice or madness had set a flame in me, I cannot say, but I wanted to find my husband, find out the truth of his action, even if I was made an utter fool in the end. Taking a shuddering breath, I began to pick my way through the shadows of the next corridor.

Nearing the last door before the stairwell that led to the lower floor, I suddenly heard a laugh from behind the stout oak. A high and flirtatious woman's laugh…followed by the burr of a deep male voice that I recognised all too well. Henry's voice, although I could not hear the words.

I paused. More laughter…and other sounds. Half of my mind screamed '*Flee, flee*', but the other roared, '*Go on! Go on*!'

I flung the door open.

On the bed was Henry, naked, the candlelight turning his skin warm copper. Beneath him lay a woman, her raven hair falling in luxuriant coils across the covers and over the edge of the bed.

It was Nest.

Worse, in her unclad state, I could see the signs of pregnancy upon her, the slight swell of her belly, the roundness of her paps.

I stood, staring, unable to find words. Nest turned her head, saw me, and gave a shriek, pushing Henry away and grabbing a coverlet around her shoulders. Henry showed no such modesty, leaping to his feet at once.

"Edith!"

"I wondered why you had scarcely seen me since my return from Sutton Courtney. I expected you would take lovers when I was absent, although the thought pained me, but Nest… *She was my friend…*"

Nest started to speak, to argue; Henry held up a hand for silence and cast her a warning glare whereupon she shut her pretty mouth with a snap. The King flung on his discarded tunic and approached me, grasping my arm none-to-gently. "We must talk."

He led me to his chamber, kicking aside his pages and squires who were asleep before the door. When they were gone, he sat down on a bench before the fire and motioned me to sit too.

"You were not meant to see that," he said gruffly.

"I can well imagine," I said, eyes narrowed. "A harlot might have shocked me, but no more than that, for a prostitute is nothing. But Nest…she is a princess and once we were friends. That is what hurts, Henry; it hurts like a sword-blow." I sucked in a shuddering breath. "And...it was clear to see that she is with child. Is it yours?"

He nodded, with some reluctance. "Yes...yes, it is mine."

"I want her gone from court, Henry. I will not countenance you swiving her when I am in attendance. Not her. Send her to some safe castle to wait out the birth of her child, then marry her off to one of your barons. At least she had proved herself fertile; some of them would be glad to have your cast off."

He glared at me, his eyes almost black. He was angry but I cared not; I was incensed too. "Very well...I will. But I was only thinking of your comfort."

"Were you?" I laughed, icily. "How considerate."

He scowled, looking fiercer than ever. "I...I did not think you really liked...it. That maybe your Aunt Cristina put it into your head that even marital congress is sinful. That maybe you were more inclined to be a nun."

I sputtered in indignation. "I have never denied you, and you know well I never intended to take the veil. You malign me. It I fully intend to give you the son and heir you need. I have heard that your brother Curthose has got fair Sybilla of Conversano with child. We must...keep up. It would not do well for him to engender a legitimate male heir when you have none."

"If it is your intention to beget my son, then who am I to shirk my husbandly duty?" He lifted a curious eyebrow, his wrathfulness abating and his dark eyes growing less cold.

"Yes, that *is* my intention," I said forcefully. "I would never lie to you, nor would I shirk my duty...to you and to England."

I slipped into his arms, not truly desiring him that night, but I refused to see my position usurped, not by Nest, not by anyone. "Hopefully our union will bear fruit as soon as soon as possible," I whispered as my robe slipped from my shoulders and pooled on the floor

Nest was sent away from Westminster the next morning. I watched her from the height of the wall, wrapped in my best winter cloak, the hood pulled up. How she felt about it I did not know or care. Henry had already started fishing around for prospective marriages for her—after the child's birth, of course. I heard the name Gerald of Windsor mooted; a fitting match. He was the Constable of Pembroke Castle in Wales, so at least Nest was back with her own people …even if Gerald was many years her senior and a dour, straightforward man. Her frivolity would soon be curbed, I wagered.

Henry and I were happy at that time and spent time together processing around the kingdom. I ordered bridges built and hospitals for the sick and those afflicted by leprosy to be raised. I courted the favour of Archbishop Anselm, and although our past was rocky, when he heard of my good works toward the poor, the last of his reservations about my past vanished…and I began to see him almost as a second father, wise, learned and holy.

All was not right within England at this time, however. Robert de Belleme was still committing criminal and treasonous activities, maiming freemen who crossed him, raiding the lands of his enemies, and building unlicensed fortresses, so Henry summoned him to court to answer forty-five charges against him. The baron refused, so Henry brought an army against his castles, first the mighty stronghold of Arundel and then Bridgwater, Shrewsbury and Tickhill. De Belleme, his English possessions lost, fled on fastest ship to Normandy, followed by his brothers Arnulf and Roger. A collective sigh of relief went up in all quarters, from peasant to king, when that troublesome family departed England's shores—but I feared we had not heard the last of them. No doubt now they were toadying up to Robert Curthose and trying to foment trouble, as was embedded in their volatile natures.

The court moved to Winchester after the banishment of Robert de Belleme and his brothers. The summer was long and tedious with Henry often far from home, mopping up after the fractious sons of the notorious Mabel. Sometimes I managed to visit Mary at Wilton, a journey I was always eager to make, for the good people of the town loved me dearly and always gave great welcome. Another light in my life was the presence of my youngest brother, David. He had come down from Scotland to experience the English court. Now aged fifteen summers, he had grown into a handsome and intelligent youth who took readily to court life but was also a reminder of my homeland and able to fill me in on events taking place there.

News arrived in October that Normandy was rejoicing and mourning simultaneously—Robert Curthose had his long hoped-for heir but his wife, the fair Sybilla, had died shortly after the birth. The infant was named William, after the Conqueror, and given the nickname Clito—*man of noble blood*, a Prince.

Now I was even more eager to give Henry a son, for William Clito would have a claim to the English throne, and Henry's only legitimate child was our daughter, Adelaide. While there was no law in England against a female monarch, what man amidst the proud, crowing barons of Norman blood would throw himself behind a woman, especially one who also bore English and Scottish blood? Fighting would ensue, civil war might well erupt...It did not bear thinking about.

My ladies-in-waiting leapt into action to help, hunting down all sorts of food and drink rumoured to aid in conception—asses' milk, fish fried with the liver of a hare, even a potion made of expensive mandrake root.

I do not know whether any of those foul-tasting remedies had any effect, but to my delight, I missed my courses once and then a second time, right around December 8, the Feast of the Conception of the Most Holy and All Pure Mother of God. Although the midwife told me it was still far too early to tell the King, I could not resist, and a Merry Yule it was that year with Henry and I in high spirits and the court full of merriment and ribaldry.

After the Twelfth Night celebrations were over, I decided to stay in Winchester rather than go to London or Windsor with my husband. As I was in a delicate condition, I had no wish to ride in a chariot over the rough and muddy road and risk the much longed-for babe. A few months later, Henry sailed to Normandy to gauge the situation there, so I remained in Winchester, walking the castle gardens as my belly grew bigger and rounder. "This one will surely be a boy," said Helisent, nodding wisely. "You carry him differently in your womb to the Lady Adelaide; I can see it."

"I thought Adelaide would be a boy, she kicked so strongly," I said ruefully as I walked through the summer flowers—beds of purple betony, the cure-all; *Oculus Christi*, which made a fine eyewash and attracted honeybees; pink, red and blue hyssop; Lady's Mantle and Tansy—the herb administered to ease the pangs of childbirth. "God will give us whatever He wills. But I do pray it is a boy, especially now that Duke Robert has a son."

Helisent sighed, plucking a yellow buttercup and twirling it between her fingers. "Ah, yes, the motherless babe of Short Legs."

I pretended to be shocked. "How rude, Helisent. Calling a royal Duke 'short legs'."

"His own father did and so does his Grace." Helisent tossed her head, nearly dislodging the veil covering her deep auburn plaits. "But I shall try to remember his proper title next time he comes up in conversation—*Royal Duke* Short Legs."

I laughed and so did Helisent but as abruptly as it came, the laughter left me. The child in my belly stirred uncomfortably. "Robert will want his son to be King of England, Helisent, as it is unlikely that he will ever sit on the throne himself. That is why it's so important I bear a son—and sooner rather than later."

Helisent looked thoughtful. "If you have no son, surely an alliance could be made. Lady Adelaide with William Clito. I know their blood is close but dispensations are given out often enough…"

"No. Halt. I do not wish to hear it." I swished my hand before her face, silencing her. "Adelaide will have better than that, Helisent."

She bowed her head, realising she had spoken recklessly on a subject far too important for light conversation. She was a diligent companion and I bore her no ill will, so I turned the subject to a pleasanter theme—a wedding.

"Did I tell you, Helisent?" I forced a friendly mile. "The Lady Mary is to wed at last. The arrangements are nearly complete."

"I-I had heard a little," said Helisent cautiously. "The Count of Boulogne, is it not?"

"Yes, it is he. A crusader…."

"But rather o…" began Helisent, who then flushed scarlet and pretended to examine a nearby rose.

My maid had been about to say 'old', and Count Eustace was indeed some years older than my sister. But like me, she had no decent dowry with both our parents dead; her main attraction to a prospective bridegroom was her impeccable bloodline. The Count seemed a moral man, as far as I knew, and Mary would live as befitting her station.

"Lady Mary is coming to see me before she leaves for France," I said. "I cannot travel to Wilton in my condition. It will be good to see her before her departure." I suddenly grew solemn, a pang of sadness darkening my mood, and cradled my growing belly beneath the rich blue satin of my gown. "Who knows once she's gone if we shall ever meet again?"

Mary arrived in Winchester with a small entourage supplied by the King, who had brokered the marriage to Count Eustace. She was ushered into my solar and curtseyed before my seat.

I gestured for Helisent and Emma to leave. "No need for such formalities, Mary," I said. "After all, look at me, hardly queenly with my swollen ankles and sweat on my brow."

Mary came over and kissed me on the cheek. "You always look queenly, Edith, whether you are with child or not. Oh...I cannot believe this is our last meeting. Tomorrow, I travel to Southampton to take ship."

"You will be well." I clasped her hand. "All will be well."

"I pray to God it will. It is hard when one has not even seen their bridegroom once. At least you...you got to know Henry at court. W-what if I should find Eustace ugly? What if I could not hold back my disgust in his presence? I know I must marry...but my husband is older and I..."

I placed a finger against her lips. "Hush, sister, you will find something to love in him, even if it takes time. Did you know that at one time our mother was horrified at the prospect of marrying Father? She thought him an uncouth barbarian..."

Mary giggled a little, though her eyes were still shining with unshed tears. "Did she truly?"

"Truly. She told me so herself."

"I wish she were here to guide me." Mary's head drooped.

"I will guide you as best I can. You must find more to Count Eustace than mere looks, which fade in all of us. He is brave—he went on Crusade with his brothers and fought at Nicaea, Dorylaeum and Antioch. He fought at Jerusalem itself, manning a great siege tower and fighting his way into the city. In Boulogne, coins are minted on his honour, bearing the figure of a lion above the walls of Jerusalem."

"It is strange he has never wed before," said Mary. "That worries me. What if…what if he is like the old King, Rufus. You know the rumours."

"I have not heard of any scandals associated with his name. It seems Count Eustace is a godly man who even considered monkhood at one time. But now he wants a wife and an heir for Boulogne."

"I will try my best to be content, then," said Mary. "But I will miss you…and St Mary's Abbey."

I drew her into my embrace, holding her tightly.

"I will miss you too, Mary. So many partings…our family is all split apart, blown on the four winds. Scotland, England, and soon Boulogne. Even Uncle Edgar has taken up new residence in Normandy." The latter had come as a shock and a blow; my uncle had decided to remain with Curthose after serving him in his Crusade. Henry now regarded me as an enemy.

"It is the way of those of our stature," said Mary. "We are fortunate in some way—food in our mouths, fine clothes, gems and jewels, tall castles, but we, especially us women, must fare forth as Fate dictates, our bodies and bloodlines bringing alliances to bring peace and riches to our respective lands. In that, we are scarcely better than the serfs that till the land. Indeed, although they must obtain their lord's permission to wed, at least they will have met the one they wish to wed and found them to their liking."

I had no words to say, remembering all too clearly when our sire wished for me to marry the odious Alan the Red.

Mary pulled away and brushed down her gown. "I must to bed early, Edith, for I cannot tarry long and need to rest before my journey. I dare not reach the harbour late; the King has arranged for a ship to bear me hence and if the weather should turn bad, I could be stranded in England for weeks. My bridegroom would not be pleased."

Nodding, I gave her hand one final squeeze. "Farewell, Mary. May the Mother of God, for whom you were named, watch over you and guide you."

She left the chamber. Outside the sun was sinking into a smoky haze and the amber light of early evening streaked the floor. Out in the town, the bells boomed in the cathedral tower and all the churches joined in, creating a clangour of great and lesser bells. Sentries cried out as they changed over at the castle gate, while below my window, someone played upon a dulcimer within the herb garden.

Suddenly I felt very alone. How quickly the ones you love most leave you, with no guarantees that you will ever meet again. The foundation of the world you knew is chipped away, bit by bit.

I reached for my missal, hating the desolate feeling that gripped my heart and made it sore. I refused, though, to let such melancholy grab hold—once my child was born, I would turn my hand to a multitude of good works for my people. From the highest to the lowest, I would regard them as dear as family, and do my best to make their lives easier. Their love would make a new foundation to shore me up, proud and true.

I would be their mother, their Good Queen.

CHAPTER FIFTEEN

"It is a prince!" Faricius's joyous cry rang through the birthing chamber.

I stared up through fazed, dimmed eyes to see the aged physician holding my wriggling, kicking son in his cupped hands. Strong. Healthy. His hair, what there was of it, was fair like mine, unlike Adelaide's, which was dark like her father's.

"Bring him to me," I gasped. My limbs felt heavy, my body like a wash cloth wrung out. I held out my arms, but they trembled as if I were made of jelly and fell limply, uselessly, to my sides.

The midwife's broad, sun-browned face loomed over me; she had taken my baby from Abbot Faricius and placed him on my chest. I wanted to reach up and hold him securely but my strength was gone.

I had not felt so weak before, not even when Euphemia was born before her time. I strove to speak; the room jiggled before my eyes. A horrid, animal iron tang hung in the air, assaulting my nostrils. "Why is it so dim in here?" I asked, blinking. "It is night? Light the candles."

"It's day, your Grace, and not yet Vespers," the midwife said, her voice grown high, tremulous. She scooped up my newborn son and glanced over at Faricius.

"You have lost much blood, my Queen," he said solemnly. "It was a hard birth, unlike the last. The bleeding has not quite stopped yet. You must not exert yourself in any way."

The midwife went away to swaddle the babe, and two laundresses accompanied by Helisent entered the chamber. Helisent took one look at me and blanched, her hand fluttering to her throat. The servants hastened to the bedside and Faricius aided by Helisent carefully rolled me aside, whilst the women removed the soiled bedding below me. Muzzy-headed, I stared at the linen with a perplexed frown. Why…why was it such a colour? I had no scarlet bedding….

The realisation hit me along with a wave of extreme dizziness and pain. I gasped as buzzing filled my ears like a thousand angry wasps and black dots flew before my gaze. I reached towards the light, but night roared in around me.

I lived, but I was bedridden for months after the birth of my child. Henry was home from Normandy, delighted to have a son, whom he had christened William after his father. I insisted that even as Curthose's son bore the nickname 'Clito', our son should be called 'Adelin', the Norman form of Atheling, the title of English princes from the royal house of Wessex. This, after three Norman kings, was an heir who bore both Norman and Saxon bloodlines, a future ruler to unite the people and bring hope to those who were downtrodden.

When I was finally well enough to rise, I called Abbot Faricius to my solar for a meeting. "In your esteemed opinion," I said, "what do you think of my chances to bear more children?"

He coughed, clearing his throat. "Your Grace, I will speak plainly. For a while, after you fell senseless on the bed, you bled profusely, and I thought you might not be saved. Your chaplain even hurried to your chamber, ready to give you the Last Rites. I would not advise another pregnancy, although of course…"

"It is my duty," I said softly. "Even if I should die. My thanks for your honest assessment, Faricius; I must now ponder your words before I speak to the King."

The Abbot bowed and left, leaving me to my thoughts. It was a wife's duty to bear children; in Genesis, it was written how God said, *Be fruitful, and multiply, and replenish the earth*…Yet I had done what was desired of a Queen—I had produced the much-needed son, as well as a daughter to make foreign alliances. For me to die producing another babe when an heir was already born seemed…wasteful. I had always looked to continue my mother's good works throughout my life and so praise God in doing so.

I had to speak to Henry, but what I was going to suggest was unlikely to please him…

I had Helisent dress my hair and help me into a rich but sombre gown without jewel or other adornment. I used no artifice, no crumbled rose petals to redden my cheeks or *blaunchet* to whiten my skin. I wanted Henry to see that I was serious about what I must ask him. Then I sent word to my husband that I wished for an audience whenever he was free of the daily duties of kingship.

I waited an hour or two for his reply, trying to keep calm...and keep my nerve. Helisent poured me sweet cordials flavoured with herbs and attempted to distract me with gossip and false jollity. I could see in her eyes that she was puzzled...and concerned.

At length, a page boy arrived, bowing. "His Grace awaits you in his apartments, madame."

I rose, brushing down my gown while attempting to hide the faint trembling of my hand. "Wait here, Helisent," I said. "And have some wine...strong wine...ready for my return."

I stood before Henry. He had spent the day listening to requests and looked weary, his hair mussed and his rich tunic rumpled. "Ah, what a day it's been, Edith. I had to listen to an old widow griping about her stolen pig. She accused her neighbour of carrying it off and making sausages of it, and no, the local authorities were not good enough for Widow Ibbot; she had to see the King and beg me to throw her neighbour into the deepest, darkest dungeon. From what I gather, her fences weren't mended and the beast ran off into the forest where it is surmised a predator ate it. I could only nod my head at her ravings...till I convinced her to see the Master of Requests, who would deliberate on the case."

"And was she happy in the end?"

"Not very...but it's all the satisfaction she's going to get." He gave a brief laugh, then his visage turned serious. "How are you, Edith, my dearest? Are you well? It is good to see you on your feet."

I swallowed. "Henry...we must talk."

"Is that not what we are doing?" He quirked an eyebrow but his lips had lost any hint of a smile. "Talk on."

I sat upon an upholstered stool; already my legs had begun to tremble, although whether from exertion or sheer nervousness I could not say. "You have spoken to Faricius, no doubt, and know that I nearly died after giving birth to William."

"Yes, I heard. I thank you for the great gift you have given me. My son, William Adelin—even though he is a little frail, I hear. I do not forget Adelaide either; such an intelligent and strong-minded maid-child."

"So…" I stared at my hands, clasped in my lap, unwilling to meet his gaze. "We now have two children, a boy to inherit, a girl to forge alliances. Do…do we need more? Sometimes, too many sons may not be such a good thing. Look how your brothers fought, and the troubles with Robert that carry on to this day."

Henry leaned back as if I had struck him. "I…I am uncertain what you are saying, Edith? Are…are you telling me you want our marriage annulled? If so, on what grounds? Or are you telling me that Anselm was right, and you are a vowed nun?" His voice began to rise, full of barely controlled fury.

"No, no…nothing like that!" I cried. "I want to remain your wife, Henry…but, I will say it—I do not wish to share your bed and produce more children. If I do, Abbott Faricius believes I will die in childbirth."

Henry looked about to explode, then suddenly the rage went out of him and he sagged on his chair. "I would not wish death on you, Edith. I love you, if in my own imperfect way."

Reaching out, I grasped his hand. To my relief, he did not pull away but wound his fingers with mine. "I would remain a good queen to you and honour you in all ways. You know I am learned; when you are away in Normandy, I can oversee the running of England. I can converse with Bishops, I have founded monastic houses, I can delegate the building of bridges and hospitals. I can dole out food and money for the poor…I can be a teacher to our children, far better than the tutors we hire. I want to be the mother of the people, much as my own mother was to the folk of Scotland."

"But, Edith…" he began, slowly disengaging his hand, "what you suggest would be highly irregular. I am no monk, as you know."

I stared down, toying with a fold in my gown. "I realise that you would need to…take concubines. I do not seek to make you chaste as a monk. I am fine with your amorous pursuits as long as I am not made to look foolish before your paramours and before the court, for my humiliation would greatly injure our children."

Henry folded his arms over his chest, brow lowered as he mulled over my words. He did not speak for what seemed hours.

Then he said slowly, "So be it. I need you, Edith, to help mend this fractured country. I have seen how the common man turns to you. And even my barons...they were dubious at first, mocking when they thought they were beyond my hearing...They have changed their position now."

"You are not angry?"

"Angry? Of course, I am angry...what man wouldn't be angry to lose a beautiful woman from his bed? But that is not what is important here; your health and life come first.   As you say, I will not go without female company."

I managed a wobbly smile. "There is a soft side to you, Henry, that few seldom see. I have noticed it in the way you care for your baseborn children; I have seen it when you visit Adelaide and little William."

"Tell no one," he jested. "I would not want such talk spread around, you understand."

"I do." I rose and kissed him on the brow. "My deepest thanks and love, my Lord King."

Later that year, after we had removed to Westminster, I heard that Nest had given birth to a baby boy. She named him, rather predictably, Henry. The King acknowledged him and hence he was surnamed 'FitzHenry' to denote his ancestry. Henry sent a rich gift of plate and then turned his attention to other more pressing matters—the lords of Normandy had grown unruly, and Curthose, under duress, had thrown his lot in with Robert de Belleme once more.

"You know what that means, Edith," Henry said, during one of our frequent discussions about the matters of the kingdom over a game of chess. "It means my brother has broken the terms of our peace treaty."

"I always thought he might" I moved my queen. Henry was not paying attention; a few more moves... "Or that you might."

"Me? I—I am honourable..." I thought he might toss the board, throwing the gleaming ivory and jet pieces across the chamber.

"Honourable, yes, but no man's fool," I smiled. "The treaty of Alton would never hold. I knew it, you knew it...and so did Robert Curthose..."

"Hmmm." A deep, indignant rumble came from Henry's sturdy throat. His eyes narrowed as he surveyed the board. "Well, I will have to invade Normandy, I suppose, and teach my brother a harsh lesson. One that will see his treachery finished for good!"

I nodded, and, to my jubilation, captured his king. I held the captive piece aloft, gleaming black in the firelight. "And then it will be...*checkmate*."

While Henry brooded over Curthose's actions and began the preparations for war, I busied myself with more cheerful pursuits. I sent to Turgot, beloved of my family and a stalwart helpmeet when it was our darkest hour, and told him I wanted him to write of the life of my mother, Queen Margaret. He agreed readily, writing, *I willingly accept these orders and rejoice that you wish to see in writing the deeds of your mother. Alas, you knew her too little, but now you shall have the fullest measure of her virtues, with aid from the Holy Ghost to narrate my words.*

I also tended to the churches I admired most, giving relics of St John the Evangelist, Mary Magdalene and the martyr Saint Christine to Westminster Abbey, along with a a black girdle embroidered with the words of the '*nesciens Mater*' and '*Deus qui salutis.*'

My greatest sorrow, though, was that the saintly Anselm had departed England and gone to Rome in high dudgeon. Problems had started two years ago when at a council his seat was placed higher than that of Gerald, the Archbishop of York. Gerald had acted the fool, shouting and kicking over benches, stools and even candlesticks in a jealous rage. Then he folded his arms, his mitre askew upon his head, pouting like an angry child, and shouted, 'I refuse to sit until both our seats of equal height!' The issue was further complicated by the presence of Ranulf Flambard, whom Henry had—unwisely, I thought—pardoned and allowed to return to court. Snake that he was, Ranulf tried to bribe us to support Anselm's claim for eminence. I supported him anyway, and refused the knave's bribe, as did the King

But my husband was less enamoured of Anselm than I. He had never forgiven him for his doubts when Henry asked to marry me, and this old wound was made raw again when Anselm and Henry clashed over the appointment of various bishops and abbots. Henry believed he had the right; Anselm vehemently insisted that only the Pope could choose an incumbent for those offices.

The situation grew so dire that Anselm fled; he claimed he was pushed, Henry insisted the Archbishop had simply leapt at the chance to visit Rome and air his grievances.

Now, I was trying my best to mediate between the King and the errant Archbishop, who had already succeeded in convincing the Pope to excommunicate any bishops made by Henry and not by the Church. *Tender Father*, I called him in my frequent letters, *Shepherd who leads the wayward flock. My joy, my hope, my refuge...* Then I added that I hoped his steely heart would soon soften toward his erring monarch...and that I would try my best to soften Henry's heart in turn.

No more than that could I do to assuage the anger of that saintly but irascible churchman. If I could keep more excommunications from happening, I would think it a job well done.

"FitzHamon has been captured!" Henry was roaring like a maddened bull, slamming his balled fist into the palm of his opposite hand over and over again. He stormed across Westminster Hall, boot thudding into a bench, which overturned, sending several young squires flying to the reeds on the ground. The castle dogs, ever eager, lurched over to lick the youths and seek for treats. "I cannot believe it! How could the fool have fallen into enemy hands?"

"Tell me what's happened, husband." I strode into the Hall, as two frightened-looking messengers, given leave to go with an agitated hand signal from the King, scuttled past, pale as wraiths.

"You heard, didn't you?" Henry's eyes were crackling with wrath. "FitzHamon has been taken by Robert. He helped to broker a truce, which my brother ignored, and FitzHamon was so incensed that he roused his Norman levies and started attacking the lands and castles of Robert's supporters. Needless to say, Robert struck back with troops from Bayeux and Caen, and FitzHamon's men were routed. He fled to safety in a church at Secqueville-en-Bessin...but his enemies set the building on fire and FitzHamon was forced to surrender. He was taken in chains to Bayeux, and only the goodwill of the mayor, Gontier d'Alney, kept him from being torn apart by the ravening mob. Oh, the old fool; he should have been sitting by the fire, not out attacking Curthose and his brother-in-law, de Belleme, without my say so."

Sighing, I thought of Sybil de Montgomery, FitzHamon's wife, my old companion from Romsey Abbey. Despite her infamous mother and brothers, she had turned out to be a steadfast wife to Robert Fitz Hamon and a highly religious woman. Evidently the evil of her mother, Mabel the Poisoner, had not rubbed off on Sybil. "So, what is to be done, Henry?"

"I rescue him," said the King. "I knew I'd have to confront my stubby-legged brother sooner or later, but I'd planned 'later' when I'd gathered more troops. But needs must...I can't have FitzHamon mouldering in a cell, can I?"

"No, you cannot," I said. "He has been loyal."

Henry nodded and drew close, placing a hand on my arm. "I leave England in your capable hands, Edith. You shall act as Regent when I am away."

I assumed the role of Regent with enthusiasm, taking on all of Henry's duties in a straightforward manner. I travelled far and wide, seeing that the walls of the Tower were repaired and the apartments at Windsor refurbished. I judged criminals in court and meted out justice tempered, I hoped, with mercy. Charters were sealed, lands granted, gifts of bells, lead and vestments given to abbeys and priories which had gained my favour through piety or good deeds. My youngest brother, David, accompanied me on my travels, riding on a grey stallion Henry had given him as a Yule gift. He was a handsome and intelligent lad, and it was my desire that he should learn of statecraft and royal duty while at my side

By Whitsun, which to the Saxons was Pentecoste, David and I were back at Westminster in time for the festivities. Although Whitsun was a holy time, commemorating the Holy Ghost coming down to the disciples of our Lord, it was a time of joy and frolicking for the ordinary people, who had a full week free from their toil. Dancing, foot races, and wrestling amongst youths took place. Ale was the drink of tradition and a couple was chosen from each village to be the Lord and Lady of the Ale, and they would process to the Lord's Hall, a barn decked in flags and ribbons, where carousing and drinking would take place.

For me, a Queen, there could be no such light-hearted celebrations. I had to show a more sedate and pious face to the masses. The lepers who tenanted the hospital of St-Giles-in-the-Fields, which I had founded in the first year of my marriage to Henry, were allowed into the palace precinct, where I would give them bread and drink…and wash their poor, ruined feet, even as Christ washed the feet of the Apostles on the night before His Crucifixion.

Dressed in solemn robes, shortly after the Prime bell had rung, I entered an ante-chamber in the royal apartments where the lepers had gathered, a white linen sash tied around my waist and a copper bowl of boiled water in my hands. I gazed upon the faces of my patients, gaunt, ravaged and white as bone, wrapped in cloths yellowed from weeping sores; many often likened the appearance of lepers to those of dead liches. Many would have fled at the sight; one man's nose was eaten away, leaving two black slits in its place, and an old woman had bent claws for hands and a single bleary blue eye.

Most folk feared the lepers, hence their lazar houses were built outside town walls; they also had bells to ring to let clean folk know they passed nearby. However, I had no fear of these tragic sufferers. I had witnessed both my parents washing leper's afflicted flesh, even kissing those clawed, twisted hands. God had protected them from harm; I had faith that He would also protect me.

As I began my task, removing the worn leather shoes of one man to reveal the stubs of missing toes, I thought suddenly of my brother David, who was still abed after a riotous evening with other young lordlings of similar age, drinking and brawling and propositioning pretty maidens. I thought it might be good to summon him, to impress upon him that life was not all singing, dancing and merriment, and perhaps persuade him to join me, as a royal son of the blessed Margaret of Scotland, in my washing of the leper's limbs.

I beckoned to my chamberlain, Ailwin. "Go summon my brother, David," I said. "He doubtless will have a sore head from drink and might bawl at you, but tell him I want to see him right away…"

Ailwin looked dubious. "Your Grace, I was a young man once and remember the vileness that comes of imbibing too much wine and ale. I fear he might refuse and raise his hand in anger."

"Tell him it is not an invitation but a command then. One that he cannot, dare not, refuse."

The corner of Ailwin's mouth rose. "As you wish, your Grace. I will go at once."

The Chamberlain exited the chamber and I sat down to my task, holding the afflicted feet of one of the lepers upon my lap. Gently, I took a rosewater-infused rag and laved his right foot, missing two toes, gnarled and discoloured, before dabbing them dry with the white linen tied around my waist.

As I worked, I became aware of a presence in the doorway. I turned my head and saw David standing there, watching my ministrations. He had leapt straight from his bed; I could tell by the way his mussed hair hung across bleary, sleep-laden eyes His tunic was rumpled and stained—and on backwards.

"Ah, David, my dear brother," I said with cheery lightness. "I thought today you might join me in caring for these poor souls, even as our mother did, God assoil her. Here…come sit beside me."

David's visage, already drained from lack of sleep and too much drink, went a shade of yellowish-grey and I feared he might spew. "Edith! What in God's name are you doing?" he cried.

"Exactly that, brother. I am doing good works in God's name. It is the duty of a ruler to minister to the poorest and most helpless among us."

David's arms flapped like a bird's wings; he was at that age when young men almost universally appeared gawky before filling out. "Does the King know about this folly? No, he cannot…otherwise he would never kiss your lips again, since they have been fouled by the putrid sores of lepers!"

"David, you are impertinent!" I warned, waving an angry finger, but then I softened. He was still a boy after all. "You must understand…the feet of He who is the Eternal King in Heaven are preferable to the lips of a mortal king who is doomed to die as all men must! Come, I beg you learn from my example. Our mother did this…"

"She also died too young," he said with bitterness. "No one knew exactly what caused her ailment. Maybe it was touching these disgusting creatures!"

"David, they are God's children, even as you and I. Come…" I put on a friendly face, still trying to convince him. "Take some rags and bathe the fellow next to me in the way I am doing now."

David looked even more horrified than before. "I-I cannot, sister, even if you command me as a Queen. These lepers are the…the living dead! You know they've had the funeral rites spoken over them already!"

"Each and every one of us has one foot in the tomb, and one day we might watch the sun in the sky with joy and the next lie below the earth with the worms. We must make do with the time that is given us, and do good works to please the Father of us all."

"I—I cannot do it…I won't," insisted David, and at that moment, the situation worsened, for his youthful companions of the previous night had begun gathering in the corridor. Ailwin kept them back with admonishments and outstretched arms, but they peered over his shoulders and were smirking and pointing at my brother.

David saw them and the sickly yellow hue of his face turned to scarlet instead. "My Lady," he said to me. "You are a far better Christian than I, and I care not who knows it. Forgive me if I anger you, but I think my time is done here. I have nought more to say about lepers." With that, he whirled on his heel and staggered out of the door, pushing a startled Ailwin aside. He vanished into his mirthful crowd of companions, who started clapping him on the shoulder while shouting 'Unclean, unclean!'

Exasperated, I ignored the unseemly racket, moving on from my last patient to yet another leper who was holding out her ruined arms for some relief, physical or spiritual. David would learn one day but that day was clearly not today.

CHAPTER SIXTEEN

"Your Grace!" Helisent was hovering in my bedchamber, a dim wraith-like figure in the grey morning light filtering through the horn panes inserted in the narrow windows. "You must come quickly!"

Groggy, I dragged myself into an upright position, pulling my hair in a straggling pale cloud over my shoulder. "What is it, Helisent? Are the children…"

"Lord William and Lady Adelaide are fine," the maid reassured me, "but an outrider has just arrived at the gates. The King and his men landed at Dover yestereven and soon will be home."

"Is there any news besides that?" I climbed from the bed and held up my arms while she dressed me in a silverish robe with long sleeves hemmed with gold curlicues. Emma appeared from the corridor beyond with my jewelled bone comb, veil and an enamelled circlet. "The King is hale and well?"

"As far as I could tell," said Helisent as Emma deftly braided my locks and put the circlet on my brow, holding the silken veil in place. "But it seems he is greatly grieved and even angrier than ever at Duke Robert."

"He did not manage to free FitzHamon, then," I breathed, imagining how distressed and angry my husband would be if that were true.

She pinned my cloak with a leaf-shaped brooch studded with glossy white pearls. "FitzHamon is with him, so I am told, but more I cannot say."

I hurried down to the hall, gowned suitably to meet the King when he arrived, and broke my fast with sops and fine white bread. Time crawled past but I dared not leave my position. I wanted my husband to see that his court—and by extension, his kingdom—was in good hands.

In the early eventide, I heard the brazen voices of the trumpets ringing in the streets of London beyond the palace walls. My breathing grew faster with both anticipation and trepidation as the main gates clanged open, guardsmen shouted, and horses stamped and whinnied as they flooded through into the inner courtyard.

Henry stalked into the Hall, pushing servants, underlings, and courtiers aside even as they bowed humbly before him. I nearly sprang from my seat in surprise, for it was like looking at a stranger. The King's appearance had changed! His shoulder-length dark hair had been crudely shorn, making him look, to my eyes, like a sheared sheep. His beard had also been hacked until it was scarce more than a black tuft on his chin. His eyes were heavy from lack of rest, ringed by dark circles and his raiment was rumpled and patched by mud.

"My...my Lord King!" I stammered, utterly dumbfounded by the change in him. "What..."

Reaching my seat, he grasped my arm, none too gently. "Matilda, you have some skills with the healing arts, do you not?"

"Yes," I said, "a little from my time at Saint Magdalen's hospital."

"Come, then. Now!" He pulled me from my seat while all within the chamber gaped to see him mishandle me so, and then he herded me through the palace corridors to his private apartments. Inside the King's bedchamber, Robert FitzHamon lay on Henry's own bed, his complexion waxy and grey, his eyes rolled back in his skull, a stained bandage circling his brow. He was neither unconscious nor asleep, however; he gave out strained moaning noises from deep in his throat and his limbs made abnormal little judders.

I rushed to the sick man's side, staring down at the drawn face, a trail of bloodied saliva dribbling from the corner of his mouth. Even as I watched he began to jerk and shudder before falling deathly still. "Jesu...what happened to him?"

"I managed to get him out of Bayeux without harm," said Henry, between gritted teeth. "At first, the city refused to surrender and I had to bring engines to smash the gates. Once inside, I let the men do as they would...and they burnt the place to the ground. I got to FitzHamon in his prison just as the smoke was getting thick. Old he might be...but he was furious, having been kept in a pit of a cell, like a common felon. He leapt up, although weak from many privations, and begged me to let him ride at my side against the Duke of Normandy. How could I say no? Battle was in his blood!"

"What happened then, to bring him to this sorry state?" I murmured, nodding toward the figure on the bed.

"We marched on towards Caen. Seeing fires leaping over Bordeaux, the town wisely opened its gates and surrendered. I had hoped to catch Curthose there, but the craven sod had turned tail and crept through a postern gate to freedom. However, Caen's capitulation meant I was able to ride straight for the stronghold of Falaise. I thought it might surrender as easily as Caen, but when we arrived, the town still held out for my brother...I ordered a ram brought to the gates."

Wearily he wiped an arm across his face. "FitzHamon was like a man possessed, taking unnecessary risks at every turn. He flung away his shield at one point while trying to scale the walls with a grappling hook...and a missile thrown from above struck him here..." He touched his temple. "I thought he was a dead man, but when I got to him, he still breathed...but he has not yet woken from that blow. Not properly."

"Did the surgeon not attend him on the field?"

"Yes," he said, almost spitting the word, "he said that FitzHamon would die that day. But he did not. A priest came to give last rites on more than one occasion, but still the tenacious old bastard clung to life. He served with my sire, you know."

"I know," I said quietly, placing a hand on his muscular arm. He had always had a fondness for Robert FitzHamon, who had not only shown loyalty to the Conqueror but even found it in him to weep over the arrow-pierced body of unpopular William Rufus. I had found him disagreeable when he came 'wooing' Sybil ...but that was years ago. I could not fault him in his loyalty to either his King or his wife.

"I held talks with Curthose while my soldiers assailed Falaise...but we could not reach terms. The weather was turning foul and Falaise's walls were strong. I decided to return home...for now."

His eyes blazed suddenly and his jaw jutted. "But I will return, next year. There will be war, and Robert will either kneel to me or I will see his head upon a spear!"

I shrank away from his wrath. "Have you called for another physician to tend poor FitzHamon?"

"I summoned one the moment I reached Dover. He bound the wound and though he was less resigned than the other one, he said that he doubted, if FitzHamon should survive, that he would have the wits of a normal man again. Sybil will end up feeding him gruel from a spoon like a babe." He stalked over to me, anger and desperation oozing from his very pores. "These so-called trained physicians, I do not trust some of them, with their arts near enough to sorcery! You have healed the sick before using simple means. Perhaps you…"

I shook my head, gazing at him with sorrow and sympathy. "Oh, my dearest lord, I was but a humble helpmeet to the nuns, with no great skill other than administering possets and washing scraps and boils. I am not a miracle worker. I fear that Robert FitzHamon's fate lies solely in God's hands."

He glared at me with such wild fury that I felt suddenly fearful, even though I had only spoken the truth. "I will examine him, of course, and do whatever is within my power."

Aware of my husband's burning gaze boring into my back, I leaned over the injured old warrior, peeling away the bandage. I winced at what I saw below; the poor soul had a jagged hole where part of his skull had caved in. No doubt shards of bone had struck into his brain like darts. I lifted his closed eyelids; he made no resistance but gave an '*Uhhnn, unhnn*' cry that sounded like a beast in pain.

I whirled about, gesticulating at a man-servant standing in the shadowy corner of the chamber. "You, sir. Make haste and go fetch some honey or elderberry oil from the herbalist. And henbane, mandrake, and…a flagon of strong wine."

The man bowed and fled the room. Henry glanced at me, brow lowering. "I have seen honey and oils used on the battlefield…but the other… Mandrake and henbane, Edith? Do not witches use such herbs to kill and aid their dark arts?"

"He will feel terrible pain without them. Too much pain for a soul to withstand."

"But such a brew might kill him." Henry's breath was hot on my neck.

"Yes, there is always that risk," I said, as calmly as I could manage, pretending I was unaware of Henry's almost menacing presence. "And if his condition is as grave as the physician at Dover believed, maybe it would be the kind thing…"

"No, I will not have it." He stomped a foot on the floor, heavy and menacing as the tread of the Bible's Goliath.

"Then you must pray to the Great Healer." I summoned the courage to look straight into his face and was surprised to see naked grief etched on his hard features. "God will determine what happens to this man."

His shoulders slouched in defeat. "I-I am a fool. What idiot imagines his Queen should know all the mysteries of leechcraft? Forgive me for such presumption, Edith."

"There is nought to forgive, husband. But, before the servant comes back with the things I have ordered, tell me—what happened to your hair and beard?"

"Oh, that," he grunted, touching the bristly tufts on his chin, dark but flecked with stray fiery red hairs. "In Normandy, I had dealings with Serlo, the Bishop of Sees. A sour fellow if ever there was one; face like a wet rag. He ranted at me that long hair on a man was fit only for those bristling in sin, and a beard longer than half a finger's length made one resemble a randy billy-goat…and hence inclined to lechery and sodomy."

"And you listened to him? The King of England listened to such insults?"

"Normally I would have mocked his foolish taunts. But in the matter with Curthose, I needed the Bishop on my side, so I hung my head in humility and decided to let the Bishop himself chop my locks off with a pair of shears. You'll notice many of my followers have now adopted the same style. Does it offend your eyes, my Lady?"

"No, of course not…but you look so *different*. Almost like a different man." I stared at the floor. "Now, if you do not mind, lord husband, I would treat Robert FitzHamon alone, so that I can use all of my concentration upon his wound…Once that is done, I will also take on the task of writing to his wife, Sybil, to tell her that he lives…but he may not be the man she once knew."

Robert FitzHamon *did* live, though I was not vain enough to believe my simple ministrations had saved his life. He awoke and even spoke a few words, but his brains were addled and he could remember little of his past life, and when he regained speech, he stumbled and stuttered over words. Finally, when he was strong enough, Henry sent him in a litter to Sybil at their manor at Tewkesbury. Nevermore would Robert FitzHamon stand strong in battle for the sons of William Bastard...

Henry was now preparing for war in earnest. I resumed queenly duties, including the construction of a bathhouse for the poor of London, and a series of privies that could be used by anyone, be he vagrant, traveller, journeyman, merchant or lord. So much more sanitary than pissing or defecating in the streets! I also built a special bridge at Stratford, near a bathing pool I liked to frequent, and gave Wiggen Mill to the Abbess of Barking in return for the upkeep of the bridge.

There were happier times, though, when Henry was not in council with his barons, deciding his next moves against Curthose. He was an attentive father to both our children, but especially, as might be expected, to little William, whom he treated with care and prudence. It brought joy to me to see him carry William on his back, shouting, "I am your warhorse, Will!' or gently teasing Adelaide because she preferred a wooden sword to a doll.

To my delight, my sister Mary, whom I had feared I might never see again, arrived in England with her husband Eustace, Count of Boulogne, and her new baby, named Matilda after me. I found Eustace a pleasant and learned companion who spoke the English tongue as well as Norman French, since he also bore royal Saxon heritage—the son of Godgifu, daughter of King Ethelred.

I travelled with my sister to the great abbey of Bermondsey, lying across the Thames from the Tower, a place of holiness opposing a castle built for warfare and authority. Mary had decided to become a patron of the order, keeping her ties with England fresh. "I am happier in my marriage than I ever thought possible," she said as we walked together through the cloisters of the abbey. "To think, I would have wriggled out of it when the King first announced the betrothal. Eustace may no longer be in the first bloom of youth, but he is loyal, kindly and valorous. He adores little Matilda...Now, all I need to do is bear a boy..."

"I am glad you brought the babe to England," I told her. "She is a beautiful child, and I was overjoyed to see my namesake. But were you not fearful for her health and safety on such a long journey?"

"Yes, but I was even more fearful of letting her out of my sight. Oh, she has the finest, most trustworthy nurses back in Boulogne, but I felt better without a raging sea between us. I wanted her to meet my dearest sister, too—her loving aunt, the Queen of England."

I chuckled remembering how when Mary had placed little Matilda in my arms, the baby's small pink hand had caught in my veil, nearly dragging it from my head. "You know," I said to Mary, "when she pulled my veil askew, I was reminded of how I did the same to Queen Matilda, my husband's mother, at my christening. Folk whispered that it meant I would become a queen one day. Mayhap your Matilda will ascend to that dignity too in the fullness of time."

Mary laughed. "I doubt that, but only God in his Almighty wisdom knows for sure."

I crossed myself. "His Will be done, whether Matilda of Boulogne grows to be countess, duchess, abbess...or queen."

Just past Candlemas, in the year of Our Lord 1106, Robert Curthose came to England bearing an olive branch. I had briefly met him once before, in the year the Treaty of Alton was signed, but I had grieved so much for my dead infant, our meeting was short and little remembered. All I could recall was that he was courteous in speech and unlike Henry in either looks or mannerisms.

I travelled with the King to the royal castle of Northampton in the Midlands where the two brothers were set to negotiate peace. Henry was in a foul mood, for he could not imagine any positive results coming from the meeting.

"A waste of bloody time," he snarled as we sat in the Great Hall, awaiting the arrival of Robert's entourage. "He has nought to bargain with...not anymore. Even his crusading feats have long been forgotten. He is weak, he is craven...yet still he needles my side like a thorn from a prickly and poisonous bush. I fear he only comes to England to stall for time while he woos that murderous carbuncle on the face of humanity—Robert de Belleme. I was ready to bring my forces to his shores and finish this charade, but God's Teeth, for the sake of the affection I felt for my dear, dead mother who bore us both and who loved the bandy-legged little wretch, I will listen one more time to what he has to say."

A trumpet blew and then another. The servants and courtiers leapt into readiness

"Here he comes, the creeping worm," said Henry through clenched teeth.

A man appeared in the doorway, accompanied by two trumpeters. Pausing briefly, he then sloped towards the dais where Henry and I reclined under a tasselled canopy. I leaned forward as he drew near, scrutinising his appearance. As his nickname suggested, Curthose was short-legged and lower in stature than the average man; indeed, he was a finger's breadth shorter than me. His hair was near-black like Henry's and worn in the old Norman fashion with the back of the neck shaved upwards. His chin was razored clean, though blue with stubble, but he had a long, drooping moustache that gave his face a strangely mournful cast. He had aged since our sole meeting, the loss of his wife Sybilla and the troubles within Normandy taking their toll.

He bowed—hesitantly, I thought—and the King alighted from his high seat to embrace him before both brothers dutifully gave each other the kiss of peace on the cheek. As they stepped apart, Robert turned in my direction, went on one knee and kissed my hand. "Greetings, your Grace, my most beautiful god-daughter, Edith."

"It is Matilda now, as surely you must know."

"Ah, yes, your regnal name, taken in honour of my gracious mother, Matilda of Flanders. It suits you well; I have heard you are near enough a saint in all things, as was your mother, the blessed Margaret. Your fame has spread far and wide across Europe; an angel to the poor, solace to the infirm, heaven-sent to abbeys and nunneries…"

"You flatter me too greatly." I cut him off in mid-flow. "I do only what is my duty as Queen as a servant of Our Lord."

"Naturally...I did not mean to..." he stammered, his ruddy cheeks almost purple.

I was aware of what some gossips said behind my back—that 'desire for glory' was my main reason to perform good works, that and a wish to rival the holiness of my mother. It was an insult that stung, and Robert Curthose had inadvertently poured salt into the wound with his excess flattery, which rightly or wrongly, sounded to my mind close to mockery.

However, the stricken expression on his face when he had realised he'd caused offence, made me think his gushing words were honest enough. I presumed he thought I'd intercede on his behalf with Henry if he spoke me fair. But I never would, goddaughter or not. The grievances between him and Henry needed to be worked out between those two alone, either at the council table or on the battlefield.

"Dear Godfather." I leaned towards Duke Robert, assuming a winsome smile. "We shall walk together in private, as soon as it is fitting to do so."

A banquet was held in Robert's honour that night. His knights looked uneasy and many times I saw their hands twitch at their sides, but their sword sheaths were empty; by strict order, all weapons were left outside the Hall. Henry was roaring with mirth as he sloshed down mugs of ale, and Robert was heartily trying to catch up. They were playing the part of good brothers, even though you could hear the falseness in their raised voices and see the tension upon their faces in unguarded moments.

"Henry, I scarce recognised you at first!" bellowed Robert, slamming down his flagon and showering ale across the high table. "That hair! You look like...a hedgehog!"

"Ah," returned Henry, his teeth flashing in an unsavoury grin, "that was the doing of Serlo, Bishop of Sees! He has a terror of men with long hair, doubtless because he is as bald as a hen's egg! You know how petty Serlo is, though, don't you, my brother? Not so long ago, he'd invited you to hear a sermon...but you'd spent the previous night guzzling drink, dandling harlots and watching a raggedy-arsed Fool caper on the table. When you fell over in a stupor, your companions dragged you to your chamber...and promptly ran off with your garments, or maybe the whores took them as payments! So there you sat, naked as the day you were born, while Serlo paced and fumed in the church."

Robert grimaced. His hand curled into a fist, then relaxed. "An unfortunate incident. He got over it."

"And have you, *dear* brother…"

"Have I what?"

"Got over it."

"I do not understand your meaning, Henry."

"Another fateful day, full of tomfoolery. That day when you were dicing with some lackey and William and I tipped a piss pot over your head…" Henry rose, arms outstretched, playing to the entire hall. "You should have seen him, good fellows! Drenched through, screaming with rage, dancing about like an ungainly marionette! He started a rebellion the next day because our sire refused to punish us!"

"Enough!" Robert's hand thudded against the table making goblets, eating daggers, and trenchers bounce. "I have not come to England to mull over the past, Henry!"

"I think the drink has gone to both your heads," I said, but lightly, so that I would seem neither overbold nor shrewish. "You must be tired, godfather." I touched Robert's arm. "Weariness from your long journey has made your temper fray. Would like me to escort you to your chambers?"

"I am not in my dotage quite yet," he snapped, but he quickly recalled his manners. "But you are right, dear goddaughter Matilda, the hour grows late and perhaps the drink is flowing a little too freely. I will retire for the night if the King gives me his leave." He glanced blearily at his brother.

"Oh, go, go, Robert." Henry waved a dismissive hand and downed another goblet of wine in one. "You never could take a jest. On the morrow, we shall talk about more serious things in the council chamber."

Robert removed himself from the Great Hall; Henry continued to drink. I sat at his side in silence, the ladies in waiting fluttering about me. Still though I was, my mind was whirring—I would have to devise a way to speak to Robert Curthose before my husband.

Just after dawn's light touched the sky, I had a page take a message to Robert's chamber, asking him to meet me in my solar. Soon the reply came, *Yes. Right away.* I was nervous but forced myself to appear at ease as my godfather entered the chamber, heavy-eyed, his tread weary.

"You wish to see me, Highness."

"Such formality is not needed, godfather. Call me Matilda. And yes, I wanted to see you before your meeting with the King this afternoon."

I snapped my fingers and a nurse entered the solar carrying my little son, William, not quite two years old. He was chubby and golden- haired, angelic in appearance, just as Pope Gregory the Great had once described English children seen in a slave market. He stared at Robert with big blue eyes, a little shy in the presence of a stranger.

"This is your nephew, William." I took my son from the nursemaid and held him up before Robert "He was named for your sire. I hear you now have a son by the same name."

"Yes, my boy is a little older. William Clito. He is strong and healthy; indeed, he quite resembles your boy, though his hair is not so gold."

"Your wife died after his birth, did she not? I heard she was very fair to behold."

A spasm of genuine grief raced over his features. "She was beautiful, Matilda. And it was a love match…at least on my side. Oh, yes, at first, I thought only of her dowry, I will admit it, but I am not young, full of great passions…I thought she would be nought but a pretty diversion, a glittering jewel who would give me legitimate sons. But when I saw Sibylla in the flesh and spoke to her, I was entranced…I loved for the first time in my life, and it was both wonderful and terrifying."

He paced the room, toying with the heavy rings he wore. "She survived William's birth and we rejoiced…but a short while after, she took a fever and died despite the physic's best efforts. Her midwife claimed her paps had been bound too tightly and she succumbed to an infection. Others whispered..." He took a deep breath. "They whisper that she was poisoned on the orders of Agnes, an old mistress of mine. I will never know the truth for Agnes herself died the next year, and if she was guilty, she carried the secret to her grave. My counsellors say I should wed again...but the time for that is past. I will face the end of my days alone."

"I feel your sorrow," I said, "and that is why I asked you to see me today. Look at my son... an innocent boy, much like your own child. His cousin. They are close kin, bearing the same blood. It would be evil to see these two boys grow into bitter enemies, fighting each other constantly. Do you not agree?"

"I do," he said, "but my brother Henry cares little for that. Perhaps you should talk to *him*."

"He knows how I feel...but you know his mind as much as I. It does no good for me to try blandishments on my husband; he is shrewd, he would see through such artifice."

"So you think that I, a knight, a crusader should try such blandishments instead? Grovel at Henry's feet?" he cried, incredulous. "I, who—forgive me for saying this—should have ruled England in my brother's stead? Henry has stolen my crown...but now it seems he desires all of Normandy too!"

"I do not expect a proud man like you to grovel." I motioned for the nursemaid to take William back to the nursery. "Only to speak with cool head...and not react to Henry's jibes. He makes them because he knows they bother you so—ignore him. Now I will speak plainly, as your goddaughter and as a queen. Your rule in Normandy had been beset by problems from the start. You have made bad friends, they've abandoned you, then you welcome them with open arms again, and the cycle of thieving, burning and violence begins anew. Henry would have let you be if your tenure in Normandy had not been so...*eventful.*"

"So, you think I should beg him for my lands back, and tell him I promise to be a good lord...or what Henry believes is a good lord?"

"If it helps, Robert."

"I do not think it will. Now I will speak plainly to you, Edith of Scotland..." He spoke my old name, which surprised me, and may have been meant insultingly; his face was uncomfortably close to mine, his breath stale and hot on my cheek. "I have a son, even as you. At one time, before your child was born, he had a good claim to the English throne. Grudgingly, I gave that idea up when your child was born, although some said I should have asserted my right...but I will not give up on Normandy and hand it to Henry on a platter. What kind of a father would I be if I gave away my son's lands? He would despise me with all his heart! Tell me truly, Lady, if the situation was reversed, would you not fight till your last breath for the wellbeing of your son?"

I bowed my head, abashed by his heartfelt words. "You know I would."

He nodded and hastened towards the doorway leading from the solar. "Then we must both accept that whatever will be, will be."

By the end of the day, the die was cast. I heard the shouting all the way in my chambers, both Henry and Robert roaring at each other like maddened bulls. Before dusk fell over Northampton, Robert Curthose had taken horse and ridden forth from the castle, galloping down country towards the nearest port.

"What happened?" I asked Henry later when darkness cloaked the castle and the halls were silent. He was still in the council chamber, a slightly miserable figure, slumped over a mazer of ale.

"He asked too much and I refused," he said. "He wanted me to grant the complete return of his paternal inheritance. What a mooncalf, to think I would do so after all that has befallen. It was all I could do not to strike him."

"And now?"

"I told you before that war was brewing. This summer, it will happen. I plan to take an army to Normandy. There shall be no more parleys, no more hastily writ treaties. Either Robert is captured and killed or I am. There can only be one victor."

Henry and I went on a swift progress around England in early June, where the King stirred the hearts of men to contribute to his projected campaign. The progress ended near Aylesbury, where

Henry owned a handsome manor house. Together we feasted in the Great Hall, and Henry announced that, at last, a compromise had been reached between him and Bishop Anselm over the investiture of bishops. The old churchman agreed to return to England, which gladdened me considerably. No more fears of excommunication would hang over Henry and his barons.

After the servants had cleared away our empty trenchers, Henry asked me to walk with him in the gardens. Dusk had fallen and moths battered themselves against the horn lanterns set in niches in the walls and above the manor's gate. The sky was clear, spangled with stars like a host of ice-pale angels. A frail crescent moon, deepened almost to burnt umber, swung across the dome of heaven, furled in fleeting clouds. Its light wavered on the fishponds.

"Henry...why have you brought me here?" I asked. "Not that I do not find it pleasant." We had not shared a bed since I had spoken to him of my fears of another pregnancy and was slightly concerned that he might seek to have me break my self-imposed vow of chastity. It would be fully within his rights if he asked me to reconsider and I'd be bound to obey.

The King smiled a little wryly as if reading my thoughts. "I have hired the services of an astrologer, Edith, and he has divined a victory by gazing upon the stars and other heavenly bodies."

My husband frequently hired astrologers, an act that did not much appeal to me; my messages would come from God Himself if He chose to give them, not from a muttering greybeard in a black robe. Nonetheless, I was curious as to what the divination foretold. "Tell me what he has foreseen."

Henry stared up at the moons sliver, still shining with a crisped burnt hue in the warm summer night. Its light reflected on his eyes, turning them into a forest beast's—a mighty stag full of strength, power and resolve. I thought of him faring into the green glades of the New Forest nigh on six years ago, alongside William Rufus...and how only one of the two brothers returned from the haunted woodlands alive. The Red King replaced by the Stag King, his very voice the bellow of the Hart in rut. William of Mortain, a much-disliked kinsman of Henry, had once mockingly called him 'Stag's

Foot' for his love of the hunt...but there would be no mockery now or in the future. The Stag King ruled.

"This year there were many portents of victory," Henry murmured. "A comet appeared in the sky with a tail like a dragon's. On Maundy Thursday, two full moons hung in the sky, one in the east, the other in the west. On top of that...it is exactly forty years since my father fought at Senlac and won his throne. That must surely be a sign that I shall prevail!"

I clasped his hands. "Maybe it is; who can truly say? All I want though is that you return to me, to England...to our children. Remember that if you should fall, fate would not be kind to them. Adelaide in a nunnery, and as for William..."

He grasped my shoulders, fingers biting into my flesh through the fabric of my bliaut. "I will win, Edith...for them, I will end this struggle once and for all."

I stared up at his intense dark face with eyes still feral, unearthly. King Stag. Over his shoulder, I caught a fleeting flash of light across the sky—a star falling from the firmament. In silence, I made a fervent wish upon it.

CHAPTER SEVENTEEN

The King left England at the end of July, the calm summer waters guiding him safely across the Narrow Sea. His intent was to capture Falaise and then march onwards to Tinchebray, where his old enemy, William de Mortain—the one who'd called him Stag's Foot, dwelt in an impressive fortress with a towering donjon and a deep ditch filled with pointed stakes.

I had been invested with the powers of regent again, aided by Robert, Bishop of Lincoln and Roger, the Bishop-elect of Salisbury. At the beginning of September, I had the pleasure of riding to the port at Dover and welcoming Archbishop Anselm back onto English soil. Hundreds of folk from the poorest to the highest gathered to watch his ship dock in the harbour. When he alighted, a frail figure whose thin hair was made a saint's halo by the sun, they all cheered and called for his blessings upon them.

I met him at the castle, knelt before him in reverence and called him Father, and he raised me up and called me 'Daughter'. I had won his full trust at long last. "I will escort you to your see of Canterbury," I told him as we dined in private that evening, discussing religious tracts and their meanings while partaking of quail and stewed conies.

Anselm shook his head, daubing his mouth with a linen napkin. "England has long been without me. I would ride forth and have the people see me, to know that I have indeed returned to serve them and bring upon them the blessings of the Lord."

So, I rode with Anselm as he progressed throughout the shires, riding ahead to castle and manor to find places to stay that were adequate for the Archbishop's needs. People swarmed out of hovel and manor to greet him, walking miles through the sticky summer heat, while monks and canons exited their monastic houses to welcome him home. He went in to visit every abbey and priory with a strength that belied his frail appearance and led the brethren in masses before sitting them down to discuss the changes that would take place amongst the clergy, confirmed and approved (if under duress), by the King himself. "It is now considered unsuitable that a priest or monk have wives or concubines," he told the churchmen. (I saw jaws drop in shock; many had mistresses and most had bastard children who often were given church positions and even inheritances.) "Men sworn to God should dedicate themselves not to fleshly lusts but to chastity and the rejection of all sinfulness. As for the children born of these illicit, unblessed unions—remember well, the wisdom of Solomon—*the brood of the ungodly shall not thrive, nor take root from bastard slips. For though they flourish in boughs for a time; yet they shall be shaken by the wind, and through the force of winds they shall be rooted out*."

Gloomily the clergy agreed with Anselm's words, although I doubted that they all would comply. At least not until they were forced.

Eventually, as Anselm headed north, I parted company with the Archbishop who, despite his age, grew stronger in his confidence in God each day, preaching sermons to vast multitudes along his route.

I returned to Westminster, full of joy at the Archbishop's triumphant return to England, but I had scarcely spent a full week there, dealing with matters of state, and when I could, visiting my children in the nursery, when a messenger arrived from Normandy. With pounding heart but serene face, I had him ushered into my presence. He was ragged, washed by the sea, smelling of salt and sweat. I surmised he had ridden straight from whatever harbour his ship had docked in.

Before the dais in the Hall, he fell to one knee. "Your Grace, I bring momentous news from Normandy…"

"Speak." My voice rang out through the high, echoing vaults of William Rufus' Great Hall.

"A battle has taken place at Tinchebray…"

The messenger hesitated, glancing down; I held my breath, willing his news to be good but fearing that it was not—and that I might be the widow of a dead King, and my children facing an unknown fate.

"His Grace King Henry wishes you to take ship as soon as possible to join him in his victory celebrations as he progresses through Normandy…"

I had never set foot on a sea-going vessel before, and it was with both excitement and trepidation that I sailed from Kent with Helisent and Emma for companionship. The ship rocked on the tides and we all shrieked at first, then, as we grew accustomed to the rolling and the drum of incoming waves, we burst into fits of laughter instead, mocking our own earlier fears. A little later, however, the listing of the vessel grew stronger again, and soon the three of us were spewing our last meal into basins. Helisent squatted behind me, holding back my waist-length braids to keep them from becoming soiled, while she fought in vain to hold back her own sickness.

"Ah, we should not have made merry and mocked the powers of the sea!" she wailed, holding her belly. "I heard tell that our ancestors once believed that a goddess called Rán hid in the watery depths with a huge net to capture sailors and drag them down to their doom. Her husband was the sea itself and the foaming waves her nine daughters."

Wiping my mouth, I laughed, but my voice was strained: "Silly heathenish tales of old, Helisent! You must forget them at once. Remember instead what happened when Our Lord faced the uncertainties of the sea—*he awoke and rebuked the wind and said to the sea, 'Peace! Be still!' And the wind ceased, and there was a great calm.* We should remember that, not childish tales of yore, and pray for our safe deliverance."

We all gathered in prayer and the sea seemed to recoil, growing far gentler in its movements, and our sickness lifted along with our hearts, and in a dawn tinted rose-gold by beams of the rising sun, we reached the port of Dives, the very place where the Conqueror had begun his journey to claim the English throne.

Stepping onto the quayside, I was escorted to a carriage and whisked away to Falaise, a town close to where the battle of Tinchebrai had taken place. In the stern castle on a height, overlooking a deep, slow-moving river, I was greeted by my husband, who embraced me soundly, his hands almost punishingly hard upon my arms. Strength and pride radiated from him, oddly infectious, and I did not flinch when he kissed my cheek with vigour.

"Normandy is mine at last. *Mine*." He swung me around the room as if we were dancing before an audience of courtiers at a feast. "There is no doubt about that now. And the people are glad! Did they cheer you as you travelled hence?"

"They did," I nodded. "They lined every route along the way. I waved from my chariot when I was able. Such a relief to find they were not outraged at the battle's outcome!"

"The common folk were as dissatisfied with my bumbling brother's bad governance as I," said Henry, "and even more repulsed by his allies such as Robert de Belleme." He released my hands and began to pace around the room, recalling the battle. "It only lasted an hour, Edith. An hour and the duchy was mine. I'd besieged the castle of that mouthy little man, the Count of Mortain, a few days prior. Since he was one of Robert's few loyal friends, he held the gates against me. Robert marched in to attempt to break the siege through a parlay, but I would not be pacified by any of his worm-like words. He then decided we should fight for our rights in plain battle…and may God smile down on the best man!" He grinned.

"And the best man was you."

"Yes. I had the better allies—Ranulf of Bayeux, the Earl of Leicester, the Earl of Surrey, the Duke of Brittany, the Count of Evreux and others. In reserve, I also had Elias of Maine, hidden from view of my enemies. I decided to employ a new tactic, one unfamiliar to my brother—I asked the knights to dismount and fight on foot."

My eyes widened in surprise. My forebears always fought afoot, and the Norman cavalry was one great advantage William's army had over them at Senlac Hill. How times had changed! The gap between English ways and Norman had already dwindled, in this and other things.

"Robert saw my men afoot and thought he could mow them down like a reaper at harvest time with his mounted knights. Instead, his horsemen smashed against the front line and their formation broke apart. Men started to fight hand-to-hand as the enemy horses were taken down with spear or arrow. Before long, all of Robert's soldiers had joined the fray, fully committed to the fight. For a time, a very brief time, he began to push my knights and foot soldiers back…but he did not know about Elias, hidden in the trees. Elias's troops were mounted and they charged into Robert's flank, throwing his men into total disarray. The battle was won that very moment; our enemies cast their weapons down and began to flee the field. That craven dog Belleme, skulking in the back like the coward he is, took flight without having struck a single blow."

"What has happened to Robert. Is he taken…or slain?" I raised my gaze to his. "And what of my uncle, Edgar Atheling?"

Henry chuckled. "My chancellor, Waldric, took Robert prisoner. He lies bound in the dungeons below this keep. The Breton knights got hold of your uncle and also captured William de Mortain. They, too, lie bound in those dark pits below our feet. I have not yet decided what to do with them." Hardness filled his eyes and his mouth grew tight and cruel. A wave of sickness rushed through me, diminishing the joy of his victory. It would not surprise me if he blinded Robert, a common practice to disable one's blood-kin foes; no murder was done, but the problem of disobedience was solved. As for my Uncle Edgar, an English prince…

"Henry…" Fighting emotion, I laid my hand on Henry's arm. "I must speak on Edgar's behalf and ask for clemency. I know not what madness possessed him, supporting Robert Curthose against all rhyme and reason."

Henry harrumphed, folding his arms and making my hand drop away. "Two old crusaders, bound together by memories of their mission, I fear. Robert can turn on the charm when he wishes—which is not that often. But it fills me with bitterness that Edgar rallied to my brother's side when I had made a queen of his own dear niece. To say nought of that fact I had found a fitting husband for his other niece and invited his nephew to my court, where he would be educated and trained as a prince…"

The murderous, angry light was hovering in Henry's eyes again and his fists clenched. "My lord King, I beg you…" I sank upon my knees, throwing my arms around his lower limbs and grovelling on the rush-strewn floor. "Have mercy. I have so few kinsmen left. The hot sun of the Holy Land must have addled Edgar's mind. He was good to me in the past, and I cannot forget that…nor can I forget the love he bore for my mother."

"Edith, Edith..." Henry pulled me up and suddenly I was in his embrace, weeping. "Christ, there is nought worse than a woman's tears... I have never seen you cry before. Look, you...I am not as hard-hearted as you might think. I...I will spare Edgar Atheling, but he must spend time imprisoned for his acts against me. I shall have him transported to England and locked in Devizes Castle for a time. He can contemplate his foolishness there..."

"And when he is released?" I glanced up and his worn, calloused thumb swept tears from my cheeks.

"I should force him into exile...but for you, I will show clemency. He can retreat to his Hertfordshire lands and live out the rest of his days there in peace, but he will have to report to my officials and he will never hold a position of importance in England again."

"T-thank you, your Grace..." I stammered, overwhelmed. I had been certain Henry would execute my uncle as an example to other traitors and rebels.

"Would you like to see him?" Henry asked. "You may impart the news that I will pardon him after his incarceration at Devizes. Let it be known that only through your intervention does he keep his head upon his shoulders."

I grabbed his hand and kissed it roughly. "Henry, I had not thought for so much. May God bless you..."

"Edith." He caught my wrist, drew me close, and suddenly kissed me hard upon the mouth. "No more weeping. Go to him. You have till the Nones bell tolls in the town." He nodded to the window; beyond I saw the spires of a monastic house. "At that time, you must return. I will send the captain of my guard to guide you thither and bring you back. A grand celebration of my victory is taking place later, and I want you seated at my side in all splendour."

The dungeon was a dank cavern hewn into the living rock below Falaise Castle. Tentatively, I descended a flight of slippery moss-clagged stairs, guided by the castle's head gaoler, a fat, waddling little man in a dinted breastplate, whose large, bulbous eyes glowed an eerie green in the light of his horn lantern. I fancied those eyes might have grown thus unnaturally from dwelling for years in the subterranean darkness and I suppressed a superstitious shudder.

"Are you well, your Grace?" the gaoler inquired, leaning forward, his lamp bobbing on its metal pole. Now its beams illuminated the short black stubs of teeth in his almost frog-like mouth, making him appear even more monstrous—a man spawned under cold stone, in the dark and the wet, half-man and half-fish. "Do not you fear, I shall not let the terrors of the night affright ye."

He was impertinent and I gathered quite enjoying my discomfiture in the chill, evil-smelling murk, but I nodded and said in an imperious tone, "Lead on, man. I am well enough."

The stair wound downwards, narrowing as it plunged into the bowels of the castle. The air was fuggy and foul, smelling of damp, urine and even worse things. As I stepped off the last stair, my foot struck cold water and I jerked back, almost falling in my haste and surprise.

The gaoler turned around, his lantern swaying and making shadows dance, twisting into lurid shapes upon the wall. "Yer Grace, don't be alarmed. We're down at the water level now, and sometimes the river next to the castle makes its way in." He smirked. "There's a series of stepping stones higher than the water level. You can walk on them so's not to wreck your pretty shoes." He swept the lantern lower, and its weak yellow light rippled over wavelets of icy river water swelling around six irregular sandstone blocks.

"Are they safe?" I inquired.

"Safe enough, your Grace. Would you like me to lay my cloak down for you?"

His tone was close to mocking, and I realised that not all men were pleased that Robert had been deposed and wished I had ordered Henry's guard, whom I had left at the top of the stairs, to accompany me—but I had wanted my meeting with Uncle Edgar to be as private as possible. Not that such privacy was possible now, with this loathsome earthworm present.

Without answering—I would not deign to answer—I pushed past him and carefully picked my way across the stepping stones. The rocky ground level rose and the water receded, and through the dimness, I saw a row of heavy doors set with iron grilles. The smell of filth grew even stronger; in one of the cells, a man groaned piteously, an almost animal sound.

I heard the gaoler stumble up behind me, his breath huffing. "Which one?" I asked in a frigid tone.

"Over there!" A pudgy finger shot out, pointing to the cell on my right. "That's where the *rosbif* lordling is…"

I turned around abruptly and slapped the man open-handed across his grinning face. "How dare you?" I snapped. "He is a prince who at one time was heir to a throne. I am minded to tell King Henry of your vile attitude and have you removed from your position."

His grin vanished instantly and he stumbled back, scowling; he knew he'd gone too far. I paid him no more heed as I hurried to the cell he'd indicated, pressing my face against the grille. As my eyes adjusted to the gloom, I saw Edgar slumped in the corner, his feet bound in chains, his hair and beard a filthy tangle, his clothes splashed with blood and mud.

My breath caught in my throat and I could utter no words, stricken to the heart to see my kinsman brought to such straits.

As I stared in shock, Edgar raised his head slowly as if it were a great weight and glanced in my direction. His eyes shone steel-blue against the bruised and begrimed skin. "Edith!" he cried in a hoarse, cracked voice. He tried to rise and rush towards me, but the chains on his legs kept him in place and he fell back with a grunt. Crumpled on the squalid floor, he bent his head into his hands, hiding his face in mortification. "I feel such shame for you to see me thus…" he groaned. "I was a fool. I should never have followed Curthose. Do not ask me why I did, niece, for I cannot truly say. Perhaps I thought he would reward me with…a high position in England if Henry fell in battle."

"So, you would have sought to replace my son," I said quietly, but with contained anger tautening my voice. I had not expected that from Edgar and wished I had not heard it. "So much for family loyalty. What you desired was a fool's dream anyway; Curthose would never have given you any part of England. He used you like a pawn. He only rewarded men of true evil…like Robert de Belleme, not a fallen prince of Saxon blood!"

He groaned again, wiping his brow. "Go then, Edith, leave this place and leave me to my deserved fate. Your presence only fills me with guilt. Soon, no doubt, Henry will make me atone for my crimes…by removing my head with an axe."

"Edgar, look at me." My tone was sharp.

Slowly he raised his head. "What? What more have you to say to me?"

"You are not going to die, Edgar."

He gasped and went white, then fell limply against the stained wall. "You…you…Tell me I have not misheard!"

"You have not misheard. I begged for your life on my knees, Uncle. Begged for a traitor. And Henry agreed that you should live."

He looked dubious as if he thought I was lying and the headsman about to appear, sneering, holding a ready axe. "How can this be? What are the terms? Edith, I tell you now that I would rather die than be imprisoned in a dungeon for life or…" He touched his face. "…or blinded so that all I'd be fit for was a monastery."

"You will be taken to England and held in Devizes castle, along with Robert Curthose. Once Henry believes you have thoroughly repented of your ways, you will be free to return to Hertfordshire—where you will stay in peace, under surveillance, away from any trouble."

Edgar clambered up again, swaying on unsteady legs. The manacles around his ankles clacked noisily. "That…that is all? There will be no tortures, no mutilation?"

"No, none, as long as you live quietly upon your lands."

Tears spilt from his eyes, making snail's tracks through the grime caked on his face. "I…I could not have foreseen…Edith, I thank you, forgive me…"

"I do not know if I can," I said. "If you want to do something for me, let it be this—stay away from court, from Henry…and from me. Forever."

Unwilling to say more, I backed away from the grille. The horrible little gaoler was silent behind me, although clearly he had listened in. On the steps down into the dungeon came the heavy tread of the guard I had left on the upper level. He appeared in the stairwell, a dark shape against the light of torches above, and said, "Your Grace, the Nones bell has struck. It is time to leave."

"Edith...wait..." began Edgar, his chains rattling like those of an angry ghost in an All Hallow's tale. A ghost was indeed what he was to me now. A *nithing*...nothing, ephemeral as the wind.

"You will address me as Matilda," I cast over my shoulder, "and as your Queen."

Tears pricked my eyes, remembering how close Edgar and Mother had been, two allies in exile, trying to make the best of their sorrowful situation. But those days were gone forever. He had chosen a different path and chose poorly.

I took a deep breath and nodded towards the captain of the guard. "Take me back upstairs to the King's chamber. I am done here."

Henry and I journeyed around Normandy, showing ourselves to our people. I marvelled at the mighty castles with their looming donjons, the rich monasteries where gems glittered amidst saints' relics, the remains of walls and baths and amphitheatres left of yore by half-forgotten peoples. Occasionally a disturbance would break out, orchestrated by some disgruntled follower of Robert Curthose, but these minor uprisings were swiftly put down and eventually dwindled away.

We spent Christmas in the castle of Rouen, and the feasting was grand and long, while snow drifted down outside, spreading an austere blanket over the town's spacious marketplace. As we dined on pork and venison, pasties and pastries, puddings and fritters, we were entertained by the famous philosopher Adelard of Bath, but it was not philosophical discussion he brought to our Christmas court. Adelard was also a musician of some note and played an instrument called the Cithara for the delight of our ears.

In January, however, that cruel month when icicles fanged the castle towers and city gateways, and the wind screamed like an angry demon, evil news arrived to burden my heart. My brother Ned—Edgar, King of Scotland—had died in Edinburgh. Rumours abounded that my Uncle Donald Bane was behind his demise, but although Donald was alive, his involvement seemed unlikely. He had been blinded and forced to take monk's vows, and by all reports remained in the solitude of his cell, attempting to live a holy life. Perhaps he still had supporters, though; men's memories were long in the far north, and seeking terrible vengeance was all too common amongst the Scottish clans.

In any case, Ned was dead, and Scotland facing new upheaval.

I sat and wept, and Henry comforted me; it was the closest we had been to true husband and wife in that time of mourning. "They called Ned 'the Valiant'," I wept. "Can my brother Alexander ever live up to him? Alex is rash and quick to wrath; I fear he will bring tumult to Scotland hunting down Ned's killers...whoever they might be."

"Alexander will learn as all kings must," Henry said, stroking my hair. "David will help him; he appears a capable youth."

I nodded, wiping my tears. "He is...maybe the most capable of all my brothers, if I am honest, even though he would not bathe the lepers' feet..." I attempted a smile; it came out a teary grimace. "Ned promised David the Kingdom of Strathclyde if he should die without heirs and also an appanage in Scotland."

"Capable? Yes. David is also the most *Norman*," said Henry, with a little grin. "All the rough edges smoothed away. As they are with you, my dearest wife..."

He lifted my arm and kissed my wrist, and for a moment, I felt a little flare of desire, which shamed me, for I had chosen chastity. I quickly drowned that pang of wantonness by recalling my brush with death when William Adelin was born. Carefully, I withdrew my hand. "I must write to Ivo, the Bishop of Chartres, with whom we held audience only last week. I feel he is a godly man. I will ask that he pray for my brother Edgar."

Henry touched my cheek in a sympathetic gesture. "Yes, do that. It will give you some consolation in this time of mourning."

Ivo soon responded to my missive. Tears fell anew as I read his kind words: *The reputation of your devotion has inspired many of the religious. We thank Lord God, bestower of all that is good, for placing the strength of a man within a woman's breast, to give aid to those in need. Therefore, we pour out prayers for the soul of your brother, Edgar of Scotland, and we are confident that, although we are sinners, his soul will repose in Abraham's bosom…*

"I will send Ivo a gift," said Henry gruffly, eyeing me. "For more prayers. More candles. It is the least I can do for your brother…and for you."

"You are good, Henry."

"Few would say so. But you are a good woman, Edith, and a good queen…You said once you wished to be seen as modern Queen Esther. Your wish, my dearest spouse, has come true."

Henry departed Normandy just prior to Lent and headed for Windsor. His prisoners went with him bound in prison carts, soon to find themselves inside the stern walls of Devizes Castle.

I spent several more weeks enjoying Rouen with Helisent, Gracia and Emma, buying cloth, cloaks, linens and fine shoes in the merchants' shops that lined the cobbled lanes. Then we moved to the castle at Lillebonne, where I issued a charter under my own seal for the town.

By Whitsun, I was back in England, joining the King at Westminster. I was glad to be at home for I missed my children, who were never far from my mind, and always a cause of worry and concern, for child lives were so precious and so fragile, often snuffed out by the simplest of illnesses.

Once I had settled into the royal apartments, I began to schedule more building works around London—Ethelred's Hythe, granted to me by the King and once held by my mother, was made a fine landing place complete with special modern privies that contained piped water for cleanliness. I desired to make it an attractive port for sailors, as I could claim duties on any goods brought into London there. I also demolished an old church to found a new monastic house of Augustinian canons and placed my own confessor, Norman, as the Prior. I called the new foundation Holy Trinity and gifted it with the first of many sacred relics—a piece of the True Cross given to me by Alexius Comnenus, the Emperor of Byzantium. Around the same time, I accepted the request of my chaplain Ersinius to leave court, which he loathed for its excesses, to join a newly consecrated

Augustinian priory in the Vale of Ewyas. I journeyed to this Welsh priory with Ersinius to meet the founder, William, a knight who had retreated from the world and embraced the hermetical life after long-serving his master, Walter de Lacey, lord of Weobley.

"Good William," I said to the humble knight, now shorn-headed in monkish style, his robes sackcloth and his feet in thin sandals, "the King and I are much taken with the Augustinian order, and would grant you rich gifts for building and for comfort."

William blushed but shook his head. "Oh no, gracious Queen, I could not accept your kind offer. I want this House to remain as intended—a place of austerity, prayer and solitude."

He moved back from me with a polite little bow, clearly ill at ease and eager to retreat from the royal presence, but as he did, I saw his flimsy robe gap open—and underneath was a coat of mail glistening dully in the light of the cressets in his chamber.

"What, good William, do I see upon you?" I walked towards him. William stood stunned, like a frightened rabbit transfixed by an oncoming hound. "The armour of war on a holy personage. What does this mean?"

"I-I was once a k-knight as you know, your Grace," he stammered. "I have hung up my sword forever…but I wear my mail close to my skin so that I might have some protection against any assault by Satan."

"May I touch it, good William?" I drew even closer to the holy man.

"You—your Grace, I do not…" he choked, his cheeks an ever-deeper shade of crimson, as I slid a hand inside the breast of his robe. I truly thought he might swoon at our close proximity. He began to sway, eyes closed, lips moving in silent prayer.

Swiftly, I withdrew my hand. "My thanks, William. I leave you now to your prayers, and I hope you will remember Matilda, Queen of the English, in them, and with fondness."

I had taken a small purse of gold and placed it within William's robe…He might not accept huge gifts, but this one was small and filled with love…

Such were the duties of a Queen, to care for all her people, great and small. My position was such now that I scarcely noticed when

Henry was away from England; more and more frequently he fared abroad.

At times, it almost felt as if I ruled the country alone.

And in my heart of hearts, I liked it—my one sin, as some of my detractors often whispered, a 'lust for glory.'

CHAPTER EIGHTEEN

Seated in my solar at Winchester, I was embroidering a fine cope for the Abbot of St Albans. In and out my needle flew, using the famed silver-gilt thread that made English embroidery famous across Europe. The cope already had Saint Michael treading upon a demon and seraphim flying all around him; I planned a nativity scene next. I had just begun to thread blue for the Virgin's robe when I was startled by loud screams and wails coming from the gardens outside. My needle slipped from my fingers and fell to the floor, rolling into a crack where I could not reach it.

Recognising the strident voices, an angry frown creased my brow. "It's the children," I said crossly to Helisent, who was sitting on a stool opposite me. "What are their nursemaids thinking to let them carry on so?"

Helisent laid down the altar cloth she was decorating and crossed to the window, pressing her eye to the thin slit. "A nurse is scolding them, your Grace. The trouble appears to be quelled, whatever it was...but Lord William is still weeping and Lady Adelaide appears angry. She is stamping her foot!"

I sighed. Adelaide was eight years of age now but seemed a good eight years older than that. Fierce and clever in turn, she rang rings around her nurses, had her sire under a spell of enchantment whenever he was in England, and in turns both frustrated me and made me proud. She already read well, spoke both French and English and had dived into Latin. Her manner held a certain imperious quality not usually seen in a child, even a royal one—I had seen serving women old enough to be her granddam retreat before her flashing eyes.

Adelaide had the air of a Queen....and a queen she would be. No, even *more* than that. My little daughter was bound to be the bride of an Emperor—Heinrich, King of Germany and Emperor of the Romans. Henry had made the final arrangements during a meeting with Heinrich at Rouen, writing home that, *By the Grace of God, we brought the matter of the marriage to a good end.*

Heinrich had then written fair and flattering words to me, as the bride's mother, and in Normandy Henry received oaths from the Emperor's officials to make the marriage binding.

I had Adelaide brought to my solar to tell her, in the kindest way I could manage, that a fitting husband had been found for her and soon she would depart for Germany to join his royal household. She had already been briefed by tutors about her worldly duties as a princess of the realm and, to my relief, there were no tears or arguments. "He is old, though, isn't he?" she had said quietly. "With a beard that makes him look like a bear."

"He is older than you, yes," I answered with honesty. I did not want to fill her head with silly notions that he was some ancient hero incarnate. "But fear not, you will not truly be man and wife for many years yet. Likely no younger than fifteen or sixteen. By then you will have grown accustomed to him, and he with you—and maybe the flame of love will even grow between you. As for the Emperor resembling a bear—I cannot say, for I have never met him. I have not heard rumours of unsightliness or untidiness, however, so I'd not worry yourself about that."

I had paused then, remembering one more condition of the marriage contract that I needed to disclose. "Oh…when you are crowned as Empress, you will be required to take a new name. Your father and Heinrich have decided on 'Matilda'—in honour of me and your grandmother. It is a highly popular and regal name in Germany too."

For the first time, I saw a flicker of rebellion in her eyes. "But I am Adelaide. There will be too many Matildas, Mother! You, my cousin of Boulogne, my half-sisters from Father's wom…" She paused, a little flushed, realising that she had almost spoken of things unsuitable for a young maiden to discuss. But I knew she was no fool; and she was good friends with her bastard half-brother, Robert of Gloucester, who lived at court.

"You could use the name 'Maude', the short form of Matilda, if you wish to avoid confusion," I told her, ignoring the more controversial parts of her brief outburst.

Adelaide had shrugged and asked if she might be dismissed from my presence, and I let her go and thought that was an end to it—perhaps, with aid from tutors and a governess, she would learn to kerb her opinions and become a little more domesticated now that she was to be married.

But now, my morning embroidery session with my ladies-in-waiting was disturbed by some kind of ruckus between Adelaide and William. They usually got on well, although Adelaide could be bossy and strong-willed. "Helisent," I said, "go find the nurse and have her bring the children into my presence."

Helisent curtseyed and hurried away. It was not long before she returned with a shame-faced nursemaid, a red-cheeked and teary William and a rather mutinous Adelaide. Sternly, I glanced from one child to the other. "What is this I hear? You two fighting like a pair of hellions in full view of all! It is unseemly for children of your stature—Adelaide, soon you will be an Empress; William, you will be a King one day…"

William pointed accusingly at his sister. "Adelaide started it, Mama. She was saying I should not be King!"

"Adelaide?" I frowned at my daughter. "What is all this about?"

She folded her arms, scowling in a manner that reminded me of her father. "I just told the truth—that if things were fair, I should be Queen of England one day. He would only be a prince then, maybe a Duke if I so decided."

"I told you, Mama!" William grabbed at my skirt and tugged on it furiously. "Make her stop!"

I gave a strained little laugh, trying to lighten the situation. "Oh Adelaide, Queens Regnant are far and few between. The Barons of this land would refuse to follow a mere woman. Fair or not, that is just the way life is."

"You manage well enough, Mama, when Father is away in Normandy."

"I…I am your father's helpmeet, which is the proper role of a wife, as ordained by God, whether she is a queen or a washerwoman living in a hut. You will be the same, Adelaide…Maude."

"Do not call me that!" she cried, while the nurse gasped in shocked disgust at her disrespect.

"Adelaide!" I shouted, as my daughter bolted from the chamber and fled down the corridor, feet pattering noisily on the floorboards.

She did not return, despite my cries. I managed a rueful smile as my ladies looked away, abashed. Adelaide was her father's daughter in both looks and temperament. She would forge her own way.

In June, the great Whitsun Court was held, and a party of German ambassadors sent to England on behalf of Heinrich brought rich gifts to honour their queen-to-be, who sat on a pearled throne, dressed in a striking green bliaut, her long, curling, dark hair twined with golden bands, her face dutifully solemn, almost emotionless. The Germans were huge men, broad-shouldered and impressive with strong, square jaws, yellow or sandy hair and startling ice-blue eyes. Their clothes were rich, fashioned from wool and silk, with braiding at neck and hem. Heinrich had given them huge collars of gold and silver, studded with gems that flashed purple, scarlet, and cerulean to impress the lords and ladies of our court.

The celebrations were of high standard, singers from afar, tumblers, actors, and all manner of foodstuffs—crane's flesh, peacocks still in opulent feathers, gilded swans, boars' heads and trotter, salted venison from the New Forest, plus salmon in pastry, bream slathered is mustard sauce, and those monstrous lampreys that Henry enjoyed so much.

At the end of the festivities, members of the court, the clergy and the Germans gathered before the door of the palace chapel. Here, one of Heinrich's envoys, a handsome young lordling named Isenhard played proxy for Emperor Heinrich and stood in as Adelaide's bridegroom. My daughter was so tiny next to him that I felt a lump rise in my throat and had to gaze over the top of their heads to fix on a carving of Christ above the chapel door. Thy Will be done....

Then the ceremony was over, and both Adelaide and Isenhard looked relieved, and the nurses whisked the little bride away to the nursery. Thanks be, Heinrich had agreed for her to stay a little longer in England because of her youth, but I knew the respite would be a short one...he wanted his folk to have a visible Queen, and even more, he desired the handsome dowry of 10,000 marks that came with her. The folk of England had sacrificed much to pay that hefty fee, and I had heard mutterings in the street against the match. To tax the already impoverished seemed wrong to me, but I had no say in the matter. A King's daughter must marry and she must come with great wealth, especially as the promised bride of the Emperor of the Romans.

Adelaide spent another few months at home, but then Heinrich began asking when we might send her on his way. He was eager for her to learn the German language and to show herself to the people they would rule together. So, when Lent had begun in the following year, I was borne in a litter to the port of Lynn, with Adelaide, dressed in vair and pale blue silk and wearing a pearled coronet upon her brow, riding in a decorated chariot next to me. William sat in the litter, attended by his nurses, still too young to ride a full-sized horse with the men.

At the port, I gazed out across the choppy grey waves of the North Sea and wondered if I might see my daughter again. I glanced over at Adelaide; she was surrounded by an escort of Germans, her care entrusted to a cleric called Burchard. It was a worthy procession of rich and noble men—bishops and priests, counts and lords, but I noted the Germans had pushed the English barons we had chosen as companions to the rear of the entourage with cold-eyed courtesy, while happily taking treasure chests full of English gifts from the baggage train to load upon their ships.

Alighting from her chariot, Adelaide appeared small and alone, but her head was held high and no tears streaked her cheeks. She did not return my glance but stared straight ahead as if transfixed, her shoulders back, her body straight as an arrow.

Nervous, I called over Henry, Archdeacon of Winchester, and a knight called Sir Drogo, who had proved himself trustworthy in the King's service. "I charge you both with the wellbeing of the Lady Adelaide…now Empress Maude, Queen of the Romans. No matter what befalls the rest of the English company, stay there with her, her fellow countrymen. If Heinrich objects to your continued presence, be strong, tell him he must deal with me. My daughter may be immersed in German ways, but by God on high, she will not forget her roots."

"It will be done, your Grace," said Sir Drogo, and he, a tall warrior built like a mountain with curls red as flame, moved his prancing black stallion over to Adelaide's side, despite the aghast looks given him by Heinrich's German nobles. The Archdeacon followed after, standing on my daughter's other side.

There was no farewell, no kisses as one might see amongst common folk about to part, as Adelaide was escorted to the waiting ship by Burchard, followed by three maidens of good birth who would attend to her personal needs.

"God save Queen Matilda, God save Empress Matilda!" the onlookers cried, the sound of their gathered voice drowning out the shrieks of the gulls about the harbour and drifting out across the rough sea.

Adelaide halted and raised her hand; although she was small, she had great presence. "Call me Maude," she said loudly. "There are other, more worthy, Matildas in my line."

To my surprise, the company, from humble servant to armoured knight to fur-clade noble, began to shout for Empress Maude, throwing their hoods into the air and raising long blades that gleamed in the dull, drizzly day.

With measured steps, her maids at her heels, holding up the train of her long gown, Adelaide ascended the gangplank into the bow of the vessel that would bear her away. She stood there for a moment like a fair ship's figurehead, the white veil fastened to her coronet flowing out over her dark curls, then she turned abruptly and vanished into the hold.

She was gone. I would see her no more.

The rest of her entourage boarded the other vessels, and then the ships cast off their mooring ropes and began to make their way out into the North Sea, headed on a swift wind for German shores.

I sighed and ruffled William's hair. His eyes were wide and wet; he cared deeply for his sister, despite their childish squabbles. "Will Addy and I meet again, Mama?" he asked.

"Only God can know such things," I said. "When you are older, maybe you will."

"I will get on a ship when I am of age and sail back and forth from Normandy!" he said brightly. "I shall command my sister to meet me, and she cannot deny me, for I will one day be a King."

I ruffled his golden curls again, inherited from the fair-haired Saxon eorls of old. He was my child in looks, just as Adelaide was Henry's. "I do not think you can command your sister to do anything she does not want to do...but I expect, for you, she would come."

I craned my head around, gazing out to where the black dots of the flotilla of ships carrying my daughter faded into a mist bank, its dense vapours tinged orange by the fading sun. Then, as blue dusk began to stretch across England and the Evenstar rose, twinkling in the west with fey brightness, I signalled to my cavalcade to move off, making all speed for London.

The day was done and so was I, a piece of my heart sent over the sea forever. Now it was time to go home.

The Lion's whelps shall be transformed into fishes of the sea, and his Eagle build her nest upon Mount Aravius—prophecy of Merlin, believed to foretell the drowning deaths of two of Henry's sons, his heir William and an illegitimate son, Richard, in the wreck of the White Ship, and the rise of Empress Maude, the Lady of the English, who fought her cousin Stephen for the English throne.

THE END

Author Notes—

Matilda of Scotland, born Edith, is one of England's most forgotten queens, despite being an ancestor of every English and British monarch and tying them into royal Anglo-Saxon and Scottish ancestry. There's not a lot written about her, one major biography, and a few chapters here and there so there was much digging to be done. The most famous part of her life seems to be when she trampled on a nun's habit her Aunt forced her to wear, but there was much more to Matilda than that. She was literate and a great builder of abbeys, bridges, hospitals…and public toilets in London!

It is not 100% certain there was a daughter called Euphemia, who did not survive birth, but several sources mention her so I include hers Matilda's surviving daughter, called Adelaide in early childhood, grew up to be Empress Maude, whose son Henry II was the founder of the Angevins/Plantagenets. Her son William died in the White Ship disaster, although Matilda had herself had died some years before he was drowned.

It is recorded that Matilda and Henry stopped sleeping together after her birth of their son and heir, and this seemed to have been a mutual decision. History does not record why. Henry I, of course, was a notorious womaniser, with at least 22 bastards. He is likely the ancestor of almost all people of western European ancestry.

Henry has long been implicated in the possible murder of his brother, William Rufus, in the New Forest, and I have followed that line, although it is by no means proven. Hunting was dangerous back then, and two other close family members had died on hunts previously.

As for 'changes' in the story, as before, sometimes I have moved events a little closer to each other that they were to avoid long, drawn out episodes.

As usual songs are real medieval ones but perhaps not quite the same centuries. Quotes to/ from bishops and archbishops in letters are the original words from documents trimmed down, in English, and in more modern language.

For those who had read my other MEDIEVAL BABES novels, you will note some people in other books tying in with this story—I have written about Henry I's illegitimate daughter Juliane, who tried to kill him, and Mabel de Belleme, notorious mother of the infamous, sadistic Robert, who is mentioned throughout for his various misdeeds.

Matilda was educated at both Romsey and Wilton Abbeys, both quite near to me. Romsey still retains its medieval character but Wilton, one of the richest abbeys in England, was sold after the Reformation and became a stately home. The only medieval feature left is the Almonry (not open to the public.)

Upon her death, Matilda was buried in Westminster, near the Shrine of Edward the Confessor. Sadly, there is no tomb or ledger, although she was remembered by Chroniclers as 'The Good Queen' Henry was buried in Reading Abbey, and perhaps now lies under the car park of the nearby disused prison which covers the ruins of the abbey.

JP Reedman, September 2023.

OTHER BOOKS BY J.P. REEDMAN:

RICHARD III and the WARS OF THE ROSES
I, RICHARD PLANTAGENET: THE PREQUELS. Richard's childhood and youth. 3 books

I, RICHARD PLANTAGENET. 3 book series. First two are Richard's life from Barnet to Bosworth; the third is a tie-in about Henry Stafford, the treacherous Duke of Buckingham.

BLOOD OF ROSES and SECRET MARRIAGES—Edward IV's battle for the throne and his tangled love life!

MEDIEVAL BABES—series of novels on lesser-known medieval women. Eleanor of Provence, Rosamund Clifford, Eleanor of Brittany, Katherine, illegitimate daughter of Richard III, Mary of Woodstock the Merry Nun, Juliane illegitimate daughter of Henry I, Mabel de Belleme the poisoner, Countess Ela of Salisbury, The Other Margaret Beaufort (mother of Henry Stafford), Dangereuse the grandmother of Eleanor of Aquitaine, and Matilda, wife of Henry I

ROBIN HOOD:
The Hood Game-3 book series set in a Sherwood full of myth and magic.

THE STONEHENGE SAGA—A novel of the Bronze Age incorporating the Arthurian myths.
UK AMAZON LINK TO AUTHOR PAGE: https://www.amazon.co.uk/J-P-Reedman/e/B009UTHBUE

USA AMAZON LINK TO AUTHOR PAGE:
https://www.amazon.com/stores/J.P.Reedman/author/B009UTHBUE

And many more!

Printed in Great Britain
by Amazon